THE
ISLAND

Also by Sarah Singleton

CENTURY

Winner of the Booktrust Teenage Book Award

Highly Commended for the Branford Boase First Novel Award

Winner of the Dracula Society's Children of the Night Award

HERETIC

SACRIFICE

THE AMETHYST CHILD

THE POISON GARDEN

THE ISLAND

SARAH SINGLETON

SIMON AND SCHUSTER

**To my remarkable niece Lydia – artist and
falconer – with lots of love.**

First published in Great Britain in 2010 by Simon and Schuster UK Ltd
A CBS COMPANY

Simon & Schuster UK Ltd
1st Floor
222 Gray's Inn Road
London WC1X 8HB

A CIP catalogue record for this book is available
from the British Library.

ISBN: 978-1-84738-296-2

1 3 5 7 9 10 8 6 4 2

Typeset by M Rules
Printed by CPI Cox & Wyman, Reading, Berkshire RG1 8EX

www.simonandschuster.co.uk

www.crowmaiden.plus.com

Otto

Monday

Otto put down his book. He could see her, the girl Maria, talking to a tall man with cropped blond hair – a German perhaps. They were sitting on the pale sand, now cooling in the brief twilight, too far away for him to eavesdrop, heads close together.

Otto was sitting at a table outside a beach shack, the only customer, drinking vodka from a tiny, smeared glass. The sky, a fierce indigo all day, had faded and now, in the minutes before the sunset, a ribbon of grainy pink burned over the horizon. The vodka flamed on his tongue and at the back of his throat. The perfume of spiced fish and woodsmoke drifted from the shack with its roof of dried palm leaves.

Without asking, the waiter refilled Otto's glass. The boy, perhaps three or four years younger than Otto, was dressed in shorts and a shirt, the ubiquitous flip-flops on his feet. A black and white puppy emerged and began snapping up the beetles that crawled, like clockwork, from the shack's crannies as the sun disappeared into the sea.

The book lay waiting on the table, opened and face down, a copy of *War and Peace* Otto had picked up from a cabin selling second-hand books off the path between his lodgings and the shack where he drank a banana lassi every morning and ate a fresh fish curry at night. He wasn't interested in the book. He couldn't take his eyes from Maria who was momentarily bathed in the golden rays of the dying day, silhouetted with her man against the backdrop of sea, a clichéd picture from a holiday brochure, a romance in paradise.

She gestured with her thin, elegant arms, tossed her head so strands of long hair swung over her shoulders. Otto sighed. It both annoyed and fascinated him that he found Maria so intriguing; he felt a sliver of jealousy, like a needle, to see her engaged in such heated conversation with this other man, the burly maybe-German, though Otto had only spoken to her twice.

He raised the glass to his lips, allowed another drop of vodka onto his tongue. Doubtless a party would kick off along the beach in the hours to come. He'd selected the quiet end for his sojourn in Goa, waiting to meet his friends. Four days into the trip, drinking alone, he realised he wasn't thinking about Jen or Charlotte very much at all.

Otto sipped his vodka. The puppy crunched another beetle. From inside the shack he heard conversation and somebody laughing. The sun sank beneath the horizon and for a moment the sky burned like a cymbal of gold, before the colour drained away and soft, indigo darkness lay over the sea. He could hear the waves, gently lapping the sand.

Maria reached for an embroidered bag resting by her side on the sand. Both people stood up, Maria hopping with an appealing mixture of awkwardness and grace as she slipped on her sandal and tipped sand from her fluttering skirt. She reached out to her companion to steady herself, fingers touching his arm momentarily. She pushed her hair behind her ears, kissed him lightly on the cheek and finally turned away.

The young waiter emerged from the shack and turned on a string of fairy lights. He raised the vodka bottle; Otto shook his head. He didn't think Maria had seen him but she was heading up the beach, away from the sea to the low enclosure and palm leaf thatch surrounding the Seaside Bar.

'Hey,' she said. 'On your own again?'

The answer was evident.

'Hey, Maria,' he said. 'Would you like a drink?' The waiter was already waiting with a glass. Maria nodded and sat on the chair the other side of the narrow table. She scrutinised Otto, a teasing smile on her face.

'So what have you been up to today?'

'Oh, the usual. Nothing much.'

She picked up the book. 'Reading?' she said. 'Oh. *War and Peace*.' The book didn't hold her interest. She wrinkled her nose and dropped it back on the table. Her skin was the colour of coffee, tanned by the Goan sun. She had long chocolate brown hair in which shone strands of burnished gold. This hair never seemed to be still, always sliding silkily over her shoulders and arms, falling across her face.

They had met two days earlier in Anjuna at the flea market. Maria had spotted him wandering alone among the traders and invited him to join her for a drink. At twenty she was two years older than Otto and had lived in Goa for several months, exactly how many she declined to say. They had met again, by chance, the following day. Otto had taken a walk along the beach and had seen her on the sand, sunbathing in a tiny blue bikini, her body all curves and hollows. She wasn't alone – two much older French women, obscured by hats and sunglasses, were sitting beside her on beach mats. Otto and Maria had conversed briefly though the French women ignored him.

Now they were alone.

'So what have you been doing?' Otto was oddly shy.

'The same,' she shrugged. 'Nothing much.' She tossed back the vodka in one gulp, grimaced, and gestured for the waiter to fill her glass again. Otto found it hard to take his eyes off her, greedily feeding on the spectacle she presented in her pink vest top and light cotton skirt with its complex hippy print of red birds and yellow flowers. She had a silver ring on one elegant finger. Her hands, like her hair, were restless, fiddling with the vodka glass or picking at the table. Otto reined in the desire to ask her about the maybe-German. He found, to his irritation, she intimidated him – perhaps because of

3

her age, or her knowledge of the place, or simply because she looked so entirely lovely. He wanted to impress but his usual sociable self-confidence faltered in her presence.

'There's a party later,' she said. 'You might like it. Not the usual tourist thing, something special. I can take you. It's a bit out of the way – at the other end of the beach. I'll show you. Why don't you move your lodgings? I could find you somewhere closer to the action. I know some good places you could stay. '

Otto shook his head. 'I like it where I am,' he said. 'It's not far to walk in any case.' He didn't want to be in her debt, didn't want to be helped. Rather, he wanted to demonstrate his competence and inde-pendence. To this end he said, 'Actually I did go to the fort this morning, before it got too hot. On the hilltop.' He gestured vaguely with his hand into the darkness. 'Built by the Portuguese in the eigh-teenth century I think. Only ruins now – have you been up there?'

Maria shook her head. The prospect of the fort and his nuggets of guidebook information made no impression. Despite Maria's indif-ference, Otto had enjoyed the walk. He was staying in a village half a mile behind the beach. The buildings making up the settlement stood in a kind of jungle to left and right of a long narrow lane that led down to a small, natural harbour. Tiny one-storey huts and brick houses stood among huge, emerald plants and strange trees with roots that seemed to grow out of the branches and down into the soil. To reach the ruined fort he'd climbed out of the canopied village and steeply up, over dry, tussocky soil to the cliff top. He had the place to himself, the ring of broken wall, the view over the ocean and a great dome of silence. A tiny island, steep-sided, jungle-crowned, rose from the sea, perhaps half a mile from the coast, mysterious and primeval. He'd sat on a turret of stone overlooking the sea and the long ribbon of white beach, soaking up the fact that, finally, he was here, in India, so far from home in this beautiful, extraordinary place. An hour passed and the heat intensified. Otto, blond and milk-skinned, felt the sting of the sun's rays on his bare shoulders and the back of his head.

4

Back in the village he was accosted by a young man who told him the trip had been dangerous because the fort was full of cobras which might, if enthusiastic, pursue him all the way back to the village, following his scent.

Otto was tempted to tell Maria this tale about the cobras, a more precious and colourful piece of information than the Portuguese provenance of the ruins since he had not uncovered it in a guidebook. But something stopped him, a nervousness that she might not respond as he would like. He would save this for Jen and Charlotte who would certainly appreciate it. By the time they arrived he would be an old hand, like Maria, easy in this place, knowledgeable and confident.

Perhaps that was part of the reason he'd booked to travel ahead of them. It hadn't exactly been part of the plan. Charlotte had been furious when she discovered he'd found a cheaper seat on a flight five days earlier than the girls' departure. It had been an impetuous, rather selfish decision but this way he got to forge the path – to be the pioneer.

'So tell me about this party,' he said. 'You're going?'

'Of course,' Maria said. 'You'll like it.'

Otto nodded. Maria had assumed he would go along. And why not? He had nothing better to do.

An hour later they were walking along the beach. Maria took off her sandals and trod in the edge of the sea so the tips of the waves played over her feet. She had an elaborate silver ornament around her ankle, chains and bells that jingled as she moved. The large, bright moon cast a long white path across the dark blue surface of the sea. As they walked further, beach shacks grew more numerous, makeshift bars and restaurants catering for the backpackers and travellers. Then came a giant holiday resort, a kind of palace fortress, an illuminated swimming pool visible through the steel railings.

'So how long are you staying in Goa?' Otto had asked the question before and Maria had avoided it, as she seemed to avoid any question relating to the banalities of life outside the present moment. Otto was dogged.

'As long as I need to,' she said.

'So how long are you travelling for? I mean, in total, before you go home?'

Maria's hair rippled over her shoulders. She stopped walking and faced the sea, arms raised as though to embrace the night sky and the endless sea.

'This is my home,' she said.

'Goa? India?'

She turned to him, exasperated. 'The world,' she said. 'What do you mean by home? Do I have a house? Do you want to know where I belong?'

Otto was chastened, tantalised and infuriated all at once.

They walked further, away from the main tourist area, around a headland with a crown of trees, and into a deeper darkness. It seemed an unlikely spot for a party, too much out the way. Otto was puzzled. He didn't like silence, and wanted to keep the conversation going.

'So who are these people we're going to meet at the party?' He didn't expect an answer though he had a premonition that Maria wouldn't stay with him for long. So it proved.

In the distance, at the back of the beach, Otto saw blazing lights and heard the low thump of amplified music. A huddle of shack bars made up the centre of the party. A low wooden platform, a dance floor of sorts, stood between them though no-one was dancing yet. A girl called out to Maria, and waved – one of a number of silhouetted figures standing at a bar. Maria waved back and ran towards her friend. Otto followed after.

'Here, have a drink!' Maria's friend, an American girl with glossy blonde hair, thrust a glass into his hand. The music was very loud, some kind of electronic dance music that was decidedly not Otto's thing though he could feel its pulse beating into his brain and his body. The American girl was swallowed by the crowd. Otto raised the glass to his lips, expecting the sting of alcohol. To his surprise, the glass contained only lukewarm water. He knocked it back, thirsty after the heat and the spicy curry.

All of a sudden he was part of a throng: young people gathering around, all talking to each other – Americans, Europeans, Indians – drinking, shouting to be heard over the music, laughing, waving to friends. For a moment, slightly disorientated by the vodka he had been drinking earlier in the evening, Otto felt slight panic. He was alone after all – knew no-one here, except Maria and she had gone. Then he felt a hand on his arm, someone pulling him.

'Maria? Maria?' He was tugged through the crowd, banging against people, weaving between them. Maria's fingers pressed into the sunburnt skin of his forearm – and then, almost magical, they were standing alone in a white place, a box of light, on smooth wood only slightly salted by sand underfoot. It took him a moment to realise she had taken him to the dance floor. They were illuminated like actors on a stage. Was she expecting him to dance? Yes. Yes indeed.

Maria danced well. She closed her eyes to begin with, shutting out everything but the sound. She was graceful and un-self-conscious. How come girls so often danced better than boys? Going to clubs and gigs in the sixth form, most male dancing seemed to involve macho displays of jumping and barging, a licence for affectionate shoving and drunken sweaty hugs. Otto, however, hadn't liked to be drunk or sweaty or barged into.

Maria opened her eyes again and she was smiling at Otto, her arms swaying above her head, inviting him to dance. What else could he do? He had no way of backing out, displayed as he was before the multitudes. And truly, why should he want to with this beautiful girl before him? Otto laughed. What did it matter what anyone else thought, the crowd of strangers? And the music caught him, beat through his limbs, his blood, into his brain. He didn't need to think what to do. He let the voice in his mind sink back.

They danced for a long time. One track followed another. They were not alone for long – soon the platform was crowded with people. Otto didn't feel tired. The more he danced, the greater the energy pulsing through his body. He had never felt so gloriously happy, as though an intense white light was shining in his chest and the pit of his belly, and similarly beaming from those dancing around him, so that together they were moving and dreaming in a brilliant lake of illumination. From time to time Maria moved away from him to dance with somebody else but each time she came back. The moon rose high in the sky. Far out to sea, a light blinked from a ship on the horizon. Along the edge of the beach palm trees stood like black cut-outs beyond which the world might have ceased to exist. A voice in his head said, remember what it feels like, to be in this place here and now.

Maria leaned towards him. 'I need another drink,' she said, holding his shoulder to speak into his ear. 'Some more water. Are you coming?'

The hard light caught the beads of sweat on her forehead. He could smell her too, some spiced perfume, sandalwood perhaps, blending with the scent of her body and hair. He nodded, unhooked himself from the music, following Maria through the dancers and off the platform. The area around the cluster of bars was busy, so many people drinking and talking. A little further away a couple of fires burned on the beach. Maria took his hand and weaved through the partygoers to one of the less crowded bars where she bought two bottles of water. The man behind the bar knew her name. He winked at Otto. The bottles were made of glass, rather than the usual plastic, and bore a plain white label upon which was written, in an elaborate Indian-style script, a single word Otto struggled to make out in the semi-darkness.

'Come on,' she said. 'I need a break. Did you enjoy that? You looked like you needed to loosen up.'

Otto laughed. 'Yeah. It was great. You look fabulous when you dance.' The excitement had loosened his tongue. Maria didn't answer. She led the way down the beach, away from the crowd and towards the sea. She plopped down onto the cool sand, opened the bottle and drank half the water in one go. She wiped her mouth with the back of her hand, a slow, sensual gesture that fascinated Otto. Then she stood the bottle in the sand and peeled off her vest top to reveal the bikini underneath. He saw, fleetingly, a small black tattoo on her back between her shoulder blades. She didn't look at Otto or ask him if he would join her. She simply dropped the skirt and ran towards the sea, the anklet jingling with every stride. Then she dived, without hesitation, into the inky night water and its mesh of reflected moonlight.

Otto opened his bottle and swigged the water. He stared at the discarded clothes. The sea called. He took off his T-shirt and cut-off jeans. Although the night was warm, a faint sea breeze plucked at his perspiring body, making him shiver. His hair clung to his scalp and the back of his neck. He ran to the water's edge.

'Maria?'

She broke the surface, some way out now, spitting and pushing back the hair from her face. Otto waded into the sea. With every movement he created a glitter of phosphorescent light, as though he had a halo around him. Even this late the water was welcoming and warm so he slipped down and began to swim, riding the slow waves. Looking back at the beach, the party with its ball of light was another world.

He swam to Maria and they trod water for a moment or two, a few metres apart.

'How are you?' Maria said.

'Very well thanks. How are you?' He couldn't stop grinning. Maria's face looked white in the moonlight. A phosphorescent glow outlined the movement of her body in the sea. Above their heads hung a dome of blazing stars.

'Can you touch the ground?' she said.

9

'Yes. Just. Can you?'

'No.'

Otto moved closer. His toes bounced on the seabed. Maria didn't take her eyes from him as he stretched out his hand and cupped the side of her face. She glided forwards, cradled by the water, and kissed him. Her lips parted and he felt all the heat of it, her mouth and her tongue, and the slickness and cool of her face. She pressed against him, the long, smooth, limber body he'd lusted after these last two days, and he had his arms around her. She tasted of the salt sea, and of vodka, and she relaxed in his arms, seemingly boneless, cleaving to him, arms around his neck.

Otto broke the kiss and drew his face away. It was too much, too overwhelming. His body was a drum in which blood was beating hard. He looked up, at the reeling stars, the beach lights smeared in the distance. Maria laughed. Otto took a deep breath. He was still holding her, his hands at her waist, supporting her in the water.

'Kiss me again,' she said. The sea moved around them. Otto heard the soft sound of the breaking waves and, distantly, the rhythmic thump of the music on the beach. He drew another slow breath, in and out, wanting to calm himself. Then he kissed her lightly and waited a moment or two with his face very close to hers.

'I like you, Otto,' she said. 'I like you very much.' She placed her hands on his shoulders and pushed herself away, sleek as a dolphin, flipping over in the water and submerging. In Maria's absence the water was cool against his belly and chest, as though contact had sensitised his nerves, an imprint of her shape now branded on his body. He wanted her back, to be in contact with her again.

Maria's head re-emerged some distance away, closer to the beach. She stood up, a silhouette, water dripping from her, hair hanging in long strands.

'Come on,' she called. 'I want another drink.' She waded out of the sea, sloshing through the low waves and onto the sand. Otto hurried after her, aching for another kiss, nervous of overstepping the mark. She picked up her discarded clothes and trotted up the beach. Goosebumps covered Otto's white skin as the seawater evaporated. Just outside of the party's light bubble Maria slipped on her skirt. Otto caught her up and she leaned on him as she struggled to pull up the skirt without covering it in sand.

'What's this? The tattoo on your back.' He placed his hand on it, feeling the warmth of her body and the cool of the evaporating seawater.

'Oh, do you like it? I got it done here,' she said. A black-ink circle with flames – soon covered by the T-shirt.

'Get us a drink, will you?' she said. 'One of the vodka mixers, whatever they've got.'

'Sure,' Otto said. He slipped his hand in his jeans pocket where a few crumpled rupee notes remained. The party was busier now, crowds of carousers gathered around the dance floor. He pushed his way to the nearest bar, where two barmen struggled to keep up with the orders from the punters, three deep, calling out what they wanted, waving money. The music was louder too – or seemed so – a physical presence thumping through warm night air which smelled of overheated bodies, perfume, cigarette smoke and alcohol. Within minutes Otto was sweating again. It took an age to be served. He was squashed in the crowd at the bar, people all around him, so much bare skin and laughter and shouting as the revellers struggled to be heard over the music. When at last he was at the front the barman still ignored him for some time, preferring to serve the women. Strings of coloured light bulbs hung beneath the thatching of dried palm leaves. Hosts of insects danced around the lights; huge spiders waited on mats of dense web. Otto looked around anxiously for Maria but his view was blocked by the people behind him. Finally, clutching two bottles, he pushed his way out from the bar and set off to find her.

The dance floor was heaving. Even the sandy area around the platform churned with people. Young people mostly, though not all. Otto could see some older ones too, old hippy types who had perhaps

11

lived in Goa for some time, or else holidayed here because they had never grown out of partying. He scanned the crowd for Maria but couldn't see her. Why hadn't she waited? The memory of their embrace in the sea was keen and he wanted to kiss her again. She'd said she liked him – and he wondered feverishly if this meant sex – sex tonight – was on the agenda. He had to find her.

Far too many people. He stomped a path through the gathering, pushing through, using his elbows. Where was Maria? He earned curses and complaints for his trouble. He circled the bar shacks, retraced his steps to the place where he'd bought his drinks in case she was waiting for him there. Nothing seemed quite normal any more. The lights were too bright, the music almost substantial. The curious energy still crackled through his body. Perhaps he was a little drunk, or overtired, or overstimulated; perhaps all three at once. He began the circuit again, still clutching the two bottles.

Then he saw her – Maria – apart from the frenzied crowd, just outside the charmed circle, sitting on the sand, with two men and a girl, beside a little fire. Otto felt a spectacular sense of relief. He headed over, dropped a bottle into Maria's lap and sat down on the sand beside her.

'There you are! I couldn't find you.' He placed a proprietary hand on her shoulder and kissed her cheek.

'Thanks.' Maria raised the bottle. She paid no particular heed to the kiss and continued her conversation with the two men sitting on the other side of the fire. Otto eyed them. He guessed they were in their twenties. One looked Indian, with a long black ponytail, the other was a European with close-cropped brown hair. They were dressed simply in T-shirts and jeans without the usual gewgaws and decorations favoured by many of the backpackers – the henna tattoos and pieces of jewellery bought from beach traders.

'Where did you go?' Otto said. 'The party's heated up hasn't it? Is it always this busy?' His voice was too loud and insistent. He was a little provoked by the two older men sitting opposite the fire and was

12

indulging a need to prove himself an alpha male. He wasn't going to defer, particularly with Maria, a tantalising prize, sitting so close beside him.

The other men considered him, seemingly unmoved by his swagger, his show of bravado.

'Aren't you going to introduce us?' Otto said, nudging Maria. 'Cheers.' He raised his bottle. They continued to regard him, the men and the other girl, who was black with long, fine braids, and an American, judging by her accent. Maria picked at something on her sandal. Otto guessed he had interrupted a conversation the others didn't wish to share. For a moment he felt a faltering inside; he sat up straighter, raised his voice.

'Well, I'm Otto, lately arrived from England – a fresh-faced beginner in all matters Goan,' he said. 'So I am a lucky man to have the lovely Maria as a guide.' He knew he sounded gauche but still he held his hand out over the fire, close enough for its heat to sting. The hand waited for a moment – until the man with cropped hair reached out to shake it.

'Max,' he said. 'And this is Kumar.' Max's accent was Irish. His friend, Kumar, nodded a greeting but didn't speak. The American girl offered: 'I'm Gina.'

She didn't say anything else. Instead she fed fragments of driftwood into the fire; the flames leaped happily onto the fresh fuel. Further away, the sea endlessly unfurled onto the beach. The music, loud as it was, did not intrude, as though the noise and the crowd lay on the other side of a barrier, a show on the television perhaps, unable to touch them. It came over him again, as it had done from time to time over the last few days, how utterly alien India was – the unknown, unimaginable stinks and perfumes of the place, the skewed sky, the swarms of people among whom, for the first time in his life, he felt he didn't belong, aware of his whiteness, his difference. Standing on the platform at a crowded suburban railway station in Mumbai he'd realised he was the only white man in sight, and it

13

struck him in a way he had never anticipated what it felt like to be the conspicuous outsider.

He'd been in survival mode for the long, solo journey – keeping focused, never letting his feelings get the better of him. Now the overwhelming shock of the place washed through his veins in a tide, a sense of his aloneness and vulnerability.

'So, when did you guys arrive in India?' He wanted to take charge of the conversation and he was curious about their intimacy, these three. Why had they clammed up? What had they been talking about when he'd arrived?

A gentle smile eased itself onto Max's face: 'Oh, I've only been here a few days.'

'Ah! Another fresh face!' Otto jumped in. 'I flew into Mumbai four days ago!'

Max laughed. 'Not a fresh face exactly. I spend a lot of time in India. Most of this last year.' He looked into Otto's eyes, a cool, measured assessment.

'And what about you, Kumar?' Some part of Otto's mind told him to cool it and take a back seat in this conversation but he couldn't let it go. He sensed he was behaving like an overenthusiastic puppy and that no-one was impressed. But Maria was by his side. He wasn't going to roll over however cool this Max and Kumar might seem. The American girl, Gina, stared away from the fire to the sea, running her fingers around the neck of her beer bottle. Kumar, who had been contemplating the flames, slowly raised his eyes to Otto's. He took a slow sip from a silver flask. He had a strong, elegant face and was evidently tall and well proportioned, his arms and shoulders strongly muscled.

'What about me, Otto?' he said. The voice surprised him. It wasn't the English of India, but of Birmingham. Something about the way Kumar had used his name made Otto feel he was back in the classroom.

'You been in Goa long?' The inanity of the question troubled him, but Otto couldn't now give it up.

14

Kumar said, 'So what do you make of the place, Otto? You having a good time? Enjoying the party?' Otto sensed some subtle put-down in the question. Clearly enjoying the party wasn't cool. So what were these three doing here, on the periphery? Otto had come across it before in his first few days – this hierarchy. Most despised were the package holidaymakers, the residents of the big hotels like the one along the beach, the gated other-worlds where low-paid Indians serviced middle-class Westerners. Otto was well read on the environmental damage these places were reputed to do, the draining of local freshwater resources, the disparity between staff wages and the price a resident might pay for a fresh lobster dinner. To be a backpacker was, of course, infinitely more cool – to travel second class, to dine at the local eateries and tread lightly: to be not a tourist, but a traveller. Names and titles were important. Again, beyond the backpackers, gung-ho, naive or self-important as they might be, were those who never intended to go home. The gap-year kids would be heading back for universities and careers after their grand tour but there were those who had cut all their ties, the perpetual travellers. Some enjoyed trust funds or inheritances. Others lived by their wits, hustling, buying and selling, trading drugs perhaps. They had as much contempt for the youthful backpackers as the travellers had for the tourists. So – was he enjoying the party? A simple question so heavily loaded Otto knew he couldn't answer it without showing himself for what he was – an innocent abroad, or else, a terrible poseur.

Beside him Maria kicked off her sandals and buried her beautiful feet in the sand. Cool, pale grains ran over her toes and clung to her calves, where the silver anklet tinkled. The spectacle of Maria's lovely feet, the contrast between the white sand and her dark honey skin, momentarily distracted Otto from his conundrum. Thoughts revolved and fitted together in his head, like Tetrus blocks.

'I'm a photojournalist,' he said.

The words dropped like pebbles into a still pond. A current

15

seemed to flow among the other three. Without speaking or visibly moving, he sensed the leap in their attention. For the first time, they heeded him. An intense silence followed – then Gina said, 'A photojournalist? That's cool. What's the assignment?' They had focused on him now, all three.

'You never told me,' Maria said. Her voice was lazy. She gazed at him, through lowered eyelashes.

'No,' Otto said. The moment of power was too delicious for him to put it aside yet, to come entirely clean. With this admission he had cut himself free of being either a tourist or a traveller. He was something else.

'So what are you working on?' Max spoke up. The Irish accent was more obvious now. He leaned forward. Firelight painted shadows on his narrow, bony face. It crossed Otto's mind he looked like a hungry prisoner of war, with his close-cropped hair. Something feverish about him too, the mad preacher perhaps, burning with zeal. Otto's confident lie began to seem like a bad idea.

'Oh,' he said, raising a hand in a nonchalant gesture, thinking on his feet. 'The party culture, the drug scene. Do you know how many Westerners have died here in the last five years?'

Again the sense of shock. Had he touched a nerve?

'Who are you writing for?' This came from Kumar. Otto was struck again by Kumar's beauty, something he usually never noticed or was indifferent to in men. He shook his head and prevaricated. A quick Google search would reveal that his employer wasn't one of the nationals but a small Bristol-based travel magazine called *Tourism West*. He'd undertaken six weeks' work experience for them over the summer just after taking his A levels. The first week he'd shadowed the staff photographer, taking photos of Wiltshire morris men and Somerset's stately homes. In the later weeks, having proved himself, the editor let him loose on solo assignments. Several of his pictures made it into the magazine, making up the beginnings of a professional portfolio. And there was some truth in his assertion.

16

Travel West did publish features on overseas travel and had expressed an interest in anything exotic Otto might come up with on his Indian odyssey.

'A British magazine,' he said.

'Which one?'

This time it was Otto who waved his hand in dismissal. 'At this stage of the game, I'm not in a position to say,' he said. The evasion risked any credibility he'd built up with Max, Kumar and Gina. He sensed a silent communication pass between them, quiet glances, a shared summing-up. Was his mission statement enough to win an access pass to this clique of uber-travellers? He wondered, briefly, why it mattered so much to be accepted by this little coterie. After all, young people crowded the beach and he had never found it difficult to make friends. In fact he prided himself on it, his social confidence. Not like Jen, who found every new encounter incomprehensible agony, or even Charlotte who was very choosy about the people she befriended. It was the challenge, wasn't it? He was used to winning people over and taking the lead. Now, in this new environment, among men and women older and more experienced than himself, he had to stretch. He didn't want to be overlooked. And of course, he wasn't going to back off in front of Maria.

Kumar unscrewed the top from his silver flask and held it out. Otto nodded, took the flask and raised it to his lips. Whisky seared his lips and tongue, caught the back of his throat. He took another sip, wiped the mouth of the bottle and offered it to Maria. It was another indication of his confidence, to make free with Kumar's whisky.

Maria shook her head. 'I want some beer,' she said. 'Come with?'

Otto was torn between his lust for Maria and his curiosity about Gina, Max and Kumar. Maria stood up, stretching out her legs, brushing the sand from her skirt. There she stood, sleek and perfect. The memory of her body pressed against him in the voluptuous sea

17

rose up in his mind with such blood-heating intensity it was suddenly no contest at all.

'Of course,' he said, climbing to his feet. 'Great to meet you guys. We'll catch up another time.' He made it a statement rather than a request. He would find them again. Neither Max nor Kumar answered but they shared a look. Gina stood up.

'I'll go with them,' she said.

They headed back into the theatre of noise, leaving the two men sitting by the fire. Once Otto glanced back to see their fronts and faces picked out by the flickering red and gold light, their backs pressed against the darkness. It was a scene immemorial, men around a fire, encircled by the night. And they were talking.

More beer, then Maria pulling him into the crowd to dance. They lost Gina on their second trip to the bar, where Maria flirted with whomsoever she met. Otto was intent, however. He wanted her and he wasn't going to give up. The drink removed any inhibitions and he laid on the charm, teased and flattered. The night stretched on, the music swam around them, ubiquitous and unavoidable, soaking into him. One track melted into the next. They danced together, Maria's movements, her grace, the form of her unfathomably lovely body branded on his brain. He had to have her.

Dawn came, at last, not as light but as a perfume from the sea, a freshening that seemed, perversely, to weary the party people. The dance floor began to clear and slowly groups of people departed. Otto stepped towards Maria and put his arms around her waist, pulling her towards him.

'I'd like to go home,' he said. 'Come with me.'

She leaned against him, all of her slight weight, and rested her head on his shoulder. He breathed the scent of her sea-salty hair, the darker perfume of her tired, overheated body.

'I want to kiss you,' she said, raising her face and flicking the hair from her eyes. It was a hard, assertive kiss, close-mouthed. He could feel her teeth through her lips.

'Let me get my bag,' she said, pulling away. 'Wait here.' She stepped back into the thinning crowd of dancers, turned away and skipped off the platform onto the beach and disappeared into the darkness.

Otto

Tuesday: early hours

Otto stepped down from the platform onto the sand and flopped down to rest while he waited for Maria to return. Now he'd stopped dancing his body ached. His head buzzed with the effects of the drink and the night's excitement. He felt very heavy, half lying on the beach.

Otto took a deep breath. The beach was almost entirely deserted now. In the last few minutes the crowds had miraculously disappeared, to sleep away the day no doubt. The music stopped. Its presence had become so habitual the sudden silence was a shock, as though the beach scene might suddenly fall to pieces in its absence. A shock and then a huge relief. Peace, a balm, restored to the gentle scene of sand and sea. Gradually the smaller sounds reasserted themselves – the shush of the waves, the peeps and chirps of a few very early birds, the weary conversations of the barmen as they washed glasses and cleared up. The darkness faded and the sun rose behind the beach, painting the sea in stripes of cobalt and turquoise. In the distance a group of fishermen tugged a small boat into the sea. How did they sleep, he wondered, the villagers living nearby, pounded nightly by the music?

Where was Maria? He wanted to be home, in bed, and wondered vaguely if she'd already gone, slipped away without him, perhaps found someone else – someone better. Then again, perhaps she'd just

21

got caught up. Having held out so long, he decided to wait a little longer. Weariness overwhelmed him. Otto laid his head on his arm and closed his eyes.

He woke with a jump, disorientated. The journey, Goa, the night with Maria, unfolded themselves in his mind like a map. How long had he been asleep? He looked at his watch. About an hour. When he sat up his body creaked and protested. His neck hurt too, from his awkward position sleeping on his arm. Dry-mouthed, vaguely nauseous, he rubbed his face with the palms of his hands and ruffled his hair, massaging his scalp, hoping to divert the oncoming headache.

No sign of Maria.

What a bitch, he thought, to tell him to wait and then to slope off without him. The rejection stung, an insult added to the injury of his hangover. She'd led him on all night and finally swanned off without even saying goodbye. Perhaps she'd met up with Gina or Max or any of the hundred other people she had spoken with during the course of the night. Otto sighed. He slowly clambered to his feet and shaded his eyes against the fierce heat of the early sun. The bar shacks and the dance platform looked eerily empty and abandoned, like the remnants of a beached ghost ship – as though the night's revelry hadn't happened, had been, perhaps, a dream. Only the sea remained, eternally unravelling at the edge of the shore.

Otto ambled over to the nearest bar. He wasn't entirely alone. One solitary, shadowed figure moved beneath the canopy of dried palm leaves, tidying up or making preparations for the day. Otto leaned on the bar. The pelts of cobweb he had noticed in the electric light the night before had faded into nothing, made invisible by sun and shadow. The barman, in shorts and shirt, had his back to Otto. He was busy unloading crates of bottles from a 4×4, while a young white man stood and watched. Then the barman opened the till, took out a huge roll of rupee notes and handed them to the driver of the 4×4. The vehicle, glossy and new-looking, laboured back across the sand and into the trees.

'Excuse me,' Otto said. The man took his time, maybe thinking himself off duty.

'What would you like?'

'A bottle of water please.'

'Water?'

'Yes, water.'

The barman shrugged, reached below the wooden counter and dumped the bottle in front of Otto. An ordinary plastic bottle, not like the glass bottle he'd drunk from the night before. He scrabbled in his pocket for a rupee note so old and well used it had the texture of silk, sliding between his fingers. The barman picked up the note and was turning away when Otto said suddenly, 'Hey, do you know a girl called Maria? She was here last night – long brown hair.'

The barman looked at Otto.

'Maria? Everyone knows Maria,' he said. A ghost of a smile.

'D'you know where she lives?' The question tumbled out before he thought about it. She'd dumped him, hadn't she? What good would it do crawling round to her house, chasing after her? The barman eyed him.

'You fallen in love with Maria? She's a beautiful girl. Everyone falls in love with her.'

'No, no.' Otto shook his head, his face burning. 'I only met her last night.' He took a swig of water from the bottle.

The barman hesitated. 'She'll be back on the beach tonight. You find her then.' He continued to look at Otto for several moments, his hands busy wiping a glass with an unclean cloth. He put the glass down, stepped closer to Otto and said, 'Go home now. You don't look good. Go home and sleep. Maybe you'll see her later.' Otto scowled, not liking to be so transparent. He picked up the bottle and turned away. Maria's disappearance disturbed him. She was gregarious, he had seen, but she hadn't seemed the sort of person who would go off without him, not when she had specifically told him to wait. He remembered their embrace in the sea. The memory was potent, physically felt, a heat passing through him. He couldn't believe – simply didn't want to believe – that she would have told him to wait and then left.

Ah, more fool him. She'd been drunk too. Maybe she'd been drawn into a conversation and forgotten him, the sad Romeo. To be honest, it was more often the case that he was the leaver, rather than the leavee. He was confident with girls, at least with those his own age, or a little younger. He'd enjoyed learning the patter, getting on top of the game, seducing with words even if, generally, that didn't end in sex. He enjoyed knowing he could have them. It was the power that counted – the sense of accomplishment.

Jen and Charlotte had never approved, of course. The thought of them, even their disapproval, was now comforting, knowing they would be together so soon. He would have plenty to tell. He began the conversation in his mind, momentarily cheered as he walked away from the bar and along the beach towards his temporary home.

Otto was renting a room in a small brick and thatch home in the middle of the village. The owners were a young couple with a five-year-old daughter always dressed in immaculate white. Animals roamed between the houses: goats with drooping ears, squat black pigs with bristly backs. The house had no toilet, only a ditch full of dry leaves where you squatted, and a pig waited to gobble up the residents' turds.

His door was secured with a padlock. Otto unlocked it, stepped into the welcome cool and checked, as was his habit, that his camera bag was still stowed away under the bed. It was a simple room, with two beds, whitewashed walls and a framed picture of the Virgin Mary. Presumably the family slept in here when they weren't making extra money renting it to tourists. He went to the back of the house, filled a bucket with cool water from the tap and stripped off his clothes behind a palm leaf screen, the washing place. A metal cup hung from a hook on the wall and this he used to sluice himself with water. He used a bar of soap his mother had given him, smelling of

24

bright mint and tea tree. The perfume conjured up home and for a fleeting moment he was assailed by homesickness, thinking of his mother alone in the house now he was away. He hadn't emailed since he first arrived in Mumbai. She would be missing him, wondering how he was doing. And he had plenty more to tell, of the long train journey to Goa and the place he was staying, the village in the trees, the pig at the back of the house.

He washed away the soap, pouring cup after cup of clean, soothing water over his body, ridding himself of the sweat and smoke and drink of the night before. He replaced the cup and empty bucket, tied his towel around his waist and returned to his room. Lying in bed between the clean white sheets, he thought at first he was too alert to sleep. He could hear, very clearly, the morning sounds of the village, people talking as they walked by, the pop-pop of motor scooters, the bleat of a goat. But sleep came, after all, obliterating his thoughts.

He slept into the afternoon, surfacing from time to time into dreams of journeys, missed trains, forgotten appointments and lost tickets. He dreamed people were making demands in a language he couldn't understand, wanting something from him that he didn't have. At some point he half awoke and heard the little girl's voice, home from school, reading the story of Red Riding Hood in English to her mother on the veranda just beyond the door. A text had arrived, from Charlotte, telling him she and Jen had arrived safely and were ensconced in a Mumbai hotel. Now it seemed strange they should also be in India, these people from a faraway home. Maria and Goa had filled his mind and heart. He put the phone down, thinking he'd reply later.

He got up, pulled on a clean T-shirt and his cut-off jeans, and padded outside, barefoot.

'Hello, Otto.' The little girl was sitting beside her mother on a bench. Otto sat on a second bench, against the wall.

'Hello, how was school?'

'Good thank you. How are you?' She seized every opportunity to speak with him. 'You've just woken up?' She laughed at his idleness.

'I was out all night. I was very tired,' he said, by way of an apology. The mother disappeared into the house and returned minutes later with a cup of sweet, spiced tea for her guest. She dressed in Western-style clothing, larger versions of the neat dresses her daughter wore, and she spoke perfect English. Still she was very shy around Otto when her husband was absent, and wouldn't look him in the eye when she spoke.

'I have a letter,' the woman said. 'A girl came this morning. She said she didn't want to wake you.' There it was, in her hand, like a dove – the folded white of the paper. A tremor passed through Otto's body.

'A letter?' He took it from her hand. They stared at him, mother and daughter, waiting to see what news it might bring, but Otto, uncharacteristically self-conscious, rose from the bench and took both letter and tea into his room, shutting the door behind him. He sat on the bed holding the paper in his hand, savouring the moment of anticipation. Surely Maria had sent it. How did she know where he was staying?

There was no envelope, just a thick piece of paper folded over and over. He thought of Maria hopping through the waves into the night sea and the glow of phosphorescence around them when they'd embraced, and the tremor went through him again, the heat of wanting to be with her. He unfolded the paper, stared at it. Outside the little girl shouted out. A man's cheery voice called back from the lane. Otto sighed, breathing the village's particular flavour, of growth and rot, of incense and goat and pig, of flowers and rotting rubbish. He opened the page.

Dear Otto –

Words written in blue biro, rounded, untidy and curiously childish.

So sorry to have skipped off last night. I got caught up in an argument, silly me. I had to help a friend, ended up comforting her all night. You know what girls are like. Apologies for leaving you waiting! Hope you will forgive? Come back to the party tonight and I'll make it up to you – promise. Last night's party was

*just a taster. We have so much more to offer you! I'll be there
for ten. Kisses, Maria xxx*

She hadn't abandoned him after all. She hadn't picked up somebody else. Maria had been distracted, helping someone out. He felt a
rush of relief and gratitude.

He read the letter a second and third time, trying to unfathom from
the scant words how much she wanted to see him. Certainly the note
was promising – why go to the trouble of writing an apology and
making a date if she wasn't that bothered? He stared at the word
'kisses' and the three 'x's with absurd longing, then he refolded the
letter, slid it under his pillow and lay back on the bed, his hands
under his head, speculating about the pleasures to come. He hadn't
felt this way about a girl for a long time, not for months. And why
was that? Why did she fascinate him? He conjured up her image, the
feel of her all saltwater slippery, her hair, the elegant hands, the
smooth skin so much on display in the Indian heat, the hollows
inside her hip bones, the flat, perfect belly. Her confidence too,
relaxed and sensual, the way she would talk to everyone, her belonging in this place and her ease in it. And, so tantalising, the fact that
she was a little older than he was, a step ahead, meaning he was the
one who would have to stretch and reach and extend himself to have
her. She was a challenge, yes? Challenge and prize in one. England,
the email to his mother, the photographs he was supposed to be
taking, the imminent arrival of Jen and Charlotte receded into the distance, pushed out by this singular desire, to vault the eight hours till
he would meet her again.

Otto picked up *War and Peace* but he couldn't concentrate on reading. He'd gone ahead of his friends and booked a flight to India several
days before theirs out of this rather childish desire to be the first, the
leader. Charlotte had been annoyed – why should he make things difficult? – but he'd made excuses about limited funds and finding a
bargain ticket. This was partly correct, but the truth was, he hadn't
wanted Charlotte to run the show. He needed to prove to himself, and

27

to them, that he was a competent man, capable of taking care of himself.

He flicked through his travel guide, lay for an hour or more on his bed and tried again to read. Still the empty between-time stretched out like a desert so he left the house, locked the door behind him and walked through the village to a small single-storey cafe where he ordered a banana lassi and an hour on the internet. He'd visited the place twice already to catch up on emails and to make arrangement with Charlotte about their meeting up. The proprietor greeted him by name. Half a dozen tables stood in the shade of a flimsy thatched canopy. At one, a very lean elderly hippy was sitting, naked to the waist. Long, silver dreadlocks hung over his shoulders, his skin tanned the colour of strong tea. His name was Jim, apparently, and he was a long-term fixture at the village; a remnant from the sixties invasion. Otto raised his hand in a greeting which the hippy returned with a genial smile. He would have seen thousands of youngsters flow through Goa over the decades.

Three computers, reasonably new, had pride of place within the small single-room building. A notice admonished users not to eat or drink while using the computers so Otto drank his lassi first, sitting outside in the sun-mottled shade. Apart from the tea, it was his first nourishment of the day but he wasn't hungry – at least, not for food. The proprietor, whose name he had been told and promptly forgotten, brought over the lassi and asked how Otto was. He hadn't got used to it yet, how friendly and chatty people were. Wherever he went, on trains, in restaurants, waiting on platforms, in shops, people made him welcome and wanted to talk. He felt like a celebrity – and thought with embarrassment of Britain, how chilly its inhabitants, and frequently indifferent to foreign visitors.

He finished the lassi, went inside and logged on to his hotmail account. Six new emails – one from his mother, two from Charlotte, three from photography and current affairs newsgroups he belonged to. The one from his mother was brief and affectionate. She owned a tiny art and framing shop and had sent it during her lunch-hour, asking how he was and sending her love. The first from Charlotte confirmed she had received the information he'd sent about where he was staying and when they should meet. It contained a list of flight information and contact numbers for her parents and Jen's parents, just in case he ever needed them, she said. The tone was typically Charlotte – to-the-point, wry and self-deprecating. Her second email was headed 'Some Problems'. He clicked on the title.

Hi Otto
How are you doing? Soaking up the sun and taking lots of amazing photos? V envious. Things not great here – Jen having problems, both parent- and self-created. Her mum going through another tempestuous time and Jen losing sleep over it. Not sure whether she should leave her in this state etc. Am trying to convince her there are other people around to take care of her. Jen also anxious about the trip: whether she's brave enough to come, how she'll cope with culture shock, possibility of illness, etc etc. Feeling exasperated she's thinking of backing out so close to departure, but rest assured, I'll be there with or without her! Though hope she *doesn't* back out – was her idea after all. She needs this trip. Deserves it. Still, you know what she's like, how much she worries . . . Anyway, looking forward to seeing you soon. Missing you already. Lots of love, Charlotte

Otto sat back in his chair and straightened his legs. The three friends had been planning the trip for over a year. Charlotte had a three-month placement as a volunteer at an Indian national park on a conservation project. Jen ostensibly wanted to use this gap year voyage to inspire her artwork. She had a place on an art and textiles foundation course for the following September. Otto, of course, had his photojournalism. Beyond these reasons and pre-dating them, they had all been drawn into Jen's dream of India. It had inspired and sustained them through the second year of sixth form. It had been Jen who first sparked their interest in the country. For all her present anxiety she was the one who had inspired them; as other children had passions for Egypt, or horses, or fashion, or rock music, Jen had longed for India.

Otto emailed back:

```
Thanks for the info. Reckon you'll be here by
now. Welcome to India! Don't know if you'll
pick this up before we meet, but hope Jen is
OK. As you say, she's the one who most wanted
to come here. And it's definitely worth it! See
you soon, Oxxxx
```

Still his head swam with thoughts of Maria. He was tempted to spill the story to Charlotte and indulge himself in a rhapsody about the girl on the beach. But he refrained – knowing how callow and ridiculous he would seem. And he wanted to keep it to himself, this adventure, the insane passion blown up like a sudden storm. Let's see how things work out, he thought. His mind fast-forwarded to the friends' reunion, introducing Charlotte and Jen to the fabulous girlfriend he'd bagged in just a few days. Best wait till then, when the matter was a fait accompli.

Otto looked at his watch. Three o'clock. Still so many hours to fill. A walk in the village, a swim, some lying in the sun on the beach, another fish curry. Somehow he'd crawl through the remaining time.

At nine o'clock, an hour early and with nothing better to do, Otto had made his way along the beach, past the hotels, to the obscure party place and he was standing at the bar, a bottle of beer in his hand. The music had started up but the dance floor was empty as yet. A few dozen people clustered together, drinking and talking. Otto had shaved before setting off and his face looked slightly peculiar, the shaved area paler and less sunburnt. He felt vaguely self-conscious and kept rubbing his chin to hide it. He'd also washed his hair, which was long, and let it out of its habitual ponytail so it fell all fine and silvery-blond over his shoulders. He was uneasy about this too, wondering if it made him appear more effeminate. He tied it back again, let it loose. Tonight he had his camera, slung over his shoulder. He wouldn't drink too much, he promised himself – instead he took a few pictures, the barmen, the coloured lights and the giant spiders, the revellers.

Girls approached him a couple of times, in twos and threes, enjoying the licence of the holiday atmosphere to strike up conversations. He was polite but hadn't made much effort. The minutes ticked by. His eyes roved the gathering constantly, looking for Maria.

'Gina! Gina!'

The American girl with inky braids was walking towards the neighbouring bar. Otto ran over, camera bumping against his hip.

'Gina – is Maria with you? She arranged for us to meet tonight at ten, and it's already twenty past.'

Gina had a curious expression on her face. Was she annoyed with him? Or perhaps with Maria? She shook her head.

'No, I haven't seen her today,' she said. 'She'll be here sooner or later. It's Otto, isn't it?' She glanced at his camera, gave him a curious stare. 'The photojournalist. What's your surname, Otto? I was going to google you.'

'Why should you bother?'

'I'm interested.' She was neither offended nor intimidated. Instead she pushed him on the question.

'Go on – your surname?'

Otto had no wish to reveal his name and thereby his limited professional reputation but he felt himself backed into a corner.

'Gilmour,' he said. 'Otto Gilmour.' What would she find? A photogallery on Flickr, a rarely-used blog, a page on Facebook and perhaps some credits from *Tourism West*. Nothing incriminating per se, nothing to make him a liar. On the other hand, she would find little to impress her either – he would be revealed for what he was, an eighteen-year-old kid on a gap year who'd done some work experience for a regional magazine. He wasn't so worried about impressing Gina but he had wanted to maintain his reputation with intense, Irish Max and Kumar from Birmingham. Yet what did he know about them? Nothing at all. He might never see them again.

'Otto Gilmour,' Gina said. 'Great. I'd love to check out your work.' She smiled. Otto wondered if he was being paranoid and perhaps Gina was only interested and friendly, not trying to catch him out, but he sensed she was very shrewd and he felt on a back foot.

She remained beside him, still smiling, as though she were waiting for a conversation to begin. Otto finally noticed how pretty she was, slight but athletic with the slender muscles of a gymnast or a runner. He glanced again around the crowd to check for Maria – and then said, inanely, 'So you're American?'

'Yeah. I'm from Connecticut.'

'How long have you been in India?'

'Oh a year now. I'm on a postgraduate placement at a university in Mumbai, but I'm here in Goa, to party, like everyone else. You're a newbie, right?'

Otto nodded humbly. Gina laughed, stretched out her hand and touched him lightly on the arm. Otto looked over her head to scan the crowd again, hoping Gina wouldn't notice. No sign of Maria. It was half past ten now.

'So who were the guys you were with last night?' he asked, trying to make the enquiry sound casual.

She shrugged. 'Friends of mine.'

32

A girl by the neighbouring bar caught his eye and he turned to look. It wasn't Maria but at a first glance she looked a little like her. She was staring at Otto.

Gina shook her head, clearly aware she wasn't holding Otto's attention. 'I think I'm wasting my time here,' she said. 'Shall I leave you to wait for your date?'

Otto blushed. 'I'm sorry,' he said. 'That was very rude of me – please – I mean, don't go.' But his body was tense, primed for the encounter he had imagined so many times over the course of the afternoon, the reconnection with the glorious Maria.

Gina turned away. 'I'll see you later,' she said, good-natured. 'I hope you catch up with Maria soon.' And then she was gone, weaving through the thickening crowd.

Otto bought another beer. Annoyance began to sour his anticipation. So many lovely women here all looking for a good time and he was pining like an idiot for someone who had apparently stood him up for a second time. He wandered away from the bar, camera in hand, and took further photographs: the lights, the first dancers – so many glossy boys and girls focused on their drinking, dancing and flirting. None of them as beautiful as Maria though. Over the last three days she'd become his template for female beauty. He found himself comparing her with all the other women and always found those other women wanting.

'Hey! Hey, Maria!' There she was. He saw her, like a mirage, walking away from him.

'Maria!' he called again. Dressed in a tangerine vest top and a pair of tiny shorts, her hair sliding over her naked shoulders, she didn't hear him and continued to walk into a crowd of people beside the illuminated platform. Otto pushed his way through, careless, treading on a foot.

'Maria!' How could she hear him? The music obliterated his voice. He saw her, walking barefoot through the trampled sand, wearing her silver ankle bracelet with the tiny bells and chains. She

33

passed easily through the crowds, people making way for her then seeming to close ranks as Otto tried to follow. He ground his teeth in frustration, the two beers buzzing in his head. All the sun-heated bodies holding out against him, odd curses, a melange of perfumes, perspiration, beer, cigarette smoke. He pushed his way through. Where had she gone? He saw a girl in an orange top swooning in an embrace, shouted out and pulled her away – but the girl turned around with a look of contempt on her face and instantly Otto realised it was the wrong person. Her partner shouted some admonishment, a threat of violence. Otto held up his hands in a gesture of apology and backed away. The wrong girl shook her head and resumed the embrace.

'Otto?' He'd bumped into Gina. 'You've spilled my drink!'

'I'm sorry – I saw – I was trying to catch her.'

Gina's expression indicated both amusement and pity. He pulled himself together, furious for losing his self-control, his cool. And all over a girl he hardly knew.

'Hey, let me buy you another.' He rallied, stood up straight and put his hand on Gina's shoulder. 'Come with me to the bar.' To hell with Maria. How could he have let himself slip like this? The barman offered him two of the glass bottles of water but Otto waved them away and asked for beer. Then he and Gina walked away from the party towards the sea. Gina chatted about the place she was living in, recommended a couple of good places to eat and visit. Suddenly it was all so easy. He was back in command of himself. There was no pressure with Gina, only easy conversation.

They sat side by side, facing the long, low waves that uncurled over and over on the sand. She seemed very interested in him, teasing out information, asking him a little more about his assignments and ambitions. Then she said, 'I might have a story for you, Otto.'

'What kind of story?'

Gina tucked her knees under her chin and wrapped her arms around her legs. She looked very serious.

34

'How much do you know?' she said. 'Things go on here,' she said. 'Stuff beyond all the tourist party stuff. Well, you've seen it for yourself.' She waved her arm at the bright, noisy bubble behind them.

'What kind of stuff?' Otto frowned at Gina. She was testing him again, trying to find out how much he knew. What was she talking about?

'Have you heard the stories? Is that what brought you here?' she said.

'I've heard things,' he said, bluffing and knowing he wasn't bluffing well. For all his social confidence he was a poor liar. He shifted his legs uneasily. 'Travellers' tales, you know. So what are these stories?'

Gina pressed her lips together, apparently thinking about something. She said, 'I want you to meet some people. Would you be interested in that?'

Otto hesitated. 'What people?' Far out to sea, a light from a ship shone out. Behind them, from the party, came a raucous, masculine cheer.

'People,' Gina restated.

Otto thought of Max and Kumar. Were they part of these 'people'? He thought for a moment. Stuff goes on. What did that mean? The obvious options turned over in his head. Crime, drugs, smuggling, illegal migration. The insistent music stopped for one inexplicable moment – some interruption to the power supply perhaps – and then started again. A panorama unwound in Otto's head, his uncovering a great story, the fabulous photos, an adrenalin rush inspired by the prospect of an adventure and personal victory. Why not? What did he have to lose?

'Great,' he said. His tone was measured; professional he hoped. 'Yeah I'd like to meet these people. When and where?'

'Give me your mobile number, and your email address. Someone will get in touch.'

35

Otto raised his eyebrows.

'How mysterious,' he said. 'Isn't this a little melodramatic?'

Gina stood up. 'If you're not interested . . .'

'I am interested. Really.' He gave her the details she wanted. Was that wise? Gina tapped the information into her own mobile then rose to her feet.

'Thanks. I'm going now – I have some calls to make. See you soon, Otto.'

He watched her walk up the beach, away from the party. Maria, inevitably, sidled back into his thoughts. Perhaps she'd joined the party by now. He bought another beer and stood at the periphery, watching the crowd. An hour passed, and he gave up any last hope that Maria might appear. He felt an almost unbearable sense of disappointment. The music seemed intolerably loud, the drunken crowd utterly vulgar. What did the locals think of them, these rich boys and girls come to drink themselves to oblivion and fornicate on the beach? He hung on one last jaded half-hour before deciding to head for home.

Otto walked back along the edge of the sea, taking his sandals off to wade in the cool water. The moon, bald and oval, hung over the ocean. Loneliness overcame him for the first time since arriving in India. He wished his friends were with him, known and trusted people with whom he could relax and be himself. He'd let himself get swept up in the new adventure, and he hadn't even replied to Charlie's text.

A row of fishing boats loomed blackly, higher on the beach. Nets hung over poles. A large bird resting on the sand flew up in a clatter of feathers. The soft air smelled faintly of river mud and dead fish. Otto felt very tired – no doubt the delayed effect of the long, challenging journey, the culture shock, the constant effort to assert himself in a new place among new people.

The tide was going out. A margin of hard, wet sand lay beyond the reach of the waves, silken and shining in the moonlight. More birds, a dozen or so, small and pale, perched on fragile stick legs at the water's edge. They didn't fly when he drew near but scurried apart to let him pass. Then ahead he saw another dark shape in the water.

He knew instantly what it was – never a moment's doubt – only shock, a weight of it, like iron, taking away his breath.

He stopped short and stared. Half in, half out of the water. Feet and legs on the pearl-shining sand, torso and head face down in the sea, slowly lifted and dropped by the movement of the waves. A woman.

Thoughts turned over in his mind. He was certain she was dead – but surely he should check? Perhaps she was only unconscious or comatose from drink. He took another step closer. The girl's legs rolled slightly, side to side, carried by the water. Her hair spread in an undulating cloud. Another step. She was still a silhouette, a dark form with the shape of a woman. The moonlight caught the back of her head, the creases of her sodden clothes. At the top of the beach some two hundred metres away, Otto could see strings of coloured lights, indicating the presence of another bar. A larger wave collapsed on the beach, tumbling the woman's body over and dragging it further out to sea. Otto dropped his camera and ran forward. He jumped in, striding through the low water to grab the woman before she was swept away. He grabbed her wrist and another wave lifted her body into the moon's glare and Otto saw her face for the first time.

Maria. It was Maria.

Blood seeped blackly from a wound in her head, losing itself in the water. Dread filled Otto, like a cold frost inside his head, in his blood, an internal freezing. She was hard to hold, her body inert and heavy, so Otto seized her clothes and tried to drag her back to the shallows. The indifferent sea moved against him, tugging Maria away from the beach and towards the deeper water. For one mad moment, Otto thought perhaps he should just let her go, let the sea have her. What was she to him, anyway? No-one would know and there would be no more trouble for him. He could simply walk off.

Another big wave came and the body – Maria's body –was drawn away. Otto jumped in the water, out of his depth at the crest of the wave, salt water slapping into his face, but he didn't let her go. Instead he shifted his grip to her narrow ankle, sought for purchase in the sand with his feet and hauled Maria towards the beach. In the shallows, as her body dragged against the compact sand, Otto leaned over the picked her up. He was shaking violently. She was very heavy but he managed at last to scoop her into his arms. Her head lolled against his shoulder, eyes nearly closed, the restless hair he had admired so much hanging like torn seaweed.

'Don't worry, over the worst now, take you up the beach to the cafe,' he said, breathing heavily. Why was he talking to her? He needed the sound of his voice for his own comfort, the beach now seeming devoid of life, so quiet, empty except for the birds and they didn't care about his struggle. He carried her up the incline, struggling in the cloying sand, dripping with water, to the cafe at the top. A scruffy, unappealing place at a less popular part of the beach, a peeling sign declared the name 'Summer Holiday Cafe'. The tables were empty. As he drew near, a young Indian man stepped from the shack into the glare of makeshift terrace, staring at Otto, his arms folded. He didn't speak. Otto drew closer and the man seemed to realise something was wrong. He called out and a second man emerged and stood beside him. Otto struggled on, his muscles aching, wanting to call for help. Couldn't they see what he had? Why didn't they come and help him?

'Please! Help me please!'

Still the men didn't move, peering out from their pool of electric light into the beach's natural darkness. Perhaps they couldn't see for certain what it was he carried. They put their heads together and said something Otto couldn't hear. He drew closer, stumbling in the sand, thorns piercing his feet, and at last stepped into the light, the body spilling out of his arms. Then the men realised something terrible had happened. They ran forward, suddenly speaking very

38

loudly in a language he couldn't understand, helping him lift Maria, cradling her between them and placing her on the wooden terrace at the front of the shack.

'Have you got a phone?' Otto shouted. 'We need to call the police! We need a doctor!' They paid him scant attention, talking instead to each other. Otto continued to shake. He wanted the men to notice him and to understand what they were saying. The light at the cafe was painfully bright and buzzing with insects. Otto saw blood on his T-shirt and shoulder where Maria's head had rested. One of the men was squatting beside her now, poking at her hair, pulling her mouth open. Otto, in a sudden rage, ran over and pushed him away.

'What do you think you're doing?' he shouted. The man responded fiercely with an incomprehensible stream of invective. He stood up, shoved Otto back. The other man ran out of the shack, a mobile in his hand.

'Please! Please be calm! I have phoned the police. Sit! Wait!' Then the two Indians began arguing again. Otto pushed his way into the shack, picked up a towel and laid it under Maria's head. For the first time he looked at her properly. She had bruises on her perfect face and arms, and her lower lip was split. In the merciless light, the coffee tan leached away so her skin appeared shallow and drained. Otto stretched out his hand and pushed the hair from her forehead, stroked her cheek. He had never seen a dead body before, sheltered British boy that he was. Her face was cold and inert under his hand; the wound on her head was not clearly visible and he was too afraid to investigate it further. Maria. He had kissed her last night, obsessed about her all day, a sudden, passionate infatuation spiced by the exotic setting, the heat, by hours of leisure. Grief surged through him, a tide of it, and an unexpected rage. For the first time it flashed into his mind that someone had done this, that someone had killed Maria, hit her in the face and smashed the back of her head, had left her for dead at the edge of the sea. Had it been a sexual assault? Had she been raped? Had she taken drink or drugs? Someone had done this, someone out there probably not far away. Poor Maria. The scene played out in his mind, the blows and the struggle.

'Maria,' he said again, blinking back tears. Dimly he was aware of the heated conversation continuing behind his back. How long till the police came? He had little idea about the efficiency or otherwise of the Goan police. Would it be minutes – or hours? What would they want from him? What about Maria's family? It dawned on him that his life would never be the same. This shocking event was now a part of him and he would never forget it or be able to erase it. This woman, whom he had kissed and held and talked with and lusted after, had been hurt and killed. That was not going to change. The old easy life was over. He would carry this with him, every single day, for all the weeks and months and years of the rest of his life.

Charlotte

December 2007

It was still dark when the alarm went off on Sunday morning. Usually on Sundays Charlotte lay in, took a long run, maybe seven or eight miles, then indulged in a luxurious soak, lying in the bath in a froth of lavender foam, rubbing sea salt and olive oil into her skin, and later, a roast dinner with her parents.

Today though, no run, bath nor roast dinner. Instead, a quick shower and a coffee. She dressed in layers of warm clothes and fur-lined boots. It would be cold, standing around in London's December weather. Her rucksack was packed already: book to read, notepaper, pens, a small aluminium flask of soup, bread rolls and bananas – she had enough for the two of them, since Otto wouldn't think to take supplies. A small digital camera, a map of the march route from the internet, her mobile phone. She checked the contents one more time, stuffed her purse and bankcard in her coat pocket, picked up her winter coat, hat and mittens and stepped out into the early morning twilight.

Frosty still – a grey and silver world, like an enchantment. Stars glittered in the sky, purely white in a blue-black sky. Ice encased the dead stalks of dock and hogweed in the verge. Glamorous feathers of ice sprawled across the windscreen of her father's ten-year-old Jaguar. No wind, no sound, except the muted clop of Charlotte's boots on the pavement as she set off towards the town centre. It took her twenty-five minutes to reach the coach stop. She waited in the little cafe across the road, ordered a cup of tea and a toasted teacake. Then she saw him, tall and very skinny, emerging from the shadows with his long, loping stride. She recognised him long before his face became visible. He came across to the cafe. When he opened the door the bell jangled.

'Otto!' She was sitting alone at the old-fashioned Formica table. Otto grinned. His face was pink from the cold. He wasn't wearing a coat, just a hoodie and a zip-up jacket over the top and one of those Nepalese knitted hats which seemed, to her inexplicably, to be all the rage this winter.

'You don't have any gloves? Where's your coat? I said to dress up warm! You'll freeze!'

Otto took no notice. He leaned forward to kiss her on the cheek and give her an extravagant, rather self-conscious hug. Charlotte felt a smile stealing across her face. She couldn't help it, the sheer pleasure of being with Otto again created a sense of warmth in the pit of her belly.

'You'll get cold,' she said, scolding more gently.

'I'll be fine, don't fuss.' He flopped down on the seat opposite, hands in his pockets, sticking his long legs under the table. There remained something coltish about Otto. He'd grown so much in the last two years, shot up to six foot. But he was still physically awkward, as though the length of his limbs surprised him; his arms and legs had to be managed and accommodated. He was growing his hair, only now it was an untidy in-between length, straggling to his shoulders, falling over his face so he was always brushing it aside or tilting his head to keep it from his eyes. He'd also acquired earrings and intermittently a rash of acne across his cheeks about which he was intensely self-conscious. The pallor of his skin, and today, the cold, did nothing to disguise the blight. All of this Charlotte drank in, loved, appreciated – delighting in his presence, the unique, entirely lovely Otto-ness of him and the prospect of the day they would spend together.

They'd been friends for years, attending the same town primary school, and had stayed in touch ever since.

'You've got your new camera!' she exclaimed. He lifted the bag onto the table – a professional camera bag from which emerged the machine itself, matt darkness and silver, the lens jutting out with its complication of rings and numbers.

'Isn't it a beauty?' Otto held the camera with some reverence and tenderness, turned it about so Charlotte might admire it.

'You think it's a good idea taking it to the march? Is it insured?' she said. How precious it looked, the deep-water glimmer of the lens when Otto took the cap off and pointed it at Charlotte.

'What's the point of having a fantastic camera if you don't use it?' Otto said. 'I might get some good pictures today. It'll be good light, I reckon. Clear sky, sunshine.'

Charlotte offered him the second half of her teacake and he ordered a cup of tea. They discussed the route of the march. By ten to eight a dozen people were waiting at the coach stop so they left the cafe and joined them. The coach was timely, already half full from its previous pick-up point. The atmosphere inside was very warm and soporific. Charlotte took off her backpack and stowed it on the rack above her seat. Otto sat beside her, cradling the camera bag on his lap, loath to let it go. Everyone was subdued by the early hour. The journey began in silence. Otto soon fell asleep, hat still on, mouth dropping open. Charlotte stared through the window as they powered along the motorway, seeing the frozen fields, the huddled villages, sheep with frosty backs. The darkness dissipated and the sun rose over the hills.

They stopped once, at a motorway service station. Charlotte bought the *Observer*, Otto snaffled a bag of fries from the burger outlet. After the stop the soon-to-be marchers grew more animated and murmured conversations began. Otto and Charlotte shared the paper and fries. London slowly closed around them, the city villages making up the suburbs, ubiquitous retail and industrial parks, decayed factories, new office blocks. Charlotte felt a quiver of excitement.

'Hey, the demonstration's got a mention in the paper,' Otto said, nudging her with his elbow. 'There look, bottom left.'

Charlotte leaned over to see. A tiny paragraph, yes. Thousands expected to join London protest against the cultivation of genetically-modified crops in Britain – a couple of sentences only. Still it was a mention. Perhaps if the turnout were large enough, she thought hopefully, the march might merit further coverage.

The coach parked up alongside Hyde Park and the travellers disembarked. The cold was stunning after the fug of the journey. Charlotte tugged her scarf around her neck, pulled on her hat, coat, mittens. Still the air was sharp as a knife despite the sunshine. She watched Otto shiver but resisted the urge to worry about him, or to say she'd told him so.

The protesters wended their way like sheep hither and thither across the park, drawn to the larger assembly. Charlotte could hear loudspeakers in the distance. Excitement tingled. After the long journey, the early start, she finally felt awake.

'Look!' She pointed with her gloved hand. A man wheeled a bicycle embellished with giant papier mâché sculptures, abstract shapes in bright colours, looking surreal in the subdued and faintly misty winter park. She saw two young men dressed as polar bears, bodies swathed in white fur, carrying their bear heads under their arms, and behind them, a handful of teenage girls dressed in pink, orange and lime green, decorated and jewelled, latter-day hippies. The protesters were all ages though – Charlotte saw families with little kids, pushchairs, babies in backpacks wrapped in layers of warm clothes. Lots of older people too. Most, probably, were middle-aged, plenty of pensioners, old ladies in warm hats, smiling and waving to friends as the diverse assembly slowly congregated and became a mass in the centre of the park. Many carried placards on sticks or long banners. Here and there sellers of socialist newspapers, looking a little forlorn, offered their wares to the passers-by. Then the march began – though march seemed a curious word for the gentle flow of people along the streets. Charlotte was not well acquainted with the geography of London. She followed the crowd, seeing only vaguely the city's highways and stores, where Christmas shoppers crowded on the pavements seemingly a world apart from the protesters with their placards bobbing, banners and flags streaming above their heads, chanting, beating drums in jaunty rhythms. How many were they? Impossible to tell. She was a single cell in the body of the crowd, aware only of those nearest to her and she was happy as the march proceeded, fired by the sound of the drums and the sense of belonging. She glanced at Otto walking by her side. He had his camera in his hands and took photographs as they went.

'How are you feeling?' she said with a grin. 'Glad you came?' He had taken some persuading, his free time between school and a part-time job at the camera shop in short supply.

He raised his eyebrows. 'Actually yes!' Then he ducked away from her, spotting something evidently picture-worthy. She admired his confidence, how he was prepared to step out of line, or crouch, or simply take shots without worrying if he looked foolish. He didn't ask permission before taking pictures of people – and they rarely seemed to take offence. Why should they, after all? They were here, in public, to make a declaration. Still Charlotte didn't think she would be bold enough to put herself about as Otto did, seeing only the picture opportunity, keeping himself focused, standing on a bin perhaps to gain a higher vantage point or walking backwards to confront the protesters and grab a shot of them coming towards him.

Police officers stood at intervals, many armed not with guns but with cameras. Information was the new ammunition of course, the currency of control. Surveillance cameras punctuated the city streets, high up on posts or attached to buildings. She'd first read *1984* when she was twelve and many times since. He'd be I-told-you-so-ing from beyond the grave, George Orwell, she thought. Attacks by a shadowy terrorist organisation to keep everyone placid and afraid, a security based on the control of information, the mass media saying they had no reason to be afraid of this surveillance unless they were up to no good. Another CCTV camera swivelled and pointed its stumpy, one-eyed face seemingly at Charlotte and she shivered. And more on the way – emerging face recognition technology – perhaps chips implanted in the body. The good feeling engendered by the march melted away for a moment, overwhelmed by the cold fear of a world over which she had no control, not even the integrity of her own body.

'Otto. Otto?' She'd lost sight of him and now wanted to see him, to be reassured, if only by his presence. There he was, red-faced from the exertion of his energetic photography. He grinned and waved from the other side of the road, then weaved his way towards her, skipping from side to side through the marchers.

'Hey! I got some great shots – there was an altercation – did you see it?'

'No – what happened?'

'Some bloke started mouthing off about the protest – *Daily Mail* type, said we were all scrounging socialist scum.' He looked thrilled, the response from the forthright shopper having validated something for him, perhaps the righteousness of the cause. It affected Charlotte in quite the opposite way. She wanted to believe that everyone was really on the same side, that they all felt the same way she did.

They continued on their way in the river of people but some of Charlotte's earlier excitement had melted away. The cold was seeping through layers of clothes and into her bones by the time the march pooled into Trafalgar Square. Speakers addressed the crowd from a stage at one end. Queues of women waited outside a toilet block. Charlotte found a gathering of people from home who had travelled up on the same coach. Some of them she knew a little from Friends of the Earth and Amnesty meetings though most were the same age as her parents. She made polite conversation.

Otto had dived off again, wanting pictures of the speakers on the stage. Charlotte sat on a cold step, poured herself a hot drink from her flask and ate some food. Despite the milling thousands she felt a little lonely. If only it was warmer; the cold was a distraction, stealing all the pleasure from this last part of the day. Clouds gathered above the city skyline. By three it was getting dark. The Christmas lights came on all at once and the city became a curious chilly fairyland strung with electric jewels.

Where was Otto? The crowds began to disperse, searching for their coaches home. People streamed away. The Friends of the Earth people advised Charlotte it would soon be time to go.

'I'm just waiting for Otto,' she said. 'You go on. We'll catch up.' She took out her mobile and texted him. She said where she was and the need for urgency if they were not to miss the coach. Ten long minutes later her phone vibrated in her hand. The screen flared in the gathering darkness.

Tlkng – ppl u must meet. We cn take train bk. Ill find u.

Charlotte's heart sank. She wanted to be on the coach, safe and warm. She had school the next morning, homework to complete. Why did he have to do this? It wasn't the first time. Quite possibly the 'ppl' he referred to meant a girl. She pressed the reply button, ready to type a curt answer, telling him that she would take the coach and leave him to find his own way home. Otto was always hungry for new people, for more friends, and he was always on the lookout for girls. She started to tap out the message but didn't have the chance to complete it, because there he was, beside her, out of breath as though he had been running.

'There you are!' he said. 'I couldn't see you. Come on, stand up. Come!'

'I want to go home. I'm tired and cold. I want to get on the coach.'

Otto was momentarily nonplussed. His face crumpled into a frown in the city's electric light.

'Didn't you get my text? You have to meet these people! Come on.' So much boyish enthusiasm.

47

'What people? I've got work to do at home. I've got school tomorrow. If we don't hurry we'll miss the coach.'

Otto pulled an expression mixing impatience and irritation as though Charlotte were stupid for not already knowing what he knew.

'Trust me, please!' He looked so appealing that Charlotte's heart began to get the better of her. She always found Otto hard to resist. Slowly she rose to her feet.

'Okay,' she said. 'But I don't want to be too late home. We'd better text the others and let them know we won't be on the coach.'

She could sense Otto's excitement. He could barely refrain from jumping up and down like a kid. He set off across the empty square, the detritus of the meeting still in place, the portable iron railings, posters, some litter though not much. All around them shop windows with Christmas displays and the coloured lights beaming out in the darkness.

'So who are they, these people?'

He was three steps ahead, tugging her along with his enthusiasm.

'Come on!' he urged. 'It'll be worth it – you'll see!'

Jen

December 2007

A pigeon with amber eyes flew down from the lamp post and darted among the feet of the marchers. Jen worried it would be hurt, trampled on by the crowd. It fluttered to left and right, eager to scoop up crumbs scattered from someone's on-the-hoof lunch. Its feathers were pale grey, banded with stripes of ivory and petrol blue. The pigeon hopped into the air and dropped down again, anxious to snatch the crumbs as the people walked around it in an endless stream.

'Watch out!' Someone bumped into her as she dithered, setting off a domino pile-up among the close-packed marchers. They were good-natured though. The first man laughed, put his hand out to her shoulder and asked if she were all right.

Jen blushed in a horrible confusion, colour burning her face. She could hardly look him in the eye, ashamed to have caused the trouble.

'It's fine, I'm sorry, I mean – I was worried about the pigeon.'

'The pigeon?'

'There, in the road. I thought it was going to be hurt.' When she looked round the pigeon had gone. The man took his hand from her shoulder, grinned and waved.

'As long as you're okay,' he said, turning away.

Jen found she had gravitated to the edge of the road, the makeshift railings where the people on the pavement were separated from the protesters filing along the street. She leaned against it, feeling dizzy for a moment and wanting to regain her composure. Such a fragile thing, her composure – like walking on a tightrope when the smallest upset, suspected slight or careless word might cast her down. She didn't find the mundane, everyday world easy to inhabit. She took a deep breath. At least the pigeon was safe. If someone had hurt it – how would she have managed then? No use thinking on it, the might-have-been. No use at all. She took another breath, focused her mind on the here and now. Best get walking again, move into the current of people.

She'd had a dream once, one of those rare dreams so bright and clear it marked itself on her memory. How long ago? Several years probably. A procession of fairies, walking along a narrow lane between two high hedgerows in summer. These fairies were human-sized, silent, dressed in brilliant, jewel-like colours beneath a blue sky. They carried long banners that streamed out behind them, long, narrow, glistening flags that floated over their heads. A vision – a revelation. Something about the march reminded her of the dream. The sense of a procession of course, the banners – even though these declared: Say No to GMO. Even though dull buildings hemmed her in and the sky was the colour of iron.

From the pavement an oik in a cheap leather jacket clicked his tongue to catch her eye and winked as he drew near. Jen jumped away from the fence and pushed her way to the middle of the road, searching for safety. Drums pounded out a rhythm from behind. Her feet in their midnight blue velvet boots began to step in time.

A boy was jumping in and out of the crowd up ahead. He was pale and angular, brandishing a camera, and stopped to perch on his toes at the edge of a kerbstone. The camera rose to his eye – clicked and clicked again. The lens swivelled and Jen sensed she had become the focus of its attention. She turned her face away, ignoring it, wishing she could make herself entirely invisible. No such luck. The camera gave a succession of clicks and then she was beside him, the blond boy, and the camera was only an arm's length from her face. She raised her arm to ward him off and hurried past.

'Hey!' he said. 'Please – may I take your picture? You look fabulous!'

Jan didn't look and didn't respond, just picked up her pace.

'Hey!' he called again. She scuttled on, hoping he would leave her alone.

'Please!' He was beside her now. 'I'm sorry,' he said. 'I didn't mean to alarm you – just, you're very photogenic. I love your outfit.' The voice was warm, the compliment made an impression, to her annoyance. She glanced at him and back at the horizon. Tall, gawky, about her age she guessed, wearing one of those wool hats. Strands of white-blond hair around a strong, handsome face. She blushed, couldn't find the words for an answer.

'I'm Otto,' he said. 'Good to meet you. Where d'you come from? I came up on a coach – from Wiltshire. It's cold, isn't it?'

Jen glanced at him again, mustered the courage to nod her head. Her eyes met his for half a moment then she looked at the road before her feet.

'London,' she said. 'I live in London. Herne Hill.'

'I'd love to live in London,' he said. 'You're really lucky. So much going on!'

Jen shrugged. 'I don't like it.'

'Why not? All those concerts, exhibitions and stuff.'

She shrugged again, shrinking from making eye contact. 'I don't like cities.'

'Well I can imagine it might all get a bit much sometimes – all built up, the traffic,' he conceded. 'I'd still like it though.'

'Good for you,' she said. This last comment was more strident than she had intended but Otto didn't seem to worry.

'What's your name?'

'Jenevieve. Jen,' she said. 'With a J.'

'Jenevieve. I like that. Like Guinevere. You know, King Arthur's queen.'

'Yes I know,' she said, looking at him again, this time a little longer.

'So you're into this whole anti-GM thing?'

'Well, obviously. Why else would I be here? Aren't you?'

'Well yeah. Of course. But really, I came to take pictures. I want to be a photojournalist.'

'Ah, I see. So you're an observer.'

'Yes! Yes.' He looked thoughtful. 'I like that. An observer, yes.' Otto smiled, looking pleased with himself. Then he said, 'Who did you come with? Are you alone?'

Jen shook her head quickly. 'Came with my brother. He's around here somewhere. I lost him.'

'Easily done – so many people.'

Jen didn't know what to say next. After a moment or two Otto started telling her about his photography A level, his portfolio, even some shots he'd taken that morning on the march. Soon she began to relax. He was easy to be with. He even asked her a couple of questions about herself, what she was doing at school.

'Are you a photographer too? Art, that's it. I bet you're doing art.'

Jen smiled. 'Yes, I am. Why do you say that?'

'How you look – your outfit I mean. Creative. I like that.'

Trafalgar Square opened ahead of them, crowds and statues, the grand buildings looming over.

'Here we are,' he said. 'I'd better text Charlotte – let her know where I am.'

'Charlotte?'

'My friend. Not girlfriend,' he added. 'I lost her some way back. Better let her know I'm here.'

Jen nodded, anticipating his departure. Otto, however, wasn't eager to leave.

'Jen! Jen!' It was Niall calling out from the crowd ahead. Beside him stood his friend James, hands in pockets. Jen headed over, Otto following. She was conscious of how Otto must see them, the art freaks. Niall and James were several years older than she was, studying fashion at St Martin's. Niall wore a tight banana yellow suit, a green scarf wrapped around his neck. James had a huge white fake fur coat, and long, straight platinum blond hair. They eyed Otto, who was carelessly scruffy, a kid of sixteen, and paid him no further attention.

'Where d'you go? We lost you ages back. I told the others, you'd have wandered off in a dream somewhere.' Niall brushed his hair back from his face. Jen glanced at Otto, expecting him to be intimidated, but he stood his ground. In fact, he stepped forward.

'I'm Otto,' he said. 'You guys look great. Love the outfits.' He thrust out his hand to James, man to man.

'James,' James said dryly. 'Charmed I'm sure.'

Jen blushed. Otto kept his cool.

'Jen and I got talking on the march,' he said. Around them the crowd surged forward and as a speaker from Friends of the Earth took to the stage. A female voice boomed through loudspeakers, cutting through the conversation. Niall grimaced.

'Shall we go?' he said, pawing James's arm. 'I'm absolutely freezing. I can't spend any longer standing around with so many badly-dressed people. It's positively draining.'

Jen glanced at Otto with a smile that she hoped would say: take no notice. They're not so bad – only putting on a show. Otto grinned back.

'Where are you going?' he said.

'For a drink. And a party,' James said. Then, archly: 'Come if you like. Do you want to bring him, Jen?'

Then they were all staring at her: Niall, James and Otto.

'Well, I, if he wants to. If you want to,' she said, staring at the ground, twisting on her heel. She shrugged, indicating it was of no great matter to her either way.

'I would like to.' Otto jumped on the invitation. 'But I have to get Charlotte.'

The threesome stared at him quizzically. 'We came on the march together. She'll be waiting for me.'

'And you lost her?' Niall tutted.

'Well we lost Jen,' James responded.

'No, she lost herself.'

Jen turned to Otto.

'Will you wait? Just a minute – I'll get her. I won't be long, honestly. Just wait. Don't go away!' Before they could answer, promise or disagree he bounded off through the crowd.

James and Niall glanced at one another. Jen shifted from one foot to another. She wished they hadn't encountered Otto. They would be thinking she fancied him, wouldn't they? Niall's smirk suggested as much. James sighed, shifting his coat luxuriously over his shoulders. Jen wanted to start a conversation and lighten the atmosphere but couldn't think of what to say. Around them the crowd grew thin, people heading off for home and out of the cold.

At last he came hurrying across the square. Beside him a tallish, athletic-looking girl with dark hair, dressed in warm, unremarkable clothes.

'This is Charlotte,' he said. Charlotte didn't look entirely happy, though she gave a brief smile and nodded, swiftly appraising the company. Then they headed off across the square, Niall and James in the lead. Jen heard Charlotte whisper to Otto: 'What did you bring me for? Why would I want to miss my coach to meet this bunch of posers?'

Jen quivered. She couldn't hear what Otto replied.

They weaved their way through the busy streets, past elaborate window displays, ornamented with silver, lights, glittering plastic icicles, polar bears, recreated scenes of an ideal Christmas that perhaps had never existed, consisting of fireplaces, stockings on the mantel, perfect trees perfectly decorated, boxes (probably empty) wrapped in

54

exquisite paper and ribbon. It worked all the same, evoking a nostalgia for something. For what? A feeling, an ache, connected with Christmas and the past. A yearning for a yearning? And so many entrepreneurs eager to profit from it, with their conjuring of never-never firesides, their implied promise the goods on offer might give you the feeling you wanted. Ahead of her, Niall and James were engrossed in a conversation. Behind, Charlotte and Otto walked in silence. Caught between the groups, Jen turned her attention away from the shop windows to the sky. It was difficult to make out the stars through the glare of the city's artificial lighting. They were distant, obscured as though by smoke. The moon wasn't visible. And Jen, still caught in the trailing threads of Christmas nostalgia, closed her eyes for a moment and wished she were out in the countryside, on a hill of stone and thorn, where the wild sky burned with stars and she could smell cold earth and ice. She conjured the scene in her imagination, the expanse of it, the billow of faraway hills in the night, the complex shadow of the bare tree thrown on the frosty ground by the moonlight, the dead leaves around her feet all silvered with frost – and the sound, very distant, of church bells.

'Jen! For crying out loud.' She had bumped into Niall. 'Walking with your eyes shut? Wake up!'

Traffic streamed past, the opposing lines of headlights and red tail lights, churning out fumes. Rubbish scattered the pavement. Moor, moon and thorn dissolved. Jen glanced at Otto, and said by way of explanation: 'Take no notice. He's my brother.' As though the familial relationship excused his temper. Siblings weren't always polite to one another.

James led the way into a bar. Its warmth engulfed them. It was some trendy place James knew, with tangerine walls and shiny black floor tiles. The bar itself was also tiled, black and white like a chessboard. They all ignored the exotic bottled beers and fancy cocktails in favour of hot drinks and found a table in the far corner of the room. Through the bar's glass frontage, the passers-by on the pavement

55

were thin shadows, lacking substance. Jen sat on a soft white chair, like a marshmallow. Otto glanced at the artwork on the wall behind her, made some comment to Charlotte who was sitting beside him. Jen turned to see what it was – some plastic confection, transparent and laced through with shiny red strings. Was Otto impressed? He was the boy from the sticks, after all. She was the city sophisticate. Except that she wasn't. She'd lived in London for six years now and it had never seemed like home. She still felt like a visitor, edgy and uneasy.

They all peeled off their coats and hats. A tight, buttoned shirt emphasised James's thinness. He brushed back his long fringe from his narrow, heavy-framed glasses and draped his arm over Niall's shoulders. Then they stared, the two of them, at Charlotte and Otto, who looked very gauche and ordinary. Jen quailed on behalf of her guests – but Otto didn't seem to feel his inferiority nor was he intimidated by her brother's considered display of gayness. In fact, Otto sat up straight, leaned forward on the table, and said, 'So, tell me about yourselves.'

In the end they got on well, the three boys. Niall and James took to Otto since he refused to be daunted. They talked for ages about London, gigs, art, photography. Otto held his ground, took teasing in good humour and had the confidence to tease back. The girls took a back seat. Charlotte clearly felt out of place and resented being there and Jen didn't dare strike up a conversation with her. They ended up being a rather dreary audience. Otto did turn to Jen from time to time with a comment or question and she got the impression his display of wit and confidence was partly for her benefit; but Charlotte too seemed to notice this and glowered from the other side of the table. Did Charlotte like Otto then?

At eleven Niall said he wanted to go clubbing. Jen, tired and bored, responded that she would go home. Charlotte and Otto argued about the last train back – Otto longed to go clubbing too. Charlotte won out in the end but Jen could see how much Otto was fretting –

torn between his duty to his friend and his desire for excitement and a novel experience. Duty and friendship triumphed. Well, that was a mark in his favour, his loyalty – not wanting to let someone down. A brief farewell followed – Otto traded contact details with Niall. Jen wondered if he would ask for her too – did she want him to? In truth he hadn't paid her so much attention since her brother had appeared on the scene. Her cheeks burned in anticipation.

He swivelled towards her: 'Could I have your email address, Jen?' he said. A certain over-brightness in his voice suggested he was also anxious about asking.

'Yes, well, of course.' She fumbled the answer. He typed it into his mobile. Charlotte stood and watched and waited, eager to be off, glowing with an aura of impatience. Then they were gone, the West Country twosome, off into the night, hoping they could get to Paddington in time for a late train. Charlotte led the way, striding along the pavement. And Jen, tired and cold, began her own shorter journey home, longing for warmth and bed.

Charlotte

December 2007

They ran up the long flight of the escalator, from the depths of the London Underground, and jumped on another Tube train just as the doors were closing. The carriage was almost empty, scattered with newspaper pages. Charlotte and Otto sat on facing seats. Otto thrust his legs out like a barricade across the corridor. Charlotte folded her arms, still churning with tightly held annoyance. She was very tired, drained by the hours of walking and standing in the cold. She was also furious with herself for allowing Otto to persuade her to stay the extra hours in London. When would she ever learn? Why did she find it so hard to say no to him? All for a girl, of course, and the intriguingly gay fashion students an optional extra. Charlotte glowered but Otto, seemingly oblivious to her feelings, responded with a big grin.

'Wasn't that cool?' he said. 'I've had a fantastic day. Thanks so much for organising everything, Charlie.' His face was so bright and awake, Charlotte felt herself weakening. He sat up, leaned over and patted her on the leg.

'Did you enjoy it? Did you have a good time?'

Charlotte nodded. 'The march was great. The late drink? Well, to be honest I could have done without that, but otherwise, yes.' She wouldn't let him get away with it entirely. He liked the girl, though, that Jen. She'd seen it in the way he had glanced at her all through the conversation at the bar, as she'd seen it a hundred times before. He was like a magpie when it came to girls, attracted to every bright, shiny face he encountered. Over the last year or so this had kicked off, as though he'd noticed for the first time just how fascinating and amazing women were. He was like a child in a sweet shop. Except for Charlotte, of course. They'd been friends for such a long time. Charlotte belonged to a different category. He talked to her, laughed with her and trusted her – but he didn't look at her in the same way he looked at other women. She waited patiently, occasionally with pain, for the day when the novelty wore off and he realised the most fascinating woman had been beside him all along.

Charlotte glanced up at the Underground map above the carriage doors.

'Next stop,' she said. 'We need to get off.' Then they were running again, along the tiled, windowless corridors, through the ticket barriers and up into the cold air of Paddington station.

Otto glanced up at the departure board. 'Platform one! It's just about to leave!'

Charlotte took a deep breath and sprinted across the station, the cold air scorching her lungs, backpack bouncing on her back. A guard was walking along the length of the train, closing the doors. Otto leaped into the first carriage, Charlotte hot on his heels. The train wasn't crowded. They walked through two carriages of first class then flopped into seats by the window facing each other over a table. Relief and warmth washed over them. The train pulled away through the great city, past office blocks and flats and streets and retail parks into the darker night beyond.

They didn't speak for a while. Otto fiddled with his phone, checking messages. Charlotte stared through the window at the passing landscape. Perhaps he was texting Jen? The image of this new belle rose in her mind. Jen was someone you'd notice even in the diverse crowd making up the march. On the short side, and petite, with flawless white skin and long hair, dyed a dark crimson, she'd had an amber nose stud, another, silver, stud beneath her lower lip and wore a long, moss-green velvet skirt, a brown corduroy jacket, nipped in at the waist, and the twists of scarf in which so many autumn colours glittered, gold and auburn and chestnut and scarlet. Yes, she was gorgeous.

His phone beeped. Charlotte looked up at him, raised her eyebrows.

'Who from?' she said, with a smile. 'Jen?'

Otto nodded, solemnly. 'Wasn't she lovely?'

Child in a sweet shop, Charlotte thought again. Sometimes she felt a decade older than Otto. That didn't stop her liking him. Liking him? More than liking him. She couldn't believe that he didn't know. Then again, as she'd never said anything, how would he know? He could be annoyingly, endearingly naive at times.

'Do you think you'll see her again?' The train drew to a halt at Reading. The platform beyond the window was deserted so late on a Sunday. Further along the train a door banged, some late passenger either climbing on or disembarking.

'I don't know. I hope so.' He wasn't looking at her, his eyes focused instead on his phone as he tapped out a reply. Charlotte squeezed her hands together. She had seen how his eyes glittered as he thought of something witty or charming to text. She couldn't help how she felt about him, had long grown used to it. Sometimes it was very hard to be patient.

It was past midnight so they splashed out on a taxi to take them home from the station. The house was dark and cold and silent when Charlotte stepped inside. She dropped her bag on the floor and ran upstairs, jumped swiftly into bed. No run tomorrow, she allowed. Too tired already and a busy day at school to come.

Otto

Wednesday: early hours

The ambulance arrived first, the police car hot on its heels.

Otto was sitting on a chair. A blanket covered Maria's body. He watched from a distance as the medics uncovered her and checked her out. The scene played in front of him, a drama in which he had no part. His emotions had faded away – perhaps more accurately, they seemed to belong to someone else. What had this to do with him? The girl, the police officers, the medics, the cafe staff – they were strangers. None of them had existed a week before, not for Otto. Having emerged from nowhere, how could they mean anything to him now? The setting possessed a similar air of unreality – the night with its perversely tilted moon, the pale sand, the Indian beach. And he couldn't understand them, the men talking in an alien language, the intense, hurried conversations. The men from the cafe became agitated and gesticulated to the police. The first waved his hand at Otto, perhaps denying knowledge or responsibility. One of the medics, a woman, came over to Otto and asked him in English where he had found the body and how long ago. She took some notes, examined the body again. More phone calls were made, more talking and waiting. Otto longed to go home, for sleep and escape. He had a sudden yearning for his mother and took his mobile from his pocket intending to send a text. What time would it be, in England? But the police officer spotted him, took the mobile from his hand and held on to it. Otto protested – but the officer brushed his words aside.

Having lost his mobile it struck him – he didn't have his camera. Where was it? The events of the last hours unreeled in his head. The beach – down at the sea's edge. When he'd run into the water, Otto had dropped the camera on the sand. And he'd forgotten it in the time of shock and panic. He'd left his precious camera behind. He stood up without thinking, ready to run and retrieve it. Of course he'd only taken a step before the same police officer moved forward, raised his hands and physically pushed Otto back to his seat.

'I have to get my camera!' he shouted. 'I have to get it! I left it down on the beach! I have to find it!'

Odd now, how passionate he felt and yet still the scene seemed to unfold at a distance. He should be afraid, shouldn't he? This police officer, a tallish, middle-aged man with a salting of grey in his moustache, a belly that bulged over his beige trousers, was treating him with neither respect nor the expected compassion. Now he stood over Otto, hands on hips, pursing his mouth.

Otto changed tack. He tried to reason. 'I'm sorry – I left my camera on the beach. It's worth a lot of money – I need to go and get it right away.'

The police officer still stared. He rubbed the end of his nose with the back of his hand, his face thoughtful.

'Okay. I will come with you,' he said. 'You show me where you found her. Show me the place.'

Otto nodded and stood up. He stepped away from the cafe and onto the beach. He glanced at his watch – it was 4 am. How easy would it be to find the camera? The beach was largely featureless, his footprints hard to make out in the soft sand at the top. He took what he hoped was the right direction and headed down to the sea. The police officer walked close beside him, near enough for Otto to hear his rather heavy breathing. The radio attached to his belt bleeped –

the man took it from his belt, listened to a message and glanced across at Otto. He made an incomprehensible reply before putting it back on his belt. They reached the sea. Otto scanned the beach, up and down, the sand almost silver in the moonlight. He couldn't see the camera and wasn't entirely sure where he'd found Maria. He recalled the journey up the beach, carrying her body.

'It has to be around here somewhere,' he said. His companion made no reply, standing with his hands on his hips, belly thrust out. Otto wandered one way then another. How far could it be? He tried again, jogging along the sea's edge where the sand was dense and wet, leaving new lines of footprints, going further each time. The sea moved beside him, impervious, the sea in which he had first embraced Maria, and from which he had pulled out her body. The feeling of disembodiment persisted, some small part of him thinking how ridiculous it was, his trotting up and down the beach like a dog on an extendable leash while the fat policeman watched and waited. But his camera – he had to find his camera.

'Here! Here's the place!' Had he veered much more than he remembered, to find the cafe? This had to be it, a mash of footprints in the wet sand and a trail where he had dragged Maria from the water. The policeman lumbered over.

Where was the camera? He looked about, scoured the beach. Where was it?

'Stand back!' the policeman shouted out. 'Keep away, you fool. You're trampling the evidence! Stand back!'

'I'm trying to find my camera – I can't see it. I don't know where it's gone!' Bewildered, Otto still searched the sand. Had he got it wrong? Perhaps this wasn't the right place after all. Maybe the sea had taken the camera already. Something glittered in the sand – silver white, catching the moonlight. He dropped down and scooped it up. There, lying in his palm, was the chain that had hung so prettily about Maria's ankle.

'What is it? What have you found?'

'Nothing. I – I thought I saw the camera, thought I saw something – but I didn't.' Otto, the poor liar. He waited for the policeman to push the point, wondered why he had lied at all. What on earth had prompted him? He kept Maria's chain cupped in his hand. When the policeman turned his attention to the disturbed sand, Otto slipped it into his pocket. Another radio conversation followed. Then they stood and waited, Otto and the policeman, as the waves uncurled on the sand and the moon sank into the sea.

They drove him to the police station. The area where he'd found the body was taped off. Maria was taken away in the ambulance. The fat policeman stayed at the cafe and Otto was accompanied by two young men, neither of whom spoke much English. Otto felt very lonely in the back of the car and for the first time he felt the sting of fear. How far might he be implicated in this? Would he be blamed? Was he a suspect? He stared through the window. Soon it would be dawn. A pain gnawed in the pit of his belly. It had been niggling for the past hour or more.

A brisk conversation proceeded between the two police officers which Otto could not understand. He began to feel afraid for himself. He had no idea how honest or corrupt the Goan police might be. At home in England, he had felt himself to be inviolable – a person with rights and protection. That might not be the same here. Why hadn't he obeyed his first cowardly instinct and left Maria where she lay? These men had him in their power now. He had no-one to call on. They might do with him as they wished. But they wouldn't treat him unfairly, surely? He was a tourist – he was British. Some small part of him registered this last thought with an ironic smirk – that when the going got rough he should cling to this notion, that his Western origin and country of birth should award him special privilege and protection. The fat police man had said simply that they wished to interview him. It was made obvious that he had no choice but to go with them.

At the reception desk a man in civilian dress asked to see Otto's passport. Otto told them he'd left it at his lodgings. He was asked for a host of personal details which were entered into a form in neat, painstaking handwriting. They took photographs and fingerprints. Then he was taken to an interview room. A single table and three chairs waited. White-painted concrete block walls and a single window, small and high in the wall with a vertical bar across it and thick, opaque glass. Otto took a seat – and waited.

His head ached. The knot of pain in his belly alternately relaxed and tightened. The chair was small, hard and uncomfortable so after a time he sat on the floor, propping his back against the wall. Overwhelmed by tiredness he fell asleep for a time, his head resting on his hands. When he woke – how long later? – he was hot. The room had become an oven. He glanced at his watch. Eight o'clock. He got to his feet and tried the door, which was locked. Then he banged, calling out for attention.

'Hey! Hey! I need a drink! Why have you locked me in? How long's this going to take?' He had no idea if anyone could hear him but he continued to knock. Within a minute or two, the door opened and the man from the reception desk appeared. 'Please, be patient. Somebody will be with you soon,' he said.

'I'm a British citizen. I have my rights!' he said.

'Of course you do. Please be calm. Have we treated you badly in any way? Have you come to any harm?' The receptionist spoke with the barest thread of contempt. Doubtless he'd heard it all before, arrogant young Westerners in Goa for a holiday, getting tanked up on drink and drugs, thinking themselves above the law and then pleading for special treatment. Only Otto had done nothing wrong.

A vision of Maria rose up in his mind, the body lying on the beach in the dark, the mat of bloody hair at the back of her head.

'I need the toilet,' he said. 'Please. I need the toilet.'

The reception man nodded. He put the tray down inside the door of the interview room and beckoned for Otto to follow. He indicated a door just along the corridor. Otto dashed inside. His guts churned, cramping in a sudden agonised pain. He tugged down his cut-offs and sat down on the toilet just in time. A deluge of burning, stinking diarrhoea cascaded into the toilet bowl. He remained for a few minutes, head in his hands, waiting for the pain in his belly to subside. Another spasm knotted his insides in an agonising ball and a second cargo of reeking, liquid waste jetted from his behind. Then, miraculous, a moment of relief. The pain ebbed away. Otto took a deep breath, rubbed his face, cleaned himself with the slick, meagre toilet paper provided. He pulled the flush, washed his hands and face and stared at himself in the tiny square mirror above the sink.

He looked terrible – grey-faced, forehead red with sunburn. And blood on his shirt, long blotches of it, darkening as it dried. Had he eaten something bad? God forbid he'd contracted dysentery already. He'd read about it in the guides, the fever and pain, the passing of blood and pus. All the dire warnings, accompanied by grins and wisecracks, about the health risks of backpacking in the developing world, the diarrhoea, parasites, malaria, bilharzias, intestinal worms, stings, bites. Why did everyone seem to have a friend of a friend who had come back from India or Peru or China cursed with some exotic and terrifying health problem?

He stared at himself in the mirror– the slipperiness of his guts was due perhaps to nothing more exotic than fear.

When Otto opened the door a whiff followed him into the corridor. The man from the reception desk made the tiniest expression of distaste before he turned and escorted Otto back to the interview room.

'How long will I have to wait?' Otto said.

The man nodded his head from side to side.

'Not long.'

'May I have some water please? I'm very thirsty.'

'Of course.' The man shut the door and turned the lock. A few minutes later he reappeared with a smeared plastic jug and cup. Otto, versed in the importance of drinking only bottled water, almost raised a protest but restrained himself. He didn't want his whining to look like weakness. Taking the jug, he nodded his thanks. Alone in the room he stared at the water, dry with thirst, wondering if he dare risk drinking the water from he-knew-not-what source. In the end thirst overcame his worries. He filled the glass, drank it down, and filled it again. The water tasted soft and warm. It seemed to soak into the tissue of his mouth and throat before even reaching his stomach, as though his body were a dry sponge.

A key turned in the lock. Otto whipped round. Two men entered the room, neither of whom he had seen before. One, a slim, upright young man, was dressed in the beige police uniform. The other, perhaps in his early forties, had bad skin and wore a white shirt without a tie and a grey suit which to Otto's eyes looked distinctly cheap and unpleasant. He felt the older man's eyes on him, similarly summing him up. How unpleasant did Otto look? Another Western tourist, a privileged child come to the playground of Goa to party and indulge, thinking himself untouchable? No good Otto explaining that he wasn't like the others, that he was serious, a photojournalist, all the back-up story. Cut-offs, T-shirt stained with blood, sunburn, long hair, the unmistakable odour, doubtless still clinging to him, of drink and diarrhoea. He certainly didn't look serious. The image of Maria floated into his mind, the dead girl, the horrible mess of it. Some part of his mind still refused to admit what had happened – expected someone to tell him it was a mistake, a terrible joke, a dream. For it had to be a mistake, didn't it? How could this have happened to him? Except, of course, it had happened to Maria.

Maria, Maria. Her face slid into his mind, the slippery hair, the brown skin, the beautiful hands. All stopped now. Extinguished and stamped out. How could she be dead? She was young and precious and unique – and all that she was, every thought, dream and memory, had been obliterated and brought to an end.

Otto glanced up at the policemen. They were staring at him. The older man stepped forward, holding out his hand.

'Good morning, Otto. I'm sorry we've kept you waiting so long. I appreciate your patience.' He said it as though Otto had waited by choice. Without thinking, Otto took the outstretched hand and shook it.

'I'm Inspector Sharma, and this is Sergeant D'souza.'

Otto shook hands with the younger man. Sharma's English was flawless and seemed to him almost unaccented.

'Please take a seat,' he said. So they sat, the three, on the hard plastic chairs around the table in the middle of the room. The younger man opened his leather briefcase and extracted a pile of grey paper.

'We have to take some details,' he said, inclining his head in a kind of apology.

'I did that already – when I arrived,' Otto said.

'I'm sorry,' the sergeant said. 'This won't take long.'

Sharma smiled, waved his hand at the forms, inviting Otto to share his amusement. 'Bureaucracy, eh? All the paperwork. Of course we're famous for it.'

We. India, he meant. It was a subtle remark, making a difference between them, Otto and Sharma, because Otto wasn't included in that 'we'. Otto shifted uneasily on his chair. He felt gauche, a big kid entangled in grown-up games, aware Sharma was trying to make him comfortable while at the same time gently patronising him. The sergeant took out Otto's passport from the bag and placed it on the table. Next he placed Otto's mobile alongside it. Otto stared at it, stunned, wondering at this conjuring trick with his passport. He looked up at Sharma.

'You've been to my room,' he said.

'Of course.'

D'souza flicked the passport open and copied details onto his form. He asked Otto for his date of arrival, flight details, occupation, travel arrangements and plans for the rest of his visit. When the form was complete, the sergeant slid the papers back into his bag. Otto stared at his passport, longing to snatch it from the table and to hold it tight. He needed it, relied on it. Now it lay on the table between them, a hostage. Sharma, all the while, had been sitting back in his chair, observing Otto, gleaming with evident good humour. While Otto smelled of sweat and blood and sickness, Sharma carried the perfume of cleanliness and the merest hint of some masculine cologne.

'Now,' he said, rubbing his hands. 'Shall we have some tea?' As though he were a fond uncle, Otto the beloved nephew.

'Yes,' Otto said. 'Yes, tea would be good.' His stomach rumbled a warning, and his intestines contracted with a shadowy, remembered pain. He would have to be careful. Tea might help.

The sergeant got up and poked his head through the door, doubtless despatching one of his lackeys for refreshments. When he'd taken his place again, Sharma leaned forward with a sigh, put his hands on the table, and said, 'Now we cannot delay this unpleasant business any further, Otto. This terrible matter.' He shook his head. 'I'm very sorry for you, my friend, to have come across this. And you just walking along the beach, enjoying your holiday! And your first time in Goa.'

What, then, was the right response? Another image of Maria drifted into his mind, of her dead body lying on a table perhaps just a few walls away in this very police station. Maria's body, which had entranced him over the last few days, her perfect throat and shoulders, hips and thighs and belly, full of heat and movement, full of life, which he'd ached to touch and kiss, now dead and no longer entitled to privacy. Perhaps other men – police, a surgeon – were staring at her, poking and examining and observing, trying to pry out any secrets her body might still hold. The idea filled him with horror, this second violation.

He shook his head abruptly, scattering the thought. He had to stop this drifting off. Sharma was watching him and Otto had a strange fancy that his own face was transparent, like a sheet of glass, through which the policeman could see the progression of his thoughts. Sharma smiled.

'You know, I am new to Goa too,' he said. 'In fact, you've been here longer than me. I've been posted from Delhi and I arrived yesterday. There are matters of concern here. Do you know what I am talking about, Otto?'

Otto frowned. Clearly he couldn't mean Maria's death, but something preceding it. Was there some connection? He shook his head.

'Well then, this nasty business, the poor girl. Shall we begin with that?' Sharma said. 'The sooner we begin, the sooner we end. You must be very tired.'

'Am I a suspect?' Otto blurted.

Sharma evinced surprise. 'Good heavens, no! Why do you say so? Have we treated you badly? Has anyone made any accusations? Otto, you're our primary witness – so you're a very important person.' He said this last sentence grandly, as though conferring an honour.

Otto sighed, Sharma's reminder bringing on the mooted weariness.

Sharma sat up straight. He said, 'Did you know the dead woman before you found her on the beach? Do you know who she is?'

'Yes,' Otto nodded. 'She's called Maria. We met a couple of days ago.'

'Do you know her surname?'

Otto shook her head. 'No, actually. She never told me.'

'Well I can tell you. Her name is Maria Westland. She's British, like you. Now, as far as you can remember, I'd like you to tell me where and how you met Maria and how your friendship developed.'

All the while, his sergeant scribbled notes in his rather laborious handwriting. Otto complied in as much detail as he could remember, minus florid descriptions of how much he'd fancied her. When Sharma asked, Otto admitted they had kissed, denied they had engaged in further sexual activity. He explained about the letter, the

72

arrangements to meet that evening and Maria's standing him up. Sharma also questioned him closely about Maria's friends, all the other people she had spoken with while in Otto's company. Finally, step by painstaking step, Otto was required to tell them exactly how he had found her, what he had seen and done.

The interview took three hours. At the end of it, Otto was reeling with exhaustion. Sharma stood up and shook his hand.

'A driver will take you back to the village now,' he said. 'Have a rest, Otto. You deserve it.'

'Thank you, yes.' Otto stumbled when he rose to his feet, oddly dizzy, overwhelmed by relief that this episode was over. He reached out for the passport, but the sergeant drew it away before Otto could touch it.

'I need my passport,' Otto said. The sergeant slowly shook his head.

'Please be so kind as to let us hold it for a day or two,' Sharma said. 'It is a formality during the period of our investigation.'

Otto felt the blood rising to his face. 'So I don't leave? You're keeping me in Goa? So I *am* a suspect! You don't trust me. You think I'm going to run away!' He realised how loud his voice had become. He was shouting. Neither Sharma nor the sergeant turned a hair. The inspector inclined his head and gave a calm smile.

'Please, Otto. You've had a very trying night, I entirely under-stand. It is part of our procedure. Indian bureaucracy, yes? Just a day or two. We'll keep it safe, entirely safe. Please trust me. Soon you will be enjoying your holiday again.' He raised both hands in the air and lowered them again very slowly, like a magician. 'You may take your mobile phone however,' he added, handing it over as though conferring a favour. 'We have checked your calls.'

Otto sighed. He felt the minimal amount of fight he still pos-sessed leaking away. What could he do?

A police officer drove him back to the village, past verdant rice fields and stands of jungle. A tall, purely white bird stood on the back of a sleek water buffalo on a grass verge. The driver hooted at a bullock cart in the lane. Otto stared at the view through the car window, his stomach turning over, head tight with a low, persistent ache. He was hungry and nauseous at once. He wanted toast to eat. Proper English toast with marmalade, and then a bath and the clear, cool familiarity of home. He pressed his forehead against the glass. The unreeling view wasn't convincing. The consequence of exhaustion, sickness and shock no doubt, this sense that the alien Indian world was an image only, a scene on the television. If he closed his eyes, perhaps it would dissolve and he would find himself at home again, in the real world.

The village hove into view. The driver honked his horn again. He had beads hanging from his rear-view mirror, a picture of blue-skinned Krishna stuck on the front dashboard, and he kept glancing at Otto. The car swerved between a moped and a cow that lay, oblivious, in the middle of the road, chewing a swatch of vegetable matter. A few pedestrians glanced up and observed Otto in the back of the car. When they pulled up outside Otto's temporary home the wife came out, nervously covering her mouth with her hand. She didn't speak to the driver and wouldn't meet Otto's eye as he stepped out of the car and walked to the house. The driver spoke to her – gave some kind of orders after which she nodded, still looking at the ground. Then the car drove off and Otto went into his room.

Cool, dark, familiar, it was almost like home. He could see the room had been searched. The contents of his suitcase had been disturbed, the bed perhaps turned over and remade. Just now he was too tired to care. He wanted to talk to someone friendly – his mother, to Charlotte or Jen, just to hear their voices and for them to reassure him everything would be okay. But his mother would panic, wouldn't she? He called Charlotte's phone, and then Jen's, but couldn't make a connection. Truly he was alone. In a stupor he took off his sandals, fell onto the bed and closed his eyes.

Otto

Wednesday

Otto's eyes opened and fixed on the ceiling. For one clear, blissful moment his mind was empty. Then memories of the night tumbled over him like stones – Maria dead at the edge of the sea, the weight of her body, the police and the long hours in the interview room.

He lay rigid, holding his breath, clenching his fists, as the recollection of the previous night unreeled in his mind. His first thought was appalled shock – how could this have happened? Why, why had it happened to him? He wanted to rub it out, erase it, to be again the person of just twenty-four hours before, the Otto who had never seen a dead body or dragged a murdered girl from the sea, who had never stepped inside a police station. His heart thrummed against his ribs. He screwed his eyes shut and forced himself to take a long, slow breath.

He lay for some time, alternately staring at the ceiling and covering his face with his hands. Slowly, piece by piece, he recalled the happenings of the night before. Certain scenes flashed into his mind with particular intensity – the birds on the sand, and the dark shape of the body in the water, the sensation of grasping the girl by the ankle as the waves dragged her away, the mat of blood in Maria's hair, the particular pattern of blood on the shoulder of his T-shirt.

He swung his legs out of bed and peeled off his clothes. When his cut-offs dropped to the floor, Maria's silver anklet fell from the pocket. Otto picked it up and held it in his palm. Perhaps it was dangerous to keep – incriminating in some way – but still he didn't want to be rid of this last remaining link. He slid it from one palm to the other and dropped it into his sponge bag. Wearing only a towel about his waist he headed to the washing place at the back of the house. He cleaned himself from head to foot, sluicing away the dirt and blood and sweat and sand and seawater. Then he padded back into his room and dressed in clean clothes, his hair still dripping down his back.

It was two in the afternoon. The rest of the house was quiet. The little girl and her mother must be out somewhere. He felt utterly and entirely alone. His first and most pressing instinct was – again – to call his mother – to cry out for help like a child. The urge was so overwhelming that in suppressing it he felt physically sick. But resist it he did. What could she do? How much would it worry her? How could she help? It would be selfish of him to call, at least just now when there was nothing she could do. He ached to hear the familiar, soothing voice telling him she could sort it out and make everything okay.

What would happen now? The police had his passport so he couldn't leave. Perhaps they would find Maria's attacker, sort it all out and let him go on his way. He had done nothing wrong, only tried to help. He had nothing to hide. So why was he full of terrible anxiety? He had a nagging, stinging instinct that he wouldn't get away so easily. Already he felt himself cribbed and confined, as though by cunning ropes and traps.

And the camera. His precious camera, saved for over many months, had disappeared. It felt like an amputation. So much of his sense of purpose was tied up in his camera and now it was either drowned in the sea or suffering in the hands of some lucky thief who had happened to be walking along the beach during the time between Otto's discovery of Maria and his return to the scene with the police officer. Had the sea taken it? He tried to remember if the tide had been moving in or out.

Otto wasn't hungry but he pushed himself to leave the little house and walk through the village to the cafe, where he ordered a lassi. The waiter, the man whose name he couldn't remember, eyed him curiously. Had he heard about the events of the night? The silver-dreadlocked old hippy had his usual place and he too stared at Otto. Did he think Otto was a murderer? Had he known Maria? People would have seen the police car. Doubtless in a place like this news travelled fast. Otto took a mouthful of the lassi and struggled to swallow it. His throat felt tight as though he had a rope around his neck. He put the glass down.

What exactly had he said to the police the previous night?

He tried to remember each question, every answer. It was difficult. A fog hung over his memory of the interview, clouding his view. He had answered truthfully and in as much detail as he could remember. Did that mean Maria's acquaintances – at least the ones he had mentioned – would also be questioned? He knew only Christian names of course, had only basic descriptions of the people he'd seen Maria talking too. First there was the maybe-German (he had not even a name or confirmed nationality for him), then the American girl Gina, the two men, Irish Max and Kumar, and any number of other revellers at the beach party.

He turned the glass round and round in his hand. Behind him, inside the cafe building, the waiter and another man were talking and staring. Otto was overcome by an urge to run away – to jump on a train and leave the place behind. But of course he couldn't. They had his passport. The small, red book held him as effectively as a prison cell. Even if he left Goa he couldn't leave India. And anyway, didn't he have a duty to see this thing through, for Maria's sake?

His mobile, lying on the table beside the lassi, rang and wriggled. The noise was shrill and unexpected, making him jump. He grabbed it.

'Hello?'

'Hey – Otto, is that you?' An American accent. A girl's voice.

77

'Gina?' He felt a flood of relief to be speaking to somebody friendly. How had she got the number? Then he remembered he'd given it to her the night before, when she'd offered to introduce him to 'some people'. He waited for her to speak again, but she paused. Otto said, his voice nervous, 'You heard what happened?'

She hesitated before answering. 'Maria. Yes I heard.'

Otto fumbled for the appropriate thing to say. 'Did you know her well?'

Gina cut him off. 'Otto, d'you want to meet up?'

'Yes. Where? When?'

'You know the Seaside Bar? It's near you. Six o'clock.' Gina's voice was level but she didn't say goodbye. She simply ended the call. Otto noted her number, saved it in his contacts.

He felt again a spasm in the pit of his stomach, both a premonition of pain to come and a bruised reminder of his humiliating bellyache the night before. It was time to go. He stood up, leaving the barely touched lassi on the table, and waved a goodbye to the cafe proprietors. They were still staring as he turned away and walked back through the village to the house, conscious their eyes were fixed on him as he headed away.

Even after the short walk, sweat soaked his face, glued his T-shirt to his back. Like the inside of a steamer, the Goan afternoon. Legions of ants swarmed in the dirt at the edge of the lane by the house. A little boy, perhaps six years old, barefoot, dressed in a grimy shirt and shorts, stopped and stared at him with round, brown eyes. Otto forced a smile. No need to get paranoid – he'd often been stared at since landing in Mumbai. The boy stuck his finger in his nose and continued to stare.

The house was mercifully cool on his return. Determined to be clear-thinking, Otto decided to assess the search of his room – what the police had seen and what, if anything, they had taken. This didn't take long. He had only a backpack and its contents, and the room itself was minimally furnished. Clothes, toiletries, sleeping bag – still present and correct. Guidebook, notebook (empty as yet), a tube of biros, sun cream, iodine tablets, water bottle, mini first aid kit – all had been moved, and examined no doubt, but the police hadn't taken anything away. *War and Peace* remained on the floor where he had left it. As far as he could tell, the only thing missing was the letter Maria had sent him the previous day, arranging the meet-up that had never happened.

Hardly surprising the police had taken that. He was afraid the contents of the letter might incriminate him. Could that be true? After all, if he had killed Maria, why would he then carry her dead body to a cafe? Surely he would simply have run as the guilty party had done? Still. His naive natural instinct cried out that he couldn't possibly be blamed for something he hadn't done but he had a terrible, queasy idea the police would look for someone to blame and that the someone would be him. Perhaps it was xenophobia, pure and simple – a nasty buried voice needling him with suspicions about the competence and integrity of the Indian police. Maybe it was because here he was the outsider, the minority, and this had ramped up his sense of vulnerability. He rubbed the sweat from his face. He had to think clearly – had to clear the fog of shock and anxiety. Gina wanted to see him.

The Seaside Bar. Otto arrived early and ordered a shot of vodka. The drink seemed to bite into the lining of his sore, empty stomach but he finished it nonetheless and ordered another. Just two days before he'd been watching Maria, jealous of the attention she had been paying to some other man. How pathetic that sounded now. How utterly pointless. When he closed his eyes, Otto could imagine her vividly, sitting on the other side of the table, her restless, long-fingered hands, the particular sleek quality of her sun-gold skin, the voice that would not be used again. The sheer, incomprehensible waste of it, the end of such a beautiful, complex, seductively lovely human being, hurt like an impalement. He knocked back the second drink and ordered a third. Don't get drunk, he warned himself. You need to be clear-headed.

Gina was exactly on time. He'd been watching for her on the beach but she arrived from behind the cafe having taken, he presumed, the same path as he had from the winding road behind the coast. She gave a brief, cool smile as she approached, her braids tied back, dressed in a plain white shirt and a pair of linen trousers. Without knowing it she took the seat Maria had taken, facing Otto. The waiter came over. She ordered an orange juice. She and Otto stared at one another for a few moments, taking measure.

'How are you, Otto?' Gina's voice, with its soft American accent, was low and compassionate.

'How did you find her?' she said.

'Along the beach – I was walking. She was lying at the edge of the sea. Her face – it was all bruised. And someone had bashed the back of her head.'

Gina's self-possession faltered for a moment. He observed a barely perceptible tremor in her lower lip. It crossed his mind Gina was afraid. Was she in danger too? Why should that be?

'Did you see who did it?'

'No.' He shook his head. 'There was no-one around. It was dark, don't forget.' Otto kept his eyes on her face, and said, 'Do you know who did this, Gina?'

A thought flashed in his mind.

'Did she have a boyfriend?' A second idea followed on its tail, carrying on its back a stab of unexpected guilt. Had this boyfriend, or ex-boyfriend, been jealous, seeing Maria with Otto? Otto wondered why his thoughts seemed to lead him into self-blame. Why did he feel so guilty about what had happened to her? Why was he seeking out a reason to link her murder to something he had said or done? That was madness. He shook his head – he had nothing to do with it.

'Maria always had boyfriends,' Gina said. 'She always attracted attention.'

Otto flinched. He had helplessly flattered himself into believing he was something special. Even after a couple of days' acquaintance? He was stupid, yes, but it was always hard to believe that one's own overwrought passions had no significance for anyone else.

'Lots of boyfriends,' he echoed, more to himself than to Gina.

'And why shouldn't she?' Gina bridled. 'Are you saving yourself for marriage, Otto? Christ almighty. I thought you Europeans were a little more liberal about that kind of thing.' Her voice rose, her anger out of proportion. Otto recoiled.

'Hey, sorry, I didn't mean anything like that,' he said, holding up his hands, palms forward. 'I didn't mean to sound disapproving. It's just – well, I know I only met her a couple of days ago, but I, I liked her a lot, Gina. Too much.'

Sudden, humiliating tears sprang to his eyes. He looked away from the table, out over the beach, but he sensed Gina was still staring at him. She sighed.

'I'm sorry. It's just . . .' She hesitated. 'It's just, well, you know what the police are like. It's always the woman's fault, isn't it? If you're not holding a husband's hand and covered from head to foot then you're asking for it. You think I'm exaggerating? Well, you would. You're a man. You haven't spent your life being told how careful you have to be – you know, we women are responsible for your actions. You can't control yourselves. You are not responsible.'

Otto bristled to be lumped amongst the mass of oppressing men. He was a feminist, wasn't he? Following his mother's example and later learning from Charlotte. She'd never let him get away with anything, always questioned him, challenged his assumptions and his behaviour.

'You think she was raped?' It was hard to say this out loud. The word stuck in his throat. He felt a whelming sense of tenderness for Maria, a belated and now useless desire to treasure and protect her. Far too late. The worst had happened.

'What do you think?'

'I don't know. It's possible,' Otto conceded. 'Do her family know?'

81

'I don't think she has any – I don't have any contact details. I guess the police will sort that out.' Gina continued to study him. Her eyes searched his face for something.

'Do you think I did it? That I killed her?' His voice was too loud, a kid protesting.

Gina waited a moment, then said, 'No, Otto. No I don't think you would be capable of it.'

'So who? Any thoughts?'

Gina shook her head. 'I don't know.'

'So why exactly did you want to see me?' He was angry again. Something about this conversation wasn't making sense and his feelings were all over the place, hopping like the proverbial box of frogs. That was hardly surprising. Why – actually – had Gina asked to see him? She knew much more than she was letting on.

'You said you wanted me to meet some people,' he said. 'What people?'

Gina picked up her glass, took a sip of orange juice and rolled it around her mouth. 'I don't know if that's such a good idea anymore.'

'Why?'

'Because of what's happened. Because you're the focus of so much attention now. Everything's changed.'

'Tell me anyway. What people?'

Gina stood up. 'I'll be in touch, Otto. Let's see how things pan out, shall we? I'll do some talking.'

'For crying out loud,' he said.

Gina patted him on the shoulder. 'Please – be patient. I'll call you.'

He opened his mouth to speak again but Gina was already walking away. She hurried onto the beach and down towards the sea. She was anxious, looking over her shoulder and scanning the sand. Well, perhaps she was right to be nervous. This was a dangerous place.

Later that evening Otto wandered from the bar and down to the beach party around the headland, hidden away. He had wondered if the event would be cancelled as a mark of respect to Maria but the music played on and the revellers were as numerous as the stars. He drank a lot and wandered among the crowd. He overheard the story of Maria's death, told innumerable times, snatches of whispered accounts. The facts of the discovery had been long lost and fantastic stories were springing out of nowhere – that Maria had been raped, tortured, tied and beaten. How she had been mugged and murdered by Goan criminals, by an angry Australian ex, or in one case, by the police themselves. She was an innocent victim, or had only herself to blame. Who but a fool would be female and travelling alone? She'd been high or drunk or both. She'd made herself vulnerable. She'd been stupid – because surely these terrible things only happen to people who deserved them? It made Otto sick to hear Maria the talk of the night, mauled all over again by people who hadn't ever met her, to hear her story bounced like an entertaining ball from one loud mouth to another. What perverse reason made him listen? Perhaps to find out if his name was mentioned in the gossip, the myth-making. But no-one said his name. Some said she'd been found by a Brit, that was all. He continued to listen till his head ached and finally he had to run away over the sand or else pulverise the next person who opined about the murder.

He stood at the bar for an hour or more, watching bottles pass to waiting hands, seeing the piles of money heap up. The barmen were raking it in. It was all too similar to the happenings of the night before, so finally he walked up to the little road and back to the village. It was hard to see in the dark, shaded from the moonlight by the canopy of trees. From time to time a scooter pop-popped past him. Once a car slid by, beeping to clear him from its path. Back in his room, Otto picked up his loo roll for a visit to the back garden where the pig waited, and a fierce, biting pain blossomed in his forefinger. He dropped the roll with a curse. Dozens of tiny black quills poked from his skin. A bristly caterpillar had crawled into the cardboard tube and Otto's finger had brushed against it. With a pair of tweezers from his medical kit, he plucked, one by one, each painful spike from his fingertip. He had just drawn the last one from his stinging, red skin when someone knocked on the door. Unexpected, quiet and consequently clandestine, the sound startled Otto. He waited for a moment, not moving, but the knock came a second time.

Otto

Wednesday evening

Otto drew back the bolt and opened the door. The light from the room spilled onto long, silvery hair, a handsome, deeply-lined face. He had a dab of coloured powder on his forehead like a Hindu holy man.

'It's you,' Otto blurted, taken aback. 'I mean, what d'you want? Why are you here?' Then, realising how rude he sounded: 'I'm sorry. Can I help you?'

It was Jim, the old hippy guy he'd seen about the place. The man wasn't tall but he stood very straight, bare to the waist and without an ounce of spare flesh, as though everything superfluous had been worn away. Except for the dreadlocks of course – they were long and lush, pale ropes hanging down his back.

They stood for a moment regarding each other. A brisk smile crossed the hippy's face. He held out his hand.

'My name's Jim,' he said. 'May I speak with you, Otto?' He had a barely discernible American accent. Still Otto didn't move right away, puzzled by this stranger's presence on his doorstep. Was he after something?

'How can I help?' Otto said, standing by the open door.

Jim looked over his shoulder. Then he said in a low voice, 'Otto, you've got to get out of there. Now.'

'What? What d'you mean? Why?' He could feel the hairs standing up on the back of his neck.

'Get out. Go away. Hurry – you haven't got much time.'

'What's going on? Is it the police?'

'The police? No. Maybe you should go to the police. Make an excuse – get a taxi. Make them give you your passport back. Have you called the British Embassy yet? They might help you.'

'Who are you? Why are you saying this?' Otto felt a rising panic and a curious sense of affront. What did the old man know? Jim shook his head, unwilling to say any more.

'Please, I'm trying to help you, Otto. Get away from here. There are people trying to find you. Dangerous people. You must go now.' He turned away and slipped off into the darkness. Otto opened his mouth to call after him but already a distance lay between them.

Otto went back inside and shut the door. The house was very quiet. He felt a galloping in his chest. What should he do? Who were these people? Perhaps it was best to follow the advice and get out. If it was a false alarm, well he could always come back in the morning. What about his stuff? He dragged out the backpack from under his bed and thrust his belongings inside it. His mind felt oddly divided. One part was panicking, stirring up a flow of adrenalin; another part remained calm, a voice giving quiet instructions and telling him what he should do. This sober self, for the time being, helped keep the panicked self under control. If someone was after him it would be best if he kept out of the way. He could spend the night on the beach easily enough and return to his room in the morning. Otto zipped up the various pockets of his rucksack, fastened the strong plastic clips and hefted it onto his back. He opened the door, cautious, peering into the darkness looking out for his purported pursuer.

He couldn't see anyone. Here and there lights shone out from the windows of shacks and houses. Insects created a soft curtain of sound. Further up the lane an animal, probably a pig, was turning over piles of refuse. The air carried a cargo of scent: the breath of the moist trees, decomposing garbage, sewage, a whiff of rotten fish, and over it all, like a bright thread, the sugary perfume of some night-flowering blossom creeping over the roof. Otto took a deep breath, waiting for his eyes to adjust to the dark. He checked again, up and down the lane, then stepped out, locked the door and jogged away from the house and into the trees. He headed towards the fort ruins he'd visited before. No-one would be about at this time of night. It was the wrong end of the beach for revellers. He followed the line of the lane, keeping within the night-shade of the trees. Now and then he glanced back. He didn't see anyone, but the sense of pursuit persisted. So who was after him? Friends of Maria, perhaps, or a grief-stricken ex-lover thinking Otto responsible for her death and wanting vengeance? He hurried, somewhere between a walk and a run, the hastily-packed rucksack bouncing on his back. Darkness engulfed him like an overheated hand. He was drenched in sweat. The nylon straps chafed his sunburnt skin. And he was afraid, no getting round it. Here the rules were different. He'd seen that for himself, the body on the beach and Maria's broken skull.

The trees thinned and the path opened to the small, natural harbour where the bigger fishing boats were moored. Otto turned off the path and headed uphill to the old fort. He remembered the story about cobras – did they come out at night? Surely not, they were reptiles and cold-blooded. Would they be sluggish now? But the night was hot and humid, surely the best time for a predator to hunt? Better be careful and noisy enough to scare them away. He trotted up the dusty path, burdened by his awkward luggage. In some peculiar way though, it was comforting to carry it. All his worldly possessions, like a snail's shell. He could just take off with the possessions he was carrying, except that the police had his passport and his camera was missing.

The air freshened, out of the trees. A rolling plain of stars burned overhead. The moon lay on its back, like a golden hammock. Otto slowed, wiping perspiration from his face with the back of his hand. The broken fort wall rose and fell along the cliff edge; tough, awkward tussocks of grass covered the ground, making it difficult to walk. At last, when he reached the wall he stopped, slid the straps from his shoulders and dropped the backpack. What a relief. He stretched out his arms, loosening his bruised shoulders and aching muscles. The cooler air bathed his skin. A faint sea breeze carried the scent of the ocean. He dropped into a squat, resting his back against the wall, invisible in the shadow. A safe place, surely? Nonetheless he was watchful for an hour, alert for an enemy. Once he heard a movement in the grass (a cobra?) but he saw nothing. He sank down onto his behind, extended his legs and rested his head against the wall. His eyes closed, dreams rising up before he was even properly asleep, dreams in which he seemed to be racing along roads at high speed like a car chase in a film: roads like roller coasters, endlessly unravelling in front of him.

Voices called out. He woke with a start. How long had he been asleep? The moon had climbed over the wall of the fort, throwing its amber light on the undulating ground. Otto, tucked behind the cliff-side wall, remained in shadow but not so the three men standing on the far side, white men he thought, each some distance from the other as though they were looking for something.

Looking for him. One called out something to another but Otto couldn't hear what he said, or even the language he was using. The acoustics of the fort were curious. Otto kept very still. His pulse beat so hard and fast it seemed his blood would burst from his body. The sound of it would echo from the walls and trumpet his presence to the three men, one of whom carried a torch, as they combed the bowls and hillocks inside the ruin of a fort.

'Otto! Otto, where are you?' German-accented English. 'Otto, we want to talk to you!'

How had they known where he'd gone? Suddenly it seemed his choice of hideout was a poor one. Here he was totally alone – if they caught him these men could do as they pleased, no-one would see. Wouldn't it have been wiser to have gone to the most populous part of the beach? Safety in a crowd. No matter, it was too late now. He had to think what to do.

A conversation proceeded between the men which he couldn't understand. The tallest man called out again, the one swinging the torch from side to side. 'Otto! Come and talk to us!' It was hard to make out the tone, with the distance and the foreign accent, but Otto detected mockery; something of the playground, the ghost of a feeling from early childhood when you feel the herd has turned against you, that you are all alone. What should he do? Sooner or later they would find him. Since they were three, it was unlikely he could elude them – and how humiliating to be caught hiding, to be dragged out like a schoolboy from a cupboard. Would it be best, wisest, to step forward and confront them? Psychologically that would put him in a better place. Physically? Well, three of them and one of him, he was going to lose that one either way.

When he stood up, Otto's body felt curiously light. He shoved the backpack against the wall with his foot, took a deep breath and stepped forward.

'Otto!' came the call again, resounding oddly from the broken walls of the Portuguese fort. One of the other two men stopped suddenly. He'd seen Otto and shouted something in German. The torch-bearer swooped the light in an arc. The beam slashed Otto like a sabre. A moment's impasse – the three men, each at a different vantage point, were standing still, staring at him. Like chess pieces, on the chequered moon-and-shadow board of the ruined fort, in relation to one another, sizing up, calculating the next move.

'Ah, there you are. What are you doing up here in the middle of the night?'

'Cobras,' Otto said. 'I wanted to see cobras.' Now he'd stepped out, Otto's fear subsided a little. He couldn't fight off three, certainly, but perhaps he could talk his way out. Smart talking had always been his weapon of choice.

'Cobras?' A moment's puzzled silence, and then the man laughed. 'You wished to see cobras.'

'What d'you want?' Otto said. 'How did you know how to find me?' He took another step forward, hands in pockets, trying to look relaxed.

'Oh, someone saw you heading this way. A guy on a boat in the harbour.' Slowly, slowly, the men edged closer.

'So – what do you want?' This time Otto invested the question with a little impatience – who were these losers, disturbing him and wasting his time? Then they were in striking distance, the foursome, shifting from foot to foot, eyeing each other, shouldering up.

'I want to talk to you about Maria.' Moonlight washed the man's pale face. He had short blond hair. Otto recognised him – but from where? He wasn't always good at remembering faces, but this man, yes he'd seen him before.

'What about her?' Otto kept his voice level.

'You found her, yes? On the beach.'

'Why do you want to know? Who are you?' Then he remembered – this man, sitting beside Maria on the beach in front of the cafe, two nights before. He'd been jealous, seeing them talking so intimately.

'I want to find out who you are, what you're doing here,' the German said. 'What you know.'

'What d'you mean? You think I killed Maria?'

The German stared at him and glanced at his two lieutenants. Some communication passed between them. Otto tried to jump back but too late, the German reached out and grabbed him by the throat. The two other men seized his arms. The German squeezed his large, powerful hand, cutting off Otto's breath. He muttered to one of the other men who fished in his pocket for something. He held up a small, transparent object so for a moment the liquid inside it caught the moonlight and glowed like gem in his hand. Otto saw the silver glitter of a needle, and convulsed in primal panic, stamping on the foot of one of his captors. He struggled and freed one arm. His captors cursed, shouted out instructions he couldn't understand, and then came a sudden, sharp sting in his upper arm as the needle slammed into his flesh.

'What is it? What?' He struggled to speak, the German still grasping his throat as the chemical seemed to chill and numb his arm. They relaxed their hold, and watched him. The four walls of Otto's world contracted. He tipped his head back and stared at the plummeting sky. The moon leaned overhead, very bright, burning like phosphorus. The canopy of stars collapsed, falling on him, blotting out the men, the fort, the night itself.

His face pressed against a dusty metal surface. He was in the back of what was probably a small truck, jolting and bouncing its way along an uneven road. Otto was blindfolded, his hands tied behind him so he found it hard to protect himself against the rough journey. His face bumped against the floor time and time again. He'd bitten his tongue or his lip because his mouth was numb and tasted of blood. Worse still, his head ached furiously, making it hard to focus. The smell of engine oil, probably from some spillage in the back of the truck, and the pervasive cloud of diesel fumes turned his stomach.

Where were they taking him?

He had no idea how long he'd been unconscious nor how far they had driven. Fear overwhelmed in recurring waves, fear as he'd never experienced it before, an intense bodily sensation that squeezed his muscles, sent his stomach into spasms and extinguished his ability to think. What did they want? What were they going to do? Were they going to hurt him, kill him? It came again, the wave of panic. Behind the blindfold Otto squeezed his eyes shut. He had to control himself – had to think clearly. If he succumbed to this acute, animal terror he had no hope of dealing with situation.

Everything had gone now, all his possessions. The police had his passport, his camera had vanished, his mobile was in his backpack and that lay against the wall in the old fort above the sea. His stuff, and the scant sense of security he gained from it, was gone. He was all he had left now – body, memory, and wits. Best use them well. He passed in and out of consciousness. The piercing headache slowly evolved into a muffled pain. He lost all sense of time. When eventually the truck stopped and the engine was turned off, someone opened the truck door and hands hauled him out. He half fell onto rough ground, his legs numb and awkward. Through the fabric of the blindfold he sensed daylight and felt the sun strike his skin. He raised his head and listened, breathed in his surroundings. Moisture, vegetable growth, the sound of tumbling water and the screech of insects – they were in the jungle.

'Where are we?' he demanded. 'Why have you done this?' His mouth was dry, his voice weak and scratchy. A hand reached out and took his arm.

'This way,' a man said. 'Go carefully or you'll fall.'

'Who are you?' Otto said. He didn't get an answer. Instead he was shepherded along what he guessed was a narrow dirt path. Long grasses brushed against his legs. From time to time foliage of some kind, hanging down, glanced off his face and shoulders. Clouds of warm mist seemed to hang on the air, making it difficult to breath. A man walked before him, someone else was following close behind. Were there others? Hard to tell. Nobody spoke. They walked for ten minutes or so, an arduous journey for Otto because he couldn't see where he was going. At the end of it he was escorted into a small, low building and the blindfold was removed.

It was a huge relief to see again. A young woman stood in front of him. She resembled Maria. Dark brown hair, sleek tanned skin, slim, graceful body. But this girl, staring at him, looked fierce. He'd seen her before, staring at him from across a bar on the beach.

'Where am I?' Otto said. 'Why have you brought me here?' His eyes scanned the building. It was some kind of thatched hut, about three metres square, firmly built, no window so the interior was dim, illuminated only by strands of sunlight that pierced the thatched roof. The girl didn't answer right away. She looked Otto up and down, walked around him as though he were a horse for sale.

'May I have some water?' he said. The girl, her mouth pressed into a narrow line, gave a curt nod. She left the hut and returned a minute later with a plastic water bottle.

'I'll need my hands free to drink,' he said. But she shook her head, unscrewed the top and signalled him to drop to his knees. It was awkward, the warm, iodised water spilling over his lips and chin as she held the bottle, but he was desperately thirsty. When the bottle was empty she left him alone, dropping some kind of bar across the outside of the door to lock it. Otto took a deep breath. Who were these people? If the German guy was simply some heartbroken ex who thought Otto had murdered his girlfriend, surely he and his friends would have given him a kicking in the fort, then and there. This kidnap suggested something more complicated. Should he be less afraid then? Or more?

Otto's stomach growled. He hadn't eaten for a long time. He paced around the hut and flexed his arms, trying to wriggle his hands free of their binding. The tape chafed his skin and he fretted against the awkwardness and sense of vulnerability it created. How long till his absence was noticed? The police would think he'd done a runner. Emails, texts, calls from his mother, from Charlotte or Jen, would all go unanswered. The family at his lodgings would be first to notice his disappearance but since he'd paid in advance and taken all his belongings they too might assume he'd simply moved on. The whole beachfront community was full of travellers who came and went like a tide.

The door opened again. The blond man stood in the doorway, the woman who had given him a drink at his side. They stepped into the hut and indicated that Otto should sit on the floor. The man sat also, leaning his back against the wall. His companion remained on her feet.

'Otto Gilmour,' he said. Otto didn't respond. His instinct was to plunge in with questions but he reined back, waited for his captors to speak. He studied the blond man, who he guessed was in his early thirties. Strongly built, square-jawed, blandly good-looking – like the ideal worker portrayed in those Soviet propaganda posters in history books. Small, vividly blue eyes and pale eyelashes. Large, strong hands clasped together in front of him. He focused on Otto – and said, 'My name's Andreas. This is Kate. We'd like you to tell us who you're working for.'

'What?'

'Who are you working for?'

Otto felt an internal scrabbling, as though he were treading on the collapsing edge of a cliff.

'What do you mean?' he said. 'I'm not working for anyone.'

Andreas gave a heavy sigh. 'Yes. Yes you are.' Then, without warning and seemingly without emotion, he drew back his hand and belted Otto across the face. Otto's head whipped back painfully. His upper lip and the skin of his cheek stung. He looked at Andreas with a mingling of amazement and shock. Then he glanced at Kate. She licked her lips, a gesture of nervousness.

Otto took a deep breath. His pulse beat hard in his face, where the blow had landed. He shook his head. 'I don't know what you mean.'

Andreas raised his eyes and shrugged. Otto trembled, straining against his bonds, waiting for another blow.

'You told Maria you were a journalist,' Kate interjected. 'Who are you writing for?'

Otto almost laughed then, from relief. 'A journalist? Not really, well, I am but it's nothing serious. I'm a student on a gap year. I did some photography for a local tourist mag.' He looked from Kate to Andreas and back to Kate again. What were they thinking? That he was some undercover big shot with a mission? *What was this all about?* Maria was dead, don't forget. What was the connection?

'Do you know who killed Maria?' His voice was quiet now.

Andreas shook his head. He made some sign to Kate and she handed him a bag from which he drew out an A4 manila envelope.

'Do you recognise these?' He tipped the envelope upside down and a dozen large photographs, badly printed on low-quality paper, slid into his hand. He passed them to Otto. Even in the hut's low light, despite the smudgy reproduction, Otto knew the pictures. He had taken them the night Maria had died.

'You've got my camera,' he said. 'These are mine.' Questions unrolled in his mind. Had Andreas or one of his friends been on the beach that night, when Maria's body lay at the edge of the sea? If so, didn't that suggest whoever had stolen his camera was also responsible for her death?

'Who are you working for?' Andreas repeated, gesturing towards the pictures.

'No-one, they're just holiday snaps,' Otto said. 'It's people on the beach! What's the problem?' He could see nothing incriminating in the pictures, or even out of the ordinary. Scenes from the perpetual party – people dancing, drinking, flirting, as they did every night.

Kate sighed. 'He doesn't know anything. I told you, Andreas. He's just a kid backpacker with a camera.'

Andreas pursed his lips. 'A kid, Otto. Is that what you are?'

'Can I have my camera back?' Otto said. His voice sounded appropriately pleading and childlike. 'Take me back to the village, before the police realise I've gone.'

Andreas smiled, the benign father 'Have a rest, Otto,' he said. 'Kate'll bring you something to eat. I'll come and talk to you again a little later.'

Charlotte

Tuesday

Charlotte's father drove them to Heathrow. They left the house at five in the morning so Jen stayed over the night before. Her parents dropped her off, staying for an awkward coffee with Charlotte's dad in the kitchen during which time they talked about their daughters' forthcoming adventure and frightened each other with some kind of clumsy joke about never seeing her again. Jen's mother, fragile-looking with black shadows under her eyes, took her daughter's hands in her own and told her apocryphal tales of rip-offs, robberies and infectious diseases. Charlotte rolled her eyes.

Finally Jen's parents said goodbye. Her dad hugged her very hard, saying he loved her and wishing her many magical adventures. Jen's mother looked rather old. It was strange how much she varied, even from one day to the next. Sometimes she looked oddly girlish. Today, tired out, a greyness in her face: worn to a ravelling. At last they were gone. Charlotte could see how much of a strain it had been for Jen, the drawn-out farewells. It would have been better if her parents had simply dropped her and driven off.

Charlotte's father dropped the mugs in the open dishwasher, among the gravy-stained plates.

'I'm off upstairs,' he said, absent-mindedly. 'See you in the morning. Don't forget to set your alarms.'

The girls were alone. A look passed between them. Jen grinned.

'All systems go,' Charlotte said. Jen's backpack, brand new, royal blue, was propped against the kitchen table. 'Bring your stuff. We'll go to my room.'

Charlotte's bedroom was the only tidy place in the house. It was very large and the furniture – a double bed, dressing table and wardrobe – were antiques from the nineteenth century, made of a glossy wood like molasses. An oil painting, supposedly very valuable, of two dark-eyed ponies eating from a manger, hung over the bed. Charlotte had been very keen on ponies at one time. The twenty-first century manifested itself in the television, computer, printer and modem, the CD player and posters. No pictures of pretty-boy rock stars though – Charlotte's interests were demonstrated by the Arno Peters projection world map and a picturesque chart extolling the virtues of organic farming. On her bookshelves, besides novels, she had reports published by Amnesty and Oxfam.

Charlotte's backpack, lemon yellow and also new, stood against the wardrobe. Jen placed hers next to it and they laughed, the young women, to see them side by side.

'What have you brought?' Charlotte said. 'Did you stick to the list?'

'Pretty much. Mum helped – fussed about suncream and first aid kits. She took me to the surgery to make sure I had the vaccinations.'

Typhoid, cholera, hepatitis. Boxes of malaria tablets. Charlotte had them too, though neither of her parents had frogmarched her to the surgery. And a top-up tetanus injection on the advice of the nurse. Her body was circulating with foreign substances.

'We should go through them again – make sure we have everything we need,' Charlotte decided. 'Then we won't have a panic in the morning. I've set the alarm for four fifteen.'

They laid down the backpacks, opened and gutted them. Clothes, toiletries, towels, sleeping bags, suncream, guidebooks, passports, travel documents, mobiles, compact digital cameras. A notebook for Charlotte, a stash of art stuff for Jen. They checked off the items on the list and then carefully repacked. Everything in order and nothing to do but wait, sleep and wake up.

Charlotte had worried about Jen's nerves but Jen seemed perfectly relaxed and it was Charlotte herself who was anxious. The feeling manifested itself in an uncomfortable gnawing in the pit of her belly. What was there to fear? Apart, of course, from leaving behind everything safe and comfortable, to throw herself into the unknown? She'd always believed herself to be a confident, capable person (head girl, high achiever, organiser), but now, at this crunch point, she felt very nervous.

It was nine o'clock, too early to sleep, but they had an early morning ahead. Jen suggested they climb into bed and watch a film. She picked out *Donnie Darko* from Charlotte's very modest collection and they lay side by side under the giant duvet and faded patchwork quilt, propped by quantities of pillows. Charlotte turned the light out and the film dusted the room with flickering grey light. From time to time a car swooped by on the road outside. At around ten, a key turned in the front door and Charlotte's mother climbed the stairs, knocked on the door, and stepped into her daughter's room.

'Hello, you two,' she said. 'All packed and ready?' She sat on Charlotte's side of the bed and put her hand out to touch her daughter's hair.

'How are you feeling?'

Charlotte stared into her mother's face. 'Okay. Bit nervous.'

'Well, that's hardly surprising.' She looked wide-eyed, glamorous and worn out all at once. 'I hope you have a fantastic time. I'm going to miss you.'

'I shall miss you too.' They were not a family given to gushing, though Charlotte knew very well how much her parents cared for her. Yesterday there had been a special going away dinner at her favourite Indian restaurant in town. One of her half-brothers had come along too. They were all congratulatory and good-hearted, resolutely teasing and cheerful. Her father had drunk a little too much and fell asleep in the car on the way home. Now though, her mother seemed on the verge of tears and uncertain what to say. Charlotte recoiled from the prospect of a scene so she sat up and gave her a brusque hug.

'We'll be fine, don't worry,' she said. 'We can email and text. I'll send you pictures. We'll have a great time.'

'I know. You're a good girl, Charlotte. And this trip – well, I'm envious you know.' She stood up. 'Take care of each other, girls. And Otto, take care of him too.'

When she'd left the room, Jen, perhaps sensing her friend's anxiety, reached out for her hand and gave it a squeeze. Charlotte sank back on the pillows and fixed her eyes on the screen, wanting the anaesthetic of television. Jen had fallen asleep by the time the film had finished but Charlotte lay awake a long time, staring at her room as though to store it forever in her memory. Something about its familiar proportions seemed strange tonight – as though in leaving, she was seeing it for the first time as a visitor would. Three old teddies were sitting on the mantelpiece beside numerous souvenirs of the first eighteen years of her life – a photograph of her on a furry pony, another mounted on sleek horse, leaping over a hedge marked with flags. A Sylvanian family of otters, half a dozen Beanie babies and a trophy for swimming. This time tomorrow she'd be on the other side of the world in an utterly alien environment. The prospect thrilled and terrified in equal measure. The complexities of the journey tangled in her mind, vague worries about making times, possible delays, troubles they might or might not encounter. The voice in her head, laden with what-ifs, chatted on, warding away any possibility of sleep.

Charlotte must have fallen asleep in the end, because the shrill alarm woke her, seemingly a moment later. It was dark outside, the air in the room very cold. Jen was still sleeping despite the alarm. Charlotte pulled on her slippers and dressing gown, padded down, shivering, to the kitchen to make coffee. The night pressed against the window as she filled the kettle.

She took a coffee to her father and returned to her bedroom where Jen lay peacefully asleep, her hair spread across the pillow like a red fan.

'Jen. Jen, it's time to get up.'

Jen's eyes opened. She gave a slow smile.

'I've made you some herbal tea. Mint – is that okay? It's all we had,' Charlotte said.

Jen nodded. 'That's fine, thank you. I slept so well! I can't remember what I dreamed about.' She sat up in bed, took the mug from Charlotte. 'How are you?'

Charlotte shrugged. 'Nervous. I keep going over things in my mind.' It was odd, wasn't it, that at this moment fragile Jen should be so calm while Charlotte's thoughts were climbing over each other? Except, perhaps, that practicalities were never such a worry for Jen. She was happy to let the tide take her, to trust she would end up where she was meant to be. She would leave it to Charlotte to obsess about journey times and connections and problems and delays.

They dressed quickly, shuddering at the cold. Neither felt any inclination to eat – breakfast at the airport maybe? Charlotte's dad didn't come down till it was time to leave and the girls were standing in the hallway with their rucksacks, Charlotte fretting over and over again that something vital had been forgotten, perhaps the passports or tickets might have magically flown from their bags and materialised back in the bedroom. Worries gnawed.

'Ready, girls?' Her father looked very tired and old in the midwinter darkness, shadows lingering over his face. But he was genial enough and gave Charlotte an affectionate hug. They went outside and dumped the backpacks in the boot, while her father stood out in the agonising cold and scraped layers of ice from the windows.

Then they were off, the heaters swiftly filling the car's interior with warm air. Charlotte looked back to see the house disappear into the darkness. A curious sensation stung in her chest – severance – like a knife cut.

Nobody spoke for an hour or more. It was too early. They were all stunned by the premature awakening. But driving along the motorway, Charlotte broke the silence.

'I'm going to be sick,' she blurted. 'Please, pull over. Please stop.'

'I can't stop! I'm on the motorway!'

'Please! I'm going to throw up.' She hadn't eaten since the previous evening but her gorge rose. She pressed her hand over her mouth. The car veered over, pulled up to a halt on the hard shoulder. Charlotte jumped out and vomited on the tough, frosty grass. Jen followed her.

'Are you okay?' She placed her hand on Charlotte's arm.

'Yes. I think so. Nerves.'

'You, nerves? Should be me, shouldn't it?'

'We all get nervous.' Charlotte wiped her chin with the back of her hand. Her mouth tasted of bile. She climbed back into the car feeling empty, scoured out.

It was still dark when they arrived at the airport, the world within a world that had no night or day, only perpetual electric light and unceasing coming and going.

They were dropped outside the terminal building. Charlotte hugged her father very hard. He looked at the girls, his baby daughter and her strange little friend. What was he thinking? That this baby was too small to be travelling around the world without him? Perhaps so, because his eyes moistened and he flapped his hand to usher them away.

'Take care of each other,' he said. Charlotte swallowed hard, holding on to herself. The car pulled away and was gone.

Charlotte looked at Jen. She was smiling.

'Just you and me now,' she said. 'The adventure begins.'

It began slowly. They checked in their backpacks, passed through

102

security and settled for a two-hour wait in the departure lounge. Charlotte bought a copy of the *Guardian*. Jen stared into space. They didn't talk much. People swirled in and out, a constant stream of travellers.

Boarding was announced; the girls picked up their handbags and walked through a windowless corridor and onto the plane.

'Our last footsteps in Britain for nine months,' Jen said. 'Isn't that an odd thought?'

Charlotte looked at her feet, suspended in the belly of the plane who knows how many metres from the runway. More waiting – then at last the engines started up and the plane taxied away from the terminal building. It turned on the runway, gathered up speed and flung itself into the air. Charlotte felt the lurch away from the ground as though the plane were not taking but *falling* off. She saw Jen's hands clutching the armrests, her fingers white. Nerves at last? Jen's eyes were closed.

'You okay?'

Jen nodded. 'I've never flown before. Never been on an aeroplane.' She kept her eyes tight shut.

Charlotte considered. 'I'd forgotten that.'

'We never went abroad for holidays till I was in my teens. And then it was the ferry to France.'

'You must have an enviably low carbon footprint.'

Jen smiled. 'I suppose so. Blown it now, though. Long-haul flight to India.'

'Not for a two-week jaunt,' Charlotte said. 'This is something different. Serious. Nine months of it. It will change us.'

Jen nodded. She sighed, relaxed her hands and opened her eyes. 'Do you think so? Will it really?'

'We'll see, won't we?' Charlotte ran through the itinerary in her mind for the umpteenth time. Four weeks in Goa then a three-month placement with a wildlife conservation project at a national park. It had taken so much effort, securing this placement, and she had been

103

thrilled to get it. Jen's plans were less definite. After Goa, she had only hazy ideas. She'd told Otto and Jen she longed to visit Varanasi and Rajasthan, wanted to study Indian art and architecture. She'd grown impatient with Charlotte's insistence on timetables and planning – she'd know what to do when she got there, she'd repeated, time and time again, to Charlotte's annoyance. Fate would blow her along, a wind catching in the sails of her artistic aspirations.

The eight-hour flight was uneventful. Four thousand miles of Earth unrolled underneath them. Charlotte dozed for a while and the night faded away. They watched a film, a bad thriller, and Charlotte ate the preserved, over-processed food in its pots and sachets. Jen, allergic to so many things, picked at a fruit salad and sipped water from a plastic bottle. It was two in the Indian afternoon as the plane descended. Charlotte stared through the tiny window wanting to see it all. The slums of Mumbai stretched out, rising up to meet them. The sun hammered on the city from a burning blue sky.

Stepping from the plane, the heat and humidity instantly engulfed them. Charlotte was sweating in seconds in her unsuitable English winter clothes. They walked into the airport, wandered down long corridors where soldiers stood at intervals and watched. Wordless, nervous, they collected their backpacks from the clunky carousel. One of the side pockets had been ripped from Jen's backpack, bursting a bottle of suncream so that thick, white liquid dripped over the floor. Getting the baggage out of the airport and changing pounds into rupees involved a welter of form filling, signing and countersigning by apparently random officials. Outside the airport they looked for a bus into the city but were besieged by taxi drivers. A brief discussion about the fare ensured (Charlotte took charge of the conversation, Jen waited quietly at her side) and then they were off, the long drive through Mumbai to the Coloba Causeway where they'd booked a hotel for the night.

To the whey-faced English girls, fresh from the frosty English winter, the heat was an assault. Charlotte stared through the window, taking in the pitted road and the broken traffic lights. The driver tore along the roads, veering from lane to lane, ducking out of the path of oncoming traffic. They passed through slums, mile after mile of them, an endless forest of low, dirty hovels cunningly created from any conceivable piece of scavenged material, of waste. Crammed against each other, made of reeds, cardboard, corrugated iron, while in and around them endless people walked and talked and squatted and gesticulated; spare, lively, dignified people for the most part – children in spotless dresses, women walking through filth, yet as upright and graceful as queens.

'Look,' Jen said. She pointed at two tiny children playing in a ditch full of brown water.

As they drew further into the city, the slums began to change. The shacks still clambered over each other but possessed a little more permanence. They were built of brick, punctuated by tiny shuttered shops. The roads teemed with people. Dogs wandered among the crowds.

At last the taxi drew up at Coloba, outside the hotel, one of a line of old colonial buildings. They stepped inside, gave their names and were shown to a tiny room with two hard beds, covered with grimy sheets. A noisy fan hung from the ceiling.

Jen sat at the end of the bed. Charlotte surveyed the room.

'Well, we chose something cheap,' she said. She still felt uneasy but the precipitous nausea had gone. The waiting was over. They had taken the plunge.

'It's okay,' Jen shrugged. 'It's just somewhere to stay before we catch the train in the morning.'

'What would you like to do?' The city was both terrifying and enticing. The desire to go out vied with an urge to stay in the room, safe and locked away.

'Go out. I want to go out,' Jen said.

'Well we didn't come all this way to sit inside. At least we have somewhere to leave our stuff.' But the place, so shockingly alien, did scare her. Time to be brave.

They changed into clothes more suitable for the climate. Charlotte sent a text to Otto, telling him they had arrived safely. She said she'd call him later. Then the girls locked up the room and headed out into the city. In the hazy Mumbai heat they found their way to the Gateway of India, on the shore of the Arabian Sea. The triumphal arch, with its towers and minarets, bristled with hawkers selling postcards, foods and souvenirs. Behind it rose the grand Taj Mahal Hotel and then a tower block. Boats swarmed over the waters from which men called out offering trips along the coastline.

They decided to walk to the station so they would know the route for the morning. Charlotte held the map and pointed the way.

Crowds everywhere – a chaos of cars, cycles, motorbikes, motor rickshaws on the roads, all hurtling in a storm of noise, cutting each other up and beeping their horns. Charlotte tried to relax, to observe and soak up the atmosphere of the alien place, but she found it hard. Shops like small boxes opened onto the busy pavements, displaying clothes, books, cigarettes, watches and mobile phones. Traders had stalls from which they sold food and drink. Every tiny space was taken, every opportunity exploited. Lining the path to the station itself, people accosted the girls, wanting to buy dollars. They saw beggars at intervals, with bent, mutilated feet, holding their hands out for money.

Charlotte steeled herself against the assault of it. London had beggars too, she reminded herself. Even the sleepy market town where she lived had a young man with a dog who spent several afternoons a week in the doorway of a closed-up shop, with a hat and a cardboard sign declaring he was homeless and hungry. Often she had given him money despite friends' warnings he'd spend it on drink or drugs. Wasn't that his choice? Here though, so many extended hands. How to choose who to give to? She could hardly bear to look at them; the old woman with huge, milky cataracts, the broken man pushing himself on a trolley with uncanny speed to pester them for alms. The beggars didn't seem at all ashamed or perturbed, but

Charlotte suffered agonies, ignoring them, wanting them simply to disappear and not to trouble her any more. In the end she gave the trolley man a few rupees just to be rid of him.

The mix was extraordinary – slums and office blocks, professionals in suits and women sitting on squares of cardboard holding tiny babies. Heat and stink. Neon signs and cows wandering on the highway.

She grasped Jen's hand. 'Are you okay? It isn't easy, is it?'

'I like it,' Jen said. 'So much energy.' She stopped walking, looked around her. 'All cities are the same, aren't they? Perhaps they've all been – you know, Byzantium, Rome, Jerusalem, Jericho. Right back to Ur, the first city. The great palaces and the hovels. The roads and alleys; the merchants and traders and beggars; schools and temples and markets, the high people in their safe and gracious houses, the low people living in the street.'

'The same but different,' Charlotte said, less happily. Why wasn't Jen so apprehensive? It was time to stop worrying, to be less uptight, but that was easier to think than do.

'There's the station,' she said. Chhatrapati Shivaji Terminus – a palace of Victorian gothic, embellished and decorated with domes, columns, arches, gargoyles and glittering stained glass. Inside, crowds and chaos. A tiny girl of three or four with huge round eyes followed them about like a mute shadow, her hand held out. Women cleared the floor with stick brooms. Charlotte bought their train tickets for the next morning. The man in the ticket office spoke the English of Oxford rather than Mumbai, impeccably dressed with fingernails in perfect ovals. He ignored the queue of customers gathering behind them and patiently wrote out instructions for their journey in beautiful copperplate handwriting. How had he known it was their first trip to India? Charlotte wondered. Was their ignorance scrawled across their faces? Presumably yes – two little girls from the West. Fish out of water.

The city possessed a perfume all of its own, a stew of heat, traffic fumes and decaying rubbish. Now and then the base notes of sewage, and on top of this an embroidery of scent that drifted in and away – sweet, spicy food, incense, urine, and other nameless, never-before-encountered smells that washed over her one after another in waves.

They wandered for an hour or more, crossing a tatty playing field where numerous games of cricket went on and then along the coast by a brown sea where women crouched over cooking pots, their belongings in a bag beside them. Piles of rubble lay everywhere, and rubbish, and so many people walking, chatting, talking on mobile phones. And in every hole in a wall, each gap or archway, in the huge concrete pipes standing at the side of the road, people had constructed makeshift homes out of cardboard, plastic sheets, rags, board from signs and old hoardings.

They bought cups of tea from a stall. It tasted like warm evaporated milk laden with sugar, so sweet it was hard to drink. As the girls sipped their tea, people came up to speak, to shake hands and introduce themselves, curious about them, where they had come from and why they were visiting Mumbai.

Later in the dim hotel room, they lay on their beds, exhausted. Over their heads the fan rattled and whirred. How would they sleep through the noise? Jen and Charlotte were silent for a long while. Then Jen said, her voice childlike, 'Are we going to be all right?'

Charlotte pondered. 'I think so. Earlier today, though, I wondered. It's too much. I didn't think I could deal with it. It's even stranger and harder than I thought.'

'Yes. At first I thought I couldn't bear it.'

Charlotte tried to call Otto but didn't get an answer. Probably the phone coverage was patchy in far-flung Goa.

Silence again. Then Charlotte said, 'I know what you mean. But I feel a bit pathetic admitting it. All those millions of people, making their living, having homes. And here I am a ridiculous wilting lily.' She turned her head on the narrow pillow, to look across at Jen.

'Don't be too hard on yourself. It's different, that's all. You know, a culture shock,' Jen said.

'But you said – you know, the city's like all cities. I thought you weren't finding it a shock at all.'

A smile passed across Jen's face. 'I was encouraging myself, that was all.'

'Otto did all this too,' Charlotte said. 'And he was on his own.'

'He'd have been okay. It would be a challenge to him. A project.'

'Still, it can't have been easy.' She wondered about him leading the way, probably relishing the chance to test himself, forging a path which they might follow. He'd have stories to tell and was probably looking forward to having an appreciative audience. She ached to see him again.

They didn't stray out of the room to eat, too tired and disorientated to be hungry. Beyond the window the noise and energy of the city continued unabated and the sun went down, the sky burned a dark, dusty pink. Charlotte called Otto again, but he didn't answer. She didn't worry about it, she felt she'd never been so weary, as though rollers had crushed her body, but sleep was still elusive. Jet lag, adrenalin; her mind refusing to let go. Above them the fan creaked on and on. Darkness filled the window. Beneath, on the pavement, two men began a long, musical argument. Far away, fireworks exploded.

I'm here, Charlotte thought. After all this time, I made it happen. I'm in India. Despite her exhaustion, the shock of the city, she felt exultation.

Jen

Wednesday

Jen lay on her back in the uncomfortable bed. What had she been dreaming? She couldn't remember, whatever it was, the dream had slipped away. The fan had stopped, the three blades drooping like the wings of a dead insect. Who had turned it off? A power cut perhaps. The slanting sunlight, early in the morning, etched in the pockmarks pitting the pale plaster walls.

Jen sat up. According to her watch it was just before seven in the morning, India time. What time at home? Too hard to work out. She glanced at Charlotte on the bed beside hers, curled up on her side, knees tucked against her chest. Jen got up and walked to the window to see her first Indian morning. The city stretched away under a milky sky. Roads criss-crossed. A large, white cow, glossy-skinned, stood patiently in a central reservation, ignoring the traffic scooting past. After the first panic of the previous day, the sense of being overwhelmed had receded. She had acclimatised; as though by sleeping she had accepted the place and stopped fighting against it.

And stirring in the haze of heat and pollution, she could see presences others could not, like the pale magenta woman, hunched over as though very frail and elderly, who drifted along the path and then faded into the air. And on the rooftops, playful like puppies, three or four spirits that rolled over and over each other in some kind of game before falling and dissolving into nothing. She had always

111

seen them, these immaterial presences, since her earliest childhood. They were not alarming. Were they different, these Indian spirits? Certainly a quality about them she could only inaccurately describe as a flavour indicated so. The magenta woman briefly materialised again, glanced up at Jen in the window, and gave something like a smile.

'Jen?' Charlotte's sleepy voice. 'How's it looking out there?'

'It looks fabulous.' She spoke softly, turning to smile at Charlotte whose face was a little puffy with sleep, her hair in dark clumps. Charlotte yawned and sat up on the bed, rubbing her eyes with her knuckles.

She looked back through the window. The female spirit had gone again. She kept the visitation to herself, as she usually did. No-one believed her. She paid the price for this sensitivity to other worlds with her fragile health, her multitudinous allergies, a body that rebelled against the very things that should nourish and sustain it – as though she had only half a foot in the real world. And the real world was a demanding, difficult place where she never felt entirely at home, full of complications and insurmountable problems. She was a changeling, poisoned by the world in which she'd found herself, uneasy with its rules of engagement, confused by other people, constantly afraid she didn't understand the rules the rest seemed to know by instinct.

Except – luckily – she'd found people who got her, even if they didn't entirely understand. Her mother of course, and now Charlotte and Otto.

'It took me ages to get to sleep,' Charlotte said. She stretched her strong, muscular arms, got off the bed and clomped to the dirty little bathroom attached to the room. The toilet didn't have a bowl to sit on, only some kind of porcelain base with foot-rests where you could squat. Perhaps it would have been better to have paid a little more for salubrious accommodation, this first night? Well, they had wanted to travel on a basic level, to live frugally, so best to start as they meant to go on.

They washed, dressed and packed, signed out from the little hotel and headed out into Mumbai and along the road to the railway station. It was hot, even so early, and the streets hectic. They found the right train, climbed on board and found their second class compartment. The seats were hard.

Beyond the window the track was littered with plastic cups and other assorted rubbish. An enormous rat, paunchy and brown-coated, sat up on its haunches and rubbed its pink hands together, utterly shameless. Jen stared at it, this rat like some kind of gangland boss. He should have been wearing a smart suit, a Rolex and a gold chain. She dug into the top pocket of her backpack for her sketchbook and pencil and drew him in a few swift, apt lines. It wasn't her first Mumbai sketch – she'd done those the previous night while Charlotte lay on her bed trying to sleep; she'd drawn people, from memory – the man at the ticket office who had so kindly explained their journey to them, the boys playing cricket on the parched field, the women squatting with their cooking pots on the beach. And the little girl who had followed them in the railway station through the gothic arches, under the gargoyles. She'd drawn this last one like a scene from *Gormenghast*, or the *Lord of the Rings* – the architecture exaggerated and grotesque, the girl tiny and vulnerable, all eyes, a long plait hanging over her shoulder.

When she looked up from the rat sketch, her model had disappeared. People crowded the corridor outside the compartment. It would comfortably accommodate eight, four on either side facing each other across a little table, but another eleven people crammed in after Jen and Charlotte had taken facing seats by the window, all men, talking and gesticulating. Once the journey was underway they began long, animated conversations and all seemed to know one another. Soon Jen and Charlotte were included – so many questions about England, their trip, their lives at home. Charlotte's India guidebook provoked enormous interest. Beyond the window, the city slid past, then miles of slums through which the train wound like a snake.

Passengers disembarked and were replaced. The city yielded to the rural landscape of Maharashtra. They changed trains once but another twelve hours of travelling still lay ahead. With every mile it seemed the countryside grew more extravagantly beautiful – lush, vast and verdant. Great trees of emerald green, fields of rice stretching for miles, opulent tropical vegetation arching over wide rivers

The train stopped at many tiny villages, where people embarked carrying baskets of produce on their heads, slender, beautiful women in bright saris, dark-skinned, hair as glossy as watered silk swept off their faces. At every station, traders overwhelmed the train, offering soft rice cakes, cups of tea, bowls of spicy vegetables, fresh fruit. A woman with a huge basket of tomatoes joined Jen and Charlotte in their compartment and gave them some to eat along with a pinch of salt. Jen hesitated – should she eat this? It was impossible to resist, the woman's generosity urging her on. The tomato was sharp and sweet, utterly delicious.

The train wound its way through mountains, past huge valleys drowning in dark forests. A waterfall cascaded over rocky cliffs only metres from the railway line, where the train halted for a minute or two. A little boy grabbed Jen's hand, pulling her to the carriage's open door to see it, the white water tumbling over the blue-grey rock, while three monkeys sat side by side and chattered in the trees by the edge. Sunlight caught the scattering water drops. The little boy jumped out of the train and ran to the water, startling the monkeys who cavorted along their branch. Jen turned around, to Charlotte. She was smiling, they were both smiling, unable to say in words what they were feeling. Jen stretched out her arms – wanting to hold the view, to embrace it. The train heaved, the carriages clunked together and lurched forward. Jen called out in alarm, worrying the little boy wouldn't get back on board in time. He didn't worry – simply skipped back onto the train as it picked up speed and continued on its way.

When night came, they slept intermittently on hard bunks

unfolded from the side of the compartment. In the early morning the long train journey ended.

'Here we are,' Charlotte said, bustling and getting them organised. Was she nervous? Yes, Jen could see it, an aura of apprehension settled over Charlotte's shoulders. If it had been a colour, this emotion, it would have been lime green. Jen put out her hand, patted Charlotte's shoulder. She was tired and quiet, happy to be told what to do. She hefted her backpack onto her shoulders and climbed awkwardly onto the low platform. It was a small town, but as always, swarming with traders and hawkers.

'We need to get something to eat,' Charlotte said, wrinkling her brow. Sweat soaked her T-shirt and glistened on her face. Jen looked around vaguely. She wasn't conscious of being hungry but apart from the tomato she'd eaten nothing the previous day. Perhaps that explained why her body felt so light and the town seemed vaguely unreal. She allowed herself to be shepherded along the platform and off into the dusty street. Charlotte found a small restaurant with a veranda overlooking the road. She ordered them each a vegetable curry, rice and chapattis. The food was good, rich and spicy but not too hot. Jen ate cautiously, worried about her sensitivities. It had been a big risk for her, coming here. What if she couldn't eat anything? What if it made her ill? But eating provoked her appetite and she forgot her caution, wolfing down the curry and then mopping the metal dish with the chapatti. Charlotte, eating more steadily, observed her wryly.

'You were hungry, then.'

Jen nodded. She examined the sensations in her stomach, awaiting the warning signal, the cramps and contractions, the prickle on her tongue and the back of her throat. How dangerous to eat in that precipitous fashion – she had no clear idea what ingredients the meal contained, and she didn't want to be ill. So far so good. No immediate effect.

'You know, people have been very kind and friendly to us, haven't they?' Jen said. 'Everyone has made us welcome. All those men on the train talking to us. And the woman with the tomatoes. Can you imagine someone at home offering food to a foreigner they saw on the train?'

'No, I can't imagine it at all,' Charlotte mused. 'People have been very kind. Though a lot of them seem to want to sell us something. I can see that could get a little tiresome. Still, they have to make a living. I can hardly hold that against them.'

Jen took a deep breath. Still no sign of an allergic reaction.

'We'll see Otto soon,' Charlotte said. Did she know how much her face softened when she said his name? Jen nodded.

'I am so looking forward to seeing him,' she said. 'Won't he be full of himself, getting here first? He'll have so much to tell us.' They exchanged an affectionate glance, knowing Otto's foibles, sharing a liking for him all the same. Jen smiled. Otto. She'd be so happy to have the three of them together again. It was hard to explain how it worked, the chemistry of friendship between them. They were all so different – yet somehow these differences bound them.

Charlotte paid for the meal and found a taxi to take them to the village behind the beach where Otto had his lodgings. She had the instructions he'd emailed, the name of the beach restaurant where they were to meet that evening. The journey only took a few minutes. The taxi pulled up, and as the driver hefted the backpacks from the boot half a dozen people gathered around and began to shout out offers of accommodation. The atmosphere grew rather heated.

'And there we were worrying we'd not find somewhere,' Jen whispered. 'Who do we go with?'

Charlotte held her own, finding out what was on offer, exactly where and for how much. Finally she grabbed Jen's hand and together they followed a stout middle-aged woman in a pale cotton dress. She led them just down the road to a new building made of white-painted concrete blocks a hundred metres from the beach. She unlocked the door.

'This is great,' Charlotte said, dropping the backpack on the floor. Jen sighed with relief. It was a clean, plain room with a toilet and shower, two beds side by side over which mosquito nets hung like fragile wings. The woman took a modest rent, urged them to hide their money and passports from thieves and left them to settle in.

At six o'clock, in the fragrant dusk, soothed by the sound of the sea, Jen and Charlotte were sitting at the Seaside Bar, waiting for Otto. They had arrived some ten minutes early and Jen had seen the anticipation flare and fade in Charlotte's face, finding the place and then seeing Otto had not yet arrived. Charlotte bought a bottle of Indian cola drink. Jen sipped bottled water, distrustful of her stomach. Further along the beach, five young men were hauling a fishing boat from the waves. From time to time other tourists strolled along the sand, shadowed by the declining sun and made rosy and gold like the people pictured in holiday brochures. Only now, Jen mused, she was herself one of the people from a holiday brochure, sitting by the beach in a tropical paradise. This was it.

The waiter, brandishing a dirty rag, brought them a menu.

'We're waiting for a friend,' Charlotte said. Since they'd arrived in India Charlotte had begun to gesticulate, Jen had noticed, so intent on communicating she had begun, quite unconsciously, to signal her words with her hands. The waiter nodded and left them again. Charlotte glanced at her watch.

'He's late now. Ten minutes late.' She narrowed her eyes.

'Probably got caught up somewhere, transport problems, who knows?' Jen turned the plastic bottle around and around in her hand. Charlotte tried to call him again, but still no reply. Jen was trying to be a comfort but in that instant she knew – knew with complete conviction – that Otto wasn't going to come and that something terrible had happened. What was it? The echoes of that something still troubled the beach. An aura lay over the sea like an off-key note, so quiet it could hardly be heard and yet so penetrating it might eventually drive you mad.

Night came, a carpet of stars unrolled. Insects started to sing. The air cooled a little. Charlotte kept talking. She passed through a mood of excitement to annoyance and finally to worry. She called Otto's mobile another time and got no answer, left a message, and twenty minutes later, another message.

'What do you think's happened to him?' she kept repeating.

'I don't know,' Jen answered, again and again. This sense of a cataclysm she kept buttoned up.

The waiter returned, waving his hand at the menu. Charlotte ordered a fish curry more out of politeness than hunger. Jen asked for a bowl of plain rice.

When the waiter returned with the food, Jen stood up. She said, very gently, 'I wonder if you would help us? We're waiting for our friend. He should have been here a long time ago. I think he's eaten here before – he's called Otto. Tall, long blond hair.'

The waiter went very still. Charlotte stared up at him.

'What is it? What's happened?' Charlotte stood up too. The curry and rice waited on the table, ignored. The waiter looked away, his eyes moving nervously from place to place. He said something the girls couldn't understand, a spool of sound unravelling from his lips. Charlotte grabbed his arm.

'Do you know Otto? Where he is? Has something happened to him?' Her voice was overloud. He pulled away, hurried back to the shack and called out something to another, unseen colleague. Jen and Charlotte glanced at one another.

'They know something,' Charlotte said. She moistened her lips.

The waiter and his colleague stepped out. The second man said, 'You're looking for Otto? You're Otto's friends?'

Charlotte nodded. 'Yes we are. Where is he?'

A snatch of swift conversation then, between the two men. Then the second one said, 'Sit down. Sit down – I'll tell you what happened.' So they were sitting at the table, all three. The waiter hovered behind them.

118

'Two nights ago, a girl died on the beach,' the man said. He had his elbows on the table and his hands clasped. His voice was low and serious.

'She was a British girl – a tourist. It happens sometimes – drink, drugs, who knows? When they get here, they forget how to behave. Anyway, it was Otto who found her. He was questioned by the police. All sorts of rumours have circulated – including the possibility she was murdered. Otto spent some time with her in the days before – I'd seen him with her myself, here at the restaurant.'

Jen looked at Charlotte.

'Otto's involved? He wouldn't kill anyone. No way!'

Jen said, 'So where is he now?'

The man squeezed his hands together. He said, 'Otto was questioned by the police yesterday and they released him. I know they let him go because he was seen on the beach last night.'

'So where is he now?' Jen repeated. 'Why isn't he here? Why hasn't he got in touch?'

'I don't know where he is. Otto was staying at my cousin's house – and my cousin told me this morning that Otto had gone. His possessions, everything – gone from the house. The police are looking for him. And now you are looking for him too.'

Charlotte looked very small and pale, her face oddly flat, like a doll. She said, clearly forcing herself to speak, 'So he's done a runner? Is that what they think? Is that what he's done?' She shook her head. 'He wouldn't do that,' she said, looking at the table. 'He's not that sort of person. He'd stay put – he'd see it through. Sort it out.'

The restaurant man stood up. 'I'm sorry,' he said. 'If you want to speak to my cousin, I'll take you to his house but I don't think he'll be able to tell you anything more.'

Then Jen and Charlotte were alone. The curry cooled and congealed in front of them. The other tables emptied. They didn't speak for a time. Jen felt sick for the first time since arriving in India.

Charlotte raised her head, looked at Jen.

'I can't believe it,' she said. 'This can't be happening.' *This isn't what we planned, it isn't right, we don't deserve it, it isn't fair, we're not in control any more, I'm afraid, I can't handle it, I don't like it, I don't want this.*

Jen saw the panic in her friend's face, a mirror to her own. They had just arrived and everything was falling to pieces. Where was Otto? What was he doing? She took out her own phone and tried to call him. Then she sent a text. Where r u? R u ok?

Otto

Thursday

He must have dozed for a while, still sitting, back propped against the wall of the hut. In the evening, Kate woke him, unlocking the door and stepping inside with a bowl of rice and dahl, several chapattis rolled like a napkin, and a plastic bottle of water. She untied his hands then gave him the food a little more graciously than expected, and sat down herself on the dry ground to watch him eat. Otto didn't waste any time, gulping down half the tepid water and then tearing into the food. From time to time he glanced up at Kate but the earlier resemblance to Maria had faded. Probably it had only been a trick of his mind, part of the chemistry of infatuation that made him seize on the faintest of similarities. He was still looking for her, the woman he had met only a handful of times and who had managed in that brief acquaintance to imprint herself so strongly on his mind. He wanted her. Even though he had carried her dead body, knew she would never return, some stubborn part of him still yearned for her to step, magically, into his life again.

'How did you know Maria?' he said, between mouthfuls. The dahl was good, very rich and oily.

'She was my friend,' Kate said. 'I met her in Thailand. We travelled together.' Her expression revealed little but at least she wasn't overtly hostile. Clearly she'd believed him – knew him to be what he was, not an undercover journalist at all, simply a *kid backpacker.*

Under any normal circumstance this would have been an unbearable insult. Just now, Otto was relieved the heat was off. This gave him space for curiosity again.

'So are you going to tell me what all this is about? Who's this reporter you're scared of? What are you all doing? Where are we?'

'Andreas is going to take you back tomorrow,' she said, ignoring all his questions.

'Don't I deserve an explanation? How do you know I shan't tell the police I was kidnapped?'

Kate shrugged. 'Tell them what you like. You haven't come to any harm. What are they going to do about it? Nothing.'

Otto mopped up the bowl with his last chapatti. His brain worked quickly. Jen and Charlotte would know he was missing by now. They would try and find him. Perhaps they would go to the police. He felt a twinge of guilt that he had, inadvertently, drawn them into this web. They would be worried, wouldn't they? And with just cause. What if they emailed his mother? Matters turned over in his mind. He had stepped, an unwitting extra, into a complicated picture and he wanted to know what was going on. Clearly Maria had been involved in something – smuggling, drugs, espionage, who knows – and this had led to her death. Wasn't this what he had wanted to find, the story to tell the world and make his name? He couldn't afford to be the pawn any longer.

'I was very fond of Maria,' Otto said. 'I only knew her a few days it's true, but I fell for her, hook, line and sinker.'

'Yeah, well, you wouldn't be the first,' Kate said, disparaging. 'Don't think you were anything special. She had that effect on most men. It usually got her what she wanted, too.'

'What did she want?' Otto said. 'Tell me about her.'

Kate shrugged. She had low, dark eyebrows which now obscured her eyes as she scowled. She wrapped her arms around her shins, pressed her chin onto her knees, and stared at the ground as she spoke.

'I met her in Bangkok, in a bar, about a year ago. She's an orphan – her parents died in a car crash while she was in her teens. They were well off so she was sent to boarding schools and spent holidays with relatives. When she was eighteen she came into the money – some kind of trust fund thing. She wasn't a millionaire exactly but there is a house she has somewhere, and she would never have had to work. She'd no brothers or sisters either – so what was there to stay for? As soon as she was eighteen she dropped out of school and started to travel. That's what she'd been doing ever since.' Kate gave another aggressive sigh and dug her toes into the ground. Otto wondered how it felt, to be eighteen and entirely alone. Who would fly out to mourn and bury her? Did any of the holiday-staying relatives care enough? Maria couldn't have loved them very much if she hadn't ever returned to England.

'What about you?' Otto said. 'How long have you been travelling?'

'I spent six months in Thailand working at a holiday resort. Maria and I spent a lot of time together. When the contract was over, I went back home. A couple of months later I got an email from Maria – out of the blue, she wasn't much good at keeping in touch – telling me she was in Goa and that I had to come out and join her. I saved up some money, sold a lot of stuff and booked a flight.' Her eyes seemed to cloud over. 'We had some great times,' she said. 'No-one partied like Maria. She possessed such a passion for life, you know what I mean? No constraints, no expectations to live up to. She was perfectly free to enjoy every single day for what it was.'

Otto was about to say, Maria was uninhibited because she had nothing to lose. He stopped himself. Clearly in the end she'd had everything to lose. Her life had been taken away.

'So won't you tell me what's going on?' he said. 'What's this all about?'

Kate raised her head. 'I can't tell you now,' she said. 'That's a decision for Andreas and the others to make. Because of Maria, and your involvement, well, that makes things difficult.'

Otto persisted. 'But what are you doing with him? Why is a woman like you hanging out with a violent thug? You saw him hit me. You didn't like that, did you? What's going on here? Is it drugs or what?'

'Shut up. Don't ask questions.' Her eyes blazed, her voice was fierce. 'He's not a thug. He's a remarkable man. You don't know what he's achieved here.'

Otto saw it in an instant. She was in love with him, wasn't she? Kate might not be comfortable with Andreas's more violent tactics, but he had some kind of emotional hold over her.

'Well, could I borrow a mobile?' he said. 'I have to send a message to my friends. I want to let them know I'm okay. I was supposed to meet them this evening. They'll be worried about me. They might go to the police. They might contact my mother.'

Kate took out her own phone from a pocket in her embroidered belt. 'Tell me the number. I'll try to send them a text later.' Otto told her Charlotte's mobile number and Kate punched it into her phone.

Otto inclined his head in thanks. Would Charlotte believe it was from him? Would they be soothed? It was the best he could do for now. Kate left, closing the door behind her. Darkness seeped through the crevices in the walls of the hut. The noises from the jungle intensified. The cries of monkeys punctuated the chorus of insects. The heat in the air dispersed but even after dark it was still warm. From time to time, people moved around outside. Andreas and Kate presumably – and how many others?

Bored and weary, he curled up against the wall and closed his eyes. Mosquitoes whined in the air, feasted on his flesh, but he dozed for a while. When he woke it was still dark but he could hear vehicles outside, the revving of engines and voices shouting. A generator started up, humming in the humid darkness, and then came a flood of electric light that pierced the interior of the hut, and then the boom-boom of dance music, setting off a cacophony of hooting and screeches in the jungle. The hut door opened abruptly. Light flooded the interior, so at first he couldn't see who was standing in front of him. He shaded his eyes.

'Get up.' It was Kate. Befuddled, legs cramped, Otto struggled to his feet.

'You're letting me out? Andreas has given me the all-clear then?' He tried to sound nonchalant, but the words seemed to plead.

Kate looked him up and down and shrugged. 'I think so.' Her expression and tone of voice were faintly derogatory, as though it were obvious Otto wasn't any kind of threat. Threat to what? He rubbed his face with his hands. Sunburn and mosquito bites prickled his skin.

'So what's going on? Another party?'

Kate didn't answer, only turned away and left through the open door. Otto hurried after her.

Several huts, like the one in which Otto had been confined, huddled in the lake of electric light. Some distance away he could see half a dozen large, very glossy 4×4s parked in a row, their bonnets and windscreens faintly described at the fringes of the illuminated space. He sensed but couldn't see the jungle that engulfed this space; it was visible only as a tall, black wall above which stars glittered, the night sky an arched lid above the bowl of the clearing.

Kate had disappeared. Why had they let him out? Mightn't he just run away? He considered this option for a moment, and then dismissed it. They were miles into the pitch-black jungle and he had no idea where to go, nor what poisonous snakes or dangerous animals acted as sentinels around this artificial space. He was as effectively confined, if only by fear and ignorance, as he had been in the hut.

At the fringes of the trees he saw a gathering of people around a low shack with coloured electric lights, just like the bars on the beach. As he stepped closer, pulse rising with apprehension, he saw the shack was indeed a bar, with ranks of shining bottles on makeshift shelves. About thirty or forty people, he thought, some of whom turned as he approached, checking him out. They didn't look exactly friendly. No-one spoke. They were young people mostly, probably none much over thirty, and they looked a little different to the revellers on the beach. Hard to put his finger on exactly why – except that these people didn't look – thank you, Kate – like kid backpackers. They looked serious, and seasoned. People who could take care of themselves.

'Get yourself a drink,' someone said. Although the bar had all the usual beers and spirits ranked along the makeshift shelves, Otto noticed that everyone was drinking the same bottled water he had seen and sampled on the beach, with the plain white label. The woman behind the bar – a European – didn't ask him what he wanted to drink and simply handed him a bottle of the same. He picked it up, scrutinised the single word on the label. Although the script was Indian in flowing style, it spelled out a word he could read. The water was called Kharisma.

The woman behind the bar didn't seem to expect any payment, which was just as well because he had nothing on him. She watched him as he unscrewed the top and took a swig. The water was luke-warm and possessed a faint metallic taste. He swallowed, and took another gulp. On the other side of the shack he saw Andreas, partly shadowed, propping himself on his elbows on the bar. He was star-ing at Otto, his expression cool. Otto realised that despite his release, he wasn't invited to be one of the crowd. His attendance at the party was perhaps another test. Otto took a deep breath, raised his bottle to Andreas, and gave what he hoped was a cool smile, man to man. Andreas didn't respond. He looked at Otto a moment longer, then turned to the woman beside him. It was Kate, wasn't it? She slid her arms around Andreas's strong neck and pressed her mouth against his. Andreas made no more than a perfunctory response but Kate clung on to him anyway. Andreas looked back at Otto, Kate still hanging from him – and this time Otto had to look away. For all his bravado he couldn't compete with Andreas. He was older, stronger, and yes, Otto was afraid of him.

Otto turned from the bar, taking another swig from the bottle. He headed for a group of men, hoping they might be a little more friendly, wondering if Andreas and Kate had briefed them on who and what he was. The men seemed a little drunk, despite the fact they were drinking water. He exchanged some meaningless banter, Otto showing off his mosquito bites. He was bursting with questions but resisted the temptation to ask them, aware he was under surveillance and that too much curiosity would land him in trouble.

But he was aching to know – what exactly was going on here? What kind of operation was Andreas running? Was it drugs? Was that why they drank only water? He moved among the people at the bar. The music seemed to grow louder and he began to feel decidedly peculiar, as though he were drunk. Except that he wasn't drunk. He felt alert and wide awake, his skin sensitive to the movement of the warm night air, his mind bright, as though for most of his life he was only half awake and now, in this strange and exotic place, the muffling and clutter had been shaken out of his head and the impressions of night, stars, jungle, people were seen for the first time in stunning clarity.

He was talking to a tough young woman in combat gear about impressions of Goa. He couldn't remember how the conversation had started but it seemed to be particularly significant and intense. Looking into the girl's face, although he didn't even know her name, Otto felt he could see right into her mind and that she could see into his, so the communication between them was without hesitation and had a quality above and beyond the usual banalities people exchanged after a few beers at parties.

'So you're joining us?' the girl said.

'Joining you?'

'Isn't that why you're here? I haven't seen you before.'

Otto struggled to find the right answer, not wanting to show his ignorance.

'That's possible,' he said, with a cheeky grin he hoped indicated he was in the know.

'It's worth it,' she said. 'If you want to make money for travelling. The work's easy enough.'

'So what do you do, exactly?' he hazarded.

She looked at him then. Then she shrugged. 'Oh, a bit of driving – deliveries, you know. But it means we get the stuff free.'

Someone tapped the girl on the shoulder, looked at Otto and whispered in her ear. When the girl looked back her expression was cold and when she turned away Otto noticed Andreas standing beyond her. Had he been eavesdropping on the conversation? Otto tried to remember what they'd said in that seemingly important exchange, but found he couldn't. When he looked at Andreas again, Kate was holding on to his arm, looking at him longingly. She was speaking to him, making some kind of demand, perhaps. Andreas responded with evident irritation. Otto seized the opportunity – ducking through the crowd and away from the makeshift bar into the shadows at the fringes, overwhelmed by an urge to get away.

Glancing over his shoulder, he hurried towards the other huts. Of course he was behaving just as Andreas had suspected he would but in his curious heightened state his courage had risen. He felt strangely invulnerable and willing to take a risk. He wanted to know what was going on. Beyond the fringes of the bar the volume of the music dropped away fast. Two of the huts contained makeshift beds and sleeping stuff, backpacks and cooking equipment. The third was locked, but a kind of lean-to tilted from it, and behind the screen of dried palm leaves something glittered. He peered inside, trying to make out what it was.

Bottles. Only bottles. A store for the bar, probably. He felt a plunge of disappointment. What had he expected? Guns, maybe. Something dramatic and exciting. He looked again. The bottles stood in wooden crates, still and patient, made of clear glass with screw tops and white labels. It was the home brand of bottled water, with the strange name, Kharisma. He frowned, thinking of the 4×4 and the Indian barman unloading crates on the beach. Was it the water itself? What had they put in it?

Someone shouted out. Otto whipped round, heart stopped, afraid he been seen snooping. A disturbance in the bar, under the veranda. He hurried towards it, without thinking. Someone shouted out and an argument began.

A young man, perhaps twenty years old, was standing alone in the centre of circle created by the others. They were all staring at him. The young man had a bruise on his left cheek, and he was breathing heavily. Andreas stepped forward and kicked the young man behind his knees, knocking him to the ground. The young man moaned. Andreas's face was cold and set as he stepped closer, drew back his booted foot and drove it hard into his victim's ribs. Even from the back of the crowd, Otto heard the terrible crunch of bone and the injured man's agonising shriek though the music played on. The crowd was silent and utterly still. Andreas glanced at two other men to his left and right (were they the lieutenants from the old fort, who'd helped Andreas take Otto?) and they stepped forward to continue the work Andreas had begun. The punishment seemed to last for hours. After the first few kicks the man stopped making any noise. The others just stood and stared – as though hypnotised, or scared to death. Otto felt sick. He had never witnessed such violence before, so cold and relentless. After an interminable time, Andreas signalled for the men to stop. At the same time the music cut out, almost theatrical, as though the scene were something from a Tarantino movie. Except when the men stepped back and the results of their labour were displayed for all to see.

The young man was hardly recognisable as human any more, all beaten and bloodied. His body was broken and misshapen, his head a pulpy ball from which a liver-red liquid oozed. He didn't move or make any sound. Had they killed him? How could anyone have survived that? Otto blinked, willing the scene to disappear. His body

129

seemed to prickle, as though his nerves were registering a sympathetic pain. His hands were oddly cold.

Still no-one spoke, so many eyes fixed on the lifeless figure on the dry dirt floor. It was as though a spell had been thrown over them all, a paralysis created by the shock of the attack.

Andreas stood up straight and shook his head.

'This is what happens,' he said. 'This is what you made me do.' He addressed his comments to the creature on the floor. When he peered over the heads of the others, Otto could see darkening blood sprayed on the ground.

'You stole from me,' Andreas said. 'From us!' He included the gathering with a gesture of his hand. 'You thought you could set up on your own? You were greedy. You brought this on yourself.' This last remark he added with a tone of tenderness, a father admonishing a disappointing son.

Still no-one else spoke or moved. Then quietly, the sound of somebody crying at the back of the crowd. This plaintive sobbing signalled the end of the macabre scene. Andreas nodded.

'Clear up,' he said. The two men stooped over, grabbed the beaten man by his ankles and dragged him like a bloody, lumpen sack away from the bar and out into the darkness.

Otto remained where he was, frozen on the spot, but the others began to move and a murmur of subdued conversation rose. His eyes remained on Andreas, hypnotised, hardly able to digest what he had seen. Someone turned the music on again and the bar resumed business, handing out bottles, as though nothing had happened.

Then, perhaps sensing his gaze, Andreas looked through the crowd to Otto. Something snapped in his face. Had he forgotten Otto was present? No, Otto thought not. Andreas had wanted him to witness this. He shook his head as though the matter were of no importance but he gestured to the man beside him and pointed at Otto.

'Lock him up again,' he said. 'He's seen enough.'

Otto

February 2008

Flat, flooded fields sped past the window. Further away, low hills and bare trees slowly unwound around the train. Rooks circled against the clouded February sky. Otto thrust his feet under the table and rested his heels on the opposite chair. The carriage was almost empty this early on a Saturday morning. He had a book in his bag, something by Doris Lessing that Charlotte, always keen to develop his mind, had loaned him with an enthusiastic recommendation. Otto wasn't in the mood for reading. His mind was busy with thoughts of the day to come.

Jen. Jen with the long, dark crimson hair. How other-worldly she'd looked, the day he saw her in the march in December. Elfin. Ethereal – a Pre-Raphaelite babe, like the milk-faced, swooning maidens in the prints his mother sold so prolifically in her shop. Not that Otto had ever been a sucker for that particular brand of female, the wan, wet-lettuce variety, the weeping Ophelias. Jen though – Jen short for Jenevieve, an appropriately Arthurian name – had caught his attention. And why was that? Well, to be fair, most girls interested him these days. A revelation – the world was teeming with girls, like brilliant candles. He was constantly on the lookout, even when travelling in the car with his mother his eyes trawled the pavements. A compulsion – who was out there? Burning curiosity.

Jen was beautiful of course, a quirky beauty, with a broad forehead, enormous blue eyes and wide cheekbones narrowing down to a tiny chin and a small doll's mouth. And all that hair, thick, apparently uncombed, tending to dreadlocks and dyed that rich, dark red, spilling down to the small of her back and in disarray over her shoulders, strands poking from beneath the green woollen hat with a red silk rose pinned on it. Big silver earrings, a green velvet skirt. The picture of her, every detail, was etched on his memory. The brother too, the fashion college friend – Otto was utterly intrigued. He wanted to know more.

After the march he'd emailed Jen a few times, striking an appropriately friendly, teasing tone. Her replies had been prompt but a little evasive; her responses to his questions were elliptical. She didn't use typical email argot, instead, she wrote with great seriousness. Her spelling was a little erratic though. They talked on MSN, Otto hinting he'd like to come and see her. Finally he'd had to invite himself, near enough. He told her he was travelling to London to visit an exhibition of paintings by Millais – would she care to meet him for a coffee? Millais was a tempting choice for Jen, he thought. So it proved. She agreed readily enough so the plans expanded and Otto was invited to stay over. Still staring through the window, caught in his own thoughts and barely seeing the landscape, Otto allowed himself a private smile. He was pleasurably nervous but also immensely pleased with himself. A day in London with Jen. He'd made it happen. He'd done well.

The journey lasted an hour and a quarter. The train pulled in at Paddington; Otto leaped off and headed down into the Underground. He wanted to be the first to arrive at the gallery but Jen was already waiting in the reception area when he arrived. She looked extraordinary in a long skirt of white and ivory, a tight little jacket in the same material edged with fake fur and a white Russian hat. A long striing of pearls hung from her neck, and her hair was as he remembered, hanging down her back in all its glorious redness. How did someone so shy dare to wear such outlandish outfits? She looked like a cross between the Snow Queen and Anna Karenina – with a spicing of punk. Everyone who came in glanced over.

She looked oddly forlorn, lingering on her own, shifting her weight from foot to foot, staring at the ground. A wave of shyness came over Otto too. It had been many weeks since their first meeting and he had invested so much thought into this second encounter.

'Jen! Jen!' He pushed the shyness to one side, calling out her name.

Her head lifted and her eyes, a vivid, crystalline blue even indoors, locked on his. Then she looked away, focused on the backs of her ringed fingers.

'Otto? I wasn't sure I'd recognise you.' He strained to hear what she said, Jen kept her voice very low.

'Would you like a coffee? You look amazing,' he said, becoming master of the situation.

'A drink, yes. Herbal tea. How was the journey?'

Again he had to incline his head to hear what she said. She brushed the long, uneven fringe from her face a little nervously, waited for him to lead the way to the cafe. She did look gorgeous. Otto couldn't help it, feasting himself on the sight of her, eating her up with his eyes. 'The journey was fine, no problem at all. It doesn't take long.' He found them a table, ordered a cappuccino and Jen had a mint tea. Then he started to talk. He talked a lot and Jen, it seemed, was happy to listen. He told her about his A levels, his mother's art shop, his life in a small town, his photography, his ambitions. He wanted to win her over.

From time to time he made her laugh, asked for her thoughts, enquired as to her opinion about contemporary art. She always had an answer but never hogged the conversation. Oh she was very engaging. He was aware of the looks other people in the cafe gave them and felt a proprietary pride that this exotic creature was sitting with him.

The exhibition itself interested Otto only in part. He enjoyed seeing the famous paintings, the ones he recognised from the prints in his mother's shops, but the sheer number wore his enthusiasm down in the end. And the place was very busy, all the art lovers crammed into the windowless, overheated gallery space. Jen appeared to be very happy though so this was reward enough. Afterwards they walked along the river into the heart of London. It thrilled him, the great city and the Thames weaving amid the skyline, familiar only from pictures or scenes on television. People thronged the pavements, so many languages half heard. On an artificial ice rink environmentalists dressed as penguins skated in the cold to protest against airport expansion. The sky cleared, a cold, brilliant blue, and everything seemed a marvellous adventure.

Jen and Otto stopped for a late lunch at a crowded restaurant, braving the chilly weather to sit outside on the terrace. They dined on onion soup, Jen passing her portion of bread to Otto because, she said, wheat didn't agree with her. She told him she had allergies and had to watch what she ate. Otto paid, flourishing the earnings from his part-time job. They walked again. Jen seemed to relax and talked more freely. She told him about her art work and that her mother suffered intermittently from depression. Something about her Otto struggled to grasp, a sense that she eluded him. This heightened his interest. He wanted to know her, to unravel the complex knot of who she might be.

Later, as darkness drew on, they took the Tube to Camden. The street lights came on as they stepped from the Underground station. They walked passed tattoo parlours, piercing studios, stalls selling scarves, belts and jewellery, shop windows in which mannequins posed in outfits made of lace and brocade and patent vinyl. Then came the maze of the indoor market where monstrous chandeliers loured over narrow corridors and huge horse statues reared over passageways. Music loomed in and out of focus. Perfumes from tantalising food stalls ribboned through the partially illuminated darkness. Otto was delighted – he'd stepped into a scene from *Bladerunner*, a gothic fairyland. Why had he never come before? Except that today was the perfect day, walking beside his winter maiden with her blood-red hair. Even here, among the other teenage emos, aged punks, tourists, wannabes and otherwise curiously adorned, Jen attracted attention. Otto observed how they checked her out, the other Camdenites, though Jen herself seemed unaware of it. He was all focused on the outside, the place, other people. She was entirely inward, lost in herself, even as she moved through the noise and crowd.

They stopped for a tray of scalding noodles and tofu – at least, Otto did. He was ravenously hungry. He was always hungry these days. Jen said she didn't want to eat so they sat on a bench beneath strings of coloured fairy lights while he shovelled food into his mouth and she waited, toying with another cup of herbal tea that looked to him like dishwater. His feet were burning from hours walking on pavements. His legs ached. It had been a long day.

'Shall we go home?' Jen asked, on cue. Home – her home. Otto nodded with some relief, glad she hadn't suggested another excursion. He'd seen enough for one day, wonderful as it had been. The journey home involved another Tube trip and then a short sojourn on a train into the south of London. They stepped out onto a cold platform into the embrace of an arctic wind. Otto shivered and hugged his arms around himself, underdressed as usual for the winter weather. The house was ten minutes' walk down the road, a small terraced house made of red brick, with a tiled path.

'Who'll be home?' Otto asked, preparing himself for the encounter. He wanted, as always, to make a good impression. To impress.

'Don't know. Mum and Dad, I expect.'

'Your brother?'

Jen shrugged. 'Maybe. He's out a lot. Stays over with friends.' She unlocked the door and they stepped into warmth. Otto could smell food cooking, spicy Indian food. A plush, grey cat stalked along the corridor towards them, purring. Jen scooped it up, rubbed the dense, smoky fur of its flank against her face.

'Aren't you allergic to cats?'

'Actually, yes. But not to this one. I was at the beginning, and then I got used to him. My immune system did.' She walked ahead, carrying the cat over her shoulder. It stared back at Otto with lemon yellow eyes. The house matched his expectations. Lots of books, paintings on the walls, sofas with bright cushions, comfortable and lived in, also slightly shabby and dusty. In the kitchen at the back of the house a tall, bony woman stirred the amber and orange contents of a large, chipped saucepan. She had long black hair, in which threads of white glinted and a gaunt, rather beautiful face. Otto found her curiously attractive, despite her age. There was a familiarity about her, of course – Jen and she were much alike.

'This is my mum, Hannah,' Jen said. Otto stepped up, held out his hand.

'Great to meet you. It's very kind of you to let me stay over,' he said.

'No problem. As long as you don't mind sleeping on the sofa. It pulls out and is perfectly comfortable. Are you hungry? Do you want some curry? You can eat it too, Jen. I'll put some aside before I put the cream in.'

Otto looked for signs of this mooted depression but saw none. What had he expected? Jen had told him these times were periodic rather than continuous. On first acquaintance she seemed rather lovely – the sort of woman his mother would like. He and Jen collapsed in the sitting room, relaxing in the warmth. Jen's dad returned soon after them, and then Niall appeared after all. They sat together around a table in a dining room with a polished wooden floor and ate the vegetable curry along with quantities of fragrant rice, chapattis, popadoms, pickles and fresh yoghurt. Despite the noodles at Camden, Otto ate plenty. Jen's dad was solid and rather quiet. Niall seemed less exotic in his home environment – a more ordinary son and brother, to be nagged by his mother, teased by his sister. He'd toned down the campness. What did the parents think of his being gay? They didn't seem to be the kind of people who would worry about it. Otto enjoyed it, the company, the family atmosphere. He and his mother had lived alone for as long as he could remember. His father had left when Otto was a toddler, moved to the United States, and Otto'd had little contact with him over the intervening years. There had been no stepfathers, no visible boyfriends – so Otto and his mum had lived quietly, self-sufficient, very close. He worried about her now though. At sixteen he wanted his own life. He had friends, a social network, plans for the future. He was out most of the time. What would she do without him?

The meal didn't finish till late. Wine to drink, ice cream for pudding. Jen's dad grew more expansive after a couple of glasses, told Otto about his business designing and making stained glass, asked him about school. They had a discussion about digital photography. Hannah went out into the back garden for a cigarette, sat shivering at a wrought iron table while she puffed. Otto, washing up, watched her through the kitchen window, observed the thin hand and tiny wrist brandishing the cigarette.

When they cleared up, Jen invited Otto up to her room. She had a television and a DVD player – did he want to watch a film? She led the way up the narrow stairs, opened the door on a tiny room at the back of the house. The grey cat pushed his way in front of them and hopped lightly onto the bed.

'Wow,' Otto said, stunned. 'Your room is amazing.'

Jen gave a small smile, eyes lowered. 'Please come in,' she said.

Crimson and saffron yellow, glimmering gold, the glance of white light in tiny fragments of mirror. A room like a tent, an exotic Indian palace hung with embroidered silks, where elephants in scarlet thread paraded among elegant trees and stitched peacocks. An archway of primrose cloth hung over the door and on the mantel over the tiny iron fireplace stood a bronze statue of Shiva, perhaps thirty centimetres high, dancing on one foot in a ring of flames, four arms gesturing. Otto stared at the statue of the Hindu god, almost feminine in his grace and slenderness, his face calm and beautiful.

Two candlesticks flanked the statue, these being golden snakes that reared up, carrying candles on their heads. Jen lit them both and a cone of incense in a pale soapstone dish. On a corkboard over a desk in the corner of the room, pictures and postcards of Indian scenes, the Taj Mahal, a palace in the desert, steps leading down to a river where boats drifted in the flame-coloured dawn.

So where was the television? It seemed impossible such a mundane article could sit in this temple. Jen pulled aside one of the wall coverings to reveal this unfitting piece of technology on a shelf along with a dozen DVDs.

'What would you like to watch?' she said. Otto browsed through the titles.

'You choose,' he said. 'I've seen *The Beach* before. The others I don't know. Pick something you like.'

Jen smiled, that same discreet, shy smile, and took down, appropriately, *A Passage to India*. It didn't look promising – one of those costume dramas that women seemed to like. However.

'So what's the fascination with India?' he said. At that time the name didn't conjure up the beauty, mystery and sheer strangeness that Jen had recreated in her room, this fantasy tableau. India, to him, summoned images of slums, dirt and dust, poverty and pollution.

'I want to go to India,' Jen said. 'I will go. Maybe I was Indian in another life, maybe I lived there. I don't know exactly why I feel like that, I just know it is the most extraordinary, fascinating and magical country in the world and I have to go there.'

Jen's face glowed, her voice was resonant. It surprised him, this passionate declaration. She had been, to this point, so shy and self-effacing, seeming always to look at things sideways, always non-committal.

Otto hesitated. Then he said, 'When will you go? Who will you go with?'

Jen turned away, fiddling with the DVD.

'I don't know. When the time's right. I'll need money of course.'

The film flickered onto the screen and they sat, either side of the cat, on Jen's bed. The story unrolled, hypnotising Otto despite his doubts. It seemed a little dated to him, the production, but he was enchanted. Was that India? If so, he wanted to go to. Or was that simply because Jen wanted to go? Had he soaked up her enthusiasm? He glanced at her, the light from the screen dancing on her face. She looked utterly lovely. He liked everything about her, the modesty and strangeness, even how shy she was. Should he kiss her? Jen had been utterly charming and friendly all day, he was sure she liked him. On the other hand she hadn't behaved flirtatiously. What did she want? It wasn't worth the risk. With this girl, it would be serious and he was reluctant to be serious. He didn't want to squander his chance. Best resist the temptation for now. He would take his time.

India. The film proceeded, full of dust and heat. Miss Quested ran from the caves, distraught, through bushes and thorns. Otto felt a sensation of warmth deep in the pit of his belly, in the cradle of his pelvis, at the base of his spine, like a wheel of fire turning and turning. What did this mean? He looked at Jen and back to the film.

Later, lying on the sofa bed, light-headed from tiredness, he dozed with the lingering perfume of their curry dinner in his nostrils, the scent of Jen's incense clinging to his hair. He made the decision then, impulsive and half smitten with this lovely girl. He would go to India too. He would go with Jen.

Charlotte

Friday

Charlotte didn't sleep well. Her body clock was wildly out of synch. Worries about Otto turned over and over in her mind. Why hadn't he let them know what was going on? He didn't always think things through but it wasn't remotely like him to be so irresponsible or careless of their feelings he would just disappear without telling them. Something bad had happened to him, she was sure of it. So what should they do? Contact her parents, Otto's mum?

They were lying in the dark, on their parallel beds. Jen, also sleepless, gave an abrupt sigh.

'What are we going to do?' she said, into the night.

'First of all, we should go to the police,' Charlotte replied, with more authority than she felt. 'Report Otto's disappearance. They have to do something.'

Jen didn't answer but Charlotte picked up her doubt. She said, with more aggression than she intended, 'Well, do you have a better idea?'

Jen didn't answer for a few moments. Then she said in a small voice, 'No, I don't. You're right; we should go to the police. It's just a frightening idea. I keep thinking this is all a mistake and that Otto might turn up and laugh at us. If we go to the police we'll find out it's all real.'

Charlotte licked her lips. Her mouth was dry. She regretted her moment of annoyance.

'What – what does your intuition tell you?' Intuition was the name Charlotte gave Jen's mooted talent. Jen had told her she had a form of clairvoyance, an ability to see spirits, beyond the limits of her ordinary senses. Charlotte was tolerant of this unlikely tale; Jen was her best friend – best female friend – and she loved her. If Jen believed she could see energies and spirits, if she reckoned she could sense beyond the realm of the physical, then Charlotte was happy to accept that was part of Jen's reality. Anyway, Jen did say the most uncanny things from time to time – spied coincidences, casually made remarks about Charlotte's past and her future that later proved to be oddly accurate. That didn't mean she was psychic of course, but however Jen's intuition worked, it was not to be dismissed.

Jen didn't answer at once. The room was so quiet Charlotte could hear her breathing.

'I think he's in danger,' Jen said. Well it doesn't take psychic powers to work that out, Charlotte thought. She waited for a further revelation but nothing came.

The police station opened at nine. An old woman, very slim and neat with her long grey hair in a plait, was sweeping the doorway with a twig broom. Jen and Charlotte had taken a taxi, eating into their meagre budget rather faster than expected. It was an emergency. The taxi driver had been nosey (perhaps intending to be helpful?), asking them why they needed the police. Jen didn't answer. Charlotte fobbed him off with some weak excuse about a stolen camera.

The man at the reception desk ushered them into a private room as soon as they mentioned Otto's name. Five minutes later a policeman stepped in, holding a folder. He was a shrewd-looking man in a bad suit. He told them his name was Inspector Sharma. Jen was sitting on a plain, hard chair not looking at the inspector at all. She looked drained, grey in the face. Charlotte would have to do the talking for both of them. She stood up straight and said in a firm voice, 'We're

Otto Gilmour's friends, come from England. You must tell me what's happened. Do you know where he's gone? We're worried he's in danger.' She kept her voice steady and strong, but she could feel the blood rising in her face. The police inspector stood very still, studying Charlotte as she spoke. His self-possession made her feel like a child, as though he knew too well she was acting out a role and that she wasn't entirely convinced by her own performance.

'We took a statement from Mr Gilmour,' he said. 'He discovered a girl's body on the beach, a girl he knew and had been involved with.'

'Involved with?' Shock was evident in her voice. She tried to rein it in. She glanced quickly at Jen. 'What do you mean involved with?'

'Romantically involved.' His voice was light and level, giving nothing away.

'He can't have been that involved – he'd only been here a few days.'

The inspector shrugged, worldly-wise. Charlotte frowned. Bloody Otto – he was such an operator when it came to women. He'd run into some beach babe with a pretty face and hadn't wasted any time. It didn't look good though. A girl he'd got entangled with had been murdered – and Otto had found the body?

'Is he a suspect, then?'

Jen was standing by the wall, neither looking at the policeman nor engaging in the conversation.

The inspector shrugged. 'He hasn't been charged but he is a suspect, yes. The investigation is ongoing. We haven't remanded him in custody, but we are holding his passport as a precaution. We don't want him leaving the country just yet.'

'But Otto's gone! He's disappeared!' Charlotte said. 'Aren't you worried something's happened to him?'

'Otto was instructed to stay at his current address. Now, like some scared little boy, he's run away, taking all his possessions with him. That was ill-advised. It is very inconvenient.'

Charlotte ground her teeth in frustration. 'He wouldn't have run away!' she said. 'I know him. He wouldn't do that. He'd have stayed and got it sorted out. Something's happened to him.'

'Are you worried, perhaps, that his running away makes it seem more likely he is guilty? That he killed this young woman?' the inspector said. 'Well I would have to agree with you. It doesn't look good at all. You say you know him but I can tell you that young people can behave in very unexpected ways once they're far away from home. No restraints.'

'Otto wouldn't kill anyone. And he wouldn't have run away either,' Charlotte insisted. 'I'm telling you, something has happened to him. Please – make some enquiries – start up a search. Please do something.'

The inspector regarded Charlotte. Something close to compassion flashed in his face. 'I'm very sorry,' he said. 'There is no evidence anything has happened to Otto Gilmour. He paid his rent, packed his belongings, and disappeared. I accept that doesn't mean he was responsible for the poor girl's death, though he may well have been. Perhaps it was all too inconvenient, too frightening. He didn't want to be involved.'

Charlotte shook her head. Tears pricked her eyes but she didn't want this weakness to show.

The inspector sighed. 'If you would leave your contact details, tell me where you are staying, I will tell you if we have any news of Otto.'

'Jen, we're going,' she said. Jen had barely moved throughout the conversation. She looked at Charlotte, her eyes misty.

'We're going?' she said. They stepped out of the hot little room into the reception area. The inspector took their contact details and turned away – then he stopped, some thought striking him.

'Just a moment,' he said. 'Wait, please? I'd like to ask you something.' He disappeared into another room, an office apparently, and came out carrying a brown folder. He fished inside and drew out a large colour photograph.

144

'Do you recognise this?'

Charlotte took the photo and showed it to Jen. It was a picture of a young woman's back, with the base of her neck at the top, the narrowing waist at the bottom. Her skin was coffee brown, marked at intervals with narrow purple bruises. Between the smooth shoulder blades, on the spine, a symbol had been tattooed in black ink. It was a circle, about the size of a fifty pence piece, surrounded by flames. The tattoo was finely done, delicate and elegant. Perhaps it was relatively new?

'A tattoo,' Charlotte said. She looked from the photograph to the inspector. 'I don't recognise it. Why should I?' The inspector shrugged.

Then Jen spoke, for the first time, 'What was the girl's name?'

'Maria. Maria Westland.'

'What about her parents? Do they know? Are they coming out?'

The inspector sighed. 'We are having difficulties locating any next of kin. The British Embassy is making some investigations on our behalf.'

'Then who will bury her?' Jen sounded like a little girl. The inspector didn't answer. He took back the photograph.

'Be careful,' he said, looking at Charlotte, and then at Jen. 'May I suggest you both leave Goa?'

'Why?' Charlotte said. 'Why should we? Are you trying to get rid of us? We won't be going anywhere till we find Otto.'

The inspector gave a grave smile. 'I thought you would say that. I am new in Goa myself, so I haven't yet discovered exactly what is going on here, something the local police have been slow to pursue until now. But rumours have reached us in Delhi, and now a young girl is dead. So I shall repeat – be careful.'

'What sort of thing is going on?' Charlotte demanded. But Sharma just shook his head and indicated it was time they left.

The girls walked back to the village in the intense heat. Charlotte soaked it up, the delicious, golden sunshine. Even after two days, her skin was responding, becoming a pale honey brown. The narrow road was dry and dusty. To either side, beyond deep ditches, rice fields glowed emerald green. Papery flowers dangled among the trees.

They walked in silence for some time. Then Jen said, 'He does think Otto's in danger.'

Charlotte sighed. 'What makes you say that?'

Jen shrugged. 'It was obvious. Why would he tell us to leave? And I don't think he believes Otto's done a runner. There'll be investigations ongoing. They'll be trying to find him.'

Was that wishful thinking? Back at their room, Charlotte made an expensive mobile call to the British Embassy in Delhi. She made no progress – the polite woman at the end of the phone informed her they were aware of the murder investigation and that the police were dealing with the matter. She refused to worry about Otto's safety and told Charlotte it was more than likely that he'd simply moved on and how irresponsible that was when a murder investigation was underway. She was not sympathetic – on the contrary, she seemed to be reprimanding Otto, via Charlotte.

Charlotte clicked off her phone in frustration and flung it in her bag.

So, what to do now? The girls walked to the beach. The milky sand burned Charlotte's bare feet. The faintest of breezes brushed the surface of the sea and touched her face. Jen, white-skinned, had covered up with a light shirt and wore a floppy hat on her head. Hardly anyone about this early, except for two young Indian women, one with an infant, both carrying bags and bracelets, eager to sell them something. They were dressed in colourful Rajasthani outfits in vibrant reds and blues, glittering with fragments of mirror and a cargo of jewellery. The women were picturesque, friendly, pushy – eager to make a sale. Charlotte resisted but Jen succumbed, buying a bangle because she didn't want to offend. She slipped it over her arm. Half a dozen young boys played in the water at the sea's edge, shouting out and splashing. A goat lay on the sand and chewed what appeared to be an old newspaper.

It was too hot to sit on the beach for long, They wandered back to the Seaside Bar and sat in the meagre shade. Charlotte sipped a cool lassi. Jen ate a banana. Beyond them the beach paradise shimmered in the heat. Both had pens and notebooks on the table. Jen was drawing something. Charlotte sucked the end of her biro.

'We need a plan,' she said.

Jen drew for a few moments more, then she said, 'A plan? What sort of plan?'

'To find Otto. We can't just do nothing.'

'What can we do?' Jen lifted her arm from the table and Charlotte saw she had recreated on paper the symbol tattooed on the back of the dead girl, Maria Westland. Jen's version was larger and more elaborate, covering a page in the leather-covered sketchbook, marked in heavy black ink, the circle revolving in its circle of fire.

Jen sighed – hesitated – then said, 'I didn't say anything to the policeman but I have seen it before. In a sketchbook at home, I drew it.'

'What do you mean? You drew this same symbol? Where did you get it from?'

'I didn't get it from anywhere. It came to me.'

Charlotte sighed. 'That is quite freaky, Jen. So you know what it means? It's just a tattoo. What's it got to do with anything?'

Jen shrugged. 'I don't know what it means. Perhaps nothing. But I have seen it before.'

Charlotte took a deep breath and said, 'How did you feel, when the policeman said Otto had, you know, got involved with this girl?' She watched Jen, waiting for the barely perceptible reaction. Jen's body seemed to freeze for a moment, the hand holding the pen stopped moving. Then the emotion passed and Jen resumed her drawing. Her head gave the merest shake.

'It's fine. You know what he's like.' She raised her eyes to

Charlotte in a kind of challenge. Did Jen know Charlotte loved Otto? Surely she must do, this mooted psychic, though they'd never talked about it. But Jen had gone out with Otto for a short while, back in the summer. They'd drifted from friendship into something more, and then a month later, seemed to drift back again. Otto wasn't ready for it, Jen had reported to Charlotte. He didn't want to spoil things, would rather they were friends because friendship lasted longer. Still Charlotte understood that Jen had been hurt by this withdrawal.

Now Jen looked vulnerable so Charlotte brushed the subject aside. 'We need a plan,' she repeated. 'The cafe man said he'd take us to the place where Otto was staying. We'll go there and see what we can find out. Then we should find out where he's been hanging out these last few days and talk to people who might have seen him, or knew Maria.'

A look of fright from Jen; Charlotte scribbled notes in her book.

'What's the problem?' she said. 'We have to do something. God knows where he is – what's happened to him.' She put her pen down, drained her glass and stood up.

Charlotte

May 2008

May was her favourite month. She went running off-road along
green lanes, through tunnels of flowering hawthorn, past tiny pockets of woodland called Sheppey Holt or Lee Wood, or Spirit Copse
where bluebells glimmered between the trees. Days of sunshine,
brisk, chilly breezes, intervals of showers. Revision for AS levels.
She saw Otto most weekends. They chatted online many evenings
during the week when doing homework. She knew he'd visited Jen,
the art girl from London, earlier in the year. The Saturday after he'd
told her all about it when she'd gone to his house – told her about
the art gallery, the people dressed as penguins, Camden after dark,
Jen dressed like the snow queen and her bedroom a temple to
India . . . Charlotte wasn't jealous, or not much. She knew he'd
stored the day in all its glorious detail in order to tell her about it.
Charlotte was his best friend, his touchstone – the audience for his
stories. His conscience, even. The trip would not have been such a
pleasure for him if he hadn't had Charlotte waiting to hear about it,
to ask the right questions and respond to his opinions. And Jen, at
least she sounded more interesting than many of his crushes. Otto's
girlfriends came and went like brief flowers. He was loath to
commit himself – a child in a cake shop unable to choose which
delicious confection to buy when so many fabulous treats were
on offer. Except for Charlotte, of course. She was the only female

constant – apart from his lovely mother. That was some consolation. Charlotte could wait.

On Friday night Otto came round to her house after school. They spent an hour in her bedroom looking at Otto's latest photos. Charlotte was encouraging but critical. She had great faith in his talent but she was intolerant of his tendency to self-indulgence and pretension. He had posted on his website a series of pictures showing a field of decaying farm buildings, low, shambling corrugated iron sheds with broken windows and coils of barbed wire.

'That one's good,' she said. 'I like the composition, the brambles looping over the roof. This one – that's good too but a little flat.'

'The light wasn't so good,' Otto jumped in. 'But this one, you like that? I got the old farm sign in you see. Look at the moss and the rust on the old bolt. So you like that one?'

Charlotte nodded. 'Yes. Yes, I do.' He would delete or alter the picture she had criticised, she knew. He wouldn't say anything, but still he would do it, trusting her opinion. When they'd looked at the photos they watched an episode of *Prison Break*. At eight her mother called up the stairs. Was Otto staying for dinner?

They ate in the dark-panelled dining room. Otto never missed an opportunity to eat with her parents. They intrigued him with their crammed, untidy, dusty house, the names they dropped casually into the conversation, government ministers and media types. They were different to him. They were Old Money. While this embarrassed Charlotte, it piqued Otto's interest. They dined from plates inherited from Charlotte's paternal grandmother, used linen napkins and heavy silver cutlery though for some reason the food was always cold when it came to the table. They drank good wine and ate very slowly. Charlotte's father made genial conversation with Otto, and Otto was happy to respond with some observation or other about school or something that had happened in the news. Charlotte could see him observing, drinking it all up, as though he were a student on some kind of field trip. This was always annoying.

They ate roast beef and new potatoes with broad beans and carrots. The beef was pink in the middle, oozed bloodily on the blue and white plate.

'So what are your plans for the weekend?' Charlotte's father said.

'I've got a friend from London coming up to stay,' Otto replied. Charlotte lifted her head. He hadn't mentioned this before.

'Who's that?' Her voice came out more sharply than she had intended. Her mother glanced over.

'Oh, it's Jen. Remember? The girl we met in London.' He said it easily, without embarrassment. Charlotte swallowed but the beef caught in her throat.

'We met her and her brother on the march we went to in London in December,' Otto said. 'Well, she fancied a break in the country. I know this place isn't exactly the country but it's near enough.' He glanced over at Charlotte. 'I thought we could take her to Avebury? Do you fancy it? We could take the bus.'

Charlotte swallowed again. She picked up her glass and took a sip of wine. Her throat was rough.

'I . . . I don't know. You didn't say before. Aren't you working tomorrow?'

'I'm taking a day off.'

Charlotte frowned. So this visit had been planned for a while. Why hadn't he mentioned it before? They were mates after all. He seemed entirely oblivious to the fact that Charlotte liked him so much and always talked about the fleeting girlfriends without a thought for her feelings. So why hadn't he told her about Jen's visit? Charlotte floundered. She didn't want to play gooseberry if this were another romance – on the other hand, perhaps she should check Jen out. And why would Otto have invited her along if he was planning to get off with his guest? Normally he kept his conquests well away from her, guessing (rightly) she would disapprove of his choices. Otto was a sucker for a pretty face.

151

'If you like,' she shrugged. 'I've got a lot of homework to do but I could come – if you want me to.'

Otto smiled. The conversation moved elsewhere. They had rhubarb crumble and cream for pudding. Afterwards Otto was his usual obliging self and helped clear the table. He and Charlotte stacked plates into the creaking dishwasher then disappeared back upstairs to Charlotte's room.

Outside the light was finally fading. Otto turned the television on for another episode of *Prison Break*. They lay down side by side on Charlotte's big bed. Even though he was inches away from her, Charlotte could feel the warmth of his body. Sometimes it was hard to care about him so much, to spend time together, and yet to be so distant in the one way that seemed at times like this to be the most important of all. Why didn't he feel the same? How could he not know? Was she simply not beautiful enough? She'd stood in front of a mirror often enough, asking this question, wondering what it was Otto might see and why he didn't register her on the radar so finely tuned to the attractions of pretty much every other girl he met. Even beneath her own critical gaze she knew she had a great body – strong, honed, exercised. And her face? That was okay too. Not remarkable for either beauty or a lack of it. She had good skin. Not a girly type though – no hair dye or make-up, no jewellery (these things never felt right). Her clothes were always simple and under-stated. Fashion didn't interest her. She certainly wasn't going to dress like a WAG – even to catch Otto's eye.

'So. What time's this girl arriving?'

'Eleven.' Otto was lying on his stomach, his chin resting on his folded arms. He stared at the television.

'So how come you want me to come along?'

'She's cool. I think you'd like her. It'd be fun.'

Charlotte sighed. 'I don't want to be tagging along if you've got designs on her.'

'I haven't.' His voice was perfectly level. Finally he turned to look at her. 'Honestly. Please come – I think you'd like her. She's a very unusual person.'

Unusual. Like Charlotte and her family were unusual (to him anyway). Another oddity to be studied, she thought, in a flash of irritation. But Otto was still staring at her. Perhaps he sensed her mood because his face softened and he smiled. He stretched out his hand and patted her on the shoulder.

'Please come,' he said, all boyish appeal. 'I'd like you to.'

How could she say no?

Charlotte woke late the next morning. Otto had stayed till after midnight. She luxuriated in the lie-in, no early run, no school to get up for. She was deliciously warm, curled up under her duvet. Sunlight poked through the curtains. Elsewhere in the house, far away, someone was moving about – her father perhaps, making tea for her mother. She lay in bed for a while longer, relaxing, letting her mind drift. It wasn't often she allowed herself such an indulgence; but didn't she deserve it, once in a while? She'd worked hard this week. And today – well, who knew what today would be like?

She showered and washed her hair, moisturised her skin, put on a clean T-shirt, jeans and walking boots. She stared in the mirror as she dried her hair, scrutinising her reflection. She looked healthy. Healthy, yes. That would have to do. She'd arranged to meet Otto on the bridge at the bottom of the High Street at twelve. It was a brisk, blue day with a quick breeze and snatches of cloud. Six young swans, slush-grey, floated alongside their snowy parents on the dark green river. Town was busy – teenagers loitering by the benches, parents with pushchairs and toddlers, old people carrying bags of shopping. And there they were – Otto's tall, familiar figure and beside him, elf-like and graceful, little Jen, walking side by side along the path across the park. Otto raised his arm and waved. Charlotte waved back, her heart leaping. He grinned. Then they were all standing on the bridge. Otto introduced them for a second time. Jen stretched out her hand. It was an oddly formal gesture; even so,

Jen only briefly met Charlotte's eyes. She was very shy. There was something very fragile about her – almost lamb-like. And she had a cool, quirky beauty. Charlotte had been too tired and irritated to pay Jen much attention when they'd met in London. Now, in the clear light of day, she was intrigued.

'How was the journey?' Charlotte asked.

'Fine, yes. I slept a bit.' Jen's dark crimson hair was bound in a thick plait down her back but long threads hung loose about her face. More exotic clothes – a purple velvet skirt, a beaded blouse splashed with yellow roses, silver bangles.

They caught the bus to Avebury, some twenty minutes away. Otto delivered a commentary, pointing out landmarks and making observations. Jen was quiet, gazing wide-eyed through the window. They disembarked outside the Red Lion where drinkers were already sitting outside at wooden tables, hikers in walking gear, hippy types with long hair and crystal necklaces, elderly tourists with dogs. The hippies noticed Jen, perhaps noting one of their own?

'This way,' Otto said, self-appointed tour guide, directing them through a narrow gate into the first field. Charlotte had visited the place many times before. The uneven circle of giant stones spread over four fields, divided by the main road and the cosy village sitting at the centre. A huge soil embankment and deep ditch surrounded the stone circle and from the path at the top Otto gestured to views over wide, cultivated fields. Sheep and lambs grazed among the stones, buffeted by the breeze. Charlotte shivered, hugging her arms around herself.

Jen didn't feel obliged to keep up with Otto. She mooched around the stones in a dream, stopping at the first to place her hands against it, palms flat, studying the uneven surface and the patterns of lichen. The wind plucked at the hair around her face. Dreaming over ley lines? She made her own winding path around the circle, meandering from stone to stone, wondering and studying, occasionally holding out her fingers to brush them against the cold, rough surface. The

154

sheep, used to visitors, didn't budge. Several lambs, in a pile, huddled out of the breeze at the lee side of a standing stone. At the top of the embankment, Charlotte and Otto waited, side by side, hands in pockets.

'Not your usual type,' Charlotte said.

'I told you,' Otto answered. 'She's not a girlfriend. That's what I said.'

Charlotte didn't answer. For some reason, she didn't find Jen's communing with the stones irritating. Perhaps because it didn't seem like a pretence? She could see Jen was totally absorbed, unaware of the people around her. When they'd walked around the stones, Charlotte suggested they went to the Swallowhead Spring and the long barrow, so they headed across the fields on the footpath by the stream. Silbury Hill, the huge grassy mound, reared to their right.

'It's the largest man-made prehistoric site in Europe,' Otto commentated, signalling the extent of its size with his arms. A field of yellow rape lay beyond the green hill. The stream, the Winterbourne, gushed with clear water in which emerald weeds rippled. Cow parsley bloomed in a cream wash on the stream banks. Happiness washed over Charlotte, enjoying the walk and the panorama of this beautiful place and the sunny morning. Jen glanced over, caught her eye – an acute *seeing* – noticing her pleasure, as though properly aware of her for the first time, knowing who she was. It was a jolt for Charlotte, used to being the observer, the watcher of others. She kept herself very private – why, even her best friend Otto, her confidant, didn't know the secret of her feelings for him. She gave her head a quick, compulsive little shake.

They crossed the main road to Marlborough, the old Roman road as Otto told them, and traversed the next field, knee-deep in damp grass, to the stepping stones over the river to the broken willow growing over the Swallowhead Spring. The place was a magnet for hippies and pagans; ribbons and rusty bells dangled from the branches, offerings and adornments representing wishes and promises. Some kind of wicker sculpture lay at the willow's root. Further up, where the spring bubbled from the chalky, flint-strewn soil, several crude clay statues of the earth goddess – faceless, all breasts and thighs – presided over the water. Otto pointed them out to Jen, almost prancing with delight to reveal the place to her. Charlotte smiled to herself – his enthusiasm was very appealing even when he was trying to impress another girl.

'What do you think? Isn't it great? I thought you'd like it, I love it.'

Charlotte smiled again, knowing he hadn't been here for three years or more. The last time they'd come with his mother who had a penchant for mystical landscapes. She'd brought ribbons for the two of them to hang up on the lower branches but they were bashful, the three of them, because four decorative young people were sitting under the willow tree and one of them was twanging the strings on a dark wooden zither.

Jen crouched by the spring mouth, watching the water bubbling up from the ground and flowing through the lush grass and verdant nettles to the river.

'It is lovely,' she agreed, inclining her head. Charlotte had to pay attention to hear her; Jen's voice was low and gentle. She would, perhaps, have liked to sit awhile at the spring, to take in the atmosphere of the place and stare at the river – this much Charlotte sensed about her. It was odd; they had spoken to each other so little but since that moment by Silbury Hill Charlotte felt a connection between them, a current of sympathy. But Otto the tour guide was keen to get them on the move again to West Kennet long barrow, their final destination on the Neolithic tour.

It was quite a walk up the steep field to the long, stone-lined tunnel under a hump in the ground. Huge standing stones stood like sentinels at the entrance. Inside, it was dark and many-chambered, like a heart. Otto led the way, still talking. At the end of the barrow, under a dim skylight, burnt out candles perched on the walls.

Charlotte took a deep breath. It was very still underground. The air smelled of cold stone and earth and incense. People had been buried here thousands of years before. What had happened to their remains? she wondered. There was no sense of spookiness for her. It was entirely peaceful, a resting place. For a moment there was silence. Even Otto turned off the commentary. They stood together, the three of them, in the quiet of the ancient grave.

Jen closed her eyes.

Then opened them wide. Her pupils were huge and black, her skin very white. In the barrow's twilight, her crimson hair was dark and drained of colour.

Charlotte shivered. Something in the atmosphere of the place had altered. She glanced at Otto then said, 'Jen – are you okay?'

Jen didn't answer. In her face Charlotte saw a vacancy that unnerved her.

'Jen, do you want to get out of here?' She reached out and touched Jen's arm. Jen swayed slightly but didn't reply. Her eyes seemed to expand, filling her face.

'Jen. Jen!'

'What's the matter with her?' Otto said. 'Is she going to faint?'

'I don't know. Maybe. Put your arm around her – don't let her fall.'

Jen's head leaned forward, very slowly. Then she raised it, abruptly. She looked around wildly, from Otto to Jen, as though she didn't know who or where she was.

'Jen, are you okay?'

Something crossed her face, a procession of thoughts. She clutched Otto, as though she was indeed afraid she'd fall, blinked, and blinked again.

'Yes. Yes, I'm okay.' She took a deep breath.

'What happened? I thought you were going to faint,' Charlotte said. 'It is claustrophobic in here. The darkness, the smell – come outside. Come on – get some light and fresh air.'

Otto had yielded to Charlotte's taking charge in the face of Jen's

157

mysterious malady. She ushered him ahead, still propping Jen, out of the barrow. He sat her down on the grassy bank into sunshine more brilliant after the darkness. Jen rubbed her hands over her face as though she were very tired. Solicitous, Charlotte and Otto sat one to either side of her. Slowly colour returned to Jen's skin and the fluttering uncertainty evaporated. She took Charlotte's hand, and Otto's, so they were joined in a chain.

'What happened?' Charlotte said. 'I thought you were going to pass out!'

The Wiltshire countryside spread away from them, spring-green and windblown. Half a dozen rooks drifted over a blooming horse chestnut in the field below.

'I see things,' Jen said. She looked nervous, clutching her hands together. She looked from Charlotte to Otto and back to Charlotte again.

'What things?' Charlotte said.

'I don't know what you'd call them. Spirits. Energies. The words aren't right really.'

'You saw a ghost in the long barrow?' Otto grinned.

Charlotte scowled at him. 'Otto, please!'

'It's okay,' Jen said, squeezing her hand. 'I know how this must sound.'

'What did you see?' Charlotte asked gently.

'It's hard to explain exactly. Like a door opening.' She looked into Charlotte's face. 'There's a connection between the three of us. Do you sense that?'

Charlotte was puzzled. 'That's what you saw?'

'No.' Jen shook her head. 'It's hard to explain. I saw myself. In the future.'

Charlotte was patient but sceptical. None of this made sense. Still, she patted Jen's shoulder. Jen persisted.

'We're going to be together, the three of us. You are the people I'm taking to India.'

She flashed them a smile that made her face with radiant.

'We're going to India?' Charlotte was sceptical now. 'That's what the spirit told you? But you're crazy about India already, Otto told me.'

Jen stood up. Clearly she didn't need to be believed. She made no effort to persuade them of her truth. Instead she said, 'Can we go now? I want to go back to the village. We need to start walking.'

They went to the Red Lion where Otto bought drinks and plates of steak pie with chips and salad. Too late Jen reminded him she was unable to eat very much because of her food allergies so she picked at a few chips and nibbled at the salad, leaving Otto to polish off a second helping of pie. They didn't talk much, preoccupied by the food and tired by the walk. Charlotte was hungry though. As she ate she wondered about Jen and what she had said. Charlotte was naturally a disbeliever of such things – a pragmatist who needed evidence and proof. Horoscopes, tarot cards, dowsing with crystals – all stuff she disregarded. And a trip to India?

But she was unsettled. There was something about Jen. Her near-fainting in the long barrow – she hadn't put that on, had she? Then again, perhaps she had been overtired. The mind could play tricks.

'You're coming to India with me,' Jen said. It wasn't a request but a statement of fact, and strangely emphatic for someone so shy.

'Sure, I'll come,' Otto said. 'What about you, Charlie? Are you up for it?' He said it lightly, as though she'd proposed nothing more exciting than a trip to Bristol. Charlotte's first emotion was resistance. She didn't like being conscripted and besides, so much to think about. Money, timing, travel, purpose. And India? She'd never considered it as a destination before. She had so much of her life mapped out – university, work overseas, a career.

'Go on,' Otto urged. 'It'd be exciting.' They were both looking at her, Otto and Jen. Otto was all bouncy and enthusiastic. Jen, whom she'd met only twice, seemed perfectly relaxed and confident of her reply.

Questions and worries turned over in Charlotte's head, difficulties to be resolved, problems, the possible relationship between Jen and Otto, all that would need to be organised to make such a venture a real possibility.

'I am going to take a gap year,' she said, unwilling to commit herself.

But Jen was still looking at her, very steadily, and she seemed to possess some quality of innocence and steadfastness, so that Charlotte felt her resistance unwind and melt away.

'Look, I can't agree to something so important just like that. Let me think about it, okay? I'd need to read up, make some investigations. I've got so many plans, I want to know how India might fit into that.'

Jen smiled. 'Of course. You think about it.'

Otto bought more drinks and they made a toast over their empty plates, while the wind blew the rooks over the roof of the pub and the standing stones. Jen talked about India, describing the pictures she had seen, conjuring up her own images of the place, of the deserts and peacocks and marble palaces. Otto speculated about adventures. Charlotte listened, intrigued. Certainly the place had possibilities.

They caught the bus back to town and spent the rest of the afternoon at Charlotte's house, hanging out in her bedroom. Jen complained of a headache and in the end didn't stay at Otto's house at all, but opted to sleep the night at Charlotte's.

The girls slept side by side on the big double bed. It was odd how easy it was to be with Jen now; there was no awkwardness, as though they'd been friends a long time.

'Tell me more about these spirits,' Charlotte said as they lay in the dark. 'When did it start? What is it like?' She didn't believe but she was curious. She wanted to know more.

'It's always been there,' Jen said. 'All my life.' Charlotte could hear her breathing. She waited for Jen to say more. Outside the house a car glided past and at the bottom of the garden a fox barked. The air in the room seemed electrically charged.

'But the first time I was truly aware of it was the day my mother had a kind of breakdown. I saw a white figure moving along the side of a field. I can remember exactly what it was like.'

'Your mum had a breakdown?'

'She spent six weeks in a psychiatric ward.'

Charlotte pondered. 'My god, what was that like?'

'Horrible. I wasn't very old. I thought she wasn't coming back.'

'But she did.'

'Yes.'

'And she's okay now?'

'Most of the time. Fragile sometimes.'

The subject beckoned, the billowing, intriguing, frightening mass of it. Charlotte wanted to know more but something restrained her from asking. They lay in the darkness a while, Charlotte seeming to hear every tiny noise, every movement in the fabric of the building. She hadn't had a conversation like this with a close girlfriend for a long time. There'd been one girl, but she'd moved to another school in year 9. Afterwards, she'd had plenty of mates at school but Otto had become her only intimate. And Otto – well, he was an entirely different case. Jen cleared her throat, hesitated, preparing herself to speak.

'If we go to India, we'll have adventures.' She propped herself up on her elbow, looked into Charlotte's face through the darkness.

'You have to come, Charlie. Please come to India.'

Charlotte smiled into the darkness. She didn't like to be nagged and persuaded, but Jen's enthusiasm was flattering.

'You have to let me think about it,' she said. 'I'd want to know a whole lot more before I made a commitment like that.'

Jen dropped back onto her pillow. And when Charlotte closed her eyes a mirage of India burned before her eyes, gold and jewelled and perfumed, a tawny city in the sand, caravans of camels, tents of azure silk and tumbled villages lying in a sea of dunes. Was this the seed Jen had dropped in her mind?

161

Otto

Friday

Otto woke scratching. Angry scarlet discs the size of five pence pieces peppered his arms, shoulders and lower legs. Spikes of sunlight pierced the hut along with the dim sound of electronic dance music.

The previous night they'd dumped him back in the hut and he'd fallen asleep almost instantly, as though his mind had overloaded and crashed with all he'd seen. But he woke up again and again throughout the night, perhaps every hour, resurfacing from sleep with a gasp as the memories of the previous evening exploded in his mind.

What had happened to the punished man? What exactly had he done to deserve it? Was he dead? And if he'd survived the terrible assault, who would help him, out here?

The questions trailed through his mind each time he woke, illustrated by graphic images of the man's broken head and the splashes of blood on the ground, and the peculiar, nightmarish passivity of the other people (himself included) standing around just watching what was happening.

And the music of course, the loud, relentless dance music playing through the horror show.

He examined his mosquito bites, worrying, despite everything, that he hadn't taken his malaria tablets. Then he dozed a little longer till Kate opened the door with a cup of sweet, spiced tea and a break-fast of cold, gluey rice cakes.

She wasn't so friendly this time, avoiding eye contact.

'What's happening?' Otto asked. 'Are you taking me home today?'

'I don't know.' She was curt, dropping the food into his hands. She placed the cup on the ground.

Having seen her hanging on Andreas, and knowing what Andreas was capable of, Otto knew he couldn't trust or rely on her, despite her friendliness the previous day. Had she simply been trying to win him over? Otto's curiosity battled with cowardice – if he asked too many questions, or said the wrong thing, who knows what punishment might be meted out to him?

Was that why he'd been allowed to witness the beating?

Andreas had realised he wasn't this hotshot journalist, but wanted to give him a warning in any case. *Don't fool with us. See what I am capable of.* How invulnerable Andreas must feel, to dole out such terrible violence without fear of reprisal.

'I need to get out of here. The mozzies are eating me alive.' He said this in a jocular tone, though he stretched out one bitten leg to illustrate. Kate barely glanced at him. Instead she went out the door and shut it behind her. Ten minutes later the dance music ceased. Another ten minutes passed; in the distance he heard a vehicle engine come to life, then another. Time to go home? He waited for the hut door to open and to be bundled into the back of the truck. Instead other vehicles started up, five or six perhaps. The ambient noise of the jungle was drowned in the revving of diesel engines. Everyone was leaving. Everyone? How many people had been out here in this jungle place? The vehicles started to move, one after another, driving away. The noise rose and slowly declined. The low daytime susurrus of the jungle reasserted itself.

Otto waited for a minute or two, straining his ears for sounds of people still on the jungle site. He couldn't hear anything and sensed, with a rising panic, that he was now entirely alone. He tried the hut door but it was barred from the outside. He called out. No-one responded.

Time stretched out. The heat intensified. The hut became an oven in which he baked, sweat erupting in a tide over his skin, dripping into his eyes and making them sting. Surely, surely they wouldn't just abandon him here. He shouted out again and prowled around the hut looking for weaknesses in the wall. He pushed at the thatched ceiling, then went back to the door, drew back his foot and kicked it as hard as he could.

The door flew open.

Fierce sunlight burst in, a fire of it, momentarily blinding. Otto raised his hand to shade his eyes against the light as he stepped outside. He thought the door had been improperly fastened – perhaps intentionally so that he might escape once his captors had departed. They wanted to get away but they didn't want to be responsible for him. They'd given themselves a head start.

His eyes adjusted to the brilliant sunlight.

Tall enclosing trees rose in a circle around him from which creepers with mauve flowers were growing. Long, lush grasses hemmed the dry earth clearing on which the huts stood. Further away, dimly seen, a narrow river poured over seal-grey boulders. A trail marked by tyres led away from the encampment – the path Otto needed to follow to find his way back. But how far was back?

He returned to the bar area. All the bottles and glasses had gone. The place was empty, abandoned-looking. In bright daylight the set-up looked so much more shabby and makeshift, as though within a day or two it would have melted back into the jungle. The store of bottles in the lean-to behind the hut had also disappeared.

Sweat prickled between his shoulders, a mingling of heat and fear. They had left him in the middle of nowhere. Perhaps he was in danger. Pampered English boy, he had no experience of truly wild places. Here might be elephants, leopards, tigers even. And snakes –

more likely to be snakes. *The Jungle Book* flashed into his mind, the Disney cartoon he had watched obsessively when he was four or five, Mowgli dancing in the temple ruins with the monkeys or cradled in the python's coils. He walked down to the river, pushing a cautious path through the long grass. It was a beautiful place, clear water alternately gushing over the boulders and pooling in tempting shallows. He squatted at the river's edge, cupped water in his hands and splashed it over his face, then his head and shoulders, washing away the sweat. He longed to undress and immerse himself. The cool water promised to sooth the endless throbbing of his mosquito bites. But he was cautious – snakes, bacterial infections, who knows what. His Westerner's confidence had melted away. He didn't know anything here – what to be afraid of and what to trust.

Otto returned to the huts. He looked inside the others. All were empty now – no clues about the occupants. How many people had stayed here? Where had they gone? Still he hesitated. Perhaps he should wait – they might come back.

On the dry soil at his feet a trail of huge black ants was marching. He jumped away, unnerved, aware for a dizzying, revelatory moment that he was utterly alone and his surroundings, the creatures living here, were entirely indifferent to his fate. For a moment he seemed to be floating above his own head, in the treetops, looking down at the lonely figure beneath.

He closed his eyes and shook his arms, attempting to draw himself together. He opened and closed his hands and squeezed them into fists. No good going to pieces – he had to stop this, had to think clearly. High up in one of the trees a creature moved and made a loud whooping sound. Otto looked up, shading his eyes. A monkey dropped noisily through the leaves from one branch to another. He could see only glimpses of its limber reddish-brown body, the curl of its tail – then the pieces of the creature came together as it crouched on a low, leafless limb in brazen view, staring at Otto, peeling back its lips to reveal a row of sharp, white teeth. The monkey was no larger than a well-grown tomcat but Otto was nervous. He read hostility in the creature's grimacing and wondered what he would do if the monkey attacked. He glanced around for a branch or a stone he could use to defend himself. He wanted to run away but felt an instinctive reluctance to turn his back on the monkey as perhaps this would prompt aggression. He stood for a minute or two, waiting and watching. The monkey snarled again, moved from side to side, its eyes fixed on Otto. Stand-off. What should he do? Slowly, slowly, he stepped backwards, tiny, shuffling steps, keeping his eyes fixed on the monkey all the time. A bead of sweat dropped, stinging, into his eye but Otto kept his hands by his sides and continued to edge away. No sudden movements, no hint of threat. The monkey shook its head. Then it was gone, sliding under the canopy of leaves. The tip of its tail whisked a farewell. Higher up, a branch twitched and leaves rustled.

Otto took a deep breath. His body, stiffly held these last minutes, began to relax. When he looked around, released from the immediate threat, the greater fear clamped down – knowing he was lost and alone. The jungle hugged itself around him.

'There's only one thing you can do,' he said to himself, aloud. 'You have to start walking.' The track waited but Otto hesitated still.

'Come on. What are you waiting for?' he chided. What indeed? Some part of him still hoped Kate, Andreas and the others would return; wanted to believe they were not the sort of people to abandon him in the jungle. It was curious, wasn't it? He'd seen what Andreas could do. He knew people did bad things – criminals, murderers, pimps, illegal arms dealers – but on some deeper, emotional and entirely irrational level, he couldn't quite believe they would do bad things to him. How so? There was evidence enough on the telly, in the newspapers, in Charlotte's Amnesty journals. People did terrible, unspeakable deeds. His own life had been so sheltered. It was time he grew up and readjusted. Time to believe the worst – how else would he survive? He'd held Maria's murdered body in his arms and seen with his own eyes the consequence of intentional violence.

'Go,' he told himself. 'Go now. They're not coming back. They left you. Even Kate. She's with Andreas. She left you too.'

It wasn't a pleasant journey. The jungle was beautiful enough but the heat and worry stole any potential enjoyment from the walk. The sun hammered his uncovered head and he could feel it burning his pale, unprotected skin, warning of blisters to come. He worried about snakes and wild animals. How far till he hit a road, or a village? No way of knowing. All he could do was keep moving and hope for the best.

He tried to distract himself, playing with pieces of the puzzle in his mind. Maria and Gina, Andreas and Kate. Andreas and his friends had mistaken Otto for a journalist (a real journalist). They were afraid he knew something and was about to expose them in some way. They had his camera. So what was this all about? What were they doing here in the jungle? Some kind of drugs racket, presumably. Something important enough to warrant kidnap – and killing. His thoughts flew to Jen and Charlotte. Had they received Kate's text? They would be worrying about him but just now there was nothing he could do to prevent that. Just keep walking.

The track was easy to follow; that was a blessing at least. It wound between the trees, through light and shade, dodging occasional rocky outcrops, boulders, boggy places. From time to time he saw monkeys moving over branches. The fabric of insect noise was torn at random intervals by a hoot or screech. And once, he saw a snake coiled like a lariat on a rock in the sunlight.

How long had he been walking? Otto couldn't tell. The curious altered state of mind triggered when he saw the army of ants persisted as he trekked through the jungle. Perhaps it was a reaction to the danger of his situation – this sense of separation from himself as though he were half a step outside his own body and partly watching the story unfold: an observer, not the protagonist.

A large, ebony spider crouched on a shiny leaf. An amber butterfly hovered by the path following a peculiar staccato path through the air. Otto's vision blurred and he wiped his eyes again with the heels of his hands. The jungle darkened as the canopy closed overhead, cutting out the sunlight. Something pushed through the undergrowth creating a sudden shush of leaves. Otto peered through the thick shade. Was it a deer of some kind? The animal, whatever it was, leaped back undercover. Otto walked on.

His sense of dissociation grew stronger. The outside world receded, his own back-story of England and home faded away. Nothing seemed to exist except the damp, dense forest. Colour heightened, the palette of greens burning into his eyes, the splashes of flowers – crimson, sulphur yellow, flesh pink – flaming like jewels. Worry disappeared. Nothing mattered except the here and now, the restless chattering voice in his mind fell silent. Creature-like, simply an observing presence, a mind absorbing the welter of sensations, he moved along the path.

What was that? Otto stopped short. A darker mass rose ahead, straight edges among the mass of natural curves. The track, he could see, veered around it. A building of some kind, derelict in the jungle? Perhaps it was inhabited. Otto proceeded with caution, unsure of what he was seeing; hardly daring to hope it might be the means of deliverance. The puzzle resolved itself as he drew nearer – a temple, half tumbled, overrun with creepers. These stems lashing the broken columns were a dry red and from the ropy bark, leaves of the brightest green erupted. Otto stepped closer. Something soft exploded beneath his foot – a fruit, with thin, leather-coloured skin. These fruits were scattered over the ground, fallen from the tree that arched over the temple. Otto hesitated, torn beneath an overwhelming curiosity and a prudent fear. The building had been long abandoned, judging by the extent to which it had been swallowed by the jungle, but the dark doorway beckoned.

He stood on the threshold, staring in and waiting for his eyes to adjust. Dried leaves covered the stone floor and the air was surprisingly, deliciously cool. Otto stepped inside. At the back of the narrow room a second, larger doorway opened. A draught carried an unknown, acrid smell, something distinctly animal but not like anything he'd encountered before. He crept closer, staring into the abyss. There was no sound, no hint of movement. A warning voice in his mind told Otto to leave the place and that he had nothing to gain, but something impelled him. He crossed the threshold into the greater darkness.

Jen

Friday

The man at the cafe was reluctant to keep his promise. He'd said he would take them to Otto's lodgings in the village but when the girls returned he was evasive and made excuses. He mentioned something about the police and his business, told them he didn't want to get involved. Charlotte nagged and badgered till he gave them the address of the place. That was something. Jen, who wasn't good at persuading and cajoling, stood at Charlotte's side and left it to her.

'Well it's a start,' Charlotte said. The village lay under a loose canopy of palm trees. A scooter put-putted past them. A beige cow grazed at the side of the lane. Charlotte had her notebook in her hand where the address was written – though it was less of an address than a description. They passed a cafe-bar, and a random assortment of brick- and wood-built dwellings. Here and there rubbish in piles. A black pig, barrel-bodied, rooted through the waste. An old man walked towards them, half naked. Jen had presumed he was Indian because he was so darkly tanned. As he drew near she saw he was a Westerner with long silver white dreadlocks. Although he passed on the other side of the road he seemed to brush against her. Perhaps he sensed it too because he looked up abruptly and glanced into her face with bright blue eyes. Who was he? She felt it, a connection between them. Was he one of those rare others, sensitive, as she was, to spirits and presences others didn't see?

171

Then he was gone. Jen sighed, trying to refocus on their dilemma. She wasn't sure how she felt about Charlotte's investigative zeal. She knew Otto hadn't killed anyone. She was worried about him – the night on the beach it had been the echoes of the girl's murder she had picked up on – but were these activities going to help find him? Still, she knew Charlotte wouldn't be happy unless she was doing something positive.

'I think this is the place.' Charlotte gestured to a white, single-storey house with a thatched roof to the left of the road. Jen shaded her eyes to see but Charlotte marched to the door and gave it an assertive knock. A boy with bare, bony knees and a pair of dirty shorts stopped in the lane and watched them.

A slim, beautiful woman appeared from the back of the house, a little girl in a white dress beside her. She smiled at Charlotte.

'Are you looking for somewhere to stay?' she said. The little girl gripped her mother's hand and pressed her face against her thigh. Charlotte hesitated.

'We're Otto's friends from England,' she said. 'We were supposed to meet him.'

Jen ambled over and stood at Charlotte's side. The woman's face expressed nothing but the most honest concern.

'He isn't here any more. He left yesterday very early. Took all of his things.'

For a few moments they stood without speaking, the three young women and the little girl. Jen glanced at Charlotte and noticed the quiver in her lower lip. The Indian woman gave a brief, worried smile. She glanced beyond her visitors to the lane.

'Why don't you come in?' she said. 'Please, follow me.'

She led them to the back of the house and into a simple, white-washed room. A small television stood on a shelf in one corner, a table in the centre. A picture of Jesus and his Sacred Heart hung on the wall.

The woman invited them to sit. The little daughter clung to the table, twisting on her feet and staring at the visitors.

172

'He stayed in the other room,' she said. 'We often rent it out to tourists. He seemed such a polite, good-mannered young man. Now we hear he may have killed a girl.'

'He didn't kill anyone,' Charlotte jumped in. 'It isn't possible. Now he's disappeared and I'm worried something bad's happened to him.'

Jen, detached from the conversation, glanced around at the room. A narrow dish on a shelf beneath the picture of Jesus contained an ashy cone of incense from which the thinnest thread of perfume still rose. The wooden floor was neatly swept. Crockery and cooking pans were piled on top of an old but immaculate refrigerator: everything in its place. The woman, Otto's landlady, possessed a calm, modest grace with her wide, brown eyes and thick, glossy hair.

'So what do you want from me?' she said.

Charlotte's lip quivered again. Visibly she pulled herself together and drew out her notepad and pen.

'We have to find out what happened to him,' she said. 'I would be very grateful if you would tell me about his visit – everything you can remember.'

The woman looked at them, from Charlotte to Jen and back to Charlotte again. She gave a brief, grave smile.

'Of course,' she said. 'Otto was our guest. He seemed to me to be a good person. I'll help in any way I can.'

An hour later, walking back through the village, Charlotte seemed absorbed in her thoughts. The flavour of sugary, spiced tea still lingered in Jen's mouth. She had taken a risk, drinking it. The milk alone might be her undoing – stomach cramps, a rash perhaps. But she hadn't been able to resist it, unwilling to refuse their host or to explain, wanting the comfort of the drink itself. It was difficult always having to say no. And so far she had been fine, in India. Not one day of sickness, no allergic reactions. Why was that? Was it something about the place, or how she felt being here? She wanted to

173

test the situation, try new food, take a few risks if her health really was becoming more robust.

They'd seen the room where Otto had stayed – bare except for the bed. Apparently he'd taken all his possessions. It was hard to imagine Otto had ever stayed there – no sign of him, no sense of his presence at all. Charlotte had asked innumerable questions, taken notes. But what had they learned?

Charlotte had the notebook in her hand and studied it as she walked, furrowing her brow and intermittently chewing the end of her pen.

'So, three days ago, a girl came round to the house with a note for Otto,' she said.

'Maria?' Jen said.

'I guess so. Who else?'

The question hung upon the air, purely rhetorical. Charlotte had no more idea than she did. A herd of kids walked past, hands outstretched, crying out cheerfully for rupees and pens. Charlotte shook her head. The girls stopped outside the internet cafe; Otto's landlady had told them he had visited it. A young Indian man hurried out and urged them to step inside – did they want a drink? An hour on the internet? He'd do a special deal. Clearly business wasn't very good, tucked away here. There were no other customers.

Jen looked to Charlotte, wondering what they should say. She saw Charlotte fumbling for her phone at the bottom of her bag, turning it on – then a quick in-breath as her mobile phone beeped. They glanced at one another – could it be? Charlotte dropped the phone on the dusty ground in her rush to pick up the message.

'Ah, there, got it.' The screen flared. Jen's eyes opened wide. Is it him, is he okay, what does he say? The questions tumbled in her mind but she didn't say anything, caught in the moment of suspense. Charlotte stared at the screen, apparently reading the message over and over. Then she raised her head.

'It's him,' she said. 'I think.'

'What does he say?'

Charlotte didn't answer – instead she passed Jen the phone.

The text declared: All is well. Don't worry about me. Otto. He hadn't used his own phone – the caller number came up as unknown. Jen's first thought – he didn't write this. *All is well?* Charlotte grabbed the phone and tried to call back on the same number. She held the phone to her ear, biting her lip. She and Charlotte looked at one another. The cafe man stared too, from one to the other. Then Charlotte frowned and shook her head.

'No reply,' she said. 'The phone's turned off.'

She dropped her own into her pocket.

'We're looking for a friend,' Charlotte said to the man. 'He was staying in the village, and apparently he visited your cafe several times. In fact, he emailed me from here.'

The cafe man didn't answer right away. He looked at Charlotte and Jen.

'Who? Which friend?'

'His name's Otto. Otto Gilmour. Tall, blond.' Charlotte gestured with her hand, indicating height. The cafe man nodded.

'He found the dead girl,' he said heavily. 'It's not good for us, for Goa. Sometimes bad people come here, looking for a holiday. They want drink and drugs, and something like this happens and it is hard on all of us.'

'Otto didn't do anything wrong!' Charlotte jumped in.

The cafe man looked at her again, a long, cool assessment. 'I didn't say he did.' He shrugged. 'Yes he came here. Used the inter-net, had a drink.' He gestured to the computers visible beyond the doorway, sitting idle.

'We should go online, Charlie. Just in case he's emailed us,' Jen said, touching Charlotte's arm.

Nothing from Otto. Jen had an email from her mother hoping she'd arrived safely. Jen tapped out a brief, cheerful reply. She didn't want her getting worried. Beside her, Charlotte continued to question the cafe man – had he seen Otto with anyone? Did he know Maria? No useful information was elicited. Jen typed Maria's name and the word 'Goa' into Google. The top link took her to a small article in the *Daily Telegraph* from the previous day, reporting Maria had died in Goa and that the Goan police were conducting a murder inquiry. The article was surprisingly small and unremarkable, with a small, rather indistinct headshot of a pretty girl, her hair blowing in a breeze. Was this all the attention she merited? The piece closed with an indifferent comment from the British Embassy about the investigation taking its course and another from an Indian tourism organisation expressing regret and explaining how safe a destination India was for foreign holidaymakers.

'Look,' she said, pointing out the article to Charlotte. 'There – that's Maria.' They stared at the screen. Jen sensed the emotion that passed through her friend, at this glimpse of the young woman Otto had courted and then discovered dead on the beach. What had it been like for him?

She stared at Maria, wanting to know who she was, what she was like, but it was hard to pick up much from a grainy picture on the internet. She wriggled on her seat and glanced over her shoulder. Two young men, standing in the road outside the cafe, were looking in at her; a white man and another who looked like an Indian, with long hair in a ponytail. Even over this distance her eyes locked with the second man's, and she felt again that moment of emotional recognition she'd shared with the old hippy. Was he like her too?

'Jen, what is it?' Charlotte looked over Jen's shoulder.

Jen shook her head. 'I don't know. A couple of guys out there – staring at us.'

Charlotte looked, but they'd gone, whoever they were.

Darkness came early, falling over the sea, extinguishing the brief, golden sunset. Jen and Charlotte were sitting at a bar on the beach. A young man handed them a photocopied flyer advertising a party at the far end of the beach, beyond the usual tourist places. A hand-drawn map indicated how to find it. The word Kharisma sprawled across the top of the paper.

'Come along,' he said, smiling and flirtatious. 'It's the best place. All the coolest people go. You'll have a great time.'

Charlotte considered the paper. When the young man had moved on she said, 'Shall we give it a try? Maybe Otto went there. If someone had told him it was where the coolest people went, he'd have been there like a shot.'

Jen shrugged. 'Yes. Why not?' She stared out at the sea, where, unseen by Charlotte, a white figure danced above the surface of the water, some elemental spirit of the sea perhaps, a guide seeming to signal to her, offering a direction. The figure melted on the air.

'Well then?' Charlotte's voice intruded.

'Well what?'

Charlotte sighed with exasperation. She was standing up. 'Shall we go now?'

The place was a reasonable walk away. Several palm-thatched bars stood about a wooden dance floor but it was early yet. They were the first customers. The man behind the bar told them the party wouldn't get going till after ten. Charlotte said they should ask around, try and find out more from the partying people.

They discussed the text. It hadn't reassured either of them. It didn't sound like Otto and it wasn't from his phone. On the other hand, how had the sender obtained Charlotte's number? Should they send a reply? If Otto truly had sent it, then of course they had to respond – let him know they were trying to help. If it hadn't been Otto's message? There was nothing to lose. Charlotte called the number again but the phone was still turned off. She sent a text.

Otto – glad u r ok. Pls contact us asap. Tell us where u r. C +J xx

Jen sipped her bottled water. She hadn't eaten much but hunger didn't seem to be a problem. So far her stomach hadn't reacted badly to the milk from the tea but she didn't feel her normal self. Tiredness perhaps, jet lag and the shock of the new country and climate, and underlying it all, the gnawing anxiety about Otto. It was hard to think straight. Her thoughts were interrupted by flashes of fear.

Might Otto, too, be dead? No, no he couldn't be. She took out her art book and ink pen, turned to a new page and began to draw, trying to capture the face she had seen on the web. Maria. The murdered girl. In the effort of drawing, other images rose into her mind bringing with them a feeling of dread – the photograph the policeman had shown her, the post-mortem picture of Maria's back and the tattoo, the circle of flames.

Charlotte's mobile lay on the table, unhelpful and inert. No reply came.

Charlotte was scribbling in her journal. She looked very tired, with shadows under her eyes and a certain heaviness about her face. For a disconcerting moment Jen could see how Charlotte would look in twenty years, as though she were looking through a window in time. Then it was gone – this odd glimpse. Jen shook her head. She needed to sleep. The place was playing tricks on her. She'd travelled halfway round the world to this alien place with its unimaginable smells and colours and places.

The ocean receded into the night. The waves repeated their fall and retreat, over and over. As the darkness intensified the harsh electric light from the bars grew more distinct. Strings of coloured lights under the eaves shone like jewels. She could hear the chat of the men behind the bars, the occasional laughter, but couldn't make out what they said or even if they were speaking in English.

'Jen. Jen?' Charlotte's voice sounded far away though she was sitting next to her. Jen glanced at her watch. She had lost herself in a train of thought, half asleep probably, and an hour had passed. She shut and opened her eyes with great deliberation, trying to kick-start a more wakeful self.

'What is it?'

'I thought you were asleep.'

'I think I was for a while.' Jen looked again at her art book. The sketch was only an approximate copy of the photograph, what she could remember embellished by her imagination and what Charlotte so kindly called her intuition. Maria, whom Otto had hooked up with. She did feel a twinge to think of it. Otto had told her he loved her once. In the end, he'd claimed he loved her too much to want to risk hurting her, though of course he had done exactly that. He was hopeless, always falling in love with people. He had *un coeur d'artichaut*, as the French said – the heart of an artichoke, and a leaf for everyone. That meant fickle and inconstant. She felt the twinge again, but put this troubling emotion to one side. She needed to focus on Maria.

She wanted to know her, to understand her. A young woman without parents, living like a gypsy, utterly rootless and without a place to belong. Complete freedom. Was the idea appealing or appalling? Horrible to think you had no-one to turn to, no-one who loved you, who would be *there* no matter what.

Other people were rolling up, mostly European and American tourists. Many of them were young, turning out for the party. The bars got busy. The music started, loud dance music that seemed to seal like a lid over the end of the beach, keeping them in, keeping others out. Charlotte sat forward on her seat and peered through the crowd. Who was she looking for? Otto perhaps, hoping against hope he would just turn up. How much longer could they hold out before telling Otto's mother?

'I'm going to start talking to people,' Charlotte shouted in Jen's ear. 'Why don't you do the same? Ask them if they know anything about Otto.'

But what would she say? What would they be able to tell her? Charlotte stood up, stuffed the mobile in her pocket and launched off into the crowd. Jen stayed where she was, feeling helpless. She should help, shouldn't she? No use to anyone, sitting here, vulnerable and alone. Someone barged into her, a young man, calling out to his friends. His voice was loud and hard and he seemed not to notice her at all despite nearly dropping onto her lap. People were dancing. A circle of earnest dope smokers sat on the sand to her right. Where was Charlotte? Jen had lost sight of her. Although she hadn't touched a drop of alcohol the atmosphere of inebriation seemed to soak in, making her feel a little drunk herself.

'Hey, how are you?' A man in his late twenties and wearing a Kings of Leon T-shirt plopped into the chair Charlotte had vacated. Jen stared at him. The man said something but the music was too loud for Jen to make out his words. She shook her head and he gestured at the bar, holding out a bottle with a simple white label. It looked like water. Did she want a drink? Jen shook her head again in a panic, stood up and marched away as fast as she could. She had to get out of the place, had to escape the violent noise and the crowd. She bumped into someone, pushed her way through, hardly seeing where she was going. The sand slipped under her feet.

At last! She was out of it. The space of the uninhabited beach opened in front of her, pure and moonlit. The overwhelming music died away with every step, becoming only a background pulse. The sea lay below her, black and smooth, glittering with broken moonlight.

Jen dropped to the sand, her back to the party, gazing instead at the sea. She had her art book in her hand. She flicked through it, the drawings and scribbles arcane in the moonlight as though drawn by somebody else. She studied the fanciful sketch of Maria and then the wheel of flames, the design Maria had tattooed on her back.

Coincidence? Of course not. It was a signal.

An idea flickered across her mind and the mist that had clouded her thoughts all evening cleared. Of course – why hadn't she thought of it?

She headed back to the circle of noise, the intangible party dome. This time, keeping her wits about her, she picked out a young girl with a tattoo at the back of her neck.

'Excuse me – did you get that done here? Your lovely tattoo?' Jen raised her voice to speak above the music. The girl shook her head. Jen moved on. The fourth person she asked nodded yes – a boy of about seventeen with a shaved head. He smiled at her, stretched out his hand to touch her hair. He had a tattoo of a new moon on his arm, so fresh it was still red and sore and partly scabbed.

'Yes! Yes I did. You like it? You want one too?' He put a hand on her shoulder, his face naive and wide open. High on something or other. Jen stood her ground.

'Where did you get it done?' She cupped her hand around his ear to speak. The boy was still dancing, unable to keep still, euphoric, soaked in music.

'Over there – at the top of the beach. There's a booth on the side of the road. See?' He gestured wildly. Jen couldn't see exactly where he was pointing but she thanked him and set off in the direction he had suggested.

She found a line of three tiny shops, booths not much more than a metre wide facing onto the beach. One, a second-hand bookshop, was closed and locked up. The second, selling mobile phones, cigarettes and lighters, sunglasses and other beach paraphernalia, was open for business. The proprietor was squatting by the side of his pavement display, smoking a cigarette. The wooden door to the third – the tattooist – was closed but evidently someone was inside; the light was on and she could hear gaudy Indian pop music. Jen hesitated, shifting her weight from one foot to another. The smoker took a deep drag and glanced at Jen, making some quick appraisal.

'You want a tattoo?'

Jen shook her head nervously. 'No. I just want to talk to the tattoo man.'

The man took another slow puff on his cigarette, still staring at Jen. She wondered what he thought of them, the revellers on the beach.

'You want to buy something?' He narrowed his eyes, pointing at the wares on offer in his booth.

'No thanks.' She shook her head, reluctant to refuse.

'What do you want to talk to him about?' The end of the cigarette flared like a hot coal in the darkness. The man threw it away, spat noisily, rubbed his mouth and moustache and stood up. Jen didn't answer but the man continued anyway, 'The police came yesterday. They wanted to talk to him.'

'Yes? What about?'

The man shrugged. 'I wasn't here. My brother told me. Something about the English girl, the one who died. Did you hear about that?'

Jen nodded. 'Yes.' She didn't want to speak, afraid she might give somehow give herself away. She wanted him to leave her alone but he didn't move and continued to stare. Jen moved towards the tattoo hut and knocked on the door. Then she stepped back. The door swung open almost immediately and a young man stood on the threshold, the music blasting out behind him.

Jen felt a jolt. She'd seen him before. He was perhaps twenty, though it was hard to be sure. He had long, glossy black hair in a ponytail and an elegant, clean-shaven face. He carried with him a swirling cloud of anger. Was he annoyed she had disturbed him so late? Was he in the middle of a job, expecting someone else?

'Hello?' He couldn't see her. 'You want a tattoo?' His voice was brusque.

Jen stepped into the aura of light spilling from the open door. His eyes fixed on her.

'No, I – I mean, I wondered if I could speak to you.' Her voice faltered. She was aware of the other man observing the exchange.

The tattoo man's expression changed. He recognised her. Abruptly, he said, 'It's you. Of course it's you. Come in.'

Jen remembered where she'd seen him before. It had been earlier in the day at the cafe in the village; he'd been one of the two men looking at her when she was using the internet with Charlotte. Who was he? Why the interest?

The tiny booth was immaculate. The silver tattooing equipment lay on shelves in silver trays. Illustrations and photographs covered the walls, an array of possible tattoos ranging from traditional hearts and swallows to sprays of stars, complex tribal markings and portraits of cult film heroes. In the far corner, on another shelf, a small soapstone figurine of Ganesh, the god with the elephant head, presided over a dish of flowers and a stick of slowly burning incense.

The tattoo man turned the music down, indicated Jen should take a seat and took the other place himself.

'What would you like?' He gestured at the illustrations on the wall.

'I don't want a tattoo,' she said. 'How do you know me? Were you following us?'

He looked at her properly for the first time, studying her face with frank, open interest. Then he smiled. Jen smiled back.

'You came to find me,' he said. 'That makes sense.'

'It does? Why?'

'We've been watching out for you, since you arrived.'

He was wearing jeans and a black vest top revealing toned, sculpted arms, one of which – the left – wore a complex swirl of tattooed lines and circles, looping and intertwining in an inky sleeve. He had a thick, piratical silver hoop in his ear and three silver bangles on the untattooed arm. The ponytailed hair, black as the night sea, fell right down his back.

'I'm Kumar,' he said, offering his hand. 'How can I help you?'

'Jen.'

His hand was dry and cool. 'Your English – your accent . . .' she began.

'I lived in England for five years,' he said. 'In Birmingham. That's where I trained. But I didn't like it. Terrible weather.' This with a casual shrug. 'So, if you don't want a tattoo, what do you want?'

'What do you want? Why were you watching me?'

Kumar smiled again, and a sense of wonderful potential seemed to cloud the atmosphere, as though all sorts of unspoken but understood connections existed between them.

Jen had been unsure how to broach the subject but Kumar now seemed so friendly, so familiar, she drew out her art book and turned to the page where she'd drawn the circle of flames. She handed it over without a word. Kumar touched the page with long, elegant fingers. Then he looked up.

'When did you draw this?' he said.

'For the first time? Some months ago. Back in England.'

Kumar nodded, as though this confirmed something he already knew. 'And now you come to me,' he said.

'Have you seen it before? Have you done this design?' she said gently. 'Is that why the police came?'

'How do you know about the police?'

'Your neighbour – he told me.'

Kumar traced the design with his forefinger. 'What does it mean to you?' he said.

Jen took a deep breath. 'The guy who found Maria's body? He's my friend. Now he's disappeared and the police seem to think he had something to do with her death.'

Kumar looked back at the page. 'Your boyfriend?'

'Friend,' she repeated. 'He's in trouble. I want to help him.'

Kumar thought for a moment. Then he said, 'Yes, I knew Maria. And yes, I did the tattoo for her. She brought the design on a piece of paper, just like you.'

'So why would the police be interested in a tattoo?'

Kumar looked directly into her face. 'Obviously they think it means something.'

'Does it? Does it mean anything?'

Kumar considered. Then he said, 'I've done this tattoo at least a dozen times over the last six months. So yes, I should say it does mean something. What it means though, that I don't know. They come in with the design and ask me to print it. Usually on their backs, but sometimes on an arm or thigh. I've asked them what it means and they tell me it is just a decoration.'

'Did you tell this to the police?'

Kumar shook his head. 'I told them I did Maria's tattoo – not about the others.'

'Why not?'

Kumar clasped his hands together. 'Because Maria's dead. Maria was *killed*. I don't want that to happen to me.'

'But don't you have any idea what this is about?' she appealed. Surely he knew more. He had to know what connected them, some thought or theory? He was the closest she'd got to the reason Maria had been murdered.

'Who were the other people? Can you describe them?'

Kumar shrugged. 'Europeans, Americans. I didn't know any names except for Maria. Everyone knew her. She'd been living here a while.'

'Why are you telling me this stuff, if you wouldn't share it with the police? Mightn't I be one of them, the tattooed people?'

Kumar grinned. 'And if you were, what have you learned? That I didn't give anything away to the police?'

'True.' They smiled at each other. Jen stood up. Kumar stood up too.

'Can I have your mobile number?' he said. 'Just in case I hear any more. I can ring you.'

Jen suppressed a smile. Perhaps to some it wouldn't seem wise to give out her number to this stranger, but she sensed the depth of the connection with Kumar. She knew he was a good man, and that knowing him was important. She wanted him to call her.

Otto

Friday

The darkness seemed to move. Otto sensed the ripple over his head as though the roof itself were shifting, hundreds of puzzle pieces sliding from place to place. He was afraid. Something flew past him, almost touching his shoulder, and it dawned on him he had disturbed a colony of bats. He stood for a time, unnerved but curious, as the creatures shuffled on the temple ceiling. They were murmuring to one another – didn't bats squeak? Perhaps the murmur he heard was simply the wind blowing through the broken building.

Slowly he began to make out the architecture of the room. It wasn't entirely dark, as it had seemed at first. A little light stole through a crack in the wall to his right. At the back of the temple another dusting of light fell through a kind of chimney in the roof, another exit for the bats perhaps. He took a step forwards, wary of disturbing the bats and conscious the soft layer on the stone floor was a carpet of droppings. He could just discern carvings on the stone walls. The chimney was in fact a hole in the roof under which a pile of stone fragments lay. Roots dangled through the hole, making a veil against the light. Against the back wall stood a stone statue of Shiva, touched by the faint fall of light, balanced on one foot, his face serene despite the fact that two of his four arms were broken and his nose was smashed from his face.

Otto stood in front of the statue, remembering the metal figurine

187

Jen had in her room at home, her little pocket of a fantasy India. Yet here he was, in a ruined temple in the jungle, lost and alone, caught up like a pawn in an unknown game. The faintest movement of air carried with it from the world outside the sickly-sweet scent of flowers. The statue's still face glimmered in the faint light. A shiver passed through Otto's body. He was tired and hungry and afraid – and at the same time, he was aware, as never before, of the warmth and perfume of the air, the smell of old stone, bat droppings, the rot and growth of the jungle outside. And over it all, in this stone womb where the ceaseless jungle made its slow inroads, where the tribe of bats lived and bred and died, Shiva stood poised in his perpetual dance of making and unmaking. Otto closed his eyes, overcome, feeling his entire life had led him to this moment when the voice in his head was silent and there was only this, the huge here and now, too strange, overwhelming and miraculous to comprehend.

His body swayed and he held out his hand to the wall to steady himself. His stomach rumbled, signalling hunger. Otto opened his eyes again. The moment had passed. He couldn't just stay here – he had to walk on. Revelatory visions were all well and good but they wouldn't help him out of this situation. He turned away and in doing so noticed something strange about the wall behind the broken statue – an unevenness or mark. It was hard to make out in the temple's patchy twilight so he looked again, straining his eyes to see.

A circle on the wall, as large as the statue, drawn perhaps with spray paint. The flames on this drawn circle mirrored the carved flames dancing from the stone halo surrounding Shiva himself. And the circle burned. Maria had the same design tattooed on her back. Maria was part of all this. She and Andreas – had they been lovers too? Had she been deeply involved? Perhaps he had offered her a family of sorts. A place to belong.

Presumably one of the jungle party crowd had drawn this graffiti. Out of creative high spirits – or to warn people away? He touched the marks with his fingertips. Something caught his eye, wedged between the statue's plinth and the wall. He stared, trying to make out what it was, this low, dark shape. A backpack, wasn't it? Otto leaned forward, stretched out his hand and gingerly patted the top. A backpack, yes. He grasped a shoulder strap and pulled it up. Then he made his way out of the old temple into the heat and blinding sunlight. The heavy backpack swung against his chest as he manoeuvred through the doorway, squelching fallen fruit underfoot. He dumped it on the ground. Travel-worn though it was, Otto didn't think the black and orange backpack had been long in the temple. No dust or bat droppings. He opened the top, the plastic clips and the drawstring, and took out the contents. A man's clothes – T-shirts, shorts, a fleece, the usual traveller's accoutrements. He turned his attention to the side pockets – a notebook, United States passport and papers, a handful of coins. Otto frowned, flipping open the passport to the name and photograph. A serious young face stared out at him, belonging to one Carlo Allen. Otto narrowed his eyes and wiped his free hand over his mouth. Carlo Allen. He'd seen him before, just the night before, kicked and beaten by Andreas and his men, hurt so badly Otto found it hard to believe he could have survived. Why was his backpack here? Had Andreas hidden it? Or had Carlo left his belongings somewhere safe so he could spy on the camp unencumbered? What exactly had he done to merit such a punishment?

Otto considered the man in the photograph, whose face was no longer so handsome, absorbing the information. Then he put the passport back into the backpack and looked in the notebook. Not much to see – Otto recognised a rough map of Andreas's encampment, drawn in biro. The word Kharisma had been scribbled on another page, along with various numbers and calculations, nothing Otto could make sense of. He replaced the notebook. This Carlo had been investigating Andreas – and spying on him. Andreas had accused him of stealing, he remembered. What kind of conspiracy was this?

He replaced the belongings in the backpack and toyed with the idea of taking it with him, as evidence. But he had no idea how far he had to walk and the prospect of carrying this heavy load wasn't a pleasant one. Where was he now, Carlo? Had Andreas taken him in one of the jeeps, back to civilisation? Or dumped him in the jungle? Otto shivered. He slipped the passport into his pocket but returned the backpack to the old temple. He couldn't waste any more time.

Otto went back to the path. He was tired and wanted something to drink. A faint pain nagged in his left temple, threatening to grow worse. How long did he have to walk? What happened if night fell and he had to sleep out here? At least he had the track to follow. Without that he would have been utterly, hopelessly lost.

One step after another. He walked on autopilot and let his mind go blank. After another hour he came to a stream running over a basin of auburn rock. Dry with thirst, he put worries about bacteria to one side and drank. He took off his sandals and washed his stinging feet, bathed his hands and face. The sun was descending, closing on the treetops. As the day diminished, the inhabitants of the jungle grew noisy. The trees were alive with monkeys. Insects crept out from beneath leaves, under stones, from the crevices in dead trees and red bark.

The trees covered the plunging sun, throwing the jungle into shadow. Otto stepped up his pace despite the burn of blisters on the soles of his feet. He had to find a way out. Mosquitoes buzzed about his head. A monkey howled as it leaped from one branch to another, seeming to follow him along the path. Otto struggled to subdue his fear. He kept walking.

The perfume on the air thickened as the night released the odours lurking in the soil, the breath of the trees. It grew harder to see where he was placing each foot and he worried again about treading on a snake. At last, ahead, like a mirage, the path opened up. Approaching this lighter space Otto didn't allow himself to hope too much. It might simply be another clearing. He drew closer and the under-growth began to thin.

190

And it stopped – the jungle, just like that. He emerged from its seemingly endless depths onto a rice field. The tree line stretched to left and right. Ahead was a level field, and at its far end, a modest house with a thatched roof. Electric light beamed from a window and a dog barked. Then, to his astonishment (as it seemed the modern world had disappeared during his sojourn in the jungle) he saw car headlights in the distance. A solitary vehicle drove past the little house and disappeared again. He was close to a road.

Relief boosted his energy. Otto picked his way around the edge of the field, careful not to step on the carefully tended rice plants. Jubilant at his deliverance, he hurried to the little house, ignored the barking dog, and knocked on the door.

Someone shouted from within. A television was on. A single power line looped from the house to the wires running on poles along the road. A boy of about twelve opened the door. He stared at Otto.

'Hello,' Otto said. 'Do you speak English?'

The boy nodded.

'I have to get back to the coast,' Otto said. 'Would you be able to help me? Do you have a phone I could borrow?'

The boy looked at him with wide eyes but didn't speak. Otto repeated his request. A male voice called out from inside the house and the boy replied in a language Otto couldn't understand. Then the boy said, 'Come inside, please.'

The house had two small rooms, in the first of which a middle-aged man with a large, brown belly was lying on a low bed watching a quiz show on a small colour television. Through the door into the second room, Otto glimpsed a young woman, but she moved from his line of sight and pushed the door closed. The man on the bed stood up very slowly, watching Otto all the time. Otto was uncomfortably aware the householders were suspicious of him. He had been treated with almost universal warmth and welcome during his Indian odyssey – until now. Still, it was a little odd for him to be turning up out of the blue, after dark, on a stranger's doorstep. He brushed back his hair, trying to make himself more respectable.

The man and the boy, presumably his son, stared at Otto. Then the man spoke and the boy translated.

'He says, where have you come from?'

'The jungle. I was lost in the jungle. I've been walking for hours.'

The boy relayed this information to the man. This seemed to confirm something for both. Their air of wariness increased.

'What do you want?' the boy said.

'I need to get to the coast, to the tourist resort. Can I call a taxi? If you have a phone I could call my friends.'

The man made an angry gesture and raised his voice.

Otto tried to restrain the quiver in his voice when he said, 'Is there a problem? Is something wrong?'

The boy didn't answer right away. Then he said, 'Why did your friends leave you behind?'

'They're not my friends!' Otto said. 'I was taken by people I don't know, they drove me here tied up in a truck and then they abandoned me in the jungle, miles from anywhere! I could have died!'

In saying the words out loud, admitting his plight to himself as well as the man and his son, Otto's self-control crumbled. Tears filled his eyes. He heard himself sob, like a baby, but he swallowed the sound and pressed his hands against his eyes to hold back this show of weakness, the childish weeping.

The man widened his eyes as the boy swiftly translated what Otto had said. The man didn't say anything but the two of them stared at him and the man's face softened. He stepped forward and patted Otto's arm. When he spoke again his voice was angry but Otto sensed the anger wasn't directed at him.

'What did he say? Your father?'

The boy shook his head. 'He says they are bad people. They come here, make trouble and disturb us. They hurt people. How do you know them? How did this happen? Did they hurt you?'

Otto shook his head. 'Except, well, leaving me in the jungle.' He looked at his feet which were covered in blood where his sandals had worn blisters and then through the skin itself. And the peppering of mosquito bites, old and new, on skin burned lobster-red by the sun. Hadn't hurt him? He'd certainly sustained physical damage. His headache cranked up a notch too.

The man peered into Otto's face and made another comment. Otto held out his hands and realised his entire body was trembling. Shock? Sunstroke? Perhaps only exhaustion and hunger. Perhaps it was relief, finally letting go, but Otto's vision swam and he thought he would faint. The man took him firmly by the arm and helped him over to the bed.

'Sit down, sit down please,' the boy said. The man called out a name and the woman from the back room opened the door and stepped inside – perhaps she had been hiding and listening? Now she took charge of the situation, giving quiet instructions, putting a large kettle on the stove and making tea. She scooped a meal of cold rice and fish curry from a pan and filled a tin dish. The man took it from her hand and passed it to Otto.

'Eat, drink,' the boy said. Never had a cup of tea tasted so good. Otto ate slowly at first, afraid he might be sick, but hunger got the better of him and he swiftly polished off the dinner. When he'd finished the tea he asked for water, and again forgetting the need for plastic bottles or iodine tablets, he drank three cupfuls, one after the other. The worst of the headache receded and instead a tide of exhaustion came over him.

'I need to speak to my friends,' he said. 'Do you have a phone?' He mimed a mobile phone call and the man nodded vigorously.

'Yes, yes,' he said, before speaking to the boy again. Otto, lying on the bed, was struggling to keep his eyes open. The man and his wife began a hurried conversation. Outside the door the dog barked and dimly Otto heard the sound of a motor scooter on the road outside. He had to phone Charlotte and Jen. Had to. Otto closed his eyes.

Sleep dragged him down, a swamp of it. He dreamed darkly, of monkeys and snakes and black trees, of a path that unwound forever no matter how fast he ran, of a man with a bloody face and a temple in a chasm where a cloud of bats flew around him, and Shiva, drumming a ceaseless rhythm, stepped from his arch of fire and kissed Otto on the forehead. A kiss like a flame, hot and bright.

He woke with a start. How long had he been asleep? It felt like hours but the family were still up and about, the woman attending to jobs in the kitchen, the boy working on some homework with his father. They spoke with low voices, out of consideration for their sleeping guest no doubt.

Otto sat up and rubbed his eyes. His headache had blurred into a low, fuzzy pain but his burnt skin seemed to scream with every movement. Even the texture of the blanket underneath him was agonising on his bare legs.

'How long was I asleep?

His hosts turned to him. The boy said, 'About two hours.'

The man stood up and passed over a clunky mobile. Otto tapped in Charlotte's number.

The phone rang twice.

'Hello?' The sound of her familiar voice filled Otto with an overwhelming sense of relief and affection. 'Hello, who is it?' He heard anxiety in her voice.

'Charlotte, it's Otto.'

'Otto? Ohmigod! Otto? Are you okay? Where are you?'

Loud music was playing in the background, making it hard to hear her words.

'I'm okay. I'm fine. Did you hear what happened?'

She said something he couldn't make out. Then: 'Just a minute, let me get away from this noise.'

'Hurry up – I can't talk long, I'm on somebody else's phone. Is Jen there?'

'She's – she's around here somewhere. Where are you?'

Otto looked at the boy. He and his parents were all staring at Otto. 'Where are we? I'm going to ask my friend to collect me – what's the address? How can she find this place?'

The boy absorbed these questions, relayed them to his father. In the meantime Otto spoke to Charlotte again. The music was not so insistent now.

'Can you get a taxi and find me? I know it'll be expensive, but I don't know what else to do.'

But the boy interrupted him. 'No taxi,' he said. 'My father will drive you. We'll take you where you want to go.'

Otto looked at them, his kind hosts. The father was nodding.

'Charlotte? Don't worry. I'm getting a lift. I need to meet you. Somewhere quiet where they don't know me. I don't want any fuss.'

Charlotte was silent for a moment. She said in a low, serious voice, 'Everyone's talking about you, Otto, about you and that girl.'

Otto took a deep breath – it was an effort to speak.

'You know it wasn't me, don't you? You do know that.'

'Of course. You don't even need to ask.' She went quiet then. 'I'm so relieved you're okay. I was worried.' Her voice started to break. 'We'll sort it out. You got your adventure, didn't you? Your story.' It was an attempt at humour. Otto felt a catch in his own throat.

'Look, I've got to go. When I get close I'll call you again and you can meet me. Bring some money – I'll need to give this guy something for his fuel and using his phone.'

'Sure. Hey, Otto, I can't wait to see you.'

'Me too.'

They travelled in an ancient pick-up, Otto, the father and the boy all crammed in next to one another in the front. The dog jumped up into the back, uninvited, and stared through the cab window at the people inside. A small picture of Ganesh was glued to the dashboard and a string of beads dangled from the rear-view mirror. As soon as the engine started up, music erupted from a cassette tape in the car stereo, music which to Otto's ears still sounded discordant and garish. The man turned the volume down a little and the pick-up pulled away, the cab filling with diesel fumes. Otto turned to the boy.

'Could you ask your father – who are these bad people who make trouble? What do they do?'

The boy stared at him with wide, serious eyes. He repeated the question to his father without taking his attention from Otto. The man slowly shook his head. Clearly he was wary, not knowing how much to say.

'Why did they take you?' the boy said. 'What have you to do with them?'

Otto considered. He didn't want to tell them about his involvement with Maria – they had probably heard about the death in the news. What should he say then?

'They robbed me, took my camera. They thought I was a journalist, wanted to know how much I knew,' he said. So much was true.

The boy repeated something to his father.

'Are you a journalist?'

Otto shook his head. 'I'm a student. But I take photos. I want to be a journalist one day.'

Father and son exchanged words. Then the boy said, 'You should write about these people. They come from abroad and they drive into the forest to party,' the boy said. 'When we go to fetch fuel or take the goats to graze they threaten us. Sometimes they drive their vehicles over the rice fields. Sometimes bad things happen – people are beaten up and hurt. They are arrogant and selfish.'

'What do they do?' Otto said. 'Is it drink and drugs? Why do they need to come all the way out here?'

He imagined the outrage if the situation were reversed and a gang of foreigners arrived in Britain, set up camp in a forest and intimidated the locals.

'Don't the police help?' Otto asked. 'Have you reported this?'

Again the quick conversation with his father, before the boy shrugged and said, 'The police don't care. They've been getting money too. And they don't want to upset the tourists because they bring in money. Many of the people living on the coast turn a blind eye as well, because the tourists bring in so much money. The older generation don't like it, but the younger ones don't care. They want dollars.'

'It's not right,' Otto rejoined. 'Who the hell do these people think they are?'

The boy didn't answer, only shrugged again. Otto thought about Inspector Sharma, posted from Delhi. Had he been brought in because the local police had become implicated in this project of Andreas and his gang?

The drive lasted about an hour. The road grew busier as they approached the coast. They pulled up outside a little white Catholic church on the edge of town and Otto called Charlotte again telling her to come and meet him. Then they waited, the three of them, listening to the lively, gaudy music on the tape, Otto tense with anticipation at the prospect of meeting his friends again.

There they were! Walking through the patchy light from intermittent street lights, Charlotte and Jen were scanning the street, looking out for him. Otto jumped out of the cab. The dog, still in the back, began to bark again.

Perhaps they weren't sure at first who he was because Otto saw them hesitate and put their heads together.

'Jen! Charlie!' he called, waving his arm. The sound of his voice was clearly convincing. They began to run. Charlotte soon outstripped Jen. She stretched out her arms and jumped onto him, wrapping him in a hug, clinging with her legs around his waist, almost knocking him over and squeezing so hard she pressed all the breath from his body. Then Jen was there too, and they were all hugging each other and exclaiming, and Otto's relief and happiness were momentarily overwhelming. They separated a little, enough to look

197

at and pat one another and exchange almost meaningless, affectionate reassurances. Are you okay? You're okay? Are you sure you're
okay?

The father and son who had come to Otto's rescue and driven him
back watched the little scene with evident satisfaction. The father
stood with his arms folded, the boy hopped from one foot to the
other. When Otto had disentangled himself from his friends, he
introduced them and Charlotte drew out money from her wallet to
reimburse him for his petrol. The man took it quietly, stuffed the
notes in his pocket, shook Otto's hand and returned to the pick-up
with his son. They called out goodbyes, and then they were gone, the
vehicle disappearing into the soft, Goan darkness, leaving only a
lingering hint of diesel on the air.

Otto, Jen, Charlotte. Jen placed a light hand on Otto's arm.

'What happened, Otto? Where did you go?'

The question hung before them.

'Where shall we go?' Otto said. He looked up and down the street.
What if they came for him again?

'We have to decide what to do,' Charlotte said. 'We need to tell the
police you're back, Otto. It looked . . . incriminating to say the least –
your disappearing.' Her voice was level, but Otto reacted as though
she had criticised him.

'I didn't disappear, I was taken,' he jumped in.

Two young Indian men walked by. They stopped talking as they
passed, glancing at the young Westerners with some curiosity. Otto
waited till they'd moved out of earshot and said, 'Where shall we go?
Do you have somewhere to stay?'

'We rented a room by the beach. Come on, we'll take you back
there and you can tell us what happened.'

Otto talked as they walked, Jen to his right, Charlotte to his left. In
a low voice he recounted the events of the last days, beginning with
his meeting Maria, her death, the interview with the police and his
kidnap – concluding with the tale of the foreigners – the bad people –

the beating he witnessed, and their campaign of intimidation. From time to time, when he was describing some difficult moment, Jen would touch his arm in sympathy. Charlotte interjected questions several times, wanting more details.

When they got to the lodging, Charlotte unlocked the door. They stepped inside. Otto saw the shock in his friends' faces when they beheld, in the hard, electric light, the physical damage he had sustained.

Otto sat on the bed. His last reserve of energy seemed to drain out of him.

'I think I'll have a shower,' he said. 'Have you anything to eat? I'm still ravenous.'

Charlotte went out for supplies as he showered. Cool water pinged painfully on his burnt skin. Blisters had bubbled up on his shoulders and the top of his ears. Even his scalp had sunburn despite the covering of hair. The cascading water hurt his head. He gently washed his hair, borrowed Jen's toothbrush to do his teeth, and then padded out to the main room with a towel wrapped around his waist.

'I have some after-sun,' Jen said, offering a plastic bottle. Charlotte returned with chapattis and samosas wrapped in paper and foil, and a polystyrene cup of tea. Otto sat on the bed and began to eat.

Charlotte and Jen sat on the bed opposite, side by side, watching him. Charlotte appeared to be formulating her thoughts.

'We've been making some enquiries of our own,' she said. 'We can embellish your story a little. Jen, tell him about your tattoo man.'

Jen, sitting very still with her hands folded in her lap, told him about Kumar and the dozen people he had tattooed with the same symbol Maria had on her back, and that Otto had discovered in the old temple in the jungle.

Kumar. The name pricked his memory. Was this the same Kumar he'd met with Maria, Gina and the Irish guy, Max?

'So what do we have?' Charlotte said. 'A serious secret party

199

crowd whose members have adopted a wheel of fire as their symbol of belonging. Drink and drugs, presumably. Did they kill Maria? Are they serious enough to resort to murder?' She furrowed her brow.

'Yes,' Otto said. 'You should have seen them kicking this guy in the jungle. It was horrible. They may have killed him for all I know. Yes they are that serious.' He took out the passport from his pocket and passed it to Charlotte. The two young women studied the photograph.

'You need to give this to the police,' Jen said. 'Perhaps they can find him.'

'What about the man who tried to help you, the old hippy? The one who told you to clear out,' Charlotte said. 'How did he know?'

'Jim?' Otto said. 'I don't know. Apparently he's been here for years. Probably knows everyone.'

'He's not a hippy,' Jen said. 'I don't think you should call him that. Maybe he was once. I think he's a sadhu.'

Charlotte frowned. 'A what?'

'A sadhu. A holy man. They give up all worldly attachments and devote themselves to prayer and spirituality. There are millions of them in India – wandering about or maybe living in the mountains.'

'But Jim's American, I think. He's not a Hindu.'

'He still looks like a sadhu. I've read about them.'

'If we find him, perhaps he can help – if he knows everyone,' Charlotte said.

She surrendered her bed to Otto while she and Jen slept top to tail in the other. Above their heads the fan whirred, keeping the mosquitoes at bay. Otto lay in the darkness, his skin smarting, grateful and relieved to have found a place of safety with his friends. He would go to the police in the morning and tell them what had happened.

When he closed his eyes, Maria rose like a phantom in his imagination. Even though she was dead, the mere thinking of her stirred a longing. He remembered the way her hair slid over her narrow shoulders and the elegance of her bare feet in the sand and the sound of her voice, as though the strength of his desire for her had burned her, like a ghost, into his memory. How long till it faded?

Then, unwanted, followed the memory of her inert body lying in his arms, all life and warmth drained away and the breakage evident in the wounded head, the bruises. Why would anyone do that? The tattoo on her back indicated she belonged to this ugly party crowd. But why would they kill her?

Andreas had believed Otto was the journalist sniffing round this story of a secret group. Had he killed Maria, thinking she had betrayed them?

Of course the murder might have been entirely unrelated. Kate had claimed she was Maria's friend and she'd certainly seemed cut up about her death. Two friends – both of whom were attached to this thug, Andreas?

He heard Charlotte sigh and turn over. The fan hummed. Far away, only just audible, he heard the sea.

'Otto, are you still awake?' Jen whispered.

'Yes, only just.'

She stretched her hand across the gap between their beds. He reached out his own and their hands clasped.

'I'm sorry,' he said. 'I've messed up your trip, haven't I?' He sensed her smile.

'I don't know yet. We don't know what's going to happen,' she said. 'And it wasn't your fault, was it?'

'Wasn't it?' He'd behaved precipitously, indulging his crush on Maria, but he'd done nothing wrong and how could he have known what was to follow?

Jen

August 2008

Jen suddenly stopped talking, and gazed at Otto, waiting for him to notice. They were sitting at the tables outside the Red Lion at Avebury. Clouds glowered over the rooftops, though from time to time bright sunshine broke through. Tourists mooched around the stones in the field the other side of the road. Jen and Otto had spent the afternoon walking, revisiting the long barrow and the spring, at Jen's request, because she'd loved the place so much on their visit with Charlotte in May. At lunchtime they picnicked, amid the standing stones, on sandwiches and fruit, until Otto suggested a visit to the pub where he bought beer for himself and mineral water for Jen.

Jen studied Otto. He was staring over her head towards the pub, seemingly lost in thought.

'You're not listening to me,' she said, trying to keep the note of hurt from her voice. She glanced over her shoulder, wondering what had caught Otto's attention. A girl, of course. A pretty blonde girl at the table behind them.

'What?' Otto blinked.

Jen sighed. 'I said, you're not listening to me.'

'What? Oh. I'm sorry.' He shook his head. 'I'm a bit tired, that's all.' He smiled and reached out for her hand on the table. 'I had too much to drink last night. I think I'm a bit hungover.'

He didn't look great, it was true.

*

Jen had taken the train from London the night before, to spend a weekend with Otto. She'd arrived a little after eight, Otto meeting her at the station with a boyish grin and a big wave, trotting down the platform to seize her bag and escort her to his home. It was her third visit and each time she'd been made so welcome by Otto's mother, who set her up a little bed in the study, made them lovely breakfasts and altogether seemed to enjoy having a guest to stay, her son's exotic girlfriend.

On Friday night, once she'd dumped her little suitcase, Otto had taken Jen to a gathering at a friend's house, where they sat in a bedroom with a dozen of Otto's mates, male and female, listening to loud music and drinking wine before heading out to a birthday party in a bar next to the river in town. Charlotte wasn't there. The night was sultry, the High Street teeming with drunk girls in tiny dresses, tottering on high heels. Jen, who rarely drank and didn't know Otto's friends, soon felt bored and isolated. Once he'd had a drink or two, Otto didn't stay with her, wanting to talk and party, eager to chat with his mates and other girls. He thought he'd organised a treat for her, with the party and the crowd of people. And everyone else seemed to be enjoying themselves. So why wasn't it a treat? Why was she such a shy little stuck-in-the-mud, that it wasn't?

The following morning, Otto slept in much later than Jen, so she had herbal tea with his mother in the kitchen and a conversation about Italian Renaissance art. When his mother went out to open her gallery Jen lingered in the house, picking up books, looking at the pictures on the walls, flicking through magazines, thinking that although she'd been looking forward to this weekend, invested so much thought in it, she wasn't actually, so far, enjoying herself.

Otto emerged at eleven thirty, dishevelled and handsome, rubbing his face with the palm of his hand. He put his arms around her and kissed her neck, apologising for his sleeping in. Then he made them both drinks, flopped down on the sofa and asked – what would she like to do today?

'Can we go to Avebury?'

'What? You've already seen it.'

'I know. But I'd like to go again. It's such a special place. Anyway, that was three months ago.'

Otto shrugged. 'Of course. If that's what you'd like to do.' He grinned, took her face in his hands and kissed her with his coffee-flavoured mouth. 'If I'm with you, I'll be happy wherever we go,' he said. 'I've never met anyone like you, Jen. I'm a very lucky guy.'

How blue his eyes were. Jen felt her annoyance melt away.

'Did you enjoy the party last night?' he said, his face still close to hers. 'Wasn't it great?'

'Yes, sure,' she said, though she hadn't. Why lie? She didn't want to hurt his feelings. And if she hadn't enjoyed it, wasn't that her fault? Everyone liked a party. And today would be better. No distractions for Otto – she'd have him all to herself.

And it had been better, till now. Once he'd showered and dressed and they'd gone out to the bus stop, Otto was funny and lively, flirting and teasing her, so she felt happy, relaxed and appreciated. They walked around the stone circle and from time to time she'd stop to make a quick sketch, of a stone, or the sheep or a crow perched on a fence post, which Otto would examine and admire. They laughed a lot, and after the picnic he lay down on his back with his eyes closed, resting his head on her lap and the sun shone. Until, at last, he'd opened one eye and said, 'I fancy a beer. D'you mind if we go to the pub?'

'You were looking at the girl,' Jen said.

'What?'

'The blonde girl, sitting behind me.'

Otto looked surprised, then affronted.

'She's very cute,' he said. 'But that's all, don't worry. I'm with you.' He leaned forward to kiss her. 'I'm with you,' he repeated.

But Jen felt a strange, painful tightening under her ribs. Was she being unreasonable? Otto was the first boy she'd been out with. He'd flattered her with his attention and she liked him – liked him so much. How wonderful it had been, his courtship, their long email exchanges, the texts he sent her every single day for a fortnight, texts she began to long for. Such feverish anticipation – heated by the eighty miles distance between them and the long tunnel of waiting from one visit to the next. Then, in London one night at the beginning of July, a first kiss in the park near her home, a giant moon hanging over the trees and the air perfumed with summer. Liking had evolved into something more delightful, and dangerous, and painful.

So was she being unreasonable? If only there were a guidebook telling you the right way to conduct a relationship, what was acceptable and what was not, so she would know how to behave, how far to go, what she should be feeling or not feeling. If Otto said don't worry, why was she still worrying? Why didn't he understand how she felt? How would he feel if she ogled every eligible man who passed within range? And despite his wandering eye, she knew he had a good heart and that he cared for her. She gave a quick, sharp sigh, her eyes fixed on the table, pressing her hands together in her lap, out of sight. She wanted to tell him what she was thinking, but struggled to get the words out, impeded by the strength of her feelings and a worry she would cry if she started to speak. She had been looking forward to this visit for the past two weeks, longed for it, but the previous evening had been such an absurd anticlimax. Scooped up in the excitement of friends, drink, party he'd paid her so little attention, and when they got home he was too drunk to remember to kiss her goodnight. Even today, when she'd assumed they would be back to normal, he wasn't listening to what she said because a cute blonde girl had caught his eye. Her disappointment was cataclysmic.

'What's the matter?' Otto said. 'You look all tense. Are you okay?'

How hard it was to force out the words.

'I wish I was enough for you.' It came out in a rush.

'What do you mean?' He looked nonplussed.

'I wish I was enough for you. Why do you always have to be look-ing at other girls?'

'You *are* enough for me, Jen. Why are you saying this stuff?' He looked genuinely wounded.

'Last night – at the party – you just left me on my own and talked to those other girls, and even today your mind is wandering. Why did you do it? Why did you make me want you, if you didn't want me?'

'I do want you. Blimey, Jen, where's all this coming from?'

She sensed she was being unreasonable and exaggerating his mis-demeanours, but she'd dreamed and fantasised about him so much these last weeks, since the magical kiss in the park, that the Otto of her romantic imagination no longer matched the real-life boy sitting on the other side of the table. And, truth be told, she would never treat him this way – inviting him to stay, then leaving him at a party while she flirted with other guys, or eyeing up boys at the pub. Surely that wasn't a way to treat someone you cared about?

But Otto still looked hurt, as though she were the one who had behaved badly while he was the misunderstood innocent: they were working from different scripts.

'I thought we could have some fun together,' he said. 'I'm sorry, Jen, I didn't mean to upset you. Do you understand that? Was this a mistake, us getting together? I like you so much, you know that, don't you? I really don't want to hurt you. We're going to India, aren't we? I want us to be friends forever.'

Jen had been staring at the table as he spoke. Now she glanced up, seeing the confusion in Otto's face. He hadn't set out to hurt her, clearly.

'I don't think this is going to work,' she said. A sense of panic fol-lowed, a sudden desire to get out of this trap she had created for herself, tying her feelings to Otto. 'I don't think we want the same things. I just – I just hadn't realised how much power I'd given you over the way I feel, and I don't like it. I don't like it at all. It's too dif-ficult. I don't think I'm ready for it.'

Otto looked stunned, as though she'd hit him. He raised his eyebrows and sucked his lower lip.

'This is all a bit sudden,' he said, crestfallen. 'I thought things were going well. I thought we had fun together.'

She softened. 'I think that's the problem. I don't think I'm very good at fun. I get so serious about things. I can't help it.'

Otto sighed. 'So you think we should just be friends?'

Jen slowly nodded. She was overwrought and shaking. One part of her longed for him to contradict her, to say he didn't want to just be friends, that he loved her passionately, that he didn't want other girls, that he would love her forever. Instead he studied her with a very grave expression and said, 'If that's what you want. But we *will* still be friends, yes?'

'Of course, always. I know we will.'

Still Otto looked downcast for a minute or two. Then he seemed to shake himself.

'I need another drink,' he said. 'Do you want something?'

Jen shook her head. Otto picked up his empty beer glass and she watched him walk towards the pub door, dropping a glance en route at the blonde girl sitting at the table behind them. Jen felt a taut thread snap within her chest. Hurt – and relief. Let him look. It wasn't something for her to worry about any more.

Jen

Saturday

Jen woke up before the others, squeezed to the edge of the narrow bed. Charlotte, in her sleep, had appropriated more than her fair share. Her warm, brown knees were pressed into the back of Jen's thighs. Sunlight beamed through the high, unshuttered window and spread like a fan on the ceiling.

Jen looked to the neighbouring bed. Otto's burnt face lay on the white pillow; his mouth was open, his eyes shut tight. Spectacular blisters adorned his bony shoulders; the mere sight of them made her nerves tingle with sympathetic pain. Still, what a relief he was back with them, that he was – for the time being – safe.

It was only seven. Jen was too uncomfortable to sleep again so she got up very quietly, slipped on a long, cotton skirt and a T-shirt, picked up her book and pen, and headed out. The air was deliciously fresh and cool, a breeze moving from the sea. Jen slipped off her sandals to walk on the sand. The waves were bigger and fiercer than she'd seen here before, crashing down at the sea's edge. She crossed the beach and stood at the waves' limit, enjoying the spray on her face and skin.

Further along the beach half a dozen men were hauling a boat into the water, for a fishing expedition presumably. In the shade of the palm trees, the two Rajasthani women were sitting, brilliant scarlet shawls over their heads, hoops in their ears and gold in their noses, chatting volubly with one another while half a dozen children played around them. Jen ambled at the sea's hem, sandals dangling from her hand, salt water stealing over her toes. Despite their predicament and the ream of unanswered questions, she felt a sense of deep physical contentment. That was a very unusual feeling; most of the time her body seemed to be rebelling against something, resisting, fighting, suffering. And now – no rashes, no stomach pains or aching muscular weakness. Why was that? Was it the air she breathed here? Was it less polluted, was some antipathetic substance missing from the Goan environment? She was afraid to think about it too much; didn't want to tempt fate.

After a time, having a stretch of beach to herself, she sat down and began to draw. She thought about Otto and the temple in the forest, the broken statue and the echoing wheel of flame painted on the wall behind it. She closed her eyes and imagined what it would have felt like, to stand beneath the bats in the stone chamber in the shadow of the stone god.

When the drawing was done, she climbed to her feet again and walked on. Already the sun was banishing the early cool. The beach curved in a gentle arc.

She looked up from the foam tickling her feet and saw another solitary figure in the distance, walking towards her. Even from so far away she knew who it was.

Coincidence? Jen didn't believe in coincidence. Intention yes. In some way, subconsciously, she'd invited him to this meeting.

She recognised his thin figure, the long, white hair blowing over his bare shoulders. She felt a twinge of nervousness so she stopped walking, climbed up onto the beach and sat down on the sand to let him come to her.

Jim walked with a long, even pace. His body, naked except for an ochre lungi tied around his middle, was whippet-thin. He appeared to be lost in thought, focused on some inner horizon, and Jen thought for a moment he hadn't noticed her at all, but when he crossed in

210

front of her he stopped and turned. For a tantalising moment, they stared at one another, Jim and Jen. She looked away, overcome with shyness – but when she looked back he was striding up the beach towards her. He dropped into a squat, long, ropy muscles bulging from his skinny thighs, right in front of her.

'It's a beautiful morning,' he said. He had a gentle voice, an American accent smoothed by many years away from the old country. Jen glanced up at him, the vivid blue eyes in a lined, leathery face. It was curious, the contrast between the young man's body – the alive blue of his eyes – and the aged face, the old man's white hair and beard.

She returned her attention to her feet, burrowed in the sand.

'Yes it is,' she said, too shy to look. What did he want? She glanced up at him again, very quickly, taking in the dab of yellow powder on his brow, the thong around his neck from which some amulet dangled. He held out his hand, into her line of vision, and said, 'I'm Jim.'

Jen took his hand, very smooth and warm, and shook it.

'I know,' she said. 'I'm Jen.'

Jim shifted to her side and sat down, and so they remained for several minutes, without speaking; but somehow, for Jen, the atmosphere had altered and her shyness melted away.

'Why did you stay so long?' she said at last.

'Because I didn't want to go anywhere else.' He didn't ask what or how she knew about him.

'Shiva,' he said.

'What?' She glanced down. Her journal on the sand beside her had fallen open, revealing her drawing. 'Oh, yes. I have a little statue at home.'

He reached out his hand for the book, first looking to Jen for permission to take it.

'Do you know what it means? The symbolism?'

She shook her head. 'I just like it, the form of him. Balance and grace and peace and joy. That's what it says to me.'

'He's Nataraja, Lord of the Dance, source of all movement,' Jim said. 'The dance that is existence, the universe, being itself – the cycle of creation, preservation and destruction.' He placed a finger lightly on the picture. 'He has a drum in one hand, making the beat that brings the universe into being. The flame in the other hand – that's destruction, the falling back. The third hand he's holding palm out, in a blessing – that's reassurance: don't be afraid. And the fourth hand is pointing down at his raised foot. That means release. His other foot is planted in the ground, signalling embodiment in the physical realm.'

'What about the little piggy thing he's standing on? What's that?'

'It signifies ignorance – the unenlightened, earthbound soul.'

'And the circle he's standing in, covered with flames . . .'

'The cosmos and all of consciousness.' He indicated with a sweep of his arms: everything.

Jen pondered, wondering at the significance of the symbolism. Why had this group chosen Shiva's wheel? Perhaps she should ask Jim. He had no tattoo that she could see, and certainly there was little enough of him covered up.

'You're a friend of the boy who found Maria, aren't you?' Jim said. His tone was gentle and concerned. 'I heard they were after him. I tried to warn him. But I was too late, wasn't I?'

'Yes. But he's okay. They took him into the jungle but they let him go. They thought he was some hotshot journalist.'

'He is here. The journalist, I mean. The real journalist. He's staying at the West Wind Hotel. Perhaps you should speak to him.'

'Jim . . .' Jen hesitated. 'Who are *they*? What's going on?'

Jim didn't answer. He looked at Jen, his complex expression impossible to read. The blue eyes seemed to freeze.

'Jen, you have to be brave,' he said. 'I know who you are – the gifts you have. I can see it in you. And you know more than you realise – trust yourself. Trust your instincts.'

212

Jen felt a tiny emotional tremor. She opened her mouth to speak, but didn't know what to say.

Her mobile rang, vibrating in her skirt pocket. She dug it out, expecting it to be Charlotte worrying where she was, but the number on the screen was unknown.

'Hello?'

'Hey, Jen. It's Kumar. Remember me? From last night, the tattoo man.' His voice was friendly, humorous, self-deprecating. Jen felt a smile rise.

'Yes, of course. How are you?'

'Good, yes. Listen – I need to talk to you. I've been thinking. There's stuff you should know. Last night, well, I didn't know how much to say. But I've been talking to my friends, and they agree it's okay.'

Jen felt a prickle of unease, and excitement. 'Say about what?'

'Look, where are you now?'

'On the beach.'

Kumar hesitated then said, 'Meet me in front of the club in ten minutes.'

'The club?'

'You know, the place with the bars and the dance floor. There.'

Jen raised her eyes, realised that Jim was looking at her intently. He did interest her – she wanted to talk with him – but not in the same way she was interested in Kumar.

'See you then,' she said. The call cut off.

Jen took back her journal. 'I'm sorry, I've got to go,' she said, rising to her feet. 'Can we talk another time?'

Perhaps Jim wanted to ask who she'd been speaking with, but he refrained. Perhaps he knew – because he said, 'Be careful, Jen. It seems like a paradise, doesn't it? But there are dangerous people here. And you know I'm not being melodramatic because you've seen the evidence for yourself.'

The vision swam in her mind's eye, the photographs of Maria's back, the dead girl Otto had lifted from the waves.

'Thanks,' she said, turning away. 'I will.' But she was thinking about beautiful Kumar as she hurried along the beach, carrying journal and sandals. I should text Charlotte, tell her where I am, she thought. She took out the phone and as she walked tapped out a message: On beach, mkg enquiries. Didn't want 2 wake u – back sn. J xx

A few minutes later she saw Kumar ahead. He waved and grinned. The breeze picked up her hair, blew it around her shoulders, and beneath Kumar's gaze she was conscious of how she must look to him, rather thin and pale, the locks of wavy crimson hair floating on the wind. When she drew near he glanced over her shoulder and then behind (checking if anyone had seen them?) and said, 'Come with me. Come on. We need to talk.'

He led her to a small boat, beached just beyond the reach of the waves, and began to push it into the sea. 'Get in,' he said.

'What? Where are we going?'

'Please, trust me.'

Jen felt a rising anxiety. What did he want? The sense of attraction and emotional connection faltered. Who but a fool would get into a boat with a strange man, headed for who knows where? Think of Maria; think of Otto abducted and taken into a jungle.

'I'm not going in the boat!' she said, flustered. 'I'd be mad to – I don't know anything about you and you won't even tell me where you want to go!' Nerves made her short of breath. Don't panic, she thought. Just turn around and walk away. But her feet didn't move, rooted to the spot.

Kumar stopped pushing the boat. He stood up straight, the vessel bobbing on the waves in front of him, bunting his legs. He looked at Jen and maybe saw the distress in her face.

'I'm sorry,' he said. 'I am not explaining myself very well. I know it seems strange – but I want to show you something, Jen. You'll understand so much better. You were called here – you know that, don't you? You were brought here for a reason.'

Jen didn't move.

'What do you mean, I was called here?'

'Why did you come to India? Whose idea was it?'

'It was my idea. I've always wanted to come here. That doesn't mean anything.'

'How long have you wanted to come here?'

'I don't know.' Memories stirred in her mind, leaves shifting in a breeze. Where lay the origin of her longing to be here? She remembered, as a child, seeing India on the television – a woman in a carmine sari walking along a dusty path. She remembered the brilliant colour and the woman's slender grace, the natural elegance of her motion, and thinking, I want to go there. Jen cast her eyes down to the sea, hair blowing across her face; in the art journal, in her hand, she had drawn the wheel of flame many weeks before seeing the tattoo on Maria's back.

'You're meant to be here, Jen.'

'I'm meant to be here?'

He nodded. 'You'll see. I'm taking you to the island. I'll show you what I mean.'

Jen raised her face and stared at him. Between them, the sea was turquoise and azure in stripes. The boat fretted on the waves. The huge, burning sky leaped in a great vault over their heads. She shaded her eyes. Yes, she was meant to be here. But how did Kumar know that? How inevitable he looked, the boatman, waiting to take her who knows where. A figure from a fairy tale, a myth – the ferry to escort her on the passage from one realm to the next. Jen thought of Maria, killed at the sea's edge, and Otto taken to the jungle, but she quelled the anxious voice telling her to take care, to be afraid. Wasn't it time to trust her instincts, as Jim had urged her? She spent so much time being afraid – of people, the human-created world, frightened even of the food she ate. And on some deeper level she did trust Kumar. She took a deep breath, picked up her skirt and waded through the water. Kumar held out his hand and helped her into the boat.

Once they were away from the beach, Kumar pulled the oars into the boat, put up a mast and hoisted a small sail. The breeze plucked at the stained fabric which bellied and flapped but Kumar expertly turned the boat around and the wind carried them over the hills and valleys of the sea.

'Where are we going?' Jen said. Sunshine glittered on the surface of the water. Underneath, now and then, she could see the dark, mobile shapes of fish.

'Not far. Around the headland.' Kumar's strong, brown feet gripped the bottom of the boat. He manoeuvred the vessel easily – arms, legs, the weight of him, riding the wind and the waves. The boat bucked but he brought it back into line. The journey was exhilarating and Jen couldn't stop the smile rising to her face.

They came to the end of the beach and passed the headland. Sheer cliffs faced the sea. The walls of the old fort rose on top, just visible, and then the opening of the natural harbour where the bigger fishing boats were moored. The boat skirted another rocky promontory where the waves worried at a tumble of broken stones. Kumar held up his arm, pointing ahead.

'Can you see?'

Jen shaded her eyes. A tiny island like a castle of reddish rock rose from the sea. A blanket of greenery, rough-hemmed, topped the sheer sides. This was their destination? She looked back at Kumar and he grinned.

The boat circled the island to the side furthest from the mainland. Kumar brought the boat closer, furled the sail and took out the oars again. Jen was puzzled. How did he hope to land? The island seemed impregnable, its sheer sides like the walls of the fortress.

'Hold tight,' he warned. The boat struggled against him as they steered a course through a succession of rocks jutting sharp heads from the water. Now and then he used an oar to jab at a rock and thrust the boat away. His face was tense. Then, unexpectedly, the cliffs seemed to part before them, giving way to a small harbour space where the waves did not intrude. The boat slipped into a

216

natural enclosure where the water was shallow and smooth, perfectly clear over a bed of red stone. The walls closed in around them, cutting out the sound of the sea. Jen took a breath, stunned and lost for words.

The island, which had appeared so tiny, now reared high above her head. The cliffs were red and dun-coloured, though here and there veins of crystal glittered. Roots of trees dangled from high up. Birds, bright white, perched in sconces, and then, as one, lifted from the cliff face and flew in a swooping circle above the boat.

'Where do we land?' Jen said. Kumar didn't answer; he raised his arm and pointed ahead of them. Jen couldn't see any promising place but just as the gap in the cliffs had opened without her seeing where, now a narrow, natural pier of the same red rock extended before them. Kumar jumped out of the boat and tied it to a rusty ring embedded on its side. He held out his hand.

Jen climbed out and put her sandals on. She checked her phone for a reply from Charlotte but there was, unsurprisingly, no phone signal. She still carried her art book and pen.

'Where are we going?' she said.

'This way.' Kumar set off ahead of her, walking towards the cliff face. Jen, of course, had been asking a more general question – why are we here? It seemed she would have to be patient. This time, when the apparently impenetrable cliff revealed a stairway cut into the rock, Jen was not surprised. The stairway was evidently ancient, its rough edges worn smooth. Here and there, figures had been carved into the surface in bas-relief – Indian maidens dancing, a likeness of Ganesh with his elephant head. She stopped to trace the shape of him with her fingertips, marvelling at the quality of the work. Kumar looked back, over his shoulder.

'It's been a holy island for hundreds of years,' he said. 'Then the Portuguese found it in the nineteenth century. There's a Christian hermitage at the top, derelict now. The local people said it was a sacred place and anyone who came here was cursed. The way onto the island was forgotten for a long time.'

Jen sweated and struggled up the steps. How many were there? From time to time the stairway seemed to disappear into the cliff itself, passing through dark chimneys of rock before emerging into the sunshine again. Once, thigh muscles burning, she looked back and saw how high they had come, the shallow harbour far, far below and the boat like a toy, and she was overwhelmed by vertigo. She pressed herself against the rock and had to cling to the steps with her fingertips, eyes closed, afraid she would otherwise let go and throw herself into the void.

'Jen? Are you okay?' Ahead of her, Kumar waited. How many times had he made this climb? Jen opened her eyes again. She dropped her book on the step by her feet.

'Just a minute. How much further is it?'

'Not far now. Keep going, Jen. Nearly there.'

The stairway twisted and levelled out for a few metres, culminating in a final flight of six, steep steps.

'Here, have a rest.' Kumar gestured to a rock where she might sit. They were standing beneath trees. A narrow path led away between the trunks. Large boulders pierced the shallow soil. Flowers, salmon pink, blossomed from hanging tendrils.

When Jen had recovered her breath, they continued along the path. Kumar pointed out the broken remains of the Christian hermitage, a tiny stone hut now filled with a black carpet of fallen leaves. They climbed again, a gentle slope. From time to time the trees cleared and Jen saw a vista of cobalt sky.

Then ahead, on a stone plateau, she saw broken columns. The jungle canopy fell away. They'd come to the island's edge because through the columns Jen could see the ocean spreading.

'What is this place?' As she stepped closer, she saw several thatched huts, half concealed in the jungle's skirts. She thought, naturally, of Otto's community in the jungle, the 'bad people' he'd told

218

her of. Kumar, perhaps sensing her disquiet, put his hand on her arm.

'It's okay,' he said. They weren't alone. A white man emerged from one of the huts and then a black girl. Jen waited with some apprehension as they stepped closer.

'Hello, Jen, I'm Gina.' The young woman had an American accent. 'Welcome to the island. This is Max.'

A strong-looking man in his twenties, hollow cheeks and burning eyes, Max held out his hand to be shaken. Jen looked from one to another. Their faces were relaxed and open. They looked at her intently – hungrily. They wanted to know her.

So this was Gina – who knew Maria and had befriended Otto. What did they want from her?

'What is this place? How did you find it?' Jen was nervous, wanting to make conversation.

Kumar said, 'Come and see the temple.' He led her towards the stone plateau. It was man-made, paved with huge, plain stone slabs. Three large steps led up. Once, presumably, it had been hemmed in with columns and lintels, a roof over the top. Now only some of the columns remained standing. Several lay across the floor like fallen trees. Others had collapsed into the jungle and lay overgrown by creepers. Wind and rain scoured the temple floor. At one end was a large stone altar, though it was cracked from one side to the other. Jen stood on the plateau, staring out to sea. Sky and ocean blended together on the horizon. A breeze, blown up from the sea, pushed its fingers into her hair and cooled the perspiration on her face and arms. Max and Gina sat on the temple floor waiting for Kumar to bring her to them. Gina handed her a clay cup of tea, smokily fragrant and densely sugared. Gratefully Jen drained the cup, savouring the spicy flavours. Then Gina took the cup back and filled it again from a large rusty kettle so that Kumar could drink. Jen began to relax. The ache eased from her muscles. She leaned her back against the pedestal of a fallen column. She studied Gina. Her hair hung in narrow, glossy braids. Her face was intelligent and intense. From time to time she glanced up at Jen, seeming to scrutinise her too. They smiled at one another, both keen to show goodwill.

Jen was so tired. Stress, jet lag, broken nights. Max began talking to Gina in a low voice so she couldn't hear what he was saying. Max was Irish, wasn't he? And he shared with Gina a particular quality of intensity. He gesticulated as he spoke.

The island was very peaceful and slowly she began to relax. Almost magically her worries evaporated. She rested her head against Kumar's shoulder, not worrying how familiar this might seem. Distantly she thought about Otto and Charlotte but they were very far away. Her eyes were tremendously heavy.

'Jen – Jen? Are you okay?' She registered Kumar's voice but she was too sleepy to answer. Gina said, 'This is very fast. We haven't had time to prepare her.'

Jen wondered vaguely what Gina meant but she was too far gone to care very much. Her eyes closed and sleep swallowed her up.

'She'll be fine,' Max answered. 'We've all been through it. We're here to help her.'

She dreamed the long procession of her life. Memories opened like rooms, into which she could step and look around, no longer the central character but an audience watching. She saw herself lying in a wooden cot, a baby. Then she was a white presence skirting the edge of ploughed field, and she turned to see Jen as a young girl in the window of a house. She saw the primary school and her one gloomy friend, then the house in London, her brother, the long years at the noisy comprehensive school. She saw the city streets full of people where a blond boy accosted her with a camera, then zoomed into the earth-enclosed Wiltshire long barrow (how real this one) and looked into the eyes of the real, awake Jenevieve, whose eyes widened to see her. She drew away. It was time to wake up. Where was she?

All her life the barrier between the real and the unreal world, the material and the spirit realms, had been unresolved so this place

220

now, where she felt disembodied, didn't seem entirely strange. She did wish, however, she could remember where she was. Time to wake up. Wake up.

She opened her eyes.

Strange golden-honey light. She was sitting on the stone platform and way down, the silken sea spread away. Sunlight glanced across the surface of the water. Jen blinked. How peculiar – the air seemed cross-crossed with light, as though colour were liquid and she could see it suspended in the air. The enormous weight of blue sky pressing down and the huge, golden cauldron of the sun – and the variegated greens of the jungle around the old temple, so many greens: lime, moss, emerald, pea, and apple green. How vain an enterprise it seemed, thinking of names for all the infinitesimal gradations of one, marvellous colour.

'Jen?' A voice. Kumar was sitting to her left. She hadn't been aware of him till this moment. He was studying her.

'How are you?' he said. She heard worry in his voice. How to answer? Speaking seemed like an enormous effort – she was too busy absorbing this notion about green.

'I'm okay,' she said.

Kumar persisted. 'How are you feeling?'

Jen considered. 'I've taken something, haven't I? What is it? What did you give me?' She felt a momentary panic. She wasn't in control.

'Let me explain something, Jen.' Very slowly, deliberately, he took off his shirt and turned around.

On his back, between his shoulder blades, about five inches across, a ring of flame had been tattooed into his soft skin.

She'd been tricked.

Kumar had lied to her and now she was all alone, trapped on an island with untrustworthy strangers. She felt a curious plummeting inside and pressed her back against the stone, gripped the ground with her fingertips. As she stared at the tattoo it seemed to move, circling and shimmering.

221

Kumar put his shirt back on. Then he said, 'Don't be afraid.' He held up his hand in reassurance, and Jen remembered very vividly the conversation she'd had with Jim the sadhu on the beach that very morning, him telling her about the meaning of the dancing god, raising its hand in the same gesture. Don't be afraid.

'You're one of them,' she said. 'Like Maria and the people who took Otto.'

'Yes and no.'

Jen heard a distant thundering, like horses' hooves. The drumming grew louder and louder. Couldn't Kumar hear it? Then she realised it was the sound of her own heart, the pulse of blood through her body. She could feel it, the fierce clench of the heart muscle, over and over, over and over.

'What did you give me?' she repeated. Would her heart burst, would she die? Had they poisoned her?

'It's okay.' He stretched out his hand, almost touched her arm. Jen drew back.

'Will you stop saying that, it's not okay!' She struggled to her feet. The liquid colours in the air lurched and bled and blended as she moved.

'Wait! Wait! Let me explain!'

'Is this what you did to Maria? Is this how she died?'

Gina appeared, seemingly from nowhere, but it occurred to Jen she had in fact been present all the time. In her current state of mind it was hard to make sense of things.

'Jen, please. Sit down. Let us explain.'

Jen looked from one to the other, Kumar and Gina. Max was standing behind them, his body gaunt, eyes blazing with light.

'It was the tea, wasn't it? Something in the tea.' But they'd all had tea, poured from the one big kettle. Did that mean these three were also where she was?

Gina nodded. 'It's the water, Jen. A spring bubbles up on the island by the temple. There's something in the water. That's why it's

222

been a holy place. If you drink the water you have visions, as you're having now. This is just the beginning. It'll grow stronger.'

Jen shook her head, trying to think clearly.

'Why didn't you tell me? Why didn't you ask me? What sort of person drugs another without their consent?' Anger rolling, like waves on the sea. She could feel it rising and rising, a terrible, helpless fury.

'We had to show you. We didn't think you would take it if we told you. And if you didn't drink the water you wouldn't understand what this was all about.' Gina was very calm. She took Jen's arm, whether to soothe or restrain, Jen wasn't quite sure.

'Then what is it about?' A succession of images flashed into her mind; the police station, the photo of Maria's dead body, the revelling tourists on the beach, the face of the young man in the passport, Otto dropped by the pick-up, his face burnt red by the sun and the blisters bubbling on his shoulders.

'Sit down. Please. Calm yourself.' Gina was pressing on her arm. Jen glanced back at Kumar. She moved away from Gina but did as she was told. What choice did she have?

Then they were all sitting, facing one another in the centre of the open temple floor, in the jungle's fragrant shade, high above the sea and drowned by the sky.

Gina took a deep breath.

'This has been a holy place, on and off, for hundreds of years,' she said. 'Holy men came here and had visions. They were visited by pilgrims, who built the temple and carved the steps. Later the Portuguese set up a chapel, but it was abandoned in the last century and there were stories of demons and curses. People kept away, forgot the route to take, left the place alone.

'But in the sixties, the hippies came. They didn't respect any of the old warnings about the place. Eventually one man took a boat, swam around the island, and found the way in, and up. He lived here, alone, for a year. He didn't leave at all during that time. People found the boat and assumed he'd drowned.

223

'When he left, swimming all the way back to the coast, he was different. He kept the secret of the place to himself. He travelled around India, and across Asia, but he didn't tell anyone what he'd found, not until he fell for a French woman two years later and they came back together. They lived in Goa together for a while and they told a few close friends about the island and the spring.'

Thoughts turned over in Jen's head. So this was the secret cult? 'So, how did you find out about it?'

Kumar shrugged. 'It's hard for secrets to be kept. The story leaked out, bit by bit. And sometimes, it seems people are meant to know – the island calls them here. People like you.'

'People like me,' she echoed slowly. 'What does that mean? And how d'you know I won't just go back and blab to everyone?'

'We don't,' Max said, staring into her face. 'Perhaps you will do just that. But I don't think so. You have a gift, Jen. We knew you were coming, in the same way you drew the tattoo before you came to India.'

He drew out from his back pocket a grimy, much-folded piece of paper.

'Look at this,' he said. He opened the paper and held it in front of her face with enormous reverence, like a sacrament.

Jen swallowed. 'Did you draw this?'

He nodded feverishly. Jen stared. It was a hurried but well-executed drawing of her own face, in a swirl of twining hair. No mistaking the subject – but had he truly drawn it before her arrival, or after seeing her, in order to trick her? She took a deep breath. Jim's face flashed into her mind, telling her to be brave and to trust her instincts.

'You have a gift, like mine?' she said. Max nodded again, his eyes boring into her.

'The tattoo,' she said. 'A sign of your belonging.'

Gina turned around to show Jen the wheel marked on her back, under her shirt.

'Andreas and Kate – they are part of this too,' she said. 'But it's gone wrong. One of you killed Maria. You thought she was talking too much – giving your secrets away to a journalist. Is that what happened?'

But she lost the question, because the colour seemed to fall from the sky and a lid of darkness closed over the island. The temple floor tilted and Jen pressed herself against the fallen column, afraid she might fall off, the long plummet into an inky sea.

Gina, Max and Kumar looked at one another.

'Don't fight it,' Gina said. 'Your journey's beginning. Come on, we're going to walk now. Take my hand.'

Jen opened and closed her mouth, trying to make words: 'Is this? Are you – in this place? The same place as me?'

Gina nodded. 'I've been here before, though. We'll take care of you, Jen. Don't worry.' Her voice was solicitous. She didn't sound like a killer. What did a killer sound like? In any case, what choice did she have? Jen grasped Gina's hand and they set off along a very narrow dirt path through the trees. Clouds raced across the dark sky, far too fast, like foam on a river, glowing silver at their ragged edges as though a brilliant moon were shining behind them. Jen tipped her head back to look but almost lost her balance. Gina urged her forwards.

Despite the eerie darkness, Jen could see perfectly well. The trees, leaves, trailing flowers seemed to glow with an internal light creating a kind of wonderland. Jen's fear dissolved.

Afterwards she wondered how long the walk had lasted: not long, surely, because the island was small – but during the measureless minutes of its duration it seemed eons of time had passed. She was conscious of every long step, the details of the shifting scene with its tracery of leaves, the shapes of trees and branches, the complex surface of the dry path. The earth seemed to pulse beneath her feet, as though the planet itself had a heartbeat, a huge drum in the core of the Earth. Or was it simply her own pulse? Or Shiva's drum, the rhythm of creation.

225

The trees opened out into a glade and Gina stopped.

'We're here,' she said.

Here. She was here.

A basin of seal grey rock rose from the thin soil and a narrow stream tumbled over its side, perhaps making its way to the sea. Jen stepped closer. The natural dish from which the spring bubbled was decorated and embellished. Marble and dark blue lapis lazuli had been inlaid in the surface of the rock, creating a perfect circle where the water rose. Pieces of veined lapis, shining under the water, were shaped into flames around the circle embedded in the white marble. It formed, of course, the symbol inked into the skin of her companions. Jen leaned over the spring and dipped her fingers in the water. The cold was so intense it seemed to bite her skin.

'So what's in the water?' Jen said.

Gina shook her head. 'We're not exactly sure but I can tell you this much. Far beneath the surface of the Earth, hidden in pockets of the rock, there are bubbles of water and ice. Sometimes this water has been trapped underground for thousands, or millions of years. From time to time, as the Earth's crust moves, when plates of rock shift and drift, the water comes under enormous pressure and finds its way up through faults on the rock, and bubbles up from the deep. That has happened here, on the island. I've seen it, on a geological survey at the university.

'There's something special about this water but I'm not exactly sure how it works. I'm making a study of it. It contains a unique blend of minerals and some chemical naturally occurring in this particular spring water, which has powerful effects on the mind.'

Another powerful eruption took place inside Jen and all her thoughts and sense of self seemed to unravel. She half sat, half fell, and when the effort of holding her body became too much she lay on the welcoming ground, flat on her back, arms slightly away from her body. She felt how the island held her up like a huge hand.

226

The boundaries of her conscious mind frayed and her last coherent thoughts unknitted even as they formed. What use words? They were clumsy, lumpen things . . .

Jen opened and closed her eyes. It made no difference. The filter of her consciousness was blown open and it seemed the universe itself was pouring through her like a vast black, shining river.

Charlotte

Saturday

Where was she?

The relief of Otto's return had turned to worry about Jen. Charlotte had the text message on her phone and returned to it constantly, checking the brief words for some clue about Jen's whereabouts.

It was the middle of the day. Otto had slept late, exhausted by his adventures. Charlotte waited patiently, stealing the chance to watch him as he dozed and woke and dozed again.

When he got up they went to a cafe near the beach for a breakfast of coffee and scrambled eggs, served on strangely sweet toast. Charlotte texted Jen from the cafe, telling her where they were and urging her to join them. But they ordered, and the food came, and still Jen didn't appear. Annoyance shaded into worry. They drank cups of coffee and Charlotte sent another text.

'She'll be okay,' Otto said. 'You know what she's like. I expect she met someone interesting and got caught up in a conversation. It wouldn't necessarily cross her mind we'd be worrying. She lives in a dream world.'

'How can you say that, after what happened to you?' Charlotte jumped in. Then, repenting, 'I'm sorry. But honestly – it's not safe here.'

But she could see the worry in his face. Otto was trying to reassure himself. He knew at first hand how dangerous the people here could be.

Otto shook his head. They'd bought him a cheap shirt and hat from a little tourist stall to cover his burnt skin. He was chomping at the bit to return to the ruined fort to see if he could recover his ruck-sack. Would it still be there? Then the matter of his missing camera and his passport at the police station.

Charlotte sent a third text, telling Jen their plans and recom-mending they met up later at their lodgings. She urged her to text back right away, trying to keep any note of hysteria from her tone.

She and Otto took a taxi to the village and then set off on foot to the fort. It was hotter than ever, like a furnace. Hardly anyone was about. Even the dogs and pigs and goats were still, hiding out in whatever patches of shade they could find. Dust clung to her sweaty skin. Otto climbed up the hill with a purposeful stride. It didn't take him long to orientate himself, standing on a high point in the fort with his hand shading his eyes.

'It's over there I think. If no-one's taken it. By the wall.'

Otto half walked, half ran, despite the heat. Charlotte didn't try to keep up. He diminished into the distance.

'It's here! It's still here!' He jumped up and down, waving his arm. Charlotte felt a sympathetic relief. She watched him heft the pack onto his back and jog back towards her, jubilant, reunited with this symbol of security, his stuff, his portable home.

'Lucky I tucked it right out of the way! No-one found it.' He was pleased with himself. Charlotte turned to the matter of his passport.

'We're going back to the police,' she said. 'We'll go now. We have to get your passport.'

'What if they won't give it to me? What if they still think I killed her?'

'Then we'll need some legal representation, Otto. And we'll have to tell our parents what's happening. You've got to tell the police about Andreas and the others.'

230

Another taxi ride, more money taken from the budget. At the reception desk, Charlotte, polite, asked to see Inspector Sharma. The man on reception indicated seats and made a long phone call. They waited a long time, half an hour or more. Otto grew impatient and asked again. An ineffective fan swirled over their heads, stirring the overheated air. The man on reception shook his head and pointed at the seats.

They waited another half an hour. At last, a door opened and Sharma's familiar face peered at them through the opening. He gestured, urging them to step inside. Charlotte scrambled to her feet, Otto close behind her. Still without a word, the policeman shut the door behind them.

'Mr Gilmour, I'm very happy you decided to return. Your friends were very worried about you.' The inspector shook Otto's hand. Charlotte didn't miss the shrewd glance at the returning prodigal, despite the avuncular greeting.

'Where's your friend?' he said.

'Back at the beach,' Charlotte said unhappily. 'Otto was taken, inspector. Otto was kidnapped. I told you he wouldn't just run off. I told you something happened to him.'

The inspector flapped his hands.

'Please, calm down. Tell me, Mr Gilmour. Tell me where you've been.' Charlotte and Otto took seats on the far side of a desk on which a computer was surrounded by mountains of brown cardboard files. The inspector also sat down, leaning back on his chair. He steepled his fingers and nodded to Otto, encouraging him to start.

Otto took a deep breath. Charlotte could see he was nervous but he recounted the story again. From time to time she couldn't stop herself intervening, with a comment or an extra detail she remembered from his first telling. The inspector didn't speak or make any kind of note. When Otto told him about Carlo Allen and handed over the passport, Sharma's face was still impassive, giving nothing

231

away. She grew impatient, worried he wasn't taking the account seriously enough, afraid he wouldn't realise its significance.

When Otto stopped talking the inspector simply rose to his feet and thanked him. Charlotte couldn't contain herself.

'What do you think? Who are these people? Can you arrest them? What about this guy who was beaten up? Shouldn't you try and find him?'

'Please – please!' He raised both his hands. The passport waited on the table in front of him. 'Leave this matter in my hands. Mr Gilmour hasn't come to any harm. And I am very interested to hear what you have told me. Don't worry – this is something I have to sort out.'

'What are you talking about? Otto was assaulted and kidnapped!' Her anger was rising.

'Yet here he is,' the inspector soothed.

'What about Maria? What about the man who was beaten up in the jungle?' She struggled to lower her voice. It was rare she lost control of herself. Even Otto was staring at her oddly.

'You were brought in to sort this out, weren't you?' Charlotte said. 'The local police – they've been colluding in this. It's serious, isn't it? And now someone is dead, and the press are interested and you have to find out what's going on.'

The inspector's face froze momentarily. Then he carried on, as smoothly as before.

'We are continuing our investigation. Don't you think I can do my job? And now, if you'll excuse me, that is what I have to get on with now.' He shooed them towards the door.

'What about my passport?' Otto said.

'If you don't mind, we'll hold on to it just a little while longer. You're not in any hurry to leave?'

'You mean I'm still a suspect? You still think I killed Maria?'

'Nothing has been ruled out yet, Mr Gilmour. I want to be sure you don't try to leave the country before we have uncovered the truth. Please bear with us.'

They were almost out of the door when the inspector, glancing over his shoulder said, 'Actually, there is a journalist looking for you, Mr Gilmour. Have you spoken to him yet?'

Beyond the reception desk, where Charlotte and Otto had waited so long, a blond man was sitting. The policeman gestured.

'That's him. He's covering the murder.'

The reporter? Did he want to talk to them? Of course it would happen, sooner or later. Images of lurid front pages flashed in her mind, families fretting at home. The waiting man looked up, directly at Otto and Charlotte.

Otto frowned. 'What did you tell him – about me, I mean?'

The inspector shrugged. 'Nothing,' he said. 'I didn't even tell him your name, he got that from someone else.' Otto opened his mouth to speak again, but the inspector cut him off, closing the door. The reception man scowled but the reporter stood up and walked towards them with his hand extended and a genial, sympathetic smile.

'Otto Gilmour?' Perhaps in his early twenties, with a deep tan and sun-bleached hair, the man wore smart jeans and a tight, plain white T-shirt showing off a fit, possibly gym-honed, body. Very white, even teeth too and an accent Charlotte recognised, only faintly disguised, of public school.

Otto reluctantly shook the proffered hand. The reporter turned to Charlotte.

'And you are?' All charm and relaxed good manners.

'Otto's friend. We're travelling together.'

'Girlfriend, right?' He had a pair of smart sunglasses pushed back on the crown of his head.

'Friend,' Charlotte repeated. She looked at Otto. 'Don't talk to him, Otto. Let's get out of here. We need to find Jen.'

'Please.' The reporter angled his body, almost blocking their way, but not quite. 'Can I buy you a drink? I've got a taxi waiting outside – I can give you a lift. Let me take you to my hotel.'

'Why should we?' Charlotte said. 'You want a story to sell. What's in it for us?'

The reporter looked over her head, to Otto. 'I can pay you,' he said. 'If I sell the story. What've you got to lose? Just come back to the hotel and have a chat, talk things through. We'll take it from there.'

Charlotte glanced at Otto. She could see he was wavering, perhaps tempted by the option of a lift and a drink, and most of all, his own yearning to be a journalist. This man, whom Charlotte already detested, would possess a particular glamour for Otto.

'Why not? Nothing to lose,' he said, with an apologetic glance at Charlotte. 'We'll take the lift, and you can tell me what you know.'

Charlotte sat in the back of the car and glowered. The reporter – Mark Joyce, he told them – took the front seat but twisted himself round so he could talk to Otto. He was very matey and smiled a lot, showing off the perfect teeth. At first it seemed Mark Joyce only wanted to talk about himself – how he'd been living and working in India for the past six months, based in Delhi, from where he sold news stories to various national newspapers and web-based magazines. Of course Otto blabbed right out about his own work and aspirations and the two men were quickly immersed in a conversation about writing, photos, the internet, life as a freelance reporter. Charlotte scowled, and from time to time she nudged Otto with her knee, trying to warn him to watch himself, not to trust this operator. Otto, however, was oblivious, carried away by the other man's confidence and interest.

The car pulled up outside the gates of the West Wind Hotel. The driver made some incomprehensible comment into the intercom and the electric gates swung open. The car drove towards the main reception and the three passengers climbed out.

'Are you coming in too?' Mark said to Charlotte. 'I mean, don't feel you have to hang around if you've better things to do. Otto and I – well, it can get quite boring when we're talking shop.' Charlotte realised she wasn't wanted, but neither was she going to leave Otto at his mercy.

'Oh no, I'm coming too,' she said, keeping her voice light. 'Just let me make a call, I'll follow you in.'

She stood on the red-tiled veranda, taking in the enclosed garden of the West Wind Hotel. The building itself, white-walled, was U-shaped and enclosed the garden on three sides. A tall fence with black iron railings ran along the fourth side, along the road. The garden was breathtaking. Despite her disapproval, Charlotte couldn't help but admire it – the elegant trees with glossy, polished leaves, the oblong pools in which waxy white blossoms floated on dark water, the artfully artless drifts of flowers. How much precious fresh water, how much energy, to maintain this little oasis? The scent of rose and lemon drifted to her nose as she took out her mobile and checked again for a message from Jen. There was none. She tried to call her but succeeded only in reaching the answering service. She left a voice message, sent another, more urgent text.

Where RU??! Pls let us know asap. V worried! Xxxxx

She hurried into the hotel over the marble floor and into a spacious bar area overlooking another garden, with a pale blue swimming pool, and then, beyond it, the beach and the sea. Two glamorous young women and several couples in late middle-age were dispersed about the large, air-conditioned room with its leather chairs and dark wooden occasional tables. Pictures on the wall showed prints of an older India, rajahs on elephants, hunting on horseback or courting pale, jewelled maidens.

Mark was talking to a waiter. Charlotte pushed her way across the room and plonked herself onto the chair beside Otto. He glanced at her, the question on his face, and Charlotte gave her head a quick shake. No sign of Jen. Of course it was possible she was back at their room, returned from her walk and catching up on some sleep. She didn't always have her phone on her either: perhaps no need to worry?

Mark lounged back on his chair, arms and legs apart, making a display of his body in its too-tight clothes. His BlackBerry, a slim wallet and a room key lay on the table in front of him. Certainly, she observed, he'd struggle to fit them into his pockets. Mark, perhaps sensing her disapproval, smiled again and turned to Otto.

'Okay,' he said. 'You found her, the dead girl. That must have been terrible.' His tone changed: sympathy, gravity. Don't tell him anything, Charlotte willed. You know the sort of stuff newspapers print.

Perhaps Otto wasn't entirely under the reporter's spell because he didn't answer at once. Mark sat forward, resting his arms on his thighs, taking himself closer to Otto.

'Tell me what happened,' he said. 'I've heard talk you were seeing her, Maria. Is that right?'

Charlotte shot him a glance, Earlier he'd asked if she was his girlfriend.

'Otto – whatever this guy writes could be in the papers at home, where everyone you know – including your mum – as well as millions of strangers might read it. Be careful.'

Mark shook his head. 'Just a chat,' he said. 'Off the record. First I want to find out if there is a story.' He held up his hands. 'No notebook, see? No tape recorder. I just want to get the facts straight in my own mind. Then, well we can see where we go.'

The waiter appeared with three glasses and three bottles of beer. He placed them on the table.

'I'm sorry, I don't drink beer,' Charlotte said. Then, to the waiter, 'May I have a vodka and tonic please? With ice?'

Mark the journalist (had Otto actually seen any ID?) shrugged and began to talk again.

'I've been following a story here, on and off, for a few months,' Mark said. 'There's always stuff going on here – so many people coming and going, getting into scrapes. But something else has been happening. I've got some good contacts on the local police and I get emails from various people who live around the place. I've been hearing some strange things.' He poured the beer, took a drink and indicated to Otto he should do the same.

'What kind of things?' Charlotte prompted.

'There've always been drugs here. The dope's cheap of course but you can get whatever you want. People come here to party. Something more than that though – something organised. The word is,' he broke off to take another slow mouthful of beer, 'there's a new drug making the rounds. Something secret.' Now he had a confiding smile, bestowing this knowledge on his guests.

'You think Maria's death was connected to this new drug,' Otto said. 'Is that it?'

Mark sat back again, and shrugged. 'What do you think?'

Otto chewed over the information.

'So how well did you know her? Tell me how you found her,' Mark said.

So Otto told him, a simplified, emotion-free version. He'd met her a couple of times, the parties on the beach, the discovery of her body lying in the surf. Mark remained focused, absorbing the information.

'They thought I was you,' Otto said. 'I said something stupid to Maria about being a journalist, and they reckoned I was on to them. That's why they took me – because of you.'

Mark blinked. He went very still for a moment.

'I'm sorry,' he said, though it was hardly his fault. 'So they're on to me too. I shall have to watch my back. I should be safe enough here though.' He looked around him, at the safe, sturdy walls of the hotel. Charlotte detected nervousness though. Mark wasn't immune either.

'Tell us more about this secret drug,' Otto urged. 'What do you know?' Charlotte tried to relax and avoided looking at Otto.

'There've been parties, gatherings – in quiet places along the coast, and sometimes inland too. Complaints to the police about the intimidation of locals. Complaints from the locals the police are turning a blind eye, and speculating they were taking a cut. Some of

237

the locals – others seem keen to cash in, those who make money from tourists.' He eyed Otto. 'They've got something, and they don't want to share it. I want to find out more about it.'

'So what makes you think Maria was involved?'

The reporter shrugged but kept a beady eye on Otto. They were all silent for a moment, staring at one another. Stalemate. Then Mark picked up his BlackBerry, searched through its files and opened a picture on the tiny screen.

'See that?' He passed the device to Otto. 'You recognise it?'

Charlotte leaned over to see. How had he got hold of this picture? It was a copy of the post-mortem photograph, the tattoo on Maria's back.

'I've seen it before, yes. The police showed me the same picture.' Otto said. He handed it back. 'How did you get it? Does it mean something?'

'It was emailed to me. That's why I came down. Does it mean anything? Maybe. It certainly seems to be connected with this new substance. I think the in-crowd use it as their sign of belonging.'

'What's it called, this drug?' Charlotte said. 'What makes it different from all the others?'

'I don't know what it is exactly, or what it does,' Mark admitted. 'But I intend to find out. It's called Kharisma. Kharisma – with a K.'

The word seemed to dwell on the air before them. Charlotte felt a tremor of emotion, hard to quantify precisely. A curious cold thrill.

'Kharisma,' she said. Otto had been right.

'It's in the bottles of water,' Otto blurted. 'They supply it at the bars at the far end of the beach, at the parties. And in the jungle, there were crates of the stuff.'

Mark nodded. 'That's the stuff,' he said. 'Then you've taken it. Can you tell me what it's like?'

Otto managed a smile. 'Why don't you find out for yourself? There are parties at the end of the beach. It would be a great story – for you.'

'I never take drugs,' Mark said. 'But it would be a great story, yes.

You're going to get it first? Are we in competition?' His tone was a little patronising. Then he said, 'There's no reason why we can't work on this together, Otto. A joint byline. You know stuff I don't know, I know stuff you don't know. How about it?'

Charlotte stiffened. She could sense Otto's eagerness, the temptation to throw in his lot with this man, to nail the story. No doubt, in his mind, the newspaper spread was already unfolding, the splash, his name written in bold.

'Otto, there's the small matter of your involvement in the police investigation,' she said gently. 'Be careful what you say.'

Otto shook his head, perplexed. The reporter studied him, waiting for a response. Finally he rummaged in his pocket for a card and handed it over.

'I'll be here for a few days. Think it over, Otto. Give me a call. Drop by for a drink. We can talk again, okay?'

He left them alone in the bar. The place was quiet. Otto and Charlotte looked at one another. Charlotte was about to speak when Otto jumped in first.

'I know what you're going to say,' he said. 'I'm not stupid. You think I don't know about a man like that?'

Charlotte flinched. 'But you seemed . . .'

'Tempted? Of course I'm tempted, bloody hell. It's what I want to do.' He picked up the beer bottle and plucked at the paper label, tearing a narrow strip from the glass.

'For crying out loud, why are you taking it out on me?' she jumped back.

'Because I know all the self-righteous stuff going round in your mind right now. I can almost hear what you're thinking!'

Charlotte recoiled, as though the words had whipped her. All the tension and worry and weariness of the last days overwhelmed her, the effort to stay calm, to be controlled.

'You don't know what I'm thinking! You're so selfish and childish! It's all your fault we're in this mess anyway – if you hadn't gone

239

whoring after the first pretty girl you saw in Goa we'd be having a great adventure and not worrying about police and all the rest!'

Charlotte took a deep breath. She noticed she was now standing up. She wasn't naturally a loud person. She and Otto had never argued before and the strength of her own anger and the volume of her outburst shocked her. Otto looked stunned. The other people in the bar had paused their conversations and were staring at them.

Charlotte, physically shaking, lowered her voice. It felt like a kind of rupture, to have expressed her anger so openly.

'We don't know where Jen is, you haven't got your passport, your sudden girlfriend was murdered on the beach and the police still have you down as a suspect – and you want to get friendly with some piece-of-shit reporter? Don't trust him, Otto. He doesn't care about you. He's not your friend and he'll stitch you up. You know that as well as I do but it's easier for you to blame me for pointing it out.'

A flash of meanness crossed Otto's face. He shook his head.

'It's not my fault. I didn't ask for this to happen. And, yes, I did like Maria: I liked her a lot, okay? Why is that wrong? You're always walking around as though you have a broomstick up your backside, Miss Moral Highground. I liked her, and then someone hurt her and killed her and I was the one who found her dead on the beach. I was the one who carried her body out of the sea. Can you imagine what that was like?'

Looking into his face, outraged and hurt as she was, Charlotte saw the recollection of the terrible night wash over Otto. Perhaps on the night itself he had simply acted and survived, but in remembering the event, he was also reliving the grief and horror of finding Maria in all her glamorous youth, lying broken and inert at the sea's edge, in the darkness. The scene played itself in Charlotte's imagination, the night and the quiet, the sound of the sea, and Otto heaving the girl's body out of the water as he had described. She sat down again, looked at him – stretched out her hand to touch his arm.

'I'm sorry,' she said. 'It must have been horrible.'

240

Otto flinched away. 'I need some space,' he said. 'I'm going out for a bit. Leave me alone, will you? Your compassion is almost as hard to take as your righteousness. I know I've behaved badly.' He rose to his feet and strode out of the hotel bar, pushing the big leather chairs out of his way as he went. The disturbance seemed to hang on the air in his wake, even after he'd disappeared and Charlotte had heard the bang of the main doors out of the reception area.

She stayed where she was, utterly miserable. Tears threatened but she choked them back. The glass of vodka and tonic rested on the table in front of her, cold and glittering, so she picked it up and savoured the bright, sharp taste of it. There was no reason for her to stay in this air-conditioned, artificial environment but she couldn't muster the will to leave. Here it was at least safe and comfortable and she didn't know what to do next. The day was coming to its end and still no word from Jen. She was alone. She had nowhere to go.

Charlotte considered what Mark had told them, about the drug, Kharisma, and the group who were taking it. In the light of this information, Otto's abduction made sense. Andreas and Kate, the people he had told her about, must be members of the group and they'd feared Otto was on to them. Presumably they had heard about the investigative reporter. Was it possible they'd confused Otto (blond British would-be journalist) with Mark, who was truly on their tail?

She curled up in the safety of the chair, drank the vodka, and ordered a second. When the glass was empty, a pleasurable feeling of distance and relaxation began to blossom, blotting out some of the misery. It was nothing to do with her. She wasn't interested in drugs and as soon as they'd cleared matters up with the police she could be on her way. Goa had been spoiled.

She bought a third measure, cradled the cold glass in her hand, and closed her eyes. Why did she think she was responsible for everyone else? Otto and Jen had left her, both of them, so why should she beat herself up worrying?

Charlotte woke up. What time was it? She twisted in her seat to stare through the large window over the hotel's rear garden and the sea. Hours had passed. The sky was turquoise, darkening over the horizon. Her mind felt very clear and empty as though the drink and sleep had scoured it out. She checked her phone – no messages. The bar was busier, presumably the hotel guests, all of whom appeared well-dressed, were enjoying a drink before dinner.

'You're still here?'

Charlotte looked up.

It was Mark, of course. Now he had a white linen jacket over his T-shirt and the sunglasses had gone. He looked clean and refreshed, as though he too had slept, and then showered and anointed himself with deodorant and creams. She smelled the understated perfume of an expensive aftershave.

Charlotte shrugged. There was something intriguing about him, repellent as he was.

'Where's Otto?'

'Oh, he's gone home. Back to our lodging, anyway.' She affected nonchalance but it crossed her mind Mark had left them alone precisely so they might have an argument, that he had anticipated this. Had he even listened in, hiding around the corner?

She shook her head. Paranoid thinking. Mark wasn't as clever as all that.

'Can I buy you another drink? Same again?'

'Sure. Thanks.' What else did she have to do? She was tired of nannying Otto. Well let him take care of himself.

Mark took the seat opposite. He smiled. 'You don't like me much, do you?'

Charlotte shrugged again. 'Not really, no.'

'Why's that? You don't know anything about me.' He seemed softer this evening, his face more open.

'Cos you wanted to buy Otto. To use him. That's what you do, isn't it? I hate the tabloids. They sell fear.' She wrinkled her nose, took a swig from her glass.

'So it's what I do you don't like. I shouldn't take it personally.'

Charlotte laughed. 'But it's what you, personally, choose to do. Hard to separate that out from who you are.'

Mark considered, looking at her all the time. 'Are you hungry? Would you like something to eat? I'm on my way to dinner.'

Charlotte hesitated. Was this wise? Something chimed in her mind . . . what was that saying about supping with the devil? But she was hungry, and she didn't want to think, and she didn't want to go back to the room where Jen and Otto might or might not be.

'Okay,' she said.

Marble pillars forested the hotel restaurant and a fountain played into a pool at the centre. They dined at a table covered in a white tablecloth. The waiting staff were silent but attentive, serving up lobster and fruit and salad. Mark ordered a bottle of white wine, which, on top of the vodka, emboldened Charlotte.

Mark asked her why she'd come to India and she told him she had signed up for a tiger conservation project at a national park. He told her something about his own experiences in India then asked her more about herself and her environmental activism. Charlotte ate, ate ravenously, and drank another glass of wine. The food was fantastic.

They talked about their respective families: Mark's parents were retired and he was worried about his mother's deteriorating health. They lived in the Lake District, apparently, a region about which he waxed lyrical, suggesting Charlotte should visit it for hiking. He was warm, personable and very funny. Charlotte began to relax and enjoy herself. The problems besetting her beyond the hotel walls melted away. Through a pleasant haze of intoxication she wondered, with some surprise – is he flirting with me? And imagined what it would be like to be held by this fit, fragrant man, so much more grown-up than Otto, more assured and comfortable in the world, a man who wouldn't need to be organised and looked after.

She didn't remember ordering a dessert but a dish of chocolate, meringue and ice cream appeared in front of her, and she ate it,

243

savouring the mix of textures, crisp, smooth and soft, the melting on her tongue. Don't drink any more, a quiet voice warned from her mind's interior. You've had enough now. Don't drink any more. The glass was full again but Charlotte didn't touch it.

The meal rounded off with sugared coffee. When the waiter appeared with the cups on a tray, Mark asked him to take it outside – they would drink in the garden. They stood up, Charlotte a little unsteadily, and Mark took her hand, leading her through the tables and out of a glass door. Outside, beyond the air conditioning, the night air was warm and soft. The watered, pampered plants in the garden gave off streamers of perfume, reminiscent of frankincense. Charlotte, normally so hard-headed and scornful of romance, found herself thinking of the gardens of Rajahs, the pictures in the hotel of the pale, jewelled girls courted by princes. The hotel was a lie, of course, sucking up local resources, an oasis for the rich. Around the garden rose the metal railings, and beyond it the real world where real people struggled and worked and eked out a living. But she pushed this aside – just for now. Something about the evening reminded her of those tales of King Arthur in which knights chanced upon fair castles, where they dined and drank and were tended by the fairest of maidens – only to wake and find themselves lying on foggy, barren hillsides, all earthly pleasures vanished into the air, naked and stained with sin.

Charlotte sighed, a mixture of pleasure and regret. She was leaning against Mark, her head resting on his warm, hard shoulder. Above, black foliage edged a sky of brilliant stars. She placed her hand on his belly, feeling the muscle beneath thin layers of fabric, and a quick electric thrill passed through the pit of her own belly. Why shouldn't she? They'd come looking for adventure and here it was, waiting for her. So why on earth shouldn't she? Yes, Charlotte, who was always so good and sensible and responsible, who always did the right thing.

She raised her face to be kissed. Mark didn't hesitate. He put his hand on her cheek and pressed his mouth against hers. He tasted of

244

heat and coffee and his tongue slipped between her lips, touching the inside of her mouth very gently. Charlotte swooned (what an old-fashioned word, some cooler part of her mind observed), drowning in the mix of drink and spiralling lust, turning so she could press herself against the length of him. They remained so for a minute or two – until Mark broke away.

'What? What is it?'

'I'm sorry, Charlotte, this isn't right. Slow down.'

'What isn't right?' Already her mood was changing. The effect of the drink seemed to ebb away in just a moment or two. This was a rejection.

'How old are you?'

'Eighteen.'

'I'm twenty-three.'

'Is that a problem?'

He laughed gently. 'No, not really. But like this? You're drunk, for a start. That's a problem. I wouldn't feel happy about it.'

'So you do have a conscience.'

'In some areas, yes. Don't sound so surprised.'

Then he said, with some hesitation, 'And I don't think you would normally do this.'

'What, you mean I'm not that sort of girl?' The remark came out more sharply than she had intended. The rejection was being wrapped as something else.

'I'd hate you to do something you later regretted, that's all. I'm not that sort of man.'

They remained as they were for a few minutes, sitting together, Mark's arm still around her. Then Mark said, 'I'll take you back to your place. We can check Otto is okay.'

'And Jen. I hope Jen is back too.'

'Jen, yes. Your other friend.'

'How do you know about Jen?'

'I told you, I have my contacts here.' They were walking through the hotel. Mark had his arm around her. At the front gates several taxis waited. Mark helped her inside the first one and got in beside her.

'Your contacts – in the police?' Charlotte asked.

Mark nodded. 'Yes. And in other places. I'm good at making friends. Getting people onside. And I can help them out.'

'Pay them, you mean.'

'Sometimes.'

'So what do you know about us?'

'Just that you and Jen were very conspicuous the other night – asking a lot of questions. People noticed.'

Charlotte lapsed into silence. She was very tired and her mouth was dry. She wanted to be in bed. The journey took only a few minutes and she could see the light was on in the room she had shared with Otto and Jen the previous night.

'I'll be okay,' she said. 'They're back. Thanks for the lift, Mark.' Before she could climb out, Mark leaned over and kissed her again, lightly on the lips.

'If you still want to see me in the morning, when you've sobered up and remembered I'm an old and evil reporter, you know where to find me,' he said.

Charlotte felt a quiver of anxiety as she fumbled for her key. It was after three, later than she had realised, and she'd behaved badly. She opened the door. Would Otto and Jen be waiting for her with disapproving faces, knowing what she'd been up to? Even worse, what if they weren't there, despite the light?

She pushed the door. A young black woman she had never seen before was sitting on the side of a bed, staring at her. Charlotte drew up short.

'Gina,' she said. 'Are you Gina? Where's Otto? What are you doing here?'

Then Jen stepped from the bathroom.

'Hello, Charlie,' she said. 'I'm back.'

Otto

Saturday afternoon

Otto stormed out of the hotel, choking on anger and guilt. Why had he sounded off at Charlotte? What had possessed him? She was straight and kind and honest – and he'd been a complete shit, striking out at her because he was upset. He recalled the stricken look on her face.

He strode through the garden and out of the hotel gates, back onto the dusty road running along the coast. He walked fast, despite the heat, till perspiration dripped from his face. He hardly noticed his surroundings, caught in the black knot of his thoughts.

Who was Charlotte to be lecturing him? How did she know what he had felt for Maria? Was it jealousy, simply that? The same series of thoughts revolved in his head, stoking his anger.

He walked for a long time, and didn't stop till he reached the distant stretch of beach used for the eternal night-time party. The place was deserted in the afternoon, two of the bars closed up. The man at the one open bar eyed him suspiciously when he ordered an orange juice. No doubt this was a dangerous place for him to be, but he was beyond caring. He wanted to face them, Andreas and the crowd.

Otto sat in the shade of a palm leaf awning and stared out at the sea. Sunlight bleached the sand white, creating a haze over its surface. The heat seemed to suppress sound. The faint, perpetual scent of fish touched his nose. A brown dog, thin and whippy like a dingo, lay panting underneath the bar.

Kharisma.

He turned over in his mind the conversation with the reporter. This missing piece of the puzzle made the picture clear.

The cult of Kharisma – he'd stumbled on it, hadn't he? Clearly Kate and Andreas, his kidnappers, were part of this secret culture. The graffitied chapel in the jungle, the parties and the intimidating of local people proved this. And Maria was involved. Maria *had been* involved. Was that why she was murdered? Had she shared a secret, or conversely, refused to share it? Had she been trying to recruit him into the group running the operation, Andreas and the others with their hideout in the jungle?

Then he'd told her he was a journalist – and created the confusion with Mark, the real journalist, similarly blond and British. Andreas had found out she'd been talking to a journalist.

He remembered the story Kate had told him, Maria writing and inviting her to India. Presumably Maria's involvement had preceded Kate's. And what was this substance, surrounded by secrecy? What did it do that made it different to the other chemical highs?

And where was Jen? Worry floated in his mind. He wanted to be sure she was safe. He couldn't think why she would be in danger, but anything was possible. If she'd been asking questions, might she, like the man in the jungle, be punished and silenced? No – that couldn't happen to Jen. How much longer should he wait before going to Sharma to say she was missing? She'd been gone most of the day. Would Sharma take him seriously?

He thought about the police inspector too. No doubt Sharma knew all about this mooted party crowd and their mysterious narcotic. He'd been brought in to clean up, since the local police weren't taking care of it. When he'd shown them the picture of Maria's tattoo, probably he knew already what it signified. Had it been a test then, showing them the sign?

He remembered hearing about the warehouse parties in the nineties, when information about illegal raves was circulated just hours before people in the know converged on some out-of-the-way venue to dance and take Ecstasy. Presumably these people operated in the same fashion, with texts or messages over the internet. What would happen now if he googled Kharisma – would any reference to the drug be revealed?

He closed his eyes, draining the last drops of orange juice. It flashed into his brain that somehow, somewhere, he had already encountered Maria's killer. He'd met so many people. She'd introduced him to Gina, and the two very serious men on the beach – what were their names . . . Max. Max and Kumar. Had it been one of them? Presumably they were friends with Andreas, Kate and the others. And what about hippy Jim, who had warned him to get away? Was he part of this too? Or had it been Andreas himself? He was brutal enough. But Maria had been his girlfriend, surely that would have counted for something?

Underneath the bar, the dog snapped at something before resting its head on its front paws. The barman was sitting motionless in the deep shade, waiting for the party to come. It seemed the heat had stopped time itself. Everything was still, except for Otto, who put down the glass and headed over the burning sand to the sea.

He had sandals on his feet but the burning grains stung his sunburnt skin. He pulled off the T-shirt as he walked, dropped it along with his jeans and shoes at the rim of the sea and ran into the water wearing just his boxers. He plunged in. The water embraced him, soothingly cool, laving his sunburnt body. He dived underwater, lifted and rocked by the waves, pushing his way through the sea with strong sweeps of his arms. Then he drifted to the surface and lay, arms and legs spread, his face down into the water. Only every now and then did he turn his head to the side to take a fresh breath. The sea carried him, held him up. He couldn't see or hear anything, except for the sea.

Afterwards he returned to his seat at the bar and waited for the slow afternoon to pass. It was night he wanted, when the music started up and the party-going tourists emerged from their daytime lairs to drink and smoke and dance. He wasn't afraid any more, only furious, boiling with a feverish desire to punish Maria's killer. He was tired of being the uncomprehending victim, the kid backpacker. Gina, Kate, Andreas, the police, Mark the reporter – they had all kept him in the dark, hiding information about the murder, let him stumble along in ignorance.

He rewound the previous days in his mind, going over each conversation, sliding the pieces of the puzzle around. He called up each of the main players and questioned them in his mind. Some of their answers he knew. Some he extrapolated and guessed. They were part of this Kharisma community: Gina, Max, Kumar, Kate, Andreas and Maria.

One of them had killed Maria, thinking she'd sold the story to the British journalist – betrayed them, shared their secrets. What if he'd been seen with her, romantically involved, and she'd been murdered to keep her quiet, and out of revenge? He thought of the horrible punishment delivered to the young man in the jungle, for his betrayal.

His thoughts burned away, leaving only blank rage, and a keen sense of purpose.

The crowd assembled, as it did every night, dribs and drabs, girls in twos and threes, young men in gangs, squaring up, laughing too loudly. They were bronzed or sunburnt, mostly young, eager to get high, to dance and talk and flirt in the cool of the night.

Otto was patient. He bided his time, drinking only orange juice and keeping a careful watch on the crowd. Once or twice girls approached him but he brushed them away. As the darkness deepened, the music started up and the sound of the sea was drowned in the violent pulse of the music which beat against the bodies of the revellers, goading them to dance.

Still Otto waited. He felt himself distinct from the rest of the party. The music was around him but not inside his head. His mind was clear, bright with purpose. The partygoers, drunk or high, shadows sliding over their faces, held some resemblance to those paintings of the damned his mother liked, hell as depicted by Hieronymus Bosch.

His phone bleeped. A message from Jen. She apologised for her absence, said she was safe, with Gina, and would see him soon.

He scanned the crowd again. There – there she was. His eyes fixed on a young woman walking at the edge of the lighted area. It was Kate. She was carrying a crate of bottles, heading towards one of the bars. She spoke briefly to one of the young men behind the bar, passed over the crate, and walked away again. Otto gripped the glass tight, watching her all the while. Then he stood up, let the glass go, and strode across the sand towards her.

It wasn't easy, this pursuit. People got in his way. More than once, he lost sight of her. He pushed someone out of his path and was pushed back with a curse. He saw her again, sensed her ahead of him, as though a magic cord bound them together, drawing Otto inexorably closer.

She was wearing a pair of very short denim shorts and a vest top, held a bottle in her hand, though he could see it was beer, not Kharisma. Her hair was tied back in a careless ponytail and she walked as though she were unaware of her pursuer. They were clear of the crowd now. Otto slowed his pace a little, maintaining the distance between them. This time he wanted the upper hand. As before, a number of campfires burned on the beach, around which small groups of people gathered to talk and smoke dope. Kate walked to one of these and dropped down to the sand opposite a tall man. Even in the darkness, and from behind, Otto recognised Andreas.

251

Jen

Sunday: early hours

A single lantern hung from a rod at the front of the boat. The sea was black as jet, opaque and solid-looking, a gem that gently undulated, hunched and swelled and swooned underneath them. The sky was a dome of black, pierced by the needles of stars.

The oars dipped and rose in the water. Kumar rowed, taking them expertly from the secret harbour onto the open sea. They were heading for the mainland, Gina sitting beside her. Max remained behind.

The effects of the island's spring water were receding but hadn't entirely disappeared. Jen was still a little disorientated, the night's colours more vivid and her thoughts like trailing threads that frayed and tangled and didn't always make sense. She stared at the sea, the wrinkling surface. Her mind was like this, an unknowable dark place from which thoughts jumped, like glittering fish. Who knows where they come from or where they go?

So much made sense now. Her childhood visions, the spirits and energies she had seen, most often at times of stress or distress – they had been forewarnings, a crack in the door now opened by the water bubbling onto the holy island. Humans were animals evolved to survive in a material world and their organs of perception – eyes, ears, nose, taste, touch – had developed solely to ensure survival. How limited that made them – how much more there was to perceive. A dog's keen nose opened to it a realm of smells a human could only try to imagine. A bee, similarly, sees light and colour beyond the limits of human senses. They needed these skills to survive in the world, as a dog or a bee. Take it further than that. Imagine we are shut in dark boxes, and the boxes have only small openings that allow us to reach for food and water, and that occasionally we bump into other people and we can talk to them from our boxes, and maybe rub hands with them. Those small openings are our senses. So how can we ever know what lies beyond, what reality truly is, when our window upon it is so limited?

Jen shook her head. Wasn't that what the island water had done? Somehow it had torn away a veil from her mind (a veil which in her case had perhaps already been faulty) and revealed this to her for the first time. It was frightening, and also reassuring. She remembered the statue of Shiva, Lord of the Dance. That was what he represented, wasn't it? The drumbeat of existence, the dance of making and unmaking. Free yourself from the illusion of the material world.

'Are you okay, Jen?' Although Gina was sitting right next to her, the voice seemed to come from far away, rudely intruding. The silver fish of Jen's thought disappeared into the black water of her mind.

'Why don't you text your friends now? You should get a signal soon,' Gina said.

Jen blinked, and shook her head, not as a negative reply to Gina's question but to focus herself, to be in the world again. She took out her phone and typed a message to Otto.

'Are you feeling okay?' Gina repeated.

'Um, yes, I'm fine,' she said. The answer sounded clumsy and absurd, and she laughed. 'I'm fine.'

'We have to find your friends,' Gina said. 'They'll be worried – wondering where you've gone.'

Jen nodded. Yes, they would be worried.

'And you'll have to tell them you're going to stay with us.'

Charlotte

Sunday: early hours

Charlotte glanced from Gina to Jen. Jen looked strange: wide-eyed, fragile. It was something Charlotte had seen before, the times Jen was afflicted by her fits – her questionable visions, seeing supposed spirits and ley lines and ghosts.

'Jen, are you okay? Where have you been?' Her voice sounded rather sharper than she had intended. She tried again.

'I'm sorry, I mean, we've been worried about you.'

Jen opened and closed her mouth, as though she were trying to speak. But Gina piped up.

'She's been with us.' A smooth American accent, a confident tone.

'Are you Gina?' Charlotte repeated. Again the question sounded a little too aggressive, but anxiety was rising. She wanted to know what was going on.

Gina nodded.

'So where's Otto? Have you seen him?'

'No. We've only just arrived. There was no-one here.'

'Where have you been, Charlie?' Jen piped up. 'Why isn't Otto with you?'

Charlotte rubbed her face with the palm of her hand. She felt thick-headed, vaguely ashamed of her dinner at the hotel and its aftermath.

'We had a row,' she said. 'We met this reporter and spoke to him. Then Otto started arguing with me and he stormed off.'

255

'How long ago?'

Charlotte shook her head. 'I don't know. In the afternoon.'

They were silent for a moment, all the unanswered questions hovering in the air between them. Charlotte picked up a plastic water bottle from her bed and gulped down several mouthfuls of warmish water. She drank again, draining the bottle. Despite the afternoon nap, she longed to lie down and close her eyes and sleep for a very long time. That was not to be. Gina was still standing there, evidently waiting for something.

Charlotte walked past her into the bathroom and locked the door. She peed, washed her face, brushed her teeth and combed her hair. She wanted to be wide awake, to freshen up. She also wanted to wash away any last trace of her contact with Mark, superstitiously worried Gina or Jen would detect the connection. She didn't hurry.

When at last she was ready, Charlotte took a deep breath and stepped back into the main room. She looked at Gina and said, 'The reporter told us all about it.'

Gina and Jen were now sitting side by side on one of the beds, facing her.

'Told you what?' Gina said. Her voice was level.

'About Kharisma – the secret parties. The tattoo thing.'

Gina remained calm. Even her hands were still, cradled one in another on her lap. She raised her face and looked directly at Charlotte.

'You know a little, but you don't know it all.'

'That's why Maria was killed, wasn't it? She was involved in all this drugs stuff.' Her voice was rising again. Something sparked in Jen.

'Is that right?' Jen said. 'Is Maria . . . was Maria . . .?'

Gina raised her hand and placed it on Jen's upper arm to soothe her. It annoyed Charlotte that Gina the newcomer should seem so much in charge, that she should take it on herself to be Jen's protector.

256

Gina pressed her lips together, considering. Then she said, 'Charlotte, please, sit down.'

Charlotte didn't move.

'Please. Let me explain – at least, as much as I can.'

Charlotte glanced at Jen, who nodded encouragingly. So Charlotte did as she was told.

Gina said, 'There's a secret spring near here, from which mystics and holy men have been drinking for hundreds of years. For thousands of years, maybe. The water is special – contains something – which affects the minds of those who drink it.'

'That's Kharisma?' Charlotte interrupted, disbelieving. 'It's spring water?' She looked from Gina to Jen, and seeing her face, her wide-open expression, it occurred to her Jen had already taken this poisonous stuff, the drug, whatever it was.

'No,' Gina said fiercely. 'It's not Kharisma. The water is only truly potent if you drink it on the island. Soon after, exposed to the atmosphere perhaps, taken off the island, its particular powers decay. It only works properly if you drink the water at its source. But if you do take it away – bottle it, drink it later – it does still have an effect – just a very different effect.'

'What sort of effect?' It was Jen who asked.

'It becomes a much more regular sort of high,' Gina said, almost contemptuously. 'Like Ecstasy, but better. You can dance all night, enjoy benign hallucinations, heightened senses. Sometimes people have visions of gods fighting in the sky, that kind of stuff.'

'No wonder it's popular,' Charlotte observed. 'So the party people – they take this Kharisma water to have a good time. But you don't approve, do you? What am I missing?'

'It's not something to be squandered in parties,' Gina said, finally impassioned. 'The spring water is a gift. A sacrament. It's not a kick, not the latest designer drug. It's not to be abused.

'After two days, the water has no effect at all. Whatever it is in the spring, it becomes inert. It's very unstable. I've been studying the

257

water at the university – trying to work out the content, what chemical creates these effects. I've had some ideas, but so far nothing conclusive.'

'Why are you telling me this?' Charlotte said.

'Because you need to understand. Otto is still in danger and we need to help him.'

'Why is he in danger? He's got nothing to do with your drug stuff. Is it Andreas? The man who kidnapped Otto? Andreas is one of your lot, right?'

Gina nodded. 'To start with, he was one of us, yes, so he knows about the island and the spring. It was something we shared together. But he had other ideas. Andreas saw it was something he could exploit – that he could use to make money, big money.

'He started persuading people to his point of view. He seduced Maria, and then Kate. He is a very cold, manipulative man. He wanted to sell the water, to take it away from the island, so he bought a boat, and carried barrels of it off the island. That wasn't easy – the island is quite inaccessible, heard to reach, so he had to recruit people to help him. Then they set up parties and started selling the water. Taking money for it. Making themselves a fortune. They've quite an operation running now – a boat visits the island every two days. We've tried to stop them, but you know what they're prepared do, and there were only three of us. We were helpless.

'They called it Kharisma, the big idea. And we've heard terrible things, what Andreas is doing to keep control of the operation.'

Charlotte nodded. 'Otto told us,' she said with a shiver. 'He saw for himself, in the jungle, some guy getting beaten in the jungle.'

'It's been going on for months now,' Gina said 'At first the police turned a blind eye, silenced by a few bribes. But word got out. Apparently there's a new policeman investigating, and now this journalist too.'

Jen had been staring at the floor. Now she raised her face and gazed at Charlotte. She didn't look right – there was a terrible vacancy about her as though she were only partially awake.

'You've taken it, haven't you, Jen, this poisoned water.' Charlotte wanted to shake her. How could she have been so stupid?

'Tell her, Jen,' Gina said.

'Tell me what?'

A flutter of panic crossed Jen's face. Charlotte wanted to slap her, hug her, wake her up to her old self.

'I'm staying here, Charlie,' Jen appealed. 'This is what I came for, to India. I understand it now. This place was calling me. I had to come here and I've found what I was looking for. It all makes perfect sense. This is where I belong.'

'You're staying here?' Charlotte said. 'What are you talking about?'

'You can go on to your tiger reservation; I'm going to stay here, in Goa,' Jen said. Gina nodded approvingly.

Charlotte shook her head. 'No you're not. Don't be stupid. You don't know what you're saying. I'm not leaving you behind with her.'

'It's not up to you,' Gina said reasonably. 'It's Jen's choice to make.'

'I'm not leaving my friend with you and your druggy mates,' Charlotte said, her voice rising. 'For crying out loud, Maria was murdered. And now, Gina, I want you to leave.' She stood up and marched to the door. 'Get out, please. Get out.'

Gina remained calm. She looked at Jen, then at Charlotte.

'We have to find Otto. He might go after Andreas. I'm afraid Andreas will kill him.'

Otto

Sunday: early hours

Otto squatted in the dark, tracing patterns in the sand with his finger, keeping a close watch on Kate and Andreas. They were engaged in an animated conversation but Otto couldn't hear what they were saying. He made out Andreas's low voice, observed Kate's gesticulations and strained his ears to make out the subject of their discussion. He edged as close as possible without being seen.

'We're closing up tonight,' Andreas said. 'This is the last. No more big parties on the beach. It's too dangerous.'

Kate said something Otto couldn't hear, and Andreas responded with a shake of his head: 'The new man at the police – it's too risky.'

The little bonfires crackled, gold and orange flowers on the sand. The musky-sweet smell of dope hung on the air. Otto wasn't going to let Andreas out of his sight. He felt calm and awake, entirely present, waiting for the moment to move. The right time would come, he knew it.

After a time someone called out to Kate. She stood up, shaking her head at Andreas, and headed away from him towards the party crowd. And then Andreas was alone, staring into the fire, the light moving on his face. Still Otto waited, peering through the darkness at the man he believed had killed Maria.

Andreas raised his head as though he'd caught the scent of something. Did he sense a watcher? Otto measured him up, the strong, heavy body, the powerful shoulders and arms. What chance for Maria? He imagined it, the slender girl fighting the implacable man, a scuffle in the water, Andreas holding her wrists in one huge hand, stooping for a rock and bashing it against her head and the skull caving, the rise of blood, Maria's eyes glazing as she fell to her knees and then, native grace extinguished, down onto the sand. Had he checked she was dead? Did he run – or walk – sure of himself and certain he hadn't been seen? Either way, he hadn't gone far. Surely it had been Andreas who'd returned and taken Otto's camera.

'How long will you wait?' The solemn voice pierced the darkness. Andreas stared through the night, directly to the place where Otto crouched. His eyes glittered in the firelight. For a few moments neither Otto nor Andreas moved.

Finally Andreas shrugged. He picked up some pieces of dried stick and dropped them on the fire.

'You want to ask me something?' he said, speaking to the darkness and to Otto, waiting within it. 'Well, ask away.'

Otto rose to his feet. He stepped towards the fire and sat down beside it, facing Andreas. He felt its heat on his body, knew the light would reveal his face as it had revealed Andreas to him.

'I spoke to him today,' Otto said. 'The man you thought I was. The British journalist. He's on to you. He told me about Kharisma, and what you're doing.'

Andreas stared at Otto, with bright blue eyes. His expression didn't alter.

'It doesn't matter. We're leaving Goa,' he said. 'This isn't the only place the water flows. There are other springs in India. Too many people here – and now, too much trouble.'

'It's a risk you being here, on the beach.'

Andreas shrugged. 'I'll be gone tomorrow.' He looked incapable of fear.

The fire crackled. The other people on the beach seemed to recede into the distance. Even the backdrop of music was far away: only this one primordial scene, the two men, enemies, staring at one another across the flames.

'Why did you kill her?' Otto said. The question hovered between them, almost tangible. Andreas moved his head very slightly, indicating a denial.

'Maria was beautiful, wasn't she?' he said. 'You think you were the first boy to fall in love with her?'

Otto quivered. 'She was your girlfriend,' he said. 'Then how could you kill her?'

'What makes you think it was me?'

'Putting the pieces together. Working it out. I met the journalist today – the one who's after you. Mark Joyce, he's called. A blond British guy – like me. You thought I was him, didn't you? You thought Maria had betrayed you by talking to me – that she'd sold the story. Sold you out.'

Andreas said, 'Maria loved me, Otto. She would do whatever I asked her. Anything I wanted, I could have.' He snapped his fingers. 'She was very lonely. She didn't have anyone. She knew everyone but she had no-one to belong to. Until she met me.'

He held Otto's gaze. 'I could wind her around my little finger,' he said. 'I can see the doubt in your eyes. You're thinking – how could she have belonged to him when she flirted with me? Don't take yourself so seriously. You were nothing. We're not talking about a bourgeois marriage. I am talking about power.'

'So you must have been angry, thinking she'd broken away from you. You must have been furious, when you thought she was having an affair with the journalist trying to uncover your project.'

Andreas didn't answer. He stood up, his movements slow and deliberate.

'Shall we walk?'

Otto hesitated. He knew how dangerous the man was but he felt a compulsion to follow him. Otto's safety lay in the proximity of these

263

other people. Step away, into the anonymity of the moonlit beach, and he would be alone – and vulnerable.

That was what he wanted, wasn't it? To be alone with Andreas, despite the risk. He wanted revenge.

Otto remembered the time he'd watched Maria and Andreas sitting on the beach together, talking, while he was sitting on the terrace of the restaurant. He recalled the jealousy he'd felt seeing Maria so relaxed and intimate with this other man.

For the first time that night, Otto felt a flicker of fear. The longing to punish Andreas had grown and grown all the long, hot afternoon. Grief and anger had combusted. Andreas. Find Andreas.

It was inevitable, this walk on the beach with Andreas, the final piece of the pattern that held the three of them together, Maria and Andreas, Maria and Otto – and now, Otto and Andreas.

Otto stood up.

'This way,' he said. They would walk towards the place he had found Maria. 'Where's my camera?'

'Kate has it.' Andreas walked by his side. They were of a similar height and stride. Perhaps someone seeing them would wonder if they were brothers.

The two men skirted the bars and the crowd and headed down the beach to the sea's edge, where the wet sand shone white in the moonlight.

Jen

Sunday: early hours

They stood on the beach, staring at the inevitable party. Charlotte had her mobile pressed to her ear. She shook her head.

'He's not answering,' she said. 'His phone's switched off.'

'How are we going to find him?' Jen surveyed the crowd of revellers, intimidated by the number of them, the noise and the harsh lights. She didn't like it here – wanted to be somewhere quiet and soothing where her flayed senses wouldn't be subjected to this overload.

'You go round to the left. Jen and I will go the other way. If you see him or Andreas text me right away. I'll do the same,' Gina said.

'Jen's coming with me.' Charlotte jumped in.

Jen, worried they might start arguing, turned to Gina, 'It's okay. I'll go with Charlie.'

Was the crowd more boisterous tonight? Perhaps a crowd of the innumerable drinkers and dancers were about to leave and were enjoying a last night of abandon before returning to grey, cheerless January Britain, to jobs and responsibilities. The faces of young men, slick with sweat, leered and cheered. They leaped on the sand with bottles in their hands. Jen, mouse-like and hunched over, grasped Charlotte's arm and followed her, skirting the crowd, scanning the faces.

They weaved in and out between clots of people, peering into the brighter light nearer the dance floor and then out into the surrounding darkness, hoping to catch a glimpse of Otto, hoping they were not too late.

They completed a fruitless circuit.

'Where is he?' Charlotte's face crumpled in frustration. She looked very pale and tired, her skin bleached by the artificial light. She took out her mobile and called him again. Still no answer.

'What are we going to do?' Jen's voice quivered.

'We have to look again,' Charlotte said. 'Go through the crowd – he can't be far away.'

Jen didn't want to trawl around the beach party a second time.

'Come on then. Let's try again.'

A middle-aged man with a paunch and shaven head seized Jen. Blurred tattoos covered his arm, which she batted away, earning a stream of obscenities. Three girls in miniskirts stepped into her path, staggering and laughing. The music pulsed through her body, invaded her skull, an ocean of sound in which she was drowning.

'Charlie!' she called out. Charlotte was ploughing on ahead of her, pushing her way through the crowd, an unstoppable force.

'Charlie!' she tried again, struggling to make herself heard.

'What? What is it? Have you seen him?'

'No – no I need to get out. I feel sick. I can't stand it.'

Charlotte stared at her. She didn't look well either – pale and strained. She opened her mouth as though to say something but Jen spoke first.

'Please – you come too. He's not here.'

Something passed across Charlotte's face – dread perhaps. She pressed her lips together, making them thin. Her eyes filled.

'Come on,' Jen said. 'We'll find him. But not here. He isn't here.'

Two minutes later they were sitting on the beach beyond the reach of the worst of the music. Light from Charlotte's mobile flared into the darkness. A text.

'It's Gina,' she said.

266

'Has she found him?'

Charlotte frowned, reading the screen.

'No. But she's found Kate, Andreas's other girlfriend. D'you remember? The girl Otto told us about.' Charlotte began feverishly texting, sent a reply.

'I'm telling them where we are,' she said. 'They're coming to find us.'

A minute or so later, Gina was running towards them; following behind, a tall, fierce-looking young woman.

'This is Kate,' she said, out of breath. 'She said she was with Andreas just a few minutes ago but he's gone now, she doesn't know where.'

Charlotte looked from Gina to Kate.

'I'm calling the police,' Charlotte said.

'What? What the hell?' Kate burst out. 'Don't do that.'

Charlotte ignored her. 'That police inspector gave me a number to call. You're not going to stop me.' She held the phone to her ear and strode away from the others so they couldn't hear what she said. A minute later she returned, her face set.

'Did you say that he killed her?' Gina's voice was level and quiet. They all turned to look at her.

No-one spoke for a moment – then Kate said, 'What did you say?'

'Andreas killed Maria.'

'No, he didn't! He wouldn't do that.' Kate's voice began to rise. 'Why would he kill her? He couldn't do it, he loved her.' How much did it cost her to admit it? She was in love with a man who had killed his other girlfriend – her own friend – Maria.

'He said it was one of your crazy friends, Gina, one of those guys you hang around with. He told me not to tell the police, they would-n't believe us, that we'd have to get our own revenge.' The words came faster and faster. Perspiration broke out in beads on Kate's face. She was climbing to some emotional crescendo.

'It wasn't one of us, Kate. It had to be Andreas,' Gina said, interrupting her.

Kate continued the denials but Charlotte broke in, cutting off the flow.

'Look, we have to find Otto. Please – will you help us? Otto hasn't done anything to deserve this. He's just caught up in it because he got involved with Maria.'

Kate was brought up short. She stared at Charlotte. Jen followed up.

'He's our friend, Kate. Please.'

Kate was breathing heavily, overcome by emotion. She looked from Charlotte to Jen and to Gina, apparently confused, not knowing whom to trust or what to do.

Her voice was flat now, passion drained away. 'I don't know where they are.'

'They can't be far away,' Jen said. 'Not if you've only just left Andreas.' She turned to Gina. 'Do you know where Otto found her? Maria, I mean. Where did he find the body?'

Kate's face became very still.

Gina took a deep breath. She said, 'You think that's where they've gone?'

Otto

Sunday: early hours

They strode along the beach, side by side. Moonlight played over the surface of the water. They didn't speak for a time, simply matching stride for stride on the firm sand at the sea's edge. Nonetheless, Otto was aware of Andreas with almost passionate intensity – the shape of him, the motion of his body, the power immanent in the arms that swung by his side as he walked. It was a prelude, wasn't it? A courtship of sorts, this stroll in the moonlight. A mere handful of nights before, Andreas and Maria had taken this very path. The ghosts of this earlier pairing seemed to haunt them, walking, in Otto's imagination, just ahead, similarly side by side. Had they argued, Andreas and Maria? Had they argued about him? Maria would have denied betraying him and Andreas, believing he'd lost his power over her, had lost his temper. He'd picked her up, hit her, broken her and left her bleeding in the seawater.

Otto felt his own blood course through his veins, infusing him with strength. Andreas, beside him, seemed very calm.

A flock of white seabirds stood at the sea's edge just ahead of them, shining in the moonlight. As the two men drew near the birds took off, as one, the clatter of their wings breaking the quiet of the night.

Otto recognised the place though he couldn't say exactly why. It was beach, like the rest of the beach, but he was certain it was the place. At the top they'd find the café where he'd carried Maria's body. They both stopped walking. Andreas raised his arms from his sides.

'So, here we are,' he said. 'What do you want from me now, Otto?'

Otto didn't answer, simply stared at his opponent. Otto's body was quivering, held tight, like a bowstring stretched to its full extent the moment before the arrow is let loose.

'I want to know how you could do it,' he said. 'How could you hurt someone like that? Were you drunk? Were you high? Are you just an inhuman piece of shit without a conscience?'

Andreas shook his head, as though Otto had amused him.

'She belonged to me,' he said.

Otto blinked. 'I asked if you were high. Had you taken that stuff? Kharisma? Were you on it when you killed her?'

Andreas sighed. 'Enough now, Otto. Go home, little boy. You know what you wanted to know. There's no evidence to connect me to Maria's killing. She has no-one to mourn her. Another stupid girl who died miles from home. The matter will be forgotten in a few weeks.'

He looked away from Otto, hands in his pockets, as though the conversation had begun to bore him.

And Otto sprang – the arrow loosed.

He'd never fought anyone before, didn't know what to do, but his body seemed to act without any conscious instruction. He leaped at Andreas and grabbed the larger man's throat with both hands. Surprised, Andreas fell back onto the sand, Otto rolling on top of him. But Otto didn't maintain the advantage for long. Andreas belted him on the side of the head with his fist, a blow of such force that Otto saw red and his ears began to ring. No definite pain at first, only numbness and then a fierce animal rage. He lost control of himself, fuelled by hurt and anger, his limbs, hands and fingers becoming weapons to inflict damage on his enemy. He punched Andreas in the

270

face again and again, only barely registering the pain of the impact on his fingers and knuckles, bone against bone. Andreas grunted underneath him and the strong body bucked beneath Otto's slighter weight, struggling to be free. Otto punched again, only this time his fist landed on the sand and he was falling from Andreas, thrown off him, and Otto felt a moment's primitive panic, knowing he'd be lost if the larger man managed to pin him to the ground. Andreas lumbered, perhaps slightly stunned. He swung at Otto and missed, but the second time, his huge hand caught Otto across the jaw and Otto spun away, losing his footing and stumbling into the water. Then Andreas was on him, blood making his face piebald in the moon-illumined darkness, smashing Otto on the side of his head. Otto reeled, a crackle sounding in his ears, dimly aware blood was flowing from his own nose and that his top lip burned. He recovered enough to run at Andreas, butting his chest with his head, throwing his arms around him in an effort to knock him off his feet again. But Andreas didn't stumble. Instead he grabbed Otto by the throat and threw him back. Otto staggered again, struggling to stay upright in the water. Then he fell, landing on his behind, the wet sand dragging at his feet, and Andreas came after him, kicked him hard on the chest and knocked him back down. The impact hammered the breath from Otto's body. Andreas was leaning over him, one hand on Otto's throat, while with the other he rained down three devastating blows on Otto's face. Otto, distant with shock, caught a glimpse of Andreas leaning over him. He lay in the water, convulsing in an effort to free himself from the grip of his oppressor, but already Otto's mind was far away, observing the situation with a curious detachment. How long did this last? Perhaps only a few seconds but time stretched out. Was this how Maria had felt? he wondered. Had she seen what he was seeing, Andreas made blind and bestial by rage, perhaps by the drug he had taken, this Kharisma he was prepared to kill for?

Andreas pushed Otto's face underwater. Shallow waves washed over him, filling his nostrils, blinding his eyes. Otto coughed and fought against it, his body striving to be free of the water, but Andreas bore down on him, powerful and inevitable. Water rushed over his face and Otto couldn't breathe at all. Brilliant colours flashed into his mind, and then an image of his mother, her beloved face, and her voice telling him all would be well . . .

The brightness ebbed away; his thoughts grew indistinct and dark. Fleetingly he realised he was going to die and he felt a final flare of grief for the loss of his life burning in the darkness – and faded away into nothing.

Charlotte

Sunday: early hours

Waves washed around her ankles. She stood, feet apart, clasping the log with both hands. Andreas lay in the water in front of her, felled by the single blow she'd landed on the back of his head.

Charlotte didn't move for a moment. She had belted Andreas with all the considerable strength she possessed. Had she killed him? She dropped the log with a splash and looked around at the others, Gina, Kate and Jen, all standing and staring.

'Quick, help me!' Her voice didn't sound right, the words oddly deep and hoarse. Jen ran into the sea. They reached for Otto, trying to grab his shirt and pull him out of the water. It was difficult. He was heavy and the water dragged him away. Were they too late? Was he dead already? Blood clouded the water over his face and he was so terrifyingly still, no struggle left.

'Help us!' Charlotte called again. Gina hurried forward, and then Kate. Between them they heaved Otto out of the water so he lay inert on the sand.

'We have to get Andreas out,' Kate said. Charlotte scowled but she didn't allow herself time to think about Andreas too much, focusing instead on organising the others, issuing instructions so they could haul the second man from the sea. He was unconscious but very evidently alive despite the blow she'd inflicted.

But Otto – what about him? He wasn't breathing and she could detect no pulse.

'Is he dead? Is he dead?' Jen's voice was high-pitched, almost hysterical. Charlotte glanced at her.

'I don't know, Jen. Please – calm down. I have to resuscitate him.' She took three deep breaths. Otto lay before her, drenched, his face leached by moonlight. She held his nose and pressed her lips against his cold, salty mouth and pushed air into his lungs. Then she placed her hands on his chest, compressed it thirty times. Nothing. She tried again. The others stared at her, Gina, Kate and Jen. Tears were flowing down Jen's face though she didn't make a sound. Charlotte felt her pulse drumming up from the deep, louder and harder with every attempt she made to breathe life into the lifeless man lying on the beach.

'We're too late, aren't we?' Gina said. 'When are you going to stop? It's not working.'

Charlotte shook her head, raising her hand as though to push Gina away. Far away, at the top of the beach, lights moved and she heard the sound of voices. Had the police arrived? She glanced at Andreas, still lying on the sand, then turned her attention to Otto again.

'Come on,' she urged. 'Listen to me, Otto, you have to come back. Don't give up on me now.' She tried again, forcing air from her own lungs into his, squeezing her eyes shut, willing him to respond.

Men were hurrying down the beach, bearing flashlights. Voices called out. Kate said, her voice edgy, 'It's the police. The police have come.'

Charlotte blocked out distractions. She returned to the chest compressions. She wouldn't let him go – wouldn't give up. It wasn't possible he could die – she simply couldn't allow it. This wasn't meant to happen.

She pressed her mouth on his again – and he began to retch, seawater bubbling up from his stomach and flowing over his face. His eyes flicked open and he coughed and struggled for breath. He turned over on his side, vomiting more water, his body shaking, blood smeared over his face.

274

Charlotte began to cry, helpless as a child in the flood of joy and relief. She tried to stand up but her knees buckled underneath her and she found herself hunched on the sand, Jen beside her, and their arms around each other and around Otto. She pressed her face against his, unworried by his blood and snot and regurgitated seawater, kissing his cheek, touching his damaged skin with her fingertips, overwhelmed by his return.

Men were milling around them now, issuing instructions to one another. Charlotte paid them no attention. Having held herself together so long, she let go. Other people could sort things out because for now, Charlotte had nothing she needed to do. She'd saved Otto from Andreas and brought him back from the brink of drowning. Nothing else mattered.

Otto

Monday night

'You'll go on the record? No? I can pay you, Otto. Serious money. Well, how about giving me something to quote anonymously? Go on – don't let this be a wasted trip. I've got contacts. I can help you get on.'

They were sitting on the veranda in the beachside garden of the West Wind Hotel: Mark, Charlotte, Jen and Otto. Otto had been taken to the local hospital for observation after his revival on the beach – apparently blood poisoning was a possible complication after a near-drowning in seawater. In the morning the police inspector had come to visit him.

The night was drawing on. Inside the hotel lounge a troupe of Rajhastani dancers and musicians were putting on a show for the guests. Strains of lively, discordant music drifted through the partly open doors.

'I'm sorry.' Otto shook his head. 'I mean, thanks for dinner and everything. We've told you lots of stuff but no pictures. No names. You're not going to quote me, okay?'

Early that morning, Charlotte had found half a dozen text messages and a voicemail on her mobile, all left by Mark. His contact at the police station had tipped him off about the incident and he was champing at the bit to find out more. At first Charlotte had been reluctant to respond but Otto said – why not? Let him buy us dinner.

277

We can tell him what happened. Once he'd made this suggestion, Charlotte changed her tune and readily agreed, which Otto thought was odd considering how vehemently she'd disliked Mark at their first meeting.

Candlelight illuminated the faces of the four diners, flushed with the effects of sun and wine, except for Jen, who had been very quiet all evening. She complained of a headache and ate very little, pushing at the rice and spiced fish on her plate, seeming preoccupied. Charlotte, however, was particularly animated and Otto noticed (something he only rarely registered in Charlotte, because she was his best friend) how attractive she looked, the days of sunshine having created a particular golden sheen on her skin, and that she had a very beautiful smile, and that this evening she was smiling frequently. No doubt she was relieved they had come through. They could leave Goa. The trip would resume.

'So this German guy, Andreas, he admitted to you he'd killed Maria. Because he thought you were me?' Mark said.

Otto nodded.

'The police haven't charged him yet,' Mark said. 'I spoke to them this afternoon. Andreas denied everything when they questioned him. They're looking for evidence to link him to the killing. Sharma knows it was him, so they have to find a way to prove it. Andreas is a pretty shady character, apparently. They're not even sure who he really is. His passport looked pretty dodgy.'

Otto took another sip of wine and winced. The drink stung his broken lip and the inside of his mouth was raw. His knuckles were badly bruised and the skin scabbed over where the skin had broken. His face was shocking – mouth swollen, a mass of bruises – but his ribs were the most troublesome, where Andreas had kicked him. They weren't cracked, luckily, but every breath, laugh or movement brought a spasm of pain. It would be weeks till he was entirely recovered. People stared at him. From time to time Otto, horribly self-conscious, made cracks about how bad the other guy looked.

Mark had a laptop on the table in front of him and a folder with cuttings and printouts. He fished inside and drew out a photograph of Maria. It was a head and shoulders shot and in it she was sitting at a table with a glass raised in her hand. She looked younger and paler, rather more ordinary than she'd seemed to Otto during the brief days of their acquaintance and his infatuation. More ordinary – but strangely, just as appealing. The ordinariness invested her with a vulnerability that he hadn't recognised at the time. She had intimidated him with her hippy beach-babe beauty and the aura of confidence she had worn like a fairy glamour.

'Where d'you get the picture?'

'It's an old one, off the internet. It was posted on her friend's Facebook pages. You can keep it if you want.'

Otto stared at the picture. Sadness, like a splinter, lodged in his heart. Having glimpsed through the glamour, he would never now have the chance to know her properly. That was a selfish grief of course, mourning his loss. Maria herself had lost her life.

Charlotte leaned over, wanting to see. 'Poor Maria,' she said.

'Yes, poor Maria,' Otto echoed. He turned, awkward and wincing, to slide the picture in the back pocket of his jeans.

Charlotte

Monday night

'So do you have enough for a story?' Charlotte said.

'Yes. Trouble in paradise. That's the line. It's a tricky one though. Only rumour and hearsay. I haven't got anything very substantial about the Kharisma group. I need to find someone who was close to Andreas and will talk to me about it. Or I need to find a way into the group – see for myself what's going on. That's eluded me so far – it'll all go a bit quiet around here for a while. I'll get there in the end.'

'But you've seen what they can do. Aren't you afraid?'

Mark shrugged. 'Yes. But that's part of the job. The challenge.'

Jen shifted uneasily on her chair beside Charlotte. She was sitting across the table from the reporter. If only he knew how close he was to this wanted someone, Charlotte thought, because Jen had taken the stuff on the island, at its most potent. So far she had refused to tell Charlotte much about it and certainly wouldn't divulge to Mark. Charlotte wasn't about to spill the beans. She'd find out more from Jen sooner or later, she was sure of it.

The police had taken statements from Charlotte, Jen and Gina. Kate had eluded them, disappearing into the darkness as soon as Charlotte had resuscitated Otto. How had she managed this? Charlotte wasn't certain, though admittedly she had been so focused on Otto and then so overwhelmed by his recovery she hadn't exactly been paying attention. Kate had simply slipped away – perhaps to find Andreas's friends?

Sharma told them the police had raided the encampment in the jungle. They'd found none of Andreas's gang, but a man's body had been recovered, and identified as Carlo Allen, the man whose beating Otto had witnessed. At some point in the future, Otto might be required to attend a trial and give evidence.

Charlotte had been both excited and nervous at the prospect of seeing Mark again. She was embarrassed about the way she had behaved at the end of their previous encounter but in the end it had all been perfectly easy. Mark was relaxed and friendly. Once the conversation was underway, Charlotte found herself enjoying the interchange with Mark without the lubrication of alcohol. And he was enjoying it too, wasn't he?

'Let us know if you sell the story – we'd want to see it,' Charlotte said. Then, to Jen and Otto, 'We'd better let our parents know. Even if you aren't using our names in this story, if they see this stuff in the papers they're going to worry. We'd better send them an email tomorrow.'

She turned back to Mark. 'Keep us updated.' Us. Of course she meant 'me'. Keep in touch with me.

Mark grinned. 'Of course,' he said. 'Let me know how you get on with your conservation project. I quite fancy a trip to the south myself; I'd love to hear about it.'

Love. Fancy. The words beamed out of the sentence. Charlotte grinned back.

She felt a wash of relief and, in its wake, excitement and anticipation. Otto and Jen were safe, and having arrested a serious suspect, the police had returned Otto's passport, believing his innocence. Tomorrow they could board a train and leave Goa and this particular nightmare far behind. The adventure could resume – that is, the ordinary, safe adventure of backpacking and volunteering for a good cause.

At the end of the meal (which Mark paid for) he shared his contact details and reminded them to keep in touch. He escorted them back through the hotel to the reception area and gave Otto a thoughtless, cheery farewell slap on the back – which caused Otto to yelp with pain – then showered him with apologies. He held out his hand to Jen. How would he say goodbye to Charlotte? Her anxiety was muddled with a longing to be hugged and held. Then it was her turn. Charlotte quivered and stalled, tentatively holding out her hand and cursing herself for behaving in such an obviously goofy fashion, giving herself away. But Mark didn't hesitate. He stepped forward and engulfed her in his arms, giving her a warm, friendly hug and a kiss on the cheek. When she broke away, she saw the look of surprise on Otto's damaged face, the question written there. How come she was such good pals with the reporter?

Well, she wouldn't answer. Perhaps it was time he recognised she wasn't just reliable, earnest, always-does-the-right-thing Charlotte – that she might be attractive to someone as grown-up and glamorous as Mark Joyce. As they walked into the night garden, all three, neither Otto nor Jen said anything. Charlotte had a secret smile on her face.

Jen

Tuesday: early hours

The darkness was warm and spiced and seductive. The moon, emptied, lying on its back, had almost descended to the sea where briefly it would sit like a boat, casting a silver reflection on the water.

It was after midnight and Jen, sleepless, was sitting on the beach, all alone. She didn't like the smug reporter and hadn't enjoyed the dinner. Otto's swollen face, its shades of puce, beetroot and mauve, repelled her – she seemed more discomforted by his pain than Otto did himself. Nor did she like the falsity of the hotel, where affluent Western tourists holidayed in a safe, unreal bubble.

Now Otto and Charlotte were asleep in bed. Their backpacks were ready for an early morning departure.

Sleep eluded Jen. Memories of the previous night haunted her, spectral images of Andreas holding Otto underwater, the sound of the blow Charlotte landed on his head, the nightmare of Otto's resuscitation, the silence as Charlotte breathed into his bloody mouth and pressed down on his chest, over and over again.

What was it she felt now? Disconnection. At least, disconnection from Otto and Charlotte, her travelling companions and best friends. It was unsettling and guilt-inducing. Conversely, she felt a deep attachment to this place, Goa, the territory her friends were both so eager to leave. Well, she could hardly blame them for that.

Jen didn't want to move on. She belonged here. Goa seemed to match some internal landscape of her heart and imagination, a place she had sought and yearned for and now recognised in the lineaments of ocean, beach, the alignment of moon and stars, in the perfume of the air, the forms of the trees and flowers, even its dirt and dust and unpredictable stinks. Of course she had always wanted to visit India, so surely no surprise that she loved it. And India was vast, a subcontinent, where so many more marvels existed, waiting for her to discover. And she would discover them. Only now she wanted to tarry for a time, to revel in this one particular place.

And the island of course, with its enchanted spring. Didn't it offer a chance to explore the gifts she possessed, her ability to see beyond the mundane world, to commune with spirits?

Yes, the island called, like a siren.

The police inspector had interviewed Jen last of all. He kept her waiting a long time while he spoke to Gina, Otto and Charlotte. Andreas, apparently under observation in hospital following the blow to his head, would be seen later in the day.

Sharma invited Jen into his office and indicated she take a seat. His desk was a mess, a laptop computer hedged in with papers, box files and cardboard folders. The room smelled of tea and something spicy, his just eaten lunch perhaps. The ceiling fan whirred, slightly wonky. The inspector didn't speak right away. He stood with his hands behind his back, tummy protruding, gazing at Jen. His expression contained some warmth and a hint of amusement. Jen remained very still, her legs pressed together, shoulders rounded, hands clasped in her lap.

The inspector said, 'Well, Jenevieve. Here you are!'

Jen glanced up at him, then back to her hands. She said, 'I don't need to tell you anything, do I? You know it all. You've always known it.'

The inspector shook his head. 'You credit me with too much, Jenevieve. I most certainly do not know everything.' He grinned,

286

revealing very white teeth. His skin wasn't good though, rough and pitted, lines around his mouth.

'But you know about the island.'

The inspector's eyes darkened. Some of the good humour faded briefly. He said, 'Of course. Wouldn't it be rather strange if I didn't know? Isn't it a little arrogant of Western visitors to come here and think they have discovered something new?'

Jen gave a quick, humble nod. 'But did you know they were taking water from the island and selling it? The stuff they call Kharisma?'

'We knew this was the case. But who was taking it – and who was organising these so-called parties, causing trouble – that I was in the process of finding out. There have always been people called to the island. Indian mystics, people from far away, like you, Jenevieve. That is not a problem. The island is a holy place, a blessing. But the others – well, taking the water, selling it for money, getting high, the violence, causing trouble for our people. That is a big problem.'

Jen raised her head and looked directly at the police inspector.

'Now you know who was taking the water from the island.'

'The ringleader, yes. He wasn't alone though. The woman Kate was helping him, and Maria was involved, and many others. I don't think this is over yet.'

He took a brief statement, in which Jen described what she had seen: Andreas holding Otto under the sea, Charlotte storming to the rescue.

As she left, Sharma and Jen shook hands gravely.

'You'll be staying a while, I think?' he said.

'No. We're leaving tomorrow.'

Sharma arched an eyebrow. 'I think you'll be staying a little while, at least.'

The moon rested on the horizon and slowly began to sink into the sea. Was she brave enough to stay on her own?

What would she do here, without Charlotte and Otto? Clearly it could be a dangerous place and she was far from home. She would be alone. She might be vulnerable. On the other hand, she was determined to be braver and to trust her visions and intuitions. It was time for her to step out on her own.

In her pocket, her mobile vibrated and bleeped. A text message from Gina. Where RU? She texted back. On the beach.

Silence for a time, except for the sea. A shadow walked along the sea's edge, dreadlocks over his shoulders – Jim, of course. Who else should she expect to meet?

'May I join you?'

'Sure.'

He sat beside her. Neither spoke for a time, side by side, staring at the starlit sea.

Jen sighed. 'It was you, wasn't it? You were the Westerner who rediscovered the island, all those years ago.'

'I think the Goan population would dispute the idea of rediscovery. They have always known about it. But yes, I believe I was the first person to land on the island for a very long time. I haven't set foot on it now for more than twenty years.'

'You're still here, though.'

He nodded. 'Still here. A witness. I saw what happened, the young man and his friends taking the water, using it to make money, resorting to violence.'

'Not good.'

'Not good, no. You've seen how it ended.'

Jen considered. She said, 'Why don't you go to the island any more?'

He didn't answer immediately, perhaps thinking how best to answer. 'I don't need to,' he said. 'I know you've taken the water, Jen, and I can't judge you for that because I did the same. I understand what it shows you. But I want you to think of this: it is possible to ride a helicopter to the top of a mountain. It is also possible to climb it step by step, challenging your mind, courage and determination, testing your body and its limits. At the mountain's summit you'll enjoy the same view in both cases. Which is the better way? Too often we are fixated by the goal, when it is the path that is important.'

Jen sighed. 'The path to enlightenment,' she said. 'That's what you're saying.' She toyed with the sand, drawing spirals in its surface with her finger. 'I do want to stay.'

'Then stay.' Jim rose to his feet, staring into the darkness. 'Gina's coming,' he said. 'If you don't go – well, I shall see you again. Goodnight, Jen.'

Within a few minutes Gina was beside her, sitting on the sand.

'I couldn't sleep,' Jen said.

'Neither could I.'

They both stared at the sea. For a strange moment, only the tips of the crescent moon were visible above the horizon. After a brief silver smoky flare, the moon disappeared altogether.

'Why did Max and Kumar invite me to the island?' Jen said.

'They thought you were the right person to ask,' Gina said. 'Max recognised something about you, your gifts and sensitivities. It is something he shares with you. And Kumar too.'

'What about Kate and the others? They were working with Andreas. They know about the spring. They might carry on selling Kharisma.'

Gina shrugged. 'They might. If they do, we'll have to deal with it somehow. But without Andreas, I doubt it, and at least the police are on side now.' She turned to look at Jen.

'You will come back to the island, won't you? You're not going tomorrow?'

Jen shook her head. 'I don't know. Charlotte and Otto are catching a train in the morning, after breakfast.'

'Please. Stay for a bit. You can catch them up.'

Gina was echoing the voice in Jen's own mind, urging her to remain in Goa. It was what she wanted.

'They won't want to leave me here,' Jen said.

'You're an adult, Jen. Your own person. They can't force you. Make your own mind up.'

Jen took a deep breath, in and out. The decision was made.

'I'll have to tell them in the morning, when they wake up. They'll try and change my mind. Charlotte will.'

'D'you want me to be with you?'

Jen shook her head. 'No. I'll do it on my own.'

She stood up, brushing sand from her jeans, surveying the scene. Sea and night, the dim scoop of beach, the rain of stars, the black mass of trees beyond the sand.

'I'll speak to you in the morning,' Gina said.

Jen took out her phone and sent a text to Kumar, then waited for a reply. She didn't have to wait long, despite the hour. Her phone bleeped and the screen beamed out in the darkness. She read the answer, and set off to meet him.

Two hours later she walked back to the lodging where Otto and Charlotte lay sleeping. She met no-one. Everything was still, as though under an enchantment. Something lay on the doorstep – a squat, toad-like shape with a coiled tail. What was it? She bent down, cautious, and at once the shape resolved itself. A camera. Someone had returned Otto's camera.

Otto

Tuesday morning

Otto cradled the camera as though it were an injured animal – a much-loved, precious animal needing nurture and care and love. His fingers lingered over its smooth surface.

They were sitting under the canopy of the internet cafe, the three travellers, drinking coffee and breakfasting on bananas and warm chapattis. Otto found it hard to eat, his mouth still sore, but his spirits were rising, nonetheless. Grief over Maria's death lingered like a dark bruise, but the terrible anxiety of the last days had dissolved and he was delighted to be with Charlotte and Jen. The trip had become an adventure again.

Charlotte pored over guidebooks and maps. Jen, though, was physically restless, staring into space, hardly engaging in the intermittent conversation. She looked tired too, and told them she had slept very little.

Otto frowned. He turned the camera on and flicked through the pictures on the screen at the back. Shots of the party on the beach, bringing back memories of that magical time with Maria, when, unknowingly high on Kharisma, the night had shone, and he'd embraced her in the sea and all had seemed most perfectly magic and charged with significance. The bars, the bottles in the revellers' hands . . . except now he knew what the bottles contained, and understood a little more about its origin, and Andreas's corruption of the natural gift, for the sake of money and power.

He flicked through the pictures, one after another. Grinning faces, sunned, youthful bodies, the forest of arms caught in the strong electric light. All so happy and high . . . were these images of heaven, or snapshots of the damned?

There she was, Maria, caught in profile among the dancers. He zoomed in, staring at her. They were valuable to him, these shots, a record of a time he could never forget. He would have to download the photographs as soon as possible, to keep them safe.

Around his wrist, silver and slippery, he wore Maria's ankle chain. He'd rescued it from his sponge bag. Charlotte had looked at it, but didn't ask him where it had come from.

Jen sighed uneasily. They looked up, Otto and Charlotte.

'What is it?' he said. 'Are you okay?'

Jen swallowed. 'I want to show you something,' she said.

'What?' Charlotte's voice was brisk and impatient, as though Jen were annoying her. Jen didn't move right away. Charlotte and Otto continued to wait, and stare.

'What is it, Jen?' Otto said more gently. He felt such tenderness towards her, sitting with such fragility, clearly worried about what she had to say.

With another, convulsive sigh, Jen rose to her feet. She turned away from them and lifted the bottom of her white blouse to reveal her narrow, rather bony back. Charlotte gave a curious, choked sound. Otto blinked.

Between Jen's shoulder blades, about the size of a fifty pence piece, was a sharp, black tattoo of a circle surrounded by flames. Nobody spoke for a few moments, then Charlotte said, 'My god, when did you get that done? What were you thinking?'

Jen dropped her blouse, turned back to the table and sat down again.

'Last night. Kumar did it for me.'

'Why? Why on earth would you?' Charlotte looked furious. Otto put his hand out and touched Charlotte's arm, trying to calm her.

'Hold on,' he said. 'Charlotte, please, let her speak. Jen? What are you telling us?'

'I wish you would listen to me,' Jen said. 'I said this yesterday, so you have no reason to be surprised. I'm not going with you. I need longer in Goa, at the island. I'm staying here.'

'We're not leaving you,' Charlotte said.

'Please – Charlie – I was planning to spend time travelling alone, when you did your stint at the national park. It's only a little sooner than we planned.' Her voice was growing in strength and confidence.

Otto glanced at Charlotte. Her anger had dissolved, tears springing to her eyes and leaking onto her cheeks.

'I don't want to leave you,' she blurted. 'Why are you doing this? We planned the trip together! It was something we were going to share!'

'Then stay here with me,' Jen said. 'Stay a little longer.'

Otto and Charlotte looked at one another. 'I don't want to stay,' Otto said. 'Too much has happened. I need to get away.'

Charlotte nodded. 'I don't want to stay either. I can't understand why Jen does.'

Jen's head tipped forward. 'I'm sorry,' she said. 'I don't want to hurt you, but it's what I have to do.'

Half an hour later Otto and Charlotte stood up and hauled on their backpacks. The atmosphere was subdued.

'You can change your mind anytime,' Otto said. 'Keep in touch. Text me, let me know how you are and if you need anything. Come and find us when you're ready, okay? And be careful. Look after yourself.' He put his arms around her, hugged her hard despite the pain it caused him.

Charlotte waited to make her own goodbye. She was still struggling with tears. The two young women embraced for a long time, reluctant to separate, though Jen seemed remarkably calm and even happy.

The waiters in the cafe were looking at them. On the other side of the road the little girl from Otto's first lodging was staring and grinning and waving. Otto lifted his arm and waved back. A pig rifled through a pile of rubbish and fallen foliage on the bank under the trees, and a scooter puttered past, carrying a man, a woman, a toddler and even a tiny baby, held with one hand by the driver on the petrol tank.

'Come on, Charlie, we have to go. We'll miss the train,' Otto said. Jen nodded, releasing Charlotte.

'If you change your mind . . .' Charlotte echoed Otto's words. 'Are you sure you'll be okay on your own?'

'I'll be fine. Stop worrying. Anyway, we'll keep in touch. I'll catch up with you again later.'

Charlotte sighed. Otto took her hand. 'We have to go,' he repeated, almost pulling her away. They walked up the lane under the trees, through the now familiar heat and perfume of the Goan village. Charlotte walked with characteristic briskness, but after a minute or two they both stopped and turned around. Jen was standing where they'd left her, on the lane just outside the cafe, looking small and pale and vulnerable. She lifted her arm and waved.

TO BE CONTINUED . . .
LOOK OUT FOR THE SEQUEL TO *THE ISLAND*.
COMING SOON!

Drawn into a dark and dangerous new world
by her friend Dowdie, will Amber join
the cult of the Amethyst Child?

"This excellent novel is thoughtful and gripping."
Nicholas Tucker, The Independent

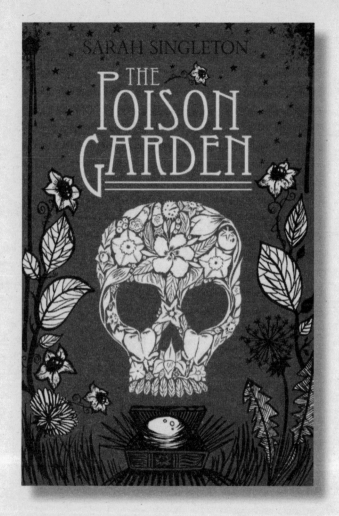

A bewitching gothic murder mystery about
a young boy who inherits a magical garden
of healing and harm.

*"Wonderful descriptions, skilful pacing and
an inventive plot make for a novel to delight
and surprise the reader."* Armadillo

SACRIFICE

SARAH SINGLETON
WINNER OF THE BOOKTRUST TEENAGE PRIZE

A gripping historical quest for a religious relic
which originally brought power to its owners,
but now only brings madness...

*"A beautifully crafted story rich in visual
imagery and gothic atmosphere."* The Bookseller

Two girls, both suffering persecution – one for being the daughter of a witch, the other for being a Catholic – unite to save a family...

"captivatingly sinister" Amanda Craig, The Times